SHADOWKINGS

Michael Cobley has had short stories published in magazines and anthologies for a number of years. He attended Strathclyde University and lives in Glasgow. *Shadowkings* is his first novel.

SHADOWKINGS

MICHAEL COBLEY

EARTHLIGHT

SIMON & SCHUSTER

London • New York • Sydney • Tokyo • Singapore • Toronto • Dublin

A VIACOM COMPANY

First published in Great Britain by Earthlight, 2001
An imprint of Simon & Schuster UK Ltd
A Viacom Company

This paperback edition published by Earthlight in 2002

1 3 5 7 9 8 6 4 2

Simon & Schuster UK Ltd
Africa House
64–78 Kingsway
London WC2B 6AH

www.earthlight.co.uk

Simon & Schuster Australia
Sydney

A CIP catalogue record for this book is available
from the British Library

ISBN 0-7434-1599-X

Typeset by Palimpsest Book Production Limited,
Polmont, Stirlingshire
Printed and bound in Great Britain by
Bookmarque Ltd, Croydon, Surrey

This book is dedicated with love
to my mum and dad,
John and Patricia Cobley

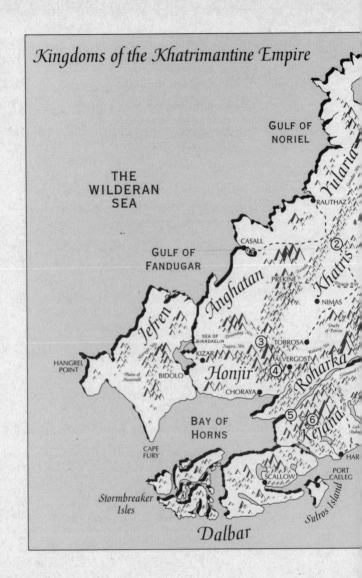

Kingdoms of the Khatrimantine Empire

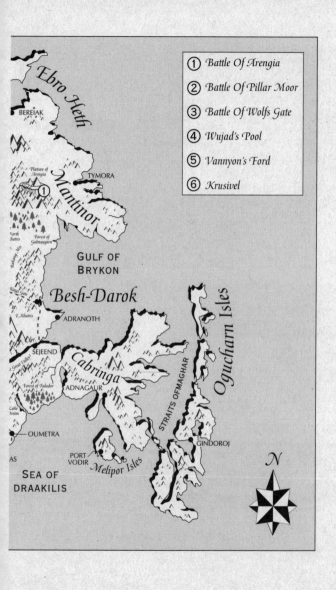

1. Battle Of Arengia
2. Battle Of Pillar Moor
3. Battle Of Wolfs Gate
4. Wujad's Pool
5. Vannyon's Ford
6. Krusivel

Part One

Chapter One

Honour the dead, for they are many and we are few.

The Book of Earth and Stone

In a high mountain valley, under the looming, starless canopy of night, campfires burned amid ancient ruins. Men, fighters all, knelt or crouched close to the flames, muttering, eating, joking, throwing dice. Off to one side, at the foot of a shattered, mossy pillar, two figures sat either side of their own fire. One was a lean-faced woman who frowned as she ran a small whetstone along the sabre that lay across her knees. The sleeveless leather jerkin she wore half-open was battered and scarred, yet carefully patched, much like the down-at-heel boots that lay on the ground nearby.

Her companion was a black-haired bear of a man, cloaked in heavy furs which only partly concealed a dented chestplate and mailed leggings. In a big, scarred hand he held a black bottle of wine but it seemed half-forgotten as he stared with amber eyes into the heart of the campfire. Flakes of ash whirled up into the cold, unforgiving night and an occasional spark flew across to land on the man's exposed hands. He appeared not to notice, just sat there with a gaze that was dark and steady, harsh as granite, sharp as a naked blade.

A burnt-through branch slumped into the centre of the fire. The flames quivered, sank a little lower. Keren Asherol paused from honing her blade, looked across, then shook her head.

3

'You're brooding again,' she said mildly.

For a moment, no reply. Then: 'Warhounds should think of the hunt, not the hunter.'

His voice was deep, with no trace of weariness, the words well formed.

'More dreams, eh?'

Byrnak, Warlord of Northern Honjir and Protector of Bidolo, drained the wine and tossed the bottle away. He gave her a surly, hooded look. 'Even the finest warhound can become a burden.'

Keren met his gaze. 'I think the word you're looking for is "warbitch".'

A glittering, dangerous smile creased Byrnak's features. 'A bitch who is lucky to have such a benevolent master.' Reflected fireglow gleamed in his eyes and cast a sulphurous tinge across his face. 'And what of you – are your own slumbers tranquil?'

'Of course,' she lied, resuming the sharpening of her sabre. Across the fire, Byrnak gave a derisive snort and went back to the flames.

Keren had last shared Byrnak's bed willingly six months ago, when it was spring and his brutal attractions had not palled. Since then she had preferred the solitude of her own bed, and the known hazards of *her* dreams. It was sixteen years since the Battle of Wolf's Gate but the horror and slaughter of it still crept up from the well of memory to fill her nights with rage and guilt.

Heat from the fire prickled her bare skin and heightened the numb ache of a scar on her lower right arm. A shaft of moist mountain air blew through the vast ruined antechamber where they sat, bringing smells of high wood and bush, earth and bark and rotting leaves. Then the wind shifted direction, drifting to her the odours of cooked meat and the sounds of the men clustered round their own fires. They were a strange mix, mostly rootless rogues from Honjir, Jefren and Anghatan, with a few odd ones like Yanama, a marsh raider from Ebro'Heth, or the daggerman Erruk from the moors of northern Yularia.

There were no Mogaun, however. Keren listened to the quiet laughter and snatches of flutesong for a moment, smiled, then turned her sword over and began to work the other side. Once into the rhythm she glanced at Byrnak again – his stare was as unwavering as before, but now there was a kind of haunted anger to it.

What do you see? she thought. *What do you fear?*

Byrnak was a living mystery. Ragtalk among the men placed him variously as a lost prince of the Imperial blood, a renegade Rootpower mage, a black sorcerer from the Erementu hinterlands, or even a formless monster from the Rukang Sagas, returned in human shape. When pressed, he claimed to have been an iron mine slave, a pit fighter, and a chief's bodyguard in Rauthaz before a misjudgement with a battlestave caused him to flee south. It was so prosaic it could almost be true.

Byrnak let out a breath of noisy impatience, rose and went over to the saddlebags piled carelessly at the foot of one of the massive pillars. Keren watched him pull out another black bottle, uncork it with his teeth and take a hefty swig. Then, bottle in hand, he prowled around the crumbling antechamber, pausing occasionally to study a worn inscription or relief carving or to pick away a patch of dark moss. These were ancient ruins, perhaps from the time of the Jefren League, but there were still older ones littering these mountains. Keren once overheard a Fathertree priest tell a mage that kingdoms, conquerors and empires had washed across the continent of Toluveraz like waves on the shore. She had thought that an exaggerated comment at the time, but her wanderings since had shown her that there was something to it.

Suddenly, Byrnak uttered a vile oath and hurled the bottle against a crumbling wall. Dark wine splashed across the ancient stones and the muted chatter of the men faded away, their uneasy eyes glancing his way.

'Where are the scouts?' he snarled, hands clenching and unclenching. 'Haven't they found that bastard scum Shaleng yet?'

Shaleng had been Warlord of Northern Honjir until two years ago when Byrnak and a band of dedicated followers infiltrated his stronghold outside the city of Kizar. Byrnak became the new Warlord, but Shaleng escaped into hiding where he gathered a gang of cut-throats and rapists whose increasingly daring – and bloody – raids were undermining Byrnak's authority.

'You're the one who taught them,' Keren muttered sourly. 'It's bound to take a little time—'

In one swift motion Byrnak stepped towards her, snatched the sabre out of her lap by the hilt and threw it point-first into the heart of the fire. Keren jerked away from the scattering of sparks, sprawling on her back.

'Gainsay me to my face once more, woman, and I'll kill you.'

The savagery of his stare burned into her skull. He seemed to tremble with contained fury and for a moment Keren thought he was going to strike her. Then there was a commotion from out in the ruined hall and he looked up, breaking the terrible spell. A slender, black-clad youth dashed in and fell to his knees before Byrnak.

'My lord, we have him!'

Byrnak stared at the youth with a joyful intensity and reached out to stroke his brown curls. Keren kept her face blank, hiding her revulsion.

'Falin, my little hawk – where?'

The youth's face glowed with adoration.

'At the village of Wedlo, Lord. The raid began less than an hour ago.'

Byrnak's grin was rapacious and with his hand still resting on Falin's head he looked at Keren.

'Take the second and third companies, cut off their retreat and any avenues of escape. I'll take the first and deal with Shaleng personally.'

The camp was suddenly alive with activity as orders were given and fires were doused. Byrnak brought Falin to his feet and they both went off to one side. Keren rose and grasped the sabre's hilt, pulling it free. The leather-wound hilt was hot from the fire, embers still clinging to the blade, and for a moment it seemed that flames were coming from the blade itself. Then she knocked the sword against a blackened stone at the fire's edge and the embers fell away.

'Keren?' said someone nearby.

No more, Keren thought, staring at her sabre. *No more.*

She turned to see Domas and Kiso, captains of the second and third companies, standing there. 'Have all the scouts returned?' she said.

Domas smiled and nodded. 'All safe, all back.'

'Then ready the men. We've a hard night ahead.'

As they hurried off she bent to pull on her boots, then took a rag from her belt and wiped the ashen smears from her sword before sheathing it at her waist. She was aware of Falin and Byrnak staring at her from across the ruined chamber but ignored them, buttoning her leather jerkin as she followed the captains out to where the horses were being harnessed and saddled.

There's nothing for me here, she thought bitterly. *Why do I stay?*

They rode down from the Nagira Mountains like vengeful wolves. A cold, steady rain was falling, turning the ground muddy, but their mounts had been bred for war and none slipped or stumbled. Wedlo was a small town squeezed between densely wooded hills and the north bank of the Dreun which coursed south-west into central Honjir. Once they had reached the hills, Keren sent Kiso and the second company to approach from the woods, with orders to eliminate any guards they encountered. As he and his men slipped away through the trees, she continued north-east with the third company.

By the light of hooded lanterns, she and one of the scouts led her thirty riders at a canter along a narrow forest path. The attack would have to be fast and savage, yet co-ordinated: they would have to seal off the north road, seize the wharfs, then move into the town itself. And it would have to be soon for in just a few minutes Byrnak and his men would come charging in from the south. 'Be there,' had been his last words. 'I don't want to have to do all the work myself.'

Keren cursed under her breath, wiping rainwater from her face with her free hand. Ahead the trees and foliage were thinning and the lights of Wedlo were becoming visible, a scattering of lampglows and an ominous funnel of smoke and sparks rising from the town's centre. The scout, a short, wiry Dalbari called Paq, turned, his waxcloth hood dripping, and raised a finger to his lips. 'Slow,' he whispered.

The order rippled back along the column as he pointed out a shack just near the town's north entrance and another over at the riverbank.

'Sentries?' Keren murmured.

Paq nodded, holding up three fingers. Keren detailed Domas and another six to take care of Shaleng's guards but no sooner had they dismounted than a warning shout went up from away to the south. The voice cut off suddenly with a choking scream, but the damage was done – figures emerged from the shacks with lit torches and more came running from the town.

'Damn Kiso,' Keren muttered, then ordered the company to head straight for the town. There were the sounds of blades drawn from scabbards as the riders turned and moved through the trees. Once out on open ground they formed up in attack pairs and charged the waiting guards.

After that it was a desperate whirl of blades as Keren's riders, some dismounted, pursued Shaleng's cut-throats and hunted for the bandit chief himself. Keren found herself cornered by a swordsman and a spearman working in unison. The swordsman slashed at her horse's face and she managed to catch the blow on her boot while parrying a thrust from the spearman. But her parry lacked force and the spear glanced off her mailed leg and gashed her horse's neck. The beast whinnied in pain and reared. Fighting to bring it under control, she made a stabbing slash at the spearman and caught him in the throat. As he went down in a spray of blood she turned to see death in the form of the swordsman's blade arcing towards her unprotected side.

Then a rider came charging out of nowhere and knocked him flying. In reflex Keren had begun to lean away but she still felt a cold sting as the sword's tip caught her upper arm. The swordsman tried to regain his feet but was cut down by the rider. It was Domas, helmetless, his blade dripping red.

'Where's that cretin Kiso?' Keren snarled.

Then, at the far end of town, she glimpsed Byrnak's company, hard-pressed by a superior number of bandits. Gathering those still on horseback she led a charge at their rear. The surprise attack scattered them, and as the riders chased them down, Keren realized suddenly that Byrnak was missing. When she questioned one of his riders he simply pointed over at a large, four-storey house whose upper windows were leaking smoke. 'He's in there – with Shaleng.'

She wheeled her horse and galloped across. She was almost at the house's tall double doors when a big man with a long, single-edged axe jumped up from behind some stacked barrels and rushed at her. He made to swing at her but tripped so that the axe bit into her horse's head. Uttering a ghastly scream the beast collapsed under her, blood jetting from its cloven skull. Keren scrambled clear of its thrashing hooves, regaining her feet in time to face her attacker. It was Shaleng.

'Slut!' he shouted, his long-jawed face contorted with fury. 'I needed the horse alive, not you!'

The heavy battleaxe seemed as light as a walking stick in his big hands. He spun it in a blurring figure-of-eight then aimed a swift crosscut at her midriff. Keren leaped backwards then ducked to avoid a second blow to her head. She snatched a handful of dirt, tossed it up into Shaleng's face and came up to shoulder-charge him. Choking, the bandit-chief staggered back but managed to grab Keren's jerkin, pulling her off-balance. Half-blinded, he swung at her as she stumbled forward, but she kept her feet, parried the axe and slid her sabre along the wooden haft and into his hand. Shaleng let out a roar of agony and the axe flew from his bloody grip. Without hesitation Keren plunged her blade into his throat and he died at her feet.

Gasping for breath, swaying where she stood, she looked up and saw Falin the scout staring open-mouthed. Muscles ached and the wound in her arm stung as she bent and picked up Shaleng's axe. It was a Mogaun-forged piece, its heavy haft carved along most of the length, its blade bearing cruel, tearing hooks at top and bottom.

'Here,' she said hoarsely. 'Take this to your lord and master . . . No, wait, I'll give it to him myself.'

She had reached the steps at the front of the house when the doors were thrown open and Byrnak stepped out. He assessed all that had happened with a single glance.

'So you took my prize for yourself, woman.'

'I had little choice in the matter,' Keren said, tossing the axe at his feet. 'But if Kiso had done as I'd ordered—'

'Yes,' he said. 'I know about that.' He reached down behind him and dragged a body out onto the veranda. Handless, footless and dead, it was Kiso. 'The fool thought I might die without his aid.' He gave the corpse a brutal kick, then grinned at Keren.

'But that's not all,' he went on. 'Look at what else I found.' He turned to one of his men. 'Bring out our new pet!' A slight figure, a young man naked from the waist up, was thrust forward and Byrnak casually threw him sprawling on the veranda. Keren immediately noticed the filthy blue breeks he wore.

'A Rootpower priest,' she said numbly.

'That's right, Keren, my lovely – the last of a dying breed, but soon to be extinct, eh?' Byrnak's malicious laughter was echoed by the crowd at his back. 'They were getting ready to torture him, but I decided to reserve that pleasure for myself.'

Keren turned away. The moans and cries of the wounded came from all around and the air stank of blood and smoke. Across the town square, one of their riders was despatching the dying of both sides with a spear. Others were looting what freshly harvested grain and roots the villagers possessed. More laughter came from behind her and she heard Falin join in from nearby.

She took a kerchief from her jerkin pocket and tried to clean her sabre. But the blade was bitten and notched and tore the cloth, leaving it in rags.

This is death's realm, Keren thought emptily. *And we are its ragged people.*

Chapter Two

Prayers are like smoke or water – they either vanish
without trace or feed what is unseen.

The Book of Stone and Fire

The birth was going badly.

For at least the tenth time that night Suviel Hantika wished
she could find within herself a shred, the merest glimmer, of
Rootpower to help heal the suffering woman. From the frail
mindbond she had already made, she could feel the awful pain
of torn inner tissues and exhausted muscles. But all she had was
the Lesser Power, sufficient only to dull the worst of the woman's
agony while praying that she would live.

Pray? she thought bitterly in a corner of her mind. *Pray to who
or what?*

Shouts and fearful cries from the street outside filtered through
to the tiny, shuttered back room, but Suviel kept the circle of her
concentration pure and unbroken. The muffled, savage sounds
told of another beating, robbery or murder, familiar evils in a
city which had changed hands twice in as many months.

There was another contraction. The woman let out a gasping
moan and Suviel fought to keep her self separate from the torment.
When the midwife and the other crones looked pleadingly at her,
Suviel masked her weariness and bent closer to the woman's ear.
Stroking the sweat-beaded forehead and neck, Suviel murmured
the thought-canto of Subdual. The half-words circled in her

mind, things of smell, sound, texture and enigma interlocking with themselves and her own being. Shared with a patient, it was meant to coax the natural healing abilities into working harder.

The Lesser Power began to chime softly through her mind and she could feel calmness edging into the woman's turbulent awareness, slow as a tentative dawn. But the waves of pain were so intense, so full of the dreadful damage taking place, that Suviel began to feel ghost twinges in her pelvis. She ignored the echoes and reached deeper into her physical and mental resources, pouring her own vitality into the Subdual canto.

Exhaustion crept slowly, inexorably upon her. Her arms grew heavy, her breathing shallow, her throat dry and aching. Yet while part of her was absorbed in the ritual of the canto, another part became aware of the details of her surroundings: the yellow glow from the wall lamps; the old women, small hooded figures clutching Earthmother amulets; the midwife, a tall, bitter woman who had once been a Khatrisian aristocrat; the pregnant woman and the scrap of life, a boy, that was struggling to be born. Across the room, in shadow, was the woman's despairing husband, a standard-bearer in Gunderlek's ill-fated rebel army; family friends had smuggled him into the city, past the Warlord Azurech's guards.

Then the vision drew further back to show her, as if through mist, the flat-roofed, two-storey house and its drab neighbours, the tiny yards, one with a scrawny dog gnawing on a bone, the dark, cobbled street littered with rubbish and the still body of a man lying near an alleyway, a death grimace on his face, a bloody tear in his ear from which some bauble had been torn . . .

At some point she was vaguely aware of being helped from the room by one of the old women, who whispered trembling thanks and comfort. The child had been born safe and well and his mother still lived. The husband came up to her as she sat before a low fire, stammering out a gratitude she could only accept with a tired nod. The fire's heat soaked into her, wrapped her in a soft warmth which somehow became thick, heavy blankets and a quilted down mattress and a cotton-covered pillow smelling of herbs. Weary through and through, she caught the faint sweetness of melodyleaf and a hint of musky rainbark and was swept off into slumber.

Daybreak's pale and haggard light seeped into her room, filling it with greyness, dissolving the last threads of sleep. Once dressed in the plain green dress and patched brown cloak of her herbwoman disguise, she left the little bedroom and found steps leading up to the roof. There had been rain during the night. The air was cold and clean and the roof's crudely mortared planks were still dark and wet. She found a fairly robust crate and sat down to look across the city, letting thoughts come to her as she watched the dawn grow.

Before the fall of the Empire, Choroya had been a prosperous, lively city port famed as much for its acting troupes as for its merchant princes. Now the theatres were burnt-out shells and the exchange halls were sullen, half-deserted places where the poor produce of the northern farmlands fetched exorbitant prices.

Suviel peered into the hazy northern distance, to the spreading patchwork of fields and smallholdings that stretched away to the far-off foothills. She could make out the dark stretches of encroaching marsh and several dull grey areas where nothing grew, ground that had been poisoned by Mogaun shamans during the invasion. Once, this land had fed fully half of Honjir but the recent harvest of inferior grain and feeble livestock would be scarcely enough to keep Choroya and its stinking shanty towns from starvation through the winter months.

This is the bane that lies across the land, she thought bitterly. *Warlords and bandit-kings who pursue their skirmishes and petty wars amid the ruins of our greatness while the people suffer and weep and bleed.*

Suviel raised a fold of her cloak to dry tears from her eyes. Then she looked into the further distance beyond the mountains and saw in her mind all the lands of Khatrimantine as they were in her youth, from the lush woods of Kejana to the vineyards and orchards of Ebro'Heth, from the singing cave-cliffs of Yularia to the windswept isles of Ogucharn. She remembered riding with the witch-horses of Jefren, sailing into the teeth of a summer storm aboard a Dalbari fishing boat, and undergoing the dreamrites of magehood on a cold mountaintop in Prekine.

Now only the foul Acolytes of Twilight trod the hallowed halls of Trevada where once mages had taught and studied, and abominations moaned in the chambers of the High Basilica.

There was a footfall behind her. Cursing herself for wallowing in memories, she dried her eyes once more and turned to see the midwife waiting, hands wringing a neckerchief, face full of uncertainty. Then she stepped forward.

'Shin Hantika,' she said tearfully, starting to kneel.

Alarmed at this use of the forbidden mage title, Suviel rose and quickly grasped her by the arms, forcing her to remain standing.

'No, Lilia,' she said. 'Not here, not out in the open. Anyone could be watching.'

The midwife began to apologize but Suviel laid a hand on her shoulder and hushed her. Lilia Maraj, she recalled, was a daughter of one of the Roharka nobles and had been a children's tutor at the palace.

'Don't worry,' she said calmingly. 'Tell me – how soon did you know who I was?'

'It was not until you used the healing lore for the second time – I remembered you from when I used to bring children to the mage halls to tend to their cuts and bruises.' Her voice grew wistful. 'They were so alive, so full of curiosity. Always getting into bother . . .'

'How are mother and child?' Suviel said.

Lilia sighed. 'Weak, but recovering. I doubt that she will be able to give birth again. Her baby is very well, though. A robust little soul he is, too.'

'Good. I'm glad,' Suviel said sincerely, then laughed softly. 'Few things these last few years have pleased me as much as helping to bring new life into the world.'

Lilia was silent a moment, a deep weariness showing in her

faintly lined features. 'It's an awful world to be born into,' she said quietly, then looked up, suddenly animated. 'Why must it go on like this, lady, why? Surely the warlords and the chieftains cannot last forever.'

Suviel sighed. 'The clans of the Mogaun have strength and a kind of unity, and their shamans have great and terrible powers, Lilia. All the things which were taken from us.'

Lilia shook her head. 'I believe that the time must come when we can regain our freedom.'

'Gunderlek thought the time was now,' Suviel murmured.

They were both silent for a few sombre moments.

'Shin Hantika, you escaped the fall of Besh-Darok,' Lilia went on. 'Did no one else survive, none of the other mages and loreweavers, none of the temple knights? Is there truly no way of bringing back the light into our lives? Is there no one to help us?'

Suviel heard the despair in her voice and for one pitying moment wanted to say, 'Yes, some of us did escape and have these sixteen long, black years remained in hiding or disguise, working selflessly towards the very end you've wished for.'

But the potential dangers were too great: if even just a rumour of still-living mages reached agents of the Acolytes, nighthunters and other sorcerous beasts would be loosed across Khatrimantine to hunt down any user of the Lesser Power. She and her colleagues would have to flee, perhaps even across the Wilderan Sea to Keremenchool. No, the risk was unacceptable.

She steeled herself. 'Lilia . . . I was near the river when the firehawks descended on the mage halls. No one could have survived that inferno. I'm sorry . . .'

Suviel saw the desperate hope in her eyes die. They both stood in silence for several moments. Suviel was about to offer words of comfort when Lilia spoke, head bowed.

'It is not you who should apologize, lady. I was wrong to burden you with my fears and longings when you have to make your way in this world without the Rootpower. I can't begin to imagine how you've coped with such a loss.'

Yes, Suviel agreed silently. *You cannot.*

'With nearly all the mages and loreweavers dead,' she continued, 'the responsibility for ridding the Empire of the foul Mogaun must lie with the people themselves. We only have to find the strength.'

Suviel heard the seed of anger in her voice and shivered. Gunderlek had voiced similar sentiments while gathering his ill-fated, ragtag army.

'Lilia,' she said. 'I have to go.'

'I understand. It's dangerous for you here.' She took a deep breath. 'Don't worry about the others speaking of you – as far as we know, you were just an old herbwoman passing through.'

'Thank you,' Suviel said and turned to leave. Halfway down the steps she looked back. Lilia was sitting on the crate, hugging herself tightly while staring past Suviel at the grey reaches of the sea.

An hour later, Suviel was riding at a steady canter along the muddy road leading north from Choroya, through one of the shanty towns that hugged the city's outer walls. All along the track was the evidence of the most recent siege: wrecked carts, broken shields and spears, the splintered remains of kegs and crates, burst wicker baskets, remnants of food and grain ground into the mire, and scorched and torn rags of clothing, a scattering of debris now being raked through and squabbled over by the desperate and the dispossessed.

Nothing she saw here, no scene of squalor or brutality, was new to her, but it could not fail to rouse her sorrow and anger. Azurech was a Mogaun chieftain, leader of the Whiteclaw clan whose savagery had struck terror into most of Honjir since their trek across the mountains from Khatris just a few years ago. An uneasy league of minor Mogaun chiefs and local warlords had kept a kind of order back then, but month by month Azurech had systematically defeated each one, absorbing their warriors into his own host. Choroya, with its encircling shanties of desperate, starving people, had been the last significant stronghold. Now it was his.

While passing through the crowded lean-tos and filthy tents, she was struck by the silence. No songs, no elders recounting the ancient stories, no chatter, only a deadening hush and resentful eyes following her. But then, the order of their lives had been shattered. Once, it had all been so faultless and clear – the spirit of the Fathertree was the overarching principle, connecting all things and all peoples through not just the priests but also the visible, tangible benefits of the Rootpower itself. In contrast, the Earthmother was the bedrock, the unseen principle of stability, both a source of life's blessings and the resting place for the spirit at life's end. They were twin forces in harmony with each other, with the people and with the world and its seasons.

Now it was all no more, and for the sixteen years since the Mogaun invasion existence had been an empty mockery of what had gone before. As Suviel rode past hollow-eyed children and old women sobbing over still, covered forms, her eyes stung with tears and she muttered bitter curses under her breath. Yet her pity was tempered by a weary sense of self-preservation that kept her riding till the shanties were behind her.

The grey sky was turning ashen by the time she reached a stretch of woods that marked the beginning of the farm holdings. Once under cover of the trees she turned off the road, carefully guiding her horse among the moss-covered roots and slippery mire till she found a westward winding path. After a two-hour ride through the rain-swept trees, she came at last to where an overgrown cart track led up into dark, bracken-cloaked foothills. Despite her sodden clothes and chilled flesh, she smiled – her memories had not misled her. Beyond the hills reared the southern spur of the Rukang Mountains, a cluster of craggy peaks riven by rocky gullies and sheer gorges. Up there lay her destination, an ancient Rootpower shrine called Wujad's Pool.

Suviel dismounted and led her horse up the track, all the while keeping alert for any sound or sign of beasts. Mountain paths like this had become dangerous since the invasion. Where merchant caravans and bands of pilgrims had once trod, now predators prowled and preyed and clumps of thorny growth blocked the route. Often she had to pause to hack a way through.

The rest of the day was spent thus, with the ceaseless rain alternating between drizzle and lashing torrents. Beneath a rocky overhang bearded with dripping moss she made brief camp to rest and feed her horse, then stopped again later under an eyeleaf tree, feeding herself and wringing out her cloak.

Night was falling but she pressed on, determined to reach the shrine before surrendering to sleep. At last she came to the opening of a ravine just visible in the poor light and after a moment's pause led her horse in.

The walls were sheer, lichen-streaked rock. When the last radiance of dusk was gone she unwrapped a tar-soaked torch, lit it and continued. The ravine floor sloped down, becoming grassy and increasingly covered in stunted trees and spiny bushes that looked black in the torchlight. The vegetation grew dense and the air took on a cold edge and an ominous musty taint. Then the path opened out and she halted, shivering in the sudden iciness, staring with deep unease at what had become of Wujad's Pool.

It was over five years since she had last visited the shrine, since when some dreadful change had taken place. Frozen grass and flowers crunched under her feet. Icicles hung from the trees and hoar-frost glittered on the shattered remnants of the small, four-pillared fane which worshippers had built on the rock out in the pool generations ago. The pool itself was an opaque mass of ice, but it appeared to have been in some kind of violent, turbulent motion at the very moment of its freezing. The wavering glow of her torch struck gleaming points of light from the solidified ripples and wavelets which radiated from a dark depression near the rock.

She hitched her horse's leads to a low branch and ventured out onto the pool, gingerly approaching the rock of the fane. There she saw a great hole in the surface of the pool, its inside full of ragged spikes and blades of ice, its edges fringed with frozen splashes and foam. An awful sense of malevolence hung over it and the coldness was so raw that she had to move back a few paces.

Appalled and shivering, Suviel wrapped her cloak tighter. Something evil had emerged from the water and in so doing had cursed the pool and its surroundings. But what, and when? The odour of musty decay, a sure sign of Wellsource sorcery, was strongest here and made her even more edgily alert for any disturbance nearby.

She came to a decision. Retracing her steps she halted at the bank, rested the torch against a small boulder, then straightened and commenced the thought-canto of Purification. The Lesser Power unfolded within her and the chill faded from her fingers and toes. At her feet, frost melted on leaves of grass and the edge of the pool began to gleam and puddle. Tiny fish became visible in the spreading patch of melting water, jerking into life, tails flapping. Then a small shape struggled free of the dissolving ice and in a flurry of wings and spray launched itself into the air. Suviel smiled as the bird, a greenwing, flew once around the glade before alighting on a branch.

But the Lesser Power canto was beginning to fail. She could feel the pressure of the Wellsource curse inexorably pushing back, freezing the waters she had freed. Mere seconds later all was as it had been, apart from the greenwing on its frosty perch. Then without warning, the bird took off and darted away among the branches. Suviel immediately felt a change in the air and across the glade saw the glow of torches approaching through the trees. Quickly she snatched up her own torch, extinguishing it in the wet grass, then went over to her horse and loosed the reins. She led the animal back along the trail and hitched it to a strong bush near the ravine entrance before creeping back to the glade to watch from behind some foliage.

Seven figures emerged from the trees opposite, one of them leading a solitary horse burdened with several bags. All were garbed in brown furs and black cloaks, the livery of Yularian merchants, but Suviel knew that these were no traders. There was an air of disciplined purpose to their movements that marked them for warriors. Five of them walked out onto the pool and positioned themselves at equal intervals around the hole in the ice.

A sixth removed a number of items from the horse's baggage then took them over to the hole where the seventh stood. This man was taller than the rest, his hair was silver and his narrow face was as lean and pitiless as a bird of prey's. Suviel began to shiver again, sure that she was looking at an Acolyte of Twilight.

Common sense told her that she should slip away while still undiscovered, but something crucial was unfolding here and she had to witness it. The Acolyte began to construct the foundations of a ritual, scattering drops from vials and powder from tiny caskets in and around the hole while muttering a continuous litany of sibilant words unintelligible to Suviel. Then he waved his assistant away, lowered his head and spread his arms, and started to speak in a guttural, droning voice. Suviel could sense the power that was gathering around the Acolyte as the musty decay became a stench that filled her nostrils and tainted her tongue.

And there was light, a pallid, greenish glow that pulsed up from the hole in the ice until it was a swirling column of nebulous skeins and hazy eddies. Within it Suviel could make out a confusion of images, a man asleep in a tent, three riders galloping across a burning desert, a skeleton clambering out of its grave . . .

The Acolyte stepped back from the column of light and a misty wave rolled out from it in all directions, coming to a halt where ice met ground, so that the pool appeared to be enclosed by an opaque wall. But when the pale wave reached the patch of water Suviel had melted, the Acolyte swung round to stare at it. An instant later his furious gaze swept unerringly to where she was crouched behind the foliage, piercing her to the soul. His eyes were dead white orbs. She gasped in fear and lost her balance, breaking that terrible link. As she regained her feet and scrambled towards the trail back out, she heard him say:

'Take her!'

Chapter Three

Who taught you the way of cruelty, and how to
scar the souls of men? Who hammered you out and
tempered your harsh edge?

The Book of Fire and Iron

Keren sat by the campfire, letting the heat sink into her face and
arms. Gasping sounds of pain were coming from the torturer's
tent down by the stream but she was working on her sabre,
running the rougher of her two wetstones along the blade for
the fifth time that night. Outwardly she seemed absorbed in the
matter of her notched blade; inwardly her mood swayed between
numbness and anger.

Byrnak was down there, personally applying the instruments
of torment. His catamite, Falin, was with him and there was
something significant about that but for now it escaped Keren's
thoughts. Only the young priest's cries filled her mind, stirring
up old doubts and the memory of honour. Hadn't there been
a time when she would have put a stop to such brutality? Why
was she able to just sit here while it continued, and how had she
come to be this way?

Shadows, she thought. *I've been living the last sixteen years in
the shadows.*

After the disastrous Battle of Wolf's Gate, she had fled with
a handful of soldiers south through the Rukang Mountains to
find refuge in the high valleys of Kejana. A short time later, on

23

hearing of the Emperor's death, she went through her equipment and buried anything that bore the Imperial sigil. Then she rode north to Anghatan in search of relatives, a long journey fraught with perils, its days a charnel display of horrors, its nights full of screams and burning fields. And everywhere, monstrous beasts commanded by the hooded, white-eyed Acolytes of Twilight.

It took her nearly three weeks, during which she lost her horse twice, took a wound in the shoulder and was caught, only to escape when her captors were ambushed. In that time she built up a picture of how the invasion had begun, how three vast Mogaun armadas had sailed out of the still morning mists to attack the cities of Casall, Rauthaz and Bereiak. Once they had been taken, three immense hordes had then surged inland to clash with the Empire's armies at Wolf's Gate, Pillar Moor and the Plateau of Arengia. By all accounts, the Grand Army of the South, Keren's army, had fared the worst, which was no surprise since more than half of its strength had been cobbled together at the last moment from Honjiran and Roharkan militia companies.

On the other hand, the Grand Army of the West, under Upekar, Duke of Kostelis, had fought the enemy to a standstill at Pillar Moor and would have turned the tide had not fire-spitting creatures attacked from the air and broken their morale. And on the Plateau of Arengia, the Grand Army of the North was crushed, the Emperor was slain and the Fathertree reduced to ash. Very few escaped that catastrophe.

When Keren finally reached northern Anghatan and the outskirts of Casall, she found that her only remaining blood relative, her dead father's brother, had fled with his family on a ship bound for Keremenchool. And with the Mogaun and the Acolytes of Twilight in firm control of the city, no passenger vessels were being allowed to leave.

With no family and no roots, Keren decided to put her own military skills to use. So, for the next twelve years she had travelled the length and breadth of the fallen Empire, fighting in the armies and warbands of the scores of feuding domains which had replaced the twelve kingdoms. Then, four years ago, the fine goods caravan she was helping to guard was ambushed on its way from Choraya to Bidolo. The bandits were a ragged but well-trained bunch, whose tall, charismatic leader offered to buy her contract, a proposal she had found surprisingly difficult to refuse.

The sobbing cries of the priest had subsided, but across the clearing Keren could see the cold look on the face of Domas, rider captain of the second company. *Yes, you know, don't you?* Keren thought. *You know just how much Byrnak has changed.*

Down by the stream two figures emerged from the torturer's tent, Byrnak and Falin. The young scout was unsteady on his feet but grinning vacantly as Byrnak, sweat gleaming on his naked upper torso, steered him up towards the rest of the camp. As they strolled over to Byrnak's tent, they shared laughs and low jests with the men: Domas and his three squad sergeants, Keren observed, did not join in the banter, offering only faint smiles in response. Then Byrnak and the scout paused at his tent and he hushed the men with a single sweep of his brawny arm.

'Listen well, you bloody rogues. The pusbag Shaleng has gone to feed the eels of the Dreun and our pet priest will spill his secrets before all of his blood . . .' He paused as raucous laughter rang round the clearing. 'But we have need of a new rider captain and after much thought I have reached a decision.' He grabbed Falin's wrist and held his arm aloft. 'Who else deserves the rank but the man who found Shaleng for us?'

There was a racket of shouts and claps of approval. Keren was careful to be seen to join in and spotted Domas and his underlings doing the same. Then Domas' grim stare came round to meet hers and with a tilt of his head indicated the bushy trees a few paces back from the encampment. Keren cursed inwardly but slipped away from the camp once Byrnak and his consort had disappeared inside his tent.

Domas was waiting alone beside a big forked, creeper-wrapped tree. He turned at her approach. 'An interesting choice for rider captain, eh?' he said bitterly. 'Should be quite a spectacle when we go out on a raid.'

She just folded her arms. 'If you've got a point to make, Domas, make it.'

The rider captain made a hissing sound through his teeth, shook his head and looked askance at her. 'I can't believe that you're going to go along with this. The man – hah, boy more like – is incompetent—'

'He did find Shaleng.'

'That means nothing,' Domas retorted. 'Falin's no rider.'

Keren shook her head. 'You think Byrnak doesn't know that?'

Domas met her gaze. 'I think that Byrnak has lost his grip.' He came a step closer. 'Come on, Keren, I joined just a few months after you and we've both seen what happened to him this past year.'

'And it's time for a change, eh? Time for a new chief?' she said disdainfully. 'Is that what this little chat is all about, Domas? Your problem is that you really don't know Byrnak at all. He is far, far more dangerous than you think. Anyone going against him will finish up with their blood in the earth, take my word for it.'

Domas laughed unpleasantly. 'How loyal, even when he's got that boy sharing his bed instead of you.'

Furious, she lashed out and caught him across the mouth with the back of her bare hand. He staggered back, sword half-drawn.

'You're a fool, Domas,' she said then walked away.

Back at the camp, she sat near the fire, gnawing on a strip of knapsack beef while staring down at the tent by the stream, now flanked by two guards. There was a low light within it, probably a candle set to keep insects from bothering any open wounds. As she sat, Domas' words came back to her, words that had so accurately echoed her own darkest thoughts. Yes, Byrnak had become a monster, but only she knew of the terrible dreams that plagued him, and the ghastly things he saw behind the wall of sleep. It had to be that which drove him to do what he did.

Suddenly she was walking towards the torture tent, moved by an awful need to see what had been done. One of the guards tried to move between her and the tent flap but when she looked him coldly in the eye he thought better of it. Pushing the flap aside, she ducked inside and came to a frozen halt, regarding with horror the sight which met her eyes.

An array of pointed and edged implements hung on a board next to a high table on which the priest's still form lay. The table's wood looked almost black in the weak glow of a tallow candle suspended in a holder at the far end of the tent. The priest's head, legs, arms and naked torso were held down with cracked leather straps, and she could detect the faint smell of scorched flesh under the candle reek.

It was the monstrous spectacle of the right arm that held her unwilling gaze. From the elbow down, the skin had been flayed and the muscles ribboned in careful, narrow strips, leaving the bones visible. Next to the arm sat two small, bronze cups, their insides smeared with traces of dark fluid. Keren shuddered – the agony must have been unimaginable. Then she noticed what resembled arteries and veins protruding from the ravaged flesh near the elbow. Their ends had been closed off with blobs of a grey substance which she saw had been used to seal other gashed, exposed areas.

Blood. They had been drinking the priest's blood.

Keren straightened, scarcely able to comprehend the hideous scene before her, but full of a cold and stirring rage. Then she heard a groan and nearly gasped as the priest turned his head to stare at her. For a moment she thought he was about to speak, but the eyes wandered unseeing, pupils dilated, eyelids half-shut. She leaned closer to sniff the prisoner's weak exhalations and caught the faint, sickly sweetness of chainberry, a powerful reverie drug.

She drew a shaky breath, wiped a hand across her face and tried to think. Death and carnage were part of the fury of battle or single combat, both of which she had experienced many times. But these lacerations were so precise and so deliberate that she could only think of the person responsible with utter loathing. The sheer vileness of it almost stripped her down to a kind of moral innocence she had thought long gone.

Her life here with Byrnak and his warband was over, irrevocably finished. She toyed with the possibility of killing him as he lay naked with his boy lover, but quickly discarded the notion. All that she really had to do was decide what kind of goodbye gift to leave for him.

She smiled hard and humourlessly, then bent and began to loosen the straps that bound the young priest to the blood-stained table.

Byrnak's dream began as it always did, with ice-cold chains.

Heavy links of iron bound him to a wide, curved rock while dense, freezing fog swirled around him. His quickened breathing chilled his chest, making him cough. Faint sounds surrounded him, murmurs growing in volume and intensity, incantations in an unknown tongue. He bellowed curses and threats then tried to laugh, but the fog swallowed the sound even as his voice died from the fear in his throat.

Fear. This was the only time Byrnak ever felt it, here in sleep's realm. When the nightmares first began nearly two years ago, he had thought it was just some shred of craven fear crawling out to disrupt the demesne of his dreams. But as the months passed the visions became ever more detailed and elaborate and took on echoes of meaning he could not understand but which aroused in him a wild, unreasoning terror.

There were metallic clinks and ticks as he moved to a sitting position, and he knew that he was wearing a suit of grey and silver battle armour. Spikes and fluted ridges adorned the weighty plates and his gauntlets seemed to resemble a pair of spiny sea creatures. He tried to stand but as usual the chains allowed only enough slack to sit or kneel. Grinding his teeth he shifted onto his knees, hunched down and waiting.

Soon the chanting voices sank back to a rhythmic whisper and the fog began to thin. Sometimes images and faces emerged from the pale wall and for a moment he thought he saw a tall, old man standing with hands upraised. But the image faded to be replaced by a rocky, sun-scoured desert stretching away to a shimmering horizon.

The three riders were already there, galloping straight towards him across the desolation. In some past nightmares they had appeared in the far-off distance, in others close enough to distinguish the grimacing mask-helms they wore and the dead white eyes of their horses. It was then that Byrnak's fear always strove to unleash its full potency: he had succumbed only once and was reduced to a shivering, shrieking state, lying curled up on the flat rock, arms covering his head. Since then he swore that he would never again buckle and break, and fought the terror of this recurring delirium.

He was fighting it now as the riders drew nearer, cloaks flapping and streaming, their horses' hooves striking up clouds of dust and grit. Fists clenched, the chains pulled tight, he knelt facing the desert. The voices still muttered on and on from the dense wall of fog at his back and he thought he could hear a note of expectation creep into the incantation. Shouts emerged from the murmuring chorus as the three riders came ever closer. Byrnak's mouth was dry and he was almost quivering with the effort of staying upright and staring ahead. The riders were drawing close enough for him to see the salient details of their own armour, how each had a different hue: gold, crimson and purple.

On they came, the rumble of hooves growing louder, the rattling of saddle harnesses becoming distinct. Any moment, he thought to himself, I shall awake beside Falin and I will reach across him for the winecup that sits on the travel chest and drain its sweet dregs . . .

The riders slowed their horses to a trot, to a walk, and brought them to a halt not half a dozen paces from him. All three grotesque mask-helms regarded him in grave silence, as did their mounts, he noticed. The horses stood stock still, tails limp, ears displaying not a twitch, while staring at him with marble-white eyes.

'Brother,' said one of the riders.

'Our forgetful brother,' said another.

'Our lost brother,' said the third with disdain.

Drawing a shuddering breath, Byrnak forced calmness into his voice and through gritted teeth spoke.

'Forgive me, lords, but I have no brothers nor any sisters.'

'Nor any parents,' said the first, 'save the sabotage of enemies and the carelessness of priests.'

With the last word the rider dug his heels into his horse's flanks. The horse uttered a ghastly groan, let its mouth hang open, and said: 'Forgive us, we beg. Day and night we strive to unshatter the Spirit of the World and remake what was and will be. Forgive us.'

'Never,' said the rider. 'The moment of my birth is seared into my mind, always there to be recalled, and I will never forgive you!' The mask came up to face Byrnak again. 'Do you know what womb delivered me into this world? It was one of those holy witch-horses from Jefren. The mess and the stench never leaves me.'

'I was born beneath some saint's carved monument,' said the next. 'It toppled and broke when I came up out of the ground.'

The third was silent a moment. 'A tree,' he said. 'I was born inside an ancient Kingsgold tree. I had to burn my way out.'

One of the other two laughed. 'And we'll never know just where that tree was, will we?'

The third ignored him, levelling a gauntleted finger at Byrnak. 'We have seen the pit of your birth, the frozen pool with its broken shrine. Do you remember?'

Byrnak was utterly still, suddenly empty of fear and trembling as deep, brittle memories struggled to surface. A dark mountainside came back to him, before that a narrow ravine, then a glade of enclosing trees. The memory was forming strongly now. He could almost remember stumbling – no, crawling – across an ice pool towards the bank. And before that? The bristling, lung-scouring ecstasy of a first breath, the claws of cold air on his naked skin. And still further back to a journey through void, and beyond that . . .

A surge of terror wrenched him back from a gravid blackness of entombed knowledge. He looked up to see the three riders watching him, tasted blood in his mouth and snarled, 'Come down, you gutterworms! Come down and free me and I'll eat the faces off you!'

The riders glanced at each other. 'He will not accept it,' said one, bluntly.

'Then he must be told,' said the second. 'The time fast approaches.'

'He's an ignorant savage,' said the first. 'How can this be one of us?'

'Why should he not be?' said the third. 'The Black Priest is in his own way just as primitive. We are all fragments of the Spirit of the World, and he was as mighty in his anger as in his intellect.' He prodded the head of his horse. 'Is this not so?'

'When the Weaving of Souls was broken,' the horse said in an iron voice that set Byrnak's teeth on edge, 'the five vessels were already brimful of his essence. Strength holds to strength so each of the five would embody an aspect of the Lord of Twilight. He lives, he resides in the House of the Dead no more, yet the Realm Between entraps him and—'

'Enough!' snapped the third rider who then regarded Byrnak. 'Do you understand what has been said here?'

'Your ravings mean nothing to me,' Byrnak said hoarsely. 'I must be mad or dreaming or both.' But that knowledge was still there, buried like a seed of poison beneath his thoughts.

'Then observe.'

Tendrils of the enclosing mist rose up and poured into his eyes. He gasped in fear but choked back the shriek that threatened to loose itself from his throat. Then images emerged from the white, a vast fleet of ships of every size and shape, their decks crowded, their sails daubed in savage symbols, their flags little more than ragged sheets fluttering madly in the stiff wind that drove the fleet forward. The view changed. Byrnak saw a huge army make its way inland, burning and pillaging as it went, then he saw that same army swarm across a flat plain towards bright, serried ranks of armour.

Byrnak watched with a mixture of anger and unease. The terror had faded but the ominous chorus had returned, voices chanting sonorous syllables with undertones of anticipation. The cold sank deeper into his bones and he felt his heart thudding as the battle scene receded, falling away beneath him, then shimmered and rippled. Hands came into view on either side of a bowl of liquid: the battle was a vision upon it, he realized as robed figures moved nearby. This was the inside of a cavernous temple, wide pillars lit around their bases by flickering torches.

'The time is near,' said a voice. 'Bring forth the vessels.'

The coldness was like lead in Byrnak's limbs and the unease had thickened to an awful dread that ate at his thoughts. Five men wearing only loinclothes were led into the temple, feet shuffling, arms hanging limply by their sides, eyes empty. All were young, their bodies strong and muscular, and Byrnak cried out as he looked at the face of the one in the middle.

'Lord of Twilight, Prince of the Realm of Dusk, Bringer of Glory,' began one of the robed priests. 'Hear us, your most faithful disciples. Those who serve your enemies are scattered, their swords and their shields are broken. See, the last of them are falling!'

In the bowl the vision showed a sea of axe- and spear-wielding Mogaun surrounding a dozen or so mail-clad Imperial soldiers and a silver-armoured man who wore a crown and carried a long battlesword. The Emperor stood beside a small tree whose foliage glittered and glowed, and as the last of his men died one by one he seemed to draw more strength from the tree and held off the engulfing attackers. Then the mass of the Mogaun drew aside as one of their number, taller and heavier than most, stepped out and hurled a fiery spear. It caught the Emperor full in the chest, pinning him to the tree, then both he and it burst into flames.

In the temple, a wordless murmuring had begun and hot green radiance was coming from a low well in the floor around which the five listless men stood. 'Your enemy dies, Lord . . . The ancient seals fall away and the gate opens! Come forth and accept these vessels for your spirit . . .'

The emerald glow brightened, swelled and put forth limbs of

light which surged towards each of the five men, enfolding them. Byrnak's breath was coming in shuddering gasps and he could not tell the priests' murmuring from the ravenous chanting of the white mists. The flowing green glow sank into the naked flesh of the men whose faces were now animated, their eyes alive with triumph. One of them lifted a hand to study it and the other four mirrored his action; another laughed simultaneously with the other four throats.

'No . . .' whispered Byrnak, feeling the event about to unfold. 'Stop . . .'

There was a shout from the rear of the temple and a figure in pale brown came darting through the sudden confusion. It was a woman wearing a tree-symbol amulet at her neck and through the disarray of his own thoughts Byrnak saw the peace, the utter calm in her face as she ran up to the blinding green well and threw herself into it.

Roaring whiteness filled his senses, then was gone. He lowered his hands from his face and looked up at the three masked riders on their motionless, dead-eyed horses.

'No . . . I'm not, I won't . . .'

'Oh yes, Byrnak. We are the shadows cast by a broken greatness. Shadowkings we are, but eventually you and we shall become one.'

It was true. Every bone and sinew and unvoiced thought said that he had been . . . a god? Something in him wanted to laugh and jeer, something savage and wary, but it was all he could do to stay upright and keep his head from bowing.

'Tell him about the priest,' said one of the other riders.

The masked rider laughed softly. 'Ah yes, your ex-lover has been in your little torture tent and when she saw what you had done to that priest, she freed him. They are both riding west.'

'I'll . . . kill them both . . . kill . . .' Byrnak gasped.

'Yes, that is what you would like to do, isn't it?' The dense mist shifted, hazing his view of the three riders. 'Do not forget, Byrnak – you and I and our brothers shall once more be that which has

the entire world as its realm. That is your destiny – acknowledge
it and be ready.'

The riders wheeled their horses and galloped away as the mist
rose up in a solid white wall. Then Byrnak was awake and sliding
off his bed of furs, half-aware of someone shaking him violently by
the shoulder. Instinctively he struck out and in the next moment
saw Falin stumble back with blood spurting from a burst lip. A
figure nearby stepped back as he came to his feet. It was the
captain of his personal guards.

'My lord, we have been betrayed!'

Byrnak gazed around him at the tent, the iron-bound chest,
his armour and weapons, the plates with half-eaten food scattered
across the dirt floor. *Shadowkings we are* . . . He looked at Falin,
then snatched up a furred cloak to covered his naked form.

'I know,' he said with a savage grin. 'Have the companies strike
camp. We've a quarry to hunt.'

Chapter Four

Fly on spirit, fly on, and stare not into Twilight's
awful eye lest it stare deep into you.

The Book of Iron and Sky

Through the mountainous night Suviel fled her pursuers, three
Acolyte guards who managed to keep track of her whatever ruse
she employed. Up rocky slopes, along narrow gullies just wide
enough to lead her horse, and across fast-running streams but all
to no avail. On they came.

Her limbs were tired and her back ached from the ride, but
her head was clear. She began to wonder if the rumours were
true, that the Acolyte guards were creatures of the hunt – dogs,
wolves and others – warped by the Wellsource into human shape.
They could not be following the odour trail left by her or her
horse since she had masked both with the Lesser Power. Perhaps
it was the Lesser Power itself that drew them after her. Or perhaps
she was deluding herself about what she could actually achieve
any more. For while the Lesser Power was a fundamental quality
of the world, like rain or grass or insects, it was a sweet valley
breeze compared to the raging gale of the Wellsource, ripples on a
pond to a mighty ocean wave. Straws for a drowning unfortunate
to grasp.

Suviel sighed and shook her head, trying to dispel her dismal
frame of mind. After all, the Wellsource was the Lord of Twilight's
power, intrinsically poisonous and corruptive while the Lesser

Power was, among other things, a fount of gentle healing that could never taint the user. It was something worth fighting for, and with.

A watery dawn was breaking through broken clouds as she topped the crest of a ridge. Below, the trail led down into a marshy, wooded vale still hazed by lingering veils of mist. She urged her mount into a canter then slowed when she entered the shadow of the trees. The faint sounds of frogs and insects were all around. The trail led among clumps of reeds and grassy hummocks and soon she came to a place where the trail narrowed to a thin strip of solid ground meandering through the mire. She slowed to a halt and sat listening, then nodded to herself. A dozen paces further on, past a huge, tangled heskel bush, she secured her horse to a tree and walked back to stand at the spot she had found.

Suviel forced calmness upon herself and let the Lesser Power fill her as she swiftly but carefully brought two cantos together in her mind, Beckoning and Constraint. The frogs and insects fell silent, but another sound reached her ears, the drumming of hooves. Confident that all was ready, she retreated behind the heskel bush, holding tight in her circling thoughts the tether of the spell she'd made.

She did not have to wait long. The three Acolyte guards rode into view, galloping along in single file. She kept the spell in check until the first rider was just coming to the narrow strip of ground, then released it. The mire on either side rustled suddenly and scores of long wriggling shapes surged out to attack. The first horse whinnied in panic, reared as the snakes struck at its legs and threw its rider. Landing, the guard cried out, a high snarling sound, then leaped to his feet covered in writhing snakes. He tried to run, tearing them from his neck and struggling to pull off his leather harness to get at the ones burrowing beneath it. Then he uttered a single shriek and fell in the mud, convulsing for a few seconds before finally lying still.

The other two riders had wheeled away from the trap. They backed off and stared impassively. Suviel watched with a grim satisfaction, but frowned as they looked at each other for several silent moments. Then in unison they turned their mounts about and rode back up the trail. Suviel sighed, hurried along to her own horse, climbed into the saddle and left the marshy vale at a canter.

She followed the track on through the mountains, keeping to the cover of trees and shadowy gullies, scrutinizing the surroundings before riding across any open ground. She knew it would not be long before the guards picked up her trail again. There was a place she had to reach, a deep, narrow gorge spanned by a huge fallen tree. Across the other side was an easier, more direct trail back to Krusivel. She just hoped that in the half-decade since she had last been there, no one had taken it into their mind to destroy it.

The morning steadily brightened and although great rafts of threatening cloud passed overhead, the rain held off. Yet Suviel felt no warmth as she passed along defiles and passes which had never been touched by the sun's rays and where tough, spiny bushes grew.

As she rode she noticed the crumbling remains of buildings, even the collapsed, pillared entrance of a temple worked into a cliff halfway up its face. She could just make out the weathered contours of steps leading up the sheer rock, impossible to scale. These were age-old ruins, decrepit fragments of some ancient kingdom from the semi-legendary Age of Wars, whose name was lost in the fog of years. She grimaced – in another three thousand years who would even remember the name of Khatrimantine?

If we fail, no one.

The path, little more than an old goat trail, led across a steep hillside, through patches of gorse and mistwrack till it dipped to join the rocky bed of a dried-up stream. Here she dismounted and continued, eyes glancing to either side, ears alert to the faintest disturbance. Except for the sound of some small creature scratching in the undergrowth, all was peace, a soothing tranquility, but she had long since learned to distrust the quiet. For a moment she yearned for the safety of Krusivel, the hidden refuge in Kejana, then she quelled it. Too much danger lay ahead for futile longing.

On either side trees leaned over, branches intertwining above her in a dense arch of leaf and bough that filtered the morning's sombre light to a shadowy dimness. After a while the cover thinned and she followed a barely distinguishable path up a grassy bank, pausing at the crest to take in the sight. Uneven ground sloped down, widening towards the edge of a wide chasm, a dark crack in the world. Steep mountain flanks rose on both sides, daunting walls of wind-scoured stone broken by patches of dark green and grey where notches trapped moisture and gave meagre shelter to weeds and bines. A few stunted bushes grew along the edge of the rocky incline and down near the dried-up stream. Only one tree had ever grown here, a giant agathon, once rooted near the brink of the chasm till some storm toppled it across the divide. Down the centuries travellers and merchants' artificers had worked on it and added to it until the great tree became a true bridge with a high-sided channel wide enough for wagons hewn along its length, and cobbled ramps at either end.

Suviel looked warily about her. Several paths and gully brooks met here, making it the perfect place for an ambush. She wished she could mount up and ride quickly down to the bridge, but her horse was near exhaustion and might stumble on the uneven slope. So she wound the traces once about her left hand and started down to the chasm.

There was a glow of sunlight from high, high above, but rags of mist hung stubbornly in this rift between the mountains. Suviel glanced from side to side, eyes missing no detail of foliage or shadow, imagination filling her with fearful images of those beast guards coming for her with whips and chains, or the Acolyte priest waiting to sear her with foul sorcery.

Her horse noticed the Acolyte guard first. As it tugged at the traces, Suviel heard a flicking sound and the animal whinnied and reared. Suviel released the reins and staggered away from the panicking horse, just as a leather-masked guard emerged from the bushes. From somewhere behind her came the sound of an approaching rider, and when the guard lunged towards her without drawing a weapon she knew they wanted her alive.

There was no time to plan. She took a step back as the guard reached her and grabbed handfuls of her cloak and jerkin. Beneath the mask a slit mouth grinned and she caught the stench of his breath in her nostrils. She bunched the knuckles of her right hand together just as she had been taught, and when the guard made to throw her on the ground she hammered her fist into his unprotected armpit. He grunted in pain and bent double, one hand going reflexively to his side. Suviel brought her knee up to connect with his chin and he went down like a sack of vegetables. Then she turned and ran.

She was almost at the bridge when the mounted guard rode up to her, trying to strike her with the flat of his sword. She ducked the blow but was knocked off her feet by the horse's hindquarters. Scrambling upright, she found herself being herded away from the tree-bridge by the rider, who transferred the reins to his sword hand and fumbled in a saddlebag. She saw him draw out the corner of a dirty trapnet and dived to the side. She heard him bark several angry syllables, and she managed almost a dozen running paces before a booted foot caught her between the shoulderblades and she sprawled, hands outstretched to break her fall. Panic seized her. She rolled clear of the horse's hooves, scrambled away on hands and knees, expecting any second a weighted mesh to land on her and tangle her limbs.

Instead she heard the clash of steel on steel and turned to see the Acolyte guard trading blows with a second rider, a lean-faced woman in quilted leather armour. A short distance away was another person on horseback, a man sitting slumped over in the saddle. The mounted guard tried to tangle the newcomer in his trapnet, but she released her reins and snatched the weighted mesh out of the air. She then swung it once about her head, leaned closer and lashed out at her enemy's sword-arm, entangling it. Then she hauled on it while making a single, deadly thrust with her own blade into his throat. She wrenched her bloody weapon free as the guard slid off his horse and landed heavily, choking his life out on the ground.

Panting, the warrior turned her attention to Suviel, taking in her manner of dress and age in a moment. 'You're a herb-woman, yes?'

Silent, Suviel nodded.

'Good. My friend is . . . very badly wounded. You must help him. Get your horse and come with me.'

'Who are you—'

'In the Mother's name, there isn't time for this!' the woman snapped. 'There's a pack of killers chasing us, and they are not far behind. We must get across the chasm, so get your mount – now.'

Suviel stared at the bloody sword's point which hovered inches away from her face. 'I'll do what I can,' she said levelly, looking the woman straight in the eye. The warrior bit her lip, and the sword lowered. Suviel nodded and hurried over to where her horse stood cropping the meagre grass. Astride the saddle, she followed the warrior and her companion across the great tree-bridge. The man, a youth, really, was semi-conscious, his eyes hardly open, his left hand limply holding the reins while his entire right arm was hidden beneath his cloak.

Once they were on the other side, the warrior dismounted and unlashed a wood axe and a long hammer.

'Here,' she said, handing Suviel the hammer. 'We'll have to wreck the bridge – it's our only chance.'

'Chance? What do you mean?'

The woman gave her a hard look, but there was something hunted at the back of it. 'The ones following after us are without pity, and would see us both killed slowly – after they had taken every pleasure they could imagine.'

Without another word the woman turned to the tree-bridge and chopped at the ground near the brink while Suviel tried to find good leverage places. The hammer was a use-blackened, slightly curved piece of seasoned torwood the length of her arm with a battered, gouged wedge of iron for a head, but it soon became clear that the bridge's weight was more than a match for it and her. Then she heard the woman curse, and looked up. A large group of riders, thirty or more, had appeared round a mountain track on the other side and were heading down the slope towards the bridge.

The female warrior spat an oath and in frustration hacked a chunk of wood out of the bridge which had stubbornly refused to shift.

'Come on,' she said to Suviel. 'We'll have to ride . . .'

Suviel could hear the exhaustion in her voice, as well as the rage that drove her. Faint pain-filled murmurs came from the youth who was over by the horses, head lolling weakly as he lay on his side. Two desperate fugitives, a female soldier and a wounded man. Without quite believing it, Suviel knew what she was going to do, what she had to do. *It's rank folly to use the Lesser Power openly*, she thought. *I could be risking everything. Yet I can't walk away from these two . . .*

'I'll take care of the bridge,' she said. 'You stay back there with your friend.'

The woman shook her head. 'In the Mother's name,' she muttered, reaching out to grab Suviel, 'Just come along, before we all get—'

Suviel caught the outstretched arm and pulled the warrior off-balance, pushing her onto her back.

'Tend to your friend, and leave this to me.'

The woman gave her a look of fury mingled with a new respect. Then she glanced at the approaching danger, came easily to her feet and loped over to the youth. Suviel turned to face the oncoming riders and coaxed forth her inner serenity, a soothing of panic, a hush in the turmoil. Almost unbidden, the Lesser Power rose to fill the calm void she had made, a sweet richness of potential which she could shape to her needs.

Quickly she envisioned the thought-canto of Cadence. As it began to coil and grow, she could feel wavelets of sound radiating from her, touching the ground, the tree-bridge, and reflecting back to her. Suddenly, she was intensely aware of the soil beneath her feet, its moist grains of earth and stones and the roots of grass and plants, a dense layer that thinned away towards the edge of the chasm. She focused the transformed Lesser Power on the brink where the tree-bridge rested, letting the ripples of sound sink into the solid rock, finding the exact pitch, the exact intensity at which the rock began to sing.

The galloping riders were moments from reaching the bridge when there was a brittle cracking sound. Suviel stepped back as the nearby lip of the chasm crumbled. The tree-bridge dropped a foot or two then, with a deep groan, it slipped off the edge, swinging down to strike the opposite face of the chasm with a shattering crash. For a second it hung there before its immense weight tore it free from the other side and sent it tumbling in a cascade of soil and rock into the depths.

On the other side most of the riders were fighting to control their panicking horses, apart from one, a tall burly man, who dismounted and uttered a wordless bellow of rage. Then to Suviel's dismay, she saw the air around him shimmer as he stretched out one cupped hand which was suddenly filled with flame. He drew back his arm and hurled the fire, not at Suviel but at her warrior companion. In an instant Suviel redirected the Lesser Power's focus and the fireball burst against the shield she had made, tendrils and sparks of flame falling to scorch the ground.

Suviel felt her limbs tremble with the strain but she held the barrier in anticipation of a second attack. The man did nothing, just stood staring across at them, dark eyes never blinking, fists clenched at his sides. Then he turned to the riders and beckoned, and a slender cloaked youth dismounted and went over to join him. The burly man put his hand on the youth's shoulder near the neck then turned.

'Keren!' he cried.

Confused, Suviel glanced round to see the female warrior sitting next to her wounded companion, her shoulders slumped, her eyes glazed. Across the chasm, the man held fast the youth, who began to shake violently, face contorted in pain, mouth wide with silent screams as the air rippled and twisted around him.

Suviel was seized by panic and horror. This was no rogue

outburst of Lesser Power, but an open display of the Wellsource. Heedless of her own safety she ran over to the woman, letting the Cadence thought-canto fade away and beginning the canto of Clarity, knowing with awful certainty that she would be too late. Suviel had just fallen to her knees when the woman's eyes showed their whites and she sprawled to one side.

'Rouse her, hedge-witch,' said the man's voice. 'Rouse my Keren so she may see what I have made for her.'

Suviel turned in slow dread and gasped. The figure that stood swaying beside the man was different, shorter in height, altered in proportions, and had lighter hair and a smaller, rounder face. The figure was female and was identical to the warrior who lay beside her. A word came into Suviel's thoughts, a word out of dark legend – *mirrorchild*.

'Or perhaps you should let her sleep,' he went on. 'Leave her in ignorance of the doom that will find her.' He gave a feral smile. 'And you, hedge-witch. I will not forget you.'

Throat dry with fear, Suviel had to swallow before speaking: 'Who are you?'

'I am Byrnak, Warlord of Honjir.' His smile widened and he laughed loudly, a brutal sound that echoed from the steep mountainsides. He glanced at the woman beside him. 'Perhaps I shall take a new title, eh, little hawk?' He lifted her lolling head. 'Look, there's your prey. Study them well.'

The woman gazed across at Suviel who shivered at that empty, void-like regard. Then those eyes moved to look at Keren, the unconscious warrior, and quivering alarm crossed the woman's features as her mouth tried to frame words.

'Hush,' said Byrnak. 'Be calm. That one is a creature of evil, a thief who stole my prize and my trust, and who means to steal your very soul. Hear me . . .' He turned her head and stared into her eyes, '. . . your name is Nerek and you are my handmaiden. I will teach you things that will help you exact vengeance—'

'Stop this!' Suviel cried.

'—and retribution against those who would deny us our destinies.'

With an arm round her waist, Byrnak led the woman back to the waiting riders, helped her onto the horse used by the youth, then mounted his own. Without a backward glance he led the band away at a gallop, heading up the track by the riverbed.

Suviel watched them ride out of sight, scarcely able to believe what she had witnessed. The creation of a mirrorchild was a violation of nature, an abomination that would have been impossible before the obliteration of the Rootpower. She had only ever heard of such a thing from her tutors, so what could Byrnak's brazen demonstration of Wellsource power mean?

Her hands were shaking. She clasped them together, knuckles whitening as she forced the turmoil of her thoughts to recede, allowing the canto of Clarity to grow in strength. Composed once more, she laid calm hands on Keren's face, massaging the temples, stroking the closed eyes.

As she worked, Keren's companion, the wounded boy, mumbled and shifted where he lay, pushing himself up on his good arm. Suviel looked at him and saw in his face a mixture of fear and exhaustion.

'Is he here?' he said in a wavering voice, and Suviel knew immediately that he meant Byrnak. 'I heard him . . . Please help me, don't let him do it again, please, oh, please . . .'

'It's all right,' Suviel said soothingly, swallowing her pity and rage. 'You're with friends. He can't get you here. We're safe.' He relaxed and sank back a little. 'What's your name?' she went on.

'Tauric dor-Barledh,' he said hesitantly. 'My father is . . . was the Duke of Patrein.'

'That's in eastern Khatris,' she said. 'How did you come to be in Honjir?'

'The warlord Gizehr attacked our keep. He claimed that we were aiding another Mogaun chief, Vashad, but we weren't, we wouldn't dare. My father's priest smuggled me out before the attack began . . .' His voice broke and tears spilled from his eyes. 'They hung the dead from the walls! My father . . . !' Weeping, Tauric lay down again, face buried in the crook of his good arm.

Suviel felt helpless in the presence of such sorrow and, sensing that Keren was beginning to recover, she reached out to gently stroke the boy's hair.

'In the Mother's name,' Keren groaned, holding her head as she sat upright. 'What did that bastard do to me?'

'Stole some of your essence,' Suviel told her. 'Oh, not much, just enough for his purpose.' And she told Keren what Byrnak had done, and all that had happened. When she finished, the warrior looked pale and shaken.

'A mirrorchild,' she muttered. 'That's only a fireside tale.'

'You saw Byrnak throw that fireball,' Suviel said. 'I assume you've never seen him do that before.'

'No, I . . .' Keren paused, warily eyeing her. 'That was clever. All right, I rode with Byrnak's warband for a few years, shared his bed, too, for a while. Does that make me untrustworthy?'

Suviel shook her head and indicated Tauric, now semiconscious again. 'You rescued him from whatever foulness was being inflicted on him. That tells me a lot about you.' She regarded Keren. 'It also gives me some idea of your resilience.'

Keren stood up, wiped hands on her grubby tunic and massaged her neck. 'So Byrnak is a mage of some kind, like you—'

'No! He's nothing like me!' Suviel said sharply. 'What he did was with the aid of the Wellsource. I, however, am a student of the Lesser Power.'

'I see,' Keren said uncomfortably. 'Well, we'd best be on our way. When Byrnak promises revenge, he's usually impatient to taste it.'

'The boy Tauric really needs proper tending,' Suviel said, bending closer to look at him. 'But you're right – it is too dangerous for us to stay here much—'

'We still need somewhere to go,' Keren went on. 'Somewhere close because I don't think the lad here can stand a long ride. Our escape from Byrnak's camp just about killed him . . .'

Suviel was not listening. She had squatted down beside Tauric and was carefully brushing the hair away from the back of his neck with trembling hands. And there, exposed to her disbelieving eyes was a purplish-brown birthmark the size of her thumb. It resembled a wolfhawk with its swept-back wings outstretched, and the last time she had seen such a mark was sixteen years ago on the bare shoulder of the Emperor Korregan as the master of the arsenal helped him into his armour before leaving for the plateau of Arengia.

'What's wrong?' said Keren. 'Is he—'

'No,' Suviel said, her thoughts whirling. 'No, he's just sleeping.'

She stood, looking down at Tauric. How could this be, she wondered. Every member of the Imperial family, no matter how minor, had been hunted down and slaughtered by the Acolytes soon after the Mogaun invasion. Was this boy the result of an Imperial indiscretion, perhaps, sent in secret to be brought up by this Duke of Patrein? He looked to be about seventeen, so it was possible. One thing was certain – she sensed in Tauric not a spark of the mage ability that was the blood heritage of the Imperial line. Clandestine enquiries would have to be made to discover just who he was, and there was only one place in the entire continent where such questions could be asked in safety.

Suviel straightened, breathed in deeply and glanced up at the sky.

'There'll be rain soon,' said Keren. She was attending to her and Tauric's horses, tightening their saddles, wiping down their flanks. 'Another reason to be on our way. North of here is the Forest of Varadin – that would offer some shelter.'

'We should head south,' Suviel said, smiling her best wise smile when Keren frowned. 'I know a place where we will be safe from Byrnak and his like.'

'Really? And what is the name of this wonderful bolthole?'

'In the old tongue it was called Krusivel but you might know of it as the Redoubt.'

Keren paused, eyes widening for a moment then narrowing. 'Another word out of legend. I suppose the Emperor lives there, waiting to ride out and retake all his lands.'

'There are no ghosts there,' Suviel said. 'Except the ones we carry with us.' She studied Keren, whose mouth was set in a bitter line as she repacked the saddlebags. 'I realize that I'm asking you to take a lot on faith. It must be difficult learning how to trust someone – or relearning.'

Keren made no answer, buckling the bags shut with a firm grip. Then she sighed and looked Suviel straight in the eye. 'Very well,' she said simply. 'We will go with you. But if he comes to any harm, I will kill you.'

Suviel met her level gaze and nodded. 'I hear what you say,' she said formally. 'Now, I think you and I had better lift Tauric onto his horse together.'

Holding the reins of Nerek's horse with his own, Byrnak rode on at the head of his riders as they cantered along a bushy ravine. He was weary to the bone yet driven by an energy that burned in his head like cold fire and gave him strength. He sensed the uneasy looks from his men and heard their whispers, but felt contempt for their fears. What could they know of the changes he was undergoing? It was as if a mighty maelstrom had snatched him into its inexorable inward swirl and was drawing him slowly into its vast heart. They were right to be afraid, for a part of him was afraid too.

He could not help recalling the dread nightmare of the three masked riders and their groaning horses. Had he been possessed by some fragment of the Lord of Twilight back at the chasm? The things he had done . . . he had not paused to think of creating a ball of fire in his hand, he had merely reached for it and it had appeared. Then there was Keren's double – a calculating fury had come over him and his mind, suddenly quicksilver and pitiless, had sorted through a number of possibilities and decided upon the creation of a mirrorchild. All done with a ruthless and cruel delight, which struck joy and fear into him in equal measure.

He glanced at her swaying drowsily in her saddle, and shivered pleasurably. His thoughts seemed bigger and stronger and the world was less daunting, more willing to be altered, directed. Byrnak grinned, wanting to throw his head back and howl with laughter, to dare the mountains, the sky, the day and the night to oppose him . . .

A horseman, one of the advance scouts, came trotting round a bend in the ravine up ahead, approached Byrnak and reined himself alongside.

'Lord, we found four men in a clearing further along. Their leader says he wishes to speak with you.'

'What are they?' Byrnak said, staring into midair as he rode on.

'They dress as merchants,' the scout said. 'But only their leader leaves his face uncovered.'

'Then let us not keep them waiting.' And he urged his mount into a gallop, as did the rest of the warband.

The clearing was dim from the ancient trees that sheltered it. Above the canopy it was raining and here and there a few rivulets of water splashed on the flattened grass. As Byrnak entered the clearing he took in the strangers in a single glance: four men in cloaks over leather armour, three of them seated on a log and wearing face-concealing helms. He dismounted swiftly and walked over to the fourth, a tall, helmetless grey-hair who stood apart from the others, head bowed.

'Who are you?' Byrnak demanded.

The tall man raised his head and Byrnak had to force himself to show no reaction: the man's eyes were completely white.

'I am Obax,' he said in a deep, steady voice. 'I was sent by your brothers to greet you in their name.'

Nightmare images filled his mind's eye, masked riders, the horses whose eyes were chalk-white orbs . . . Without looking away from those narrow, lined features he stretched out one hand and pointed at the man's three companions. 'And these?'

'My servants and guards.'

'Since you are now under my protection, you have no further need of them.' He turned to one of the company sergeants. 'Kill them.'

The fight was short but brutal. When it was over one of Byrnak's men was dead and another had lost a hand, but the three guards were slain, their helms torn away to reveal snouted, bestial faces. And through it all, the man calling himself Obax displayed no emotion of any kind. Byrnak ordered his men to make camp, then detailed two of his best fighters to stay with him as he dragged the unresisting Obax off into the darkening wood. Once out of sight of the clearing he turned to Obax.

'What are you? Why are you here?'

'I am honoured to be an Acolyte, a Nightbrother of the Twilight Path.' The pale, milky eyes seemed to stare through him. 'My duty and pleasure is to become your thrall, to carry you across the Realm of Dusk, and to show you the Great Source.'

Byrnak slowly licked dry lips. 'How will you do this?'

'I can show you,' Obax raised a long-fingered hand between them, 'now.'

He almost stepped back but held his ground, saying to his two men; 'Draw your blades and stand either side of him. If I seem to be in danger, kill him.'

When they were ready, he stared at Obax for a long moment then nodded.

'Begin.'

By the time they returned to the clearing, night had fallen and most of the men were asleep, blanket-wrapped forms clustered around a couple of campfires. Byrnak dismissed his guards and told Obax to help himself to whatever food was available and find a place to sleep. The Acolyte wordlessly bowed his head, went over to the nearest fire, ignored the gently steaming pot that rested among the coals and sat on a log, pulling his cloak tightly about himself.

Byrnak walked heavily across to his tent, the only tent, stumbled past the flaps into the lamplit interior and slumped down on the end of his fur-heaped pallet. There was movement beneath the furs and the woman sat up at the other end, startled gaze fixed on him. But his eyes were still seeing the hazy regions of the Realm of Dusk, the pale forest of skeletal trees whose brittle branch ends broke into twisted shards which scurried away into the undergrowth, the two immense towers whose pillars wept ghosts, the crumbling, hollow stone colossus with its half-mouth whispering rhymes in an unintelligible tongue. There, in the Realm of Dusk, Obax took the shape of one of the deathly steeds and carried Byrnak past all these sights and more, finally bringing him to a shattered, peakless titanic mountain and to the awesome wonder that pulsed at its core – the Wellsource.

Now, when he tried to recall its form, only fragmentary images would come to mind – was it a heart pumping iridescent flame, or a fountaining column, or a moaning whirlwind veined with lightning, or a cloudy thing of levers and crystalline planes? He did remember how it called to him, to the cold fire that blazed in his head. It had known him, and his destiny.

Byrnak became aware of the woman's unwavering stare, moved up the pallet and pulled the furs aside. She was naked, her pale-skinned, rounded form sending lust rushing through him. Then he took her, sating himself, and she made no sound. Only when he was done did she say, in a voice desperate with need: 'Who am I? Please tell me – who *am* I?'

Chapter Five

Towards the glutted margins of battle they ride, With
their greying hair and rusting blades.

Kovalti, *Ode to the Warrior*

It was a cold, grey autumn morning in the Bachruz Mountains,
cold without being icy, grey without the promise of an imminent
downpour. Mist veiled the cruel crags and pinnacles and hid from
view the few streams that wound along ravines and gorges worn
deep by uncountable summers and winters. One of these streams,
a river almost, came down from the highest snow-wrapped slopes,
tumbling through mossy, boulder-strewn gullies till it reached the
upper reaches of a high, sheltered valley called Krusivel. There, the
waters slowed and widened towards the north of the valley where
they fed a small lake and the town gathered around its banks. A
runoff stream led away from the lake's north-east bank to a notch
at the edge of a sheer drop, near the foot of a natural rock tower
rooted in the cliffs themselves. The stream flung itself over the
brink and into the air, falling from such a height that it bathed
the barren rocks below in never-ending spray.

A philosophically-minded townsperson might have pondered
that long journey and wondered why anything would travel so
far only to leap into oblivion.

That morning, two men sat on a boulder near the edge of
those falls. The taller and older of the two wore thick woollen
breeches and a battered-looking black jerkin of quilted leather.

His companion, a short, burly man in a trader's many-pocketed tunic, poured pale wine into a wooden beaker which he then handed over.

Ikarno Mazaret, Lord Commander of the Knights of the Order of the Fathertree, accepted the cup and took a mouthful. He let the pungent flavour fill his head before swallowing, then whistled.

'What a vintage,' he said. 'That has to be the finest cup of Ebroan white I've ever tasted.' He ran his tongue around the inside of his mouth. 'What a difference from these Honjir ales, which are fine in their way, you understand. And as for asmirith, that distilled furnace-milk . . .'

His companion leaned forward with the bottle but Mazaret shook his head.

'One's enough this early, Gilly,' he said. 'Besides, you didn't come all this way just to bring me a flask of wine.'

'Well, I also happen to have a piece of Cabringan cheese,' said the man called Gilly, producing a wax-paper package from a pocket and unwrapping it. 'But if you'd rather not . . .'

'Daemon in human form,' Mazaret growled with a smile, reaching for the cheese and breaking off a piece. As he chewed, enjoying the sharp tang, he regarded his companion levelly.

'So the news is bad, then?'

Gilly shrugged, then poured himself a cup of wine. He was a round-faced, bearded man whose affable demeanour belied his lethal abilities with the broadsword.

'Depends on your definition of "bad". Our sympathizers in the east have all promised to keep sending supplies through our people in Scallow, but the Sejeend and Oumetra cabals have decided to reduce their contributions.'

Mazaret's heart sank. 'Why?'

'They're impatient, Ikarno. Damn it, everyone is impatient. They all seem to think that you're sitting up here in charge of ten, fifteen, twenty thousand hardened warriors, each ten feet tall and able to blow arrows from their nostrils!' He gave a lop-sided grin. 'Of course, I couldn't confirm or deny such speculations, being a mere messenger.'

Mazaret sighed and ran a hand through his bushy, greying hair. 'What about the Mogaun troop strengths? Any reliable numbers?'

'Some, yes. In Cabringa the tribes can field about four and a half, five thousand, mostly light cavalry; in Kejana, about three and a half thousand split equally between cavalry and foot soldiers; and in Dalbar it comes to roughly nineteen hundred, again half cavalry, half on foot. The Ogucharn Isles scarcely matter – there's only a couple of minor tribes there, totalling maybe eight hundred.'

'And Yasgur?'

The trader smiled and examined his fingernails for a moment before looking up. 'At least fourteen thousand, of which two thousand are heavy cavalry, another four thousand light cavalry, and the rest foot troops.'

Mazaret looked away, not wanting Gilly to see the dismay in his eyes. Instead he gazed at the nearby stream as it rushed away over the edge of the cliff and tried to make sense of the numbers and totals that filled his head. Since the invasion sixteen years ago, the military strength of the tribes had waned, some by nearly half. Except for Yasgur.

Son of Hegroun, the warchief who led the Mogaun invasion seventeen years ago, Yasgur had held northern Khatris and all Mantinor during the chaos that followed his father's death just months after the fall of Besh-Darok. In the years since he had forged an alliance with several noble families, initially as a response to the incursions and raids by neighbouring warchiefs eager to grab Hegroun's prize. His army was now the largest of any warlord, its ranks filled with recruits drawn from the native Khatrisian and Mantinoren peoples as well as his own tribe.

'Can't be done, can it?'

'No such word as "can't", Gilly,' Mazaret said. 'They may have the numbers but we have the strategy and the unity of purpose.'

The trader gave him a piercing look. 'As well as the numbers, they also have all the towns, forts and outposts, whereas we have, what, two thousand would-be knights—'

'Two and a half thousand, plus a thousand of the Hunter's Children.'

'Ah yes, the Hunter's Children. What a unity of purpose that is!'

Gilly's face was stonelike and Mazaret glared at him, feeling a sudden resentment at the man for speaking aloud the very doubts and fears that clouded his every day. Then a ghost of a smile crept across the trader's features, and Mazaret shook his head ruefully.

'I seem to recall having a similar discussion about ten years ago,' he said. 'You were so scathing back then that I almost decided to give up any idea of resistance or rebellion, sail away to Keremenchool, perhaps. But I didn't.'

'You should have,' Gilly said softly. 'It was a madman's dream then, and it still is.' He drank off the last of his wine. 'But what sort of madmen would we be to let things stay as they are?'

They were silent for several moments before Gilly spoke again.

'Earlier, while I was on my way here, I heard a rumour that Suviel had returned last night, and not alone.'

'And what else did you overhear?' Mazaret said testily.

'That one of her companions was none other than Korregan's bastard and thus heir to the Imperial throne.' Gilly smiled widely. 'Which could upset your agreement with the Hunter's Children, if it's true.' He gave Mazaret a sidelong glance. 'Is it?'

'Bardow and the other mages certainly seem to think so,' Mazaret said. 'They also think that he will lose an arm.'

'How so?'

'Apparently the boy was tortured by his captor, one of the northern Honjir warlords, who sliced his right arm to ribbons,' Mazaret said, keeping back what he'd been told about Byrnak and the mirrorchild. 'Suviel tried to save it, but the damage is too great.'

Gilly cursed. 'Beasts, some of them. Worse than beasts.' He looked thoughtful. 'How would the people regard a crippled Emperor? Would they follow him, do you think?'

'They followed Orosiada,' Mazaret said.

'That was nearly two thousand years ago.'

Mazaret shrugged. 'For the moment I am more concerned with what Volyn and the Hunter's Children are going to say at the War Council later.'

'That's at noon, I believe . . .'

'Yes, and I would thank you to speak with Abbess Halimer before it starts,' Mazaret said drily. 'I've no wish to have to send the procurals out to find you . . .'

Gilly glanced to one side. 'We have company.'

Mazaret turned to see a staff runner approaching, pale yellow overshirt and trews flapping as he ran. The boy came to a halt a few feet away and saluted, open hand against opposite shoulder.

'Yes, lad.'

'My lord commander, there is a visitor to see you at the temple.'

'Who is it?'

'I do not know, my lord. The Rul told me to say only that it was someone of importance.'

What is Rul Dagash up to, Mazaret wondered as he stood. 'Will you join me?' he asked Gilly. 'Or are you going to stay and finish the wine?'

The trader grinned, put the bottle to his mouth and uncorked it with his teeth.

Mazaret shook his head. 'There could be only one answer, eh? All right, lad – let's be on our way.'

It was a short walk back round the lake. As he followed the runner Mazaret looked across at the town, remembering how it was when he and the ragged remnants of the Order arrived here sixteen years ago. Then there had been only a decrepit Skyhorse shrine by the small lake, along with the tumbled, mossy stones of a few abandoned huts. Now there were barracks, cabins, stables, barns, a forge, a tavern, a mill and a bakery. And the temple.

The Temple of the Earthmother was a large, single-storey building situated on a slight rise overlooking the town. It had a flattened dome at its centre and a slender tower at each corner.

Within its confines were cells and chambers, as well as a library, the main armoury, a school, the healer's chamber, and the chapel with the sacred Tabernacle of Ash. As well as the fighting yards, the temple grounds included an orchard, a vegetable plot and a burial garden. Mazaret's regard lingered on the gravestones and plinths clustered around a nearby copse of aging trees. His wife and three children lay buried there, along with several close friends and scores of brave knights. Although many had perished during the long, desperate flight from the terrible defeat at Arengia sixteen years ago, it was not till they reached Krusivel that others began to die from a contagion loosed by the Mogaun shamans. Perfect recollection brought back to him how the ghastly fever had taken hold of his loved ones and burned them from within, melting their flesh away, filling their eyes and minds with horror, destroying their memory of him before finally freeing their souls from agony.

With time the raging grief had ebbed to a dulled sorrow but he could still remember when the last of his family, little Talve, had died and how he had uttered a cry of anguish and run out into the night, stumbling among the trees and bushy undergrowth, losing himself. At some point he had staggered, scratched and bleeding, out of the dense forest and found himself beside a deep pool into which a waterfall poured with an embracing, rushing sound. Madness was upon him and, filling his tunic and his pockets with stones, he threw himself into the pool. There had been a blinding pain in his head and he had known no more until he woke on his back, lying on the rocks behind the waterfall with sunlight shining down through the spray. Then out of the hissing cascade had come a voice: **'Death is not for you, son of my daughters. Much has been lost, yet the fight is not done, the race is not yet run.'**

A swirl of odours had filled his head: earth, roots, the heavy moist smell of growing things. A cold fear had made his heart pound. 'Who speaks?'

'You know me, and my beloved who was slain with your Emperor at Arengia. Bitterly have I wept for my heart's desire

whose spirit is no more but who I cannot forget. Know that your sorrow is as my own, black and tenacious, yet my hunger for vengeance is more than its equal. So hear me, Ikarno Mazaret, choose life so that life may yet triumph. For although the Lord of Twilight appears to have been victorious, his darkest strategy has failed. And a day will come when the Lord of Twilight's baleful workings shall again twist the world and war shall eat the weak and the innocent. So live, son of my daughters – live and prepare for that day. And avenge our loss.'

Searchers had found him later, half-dazed and slumped by the side of the pool. A brooding darkness of spirit had gripped him for weeks thereafter, during which the guidance and command of the survivors was in the hands of the Order's Shield-Prior, Attal. Mazaret frowned, trying to recall Attal's likeness, then sighed in regret. Poor Attal's remains lay in the burial garden with the rest now, dead from a spearthrust that should never have reached him.

But the memory of that voice speaking in his head, and of the intense, eldritch smells of leaves and wood, would remain undimmed by the passing years.

Mazaret and the runner followed the quicker path to the temple, leading round the town and through a small orchard. About two score novitiates and knights were practising swordcraft in the temple's main yard as they hurried by, heading for the vestry-gate. Rul Dagash was waiting in the archway as they approached.

'See Tol Urzik,' he said to the boy. 'He has other tasks for you.'

The runner saluted and darted away. Dagash watched him disappear round a corner before turning to Mazaret.

'My lord,' he said quietly. 'A visitor is waiting in your ante-chamber—'

'Good,' Mazaret said, following the Rul into the dim interior.

'—where I have him closely guarded by two senior novitiates.'

Mazaret paused, staring at Dagash. 'Why? Who is he?'

'A patrol encountered him and another, an elderly manservant as it turned out, riding in along one of the ravine paths in the middle of the night. After hearing the man's explanation, the Tol in charge of the patrol had them bound, gagged and blinkered then brought up to Krusivel.'

'So who is he?'

'My lord, he claims to be your brother.'

Mazaret went very still, gaze averted from Dagash. 'Describe him.'

'A man in his forties, shorter than yourself, carries more weight than is good for him, has a sallow complexion, and shoulder-length black hair tied back. He was carrying a sabre and a sleeve dagger when the patrol found them.'

Mazaret nodded, holding up his hand. 'Thank you, Dagash. You've done very well. I'll deal with this matter immediately.'

Without another word, he turned and stalked off down the corridor, bootheels loud on the floor planks. Emotion surged through him in varying shades of anger, and as he came to his antechamber he slowed, trying to regain his equilibrium. Then he opened the door.

Salutes came from the two guards within, and a figure sitting at the room's single long table rose as he entered and took a couple of steps towards him, smiling, with hand outstretched. The smile faltered when Mazaret's demeanour remained grim and the hand fell to fingering the edge of a shabby brown cloak. Mazaret dismissed the guards and closed the door behind them. Then he turned back to his younger brother.

'So – you're here,' he said. 'Now, what do you want?'

Coireg Mazaret resumed his seat at the end of the table, leaned one elbow on it and stroked his chin. 'The tapestries in here are quite rare, did you know that? And as for that Order banner over there – there are collectors in the north who would really pay—'

'Right, I'll call the guards—' Ikarno Mazaret reached for the door.

'No! Wait! Damn, but you never did have a sense of humour.'

The younger man sighed, took a handful of his cloak and rubbed his face on it. 'I'm . . . sorry, I forget how badly we get on usually.'

'Another thing you forget is what I said I'd do if I ever saw you again,' Mazaret said, hand straying to the dagger at his waist.

Coireg's eyes widened in alarm. 'In the name of the Mother, Ikarno, it was an accident!' He rose from his chair and backed away as Mazaret advanced. 'It was eight years ago, for pity's sake!'

'She was our sister and you let those Mogaun scum take her . . .'

'There was nothing I could do, do you hear me? Nothing!' Trembling, Coireg tore the cloak from his shoulders, flung it on the floor then walked up to Mazaret and looked him in the eye. 'There! You want to gut me? Well here I am, and you won't even have to reach very far. But before you do anything, you better listen because there's something you should know.'

Staring back, Mazaret was unsettled to see despair and sorrow naked in his brother's face. 'What could you have to say that would interest me?' he muttered.

'He's dead,' Coireg said, falling into a chair at the table. 'Father's dead.'

An awful, empty silence came in the wake of those words and a sense of hollowness and a kind of panic filled Mazaret. This was no ruse. He could hear the truth in Coireg's voice.

'How . . . ?' he said.

'Poison in his food. He hadn't been well for quite a while, and the Mother knows how many times I begged him to leave Casall and join you here. He'd have none of it, of course, always claiming that the Midnight Ships would come to a halt without his personal direction.'

Mazaret leaned on the table. It was as if it were someone else hearing the terrible news and feeling this powerless anger and grief. Out of a numb stillness he tried to remember the last time he had seen his father, during a secret journey to the north five years ago. Hevelik Mazaret, a baronet to the ancient crown of

Anghatan, was also Master of Harbours for the city of Casall. Instead of fleeing the invasion, he had appeared to bend the knee to the conquering Mogaun, offering to manage the harbours and docks on their behalf. In reality he was assembling a clandestine organization called the Midnight Ships, dedicated to providing an escape route for refugees, particularly nobles, desperate to leave. In the years that followed, the risk of being unmasked grew steadily but despite that, and his advancing age, he refused to step down.

'If I retired,' he had told Ikarno during that last visit, 'they would put some spineless fool in my place, a puppet for this Thraelor they've made High Captain. If that happened, many traders would opt for Rauthaz instead, or even some of the Jefren ports, and then where would they be, hmm?'

For a moment or two, Mazaret listened to the sound of his own breathing. Then he said: 'Did they catch whoever did it?'

'A kitchen servant was found dead the next morning.' The younger Mazaret shrugged. 'Maybe it was because too many refugees were turning up across in Keremenchool. Or perhaps one too many high-ranking prisoners had been spirited out of the Red Tower, and someone close to Thraelor decided that old man Mazaret should be made an example of . . .'

His voice tailed off in a quiet, gasping sob, quickly stifled. Ikarno Mazaret regarded him with sorrow and pity, recalling how deeply Coireg had been affected by their mother's death sixteen years ago. They had, he realized, both drunk deeply from the cup of grief. He released a shaky sigh and reached out to rest a hand on his brother's shoulder. Coireg looked up with reddened eyes.

'I was nearing Casall when word reached me. I stayed there a day and a night before deciding to ride south to tell you. Five weeks is a long journey on horseback, especially for Olgen, my servant. When I started out, all I intended was to find you and deliver the news. But I dwelled on what had happened and now, as I sit before you, all I know is that I want someone to pay.' His fist clenched. 'I want the chance to hit back, Ikarno, you understand? That's the other reason why I'm here, to ask you to let me join you. Oh, I know I'm no knight, but I am a good scout and I know how to fight dirty. At the very least, I could teach some of your people a few tricks, perhaps go on a raid here or there . . .'

His voice was level and serious, but Mazaret knew with a kind of shock that his brother was begging. He thought of his mother and sister, of the graves behind the temple, and of his father, then considered the arrival of Suviel and the boy Tauric and found himself with the seed of an idea. With a hand on Coireg's shoulder, he drew him to his feet.

'There *is* a way that you can help us.'

Chapter Six

When deceit makes a mask,
Trust makes us dance.

Avalti, *Song of the Blade*

The east corridor of the Temple of the Earthmother was long and windowless, yet devoted to artistic expressions of devotion. Dozens of glass lamps hung from delicately ornate wall stanchions, shedding plentiful golden light on the paintings, carvings, sculptures and illuminated parchments. Suviel was standing before one of the niches, examining a portrait of the Emperor Korregan, when she saw the Lord Commander and another man emerge from his chambers. The man was heavy-set, aged about forty and carrying a dark cloak over his shoulder. In the torchlight they exchanged muttered words, then the stranger nodded and glanced at her before walking away to disappear down a branch passage.

'Fair morning, my Lord Mazaret,' she said with mock solemnity.

'Shin Hantika,' he replied with a faint smile, looking either way along the corridor before drawing her to him.

Suviel hugged him, her face against his, enjoying the broadness of his back through his leather jerkin. Then she pulled back slightly, frowning.

'Is something wrong?'

Mazaret sighed. 'My father is dead, poisoned while in Casall. That was my brother you saw – he brought the news.'

63

'Your brother Coireg? Was he not responsible for—'

'Yes . . . yes, I know. But he is not as he was. Something in him has changed.' He looked at her. 'He is all the family I have left, Suviel. I must try to heal the rift between us.'

She put her hand gently on his cheek. 'I am so sorry about your father,' she said, wanting to say much more but knowing it would be unnecessary.

He went silent for a moment then said: 'There is never enough time to get to know someone, Suviel. I do not even know if my father approved of what I have been doing here, and we met at least twice a year since the invasion . . . since our mother died.' He laughed, a quiet, dry sound. 'Now she would have approved. We always knew what she thought about anything which involved right and wrong because she was quick to speak her mind . . .' He breathed in deep and seemed to gather himself together. 'How is Tauric?'

She smiled wanly. 'He is still full of grief about his father – well, the man he knew as his father. We have not mentioned the matter of his lineage yet. It would just add to his sorrow and confusion.'

Mazaret nodded sadly. 'I met the Duke of Patrein several times. He was a good man. What of the boy's arm?'

'It cannot be saved. Bardow and the chief surgeon intend to amputate it below the elbow this evening.'

'He is young. He will overcome these . . . losses.'

Suviel felt otherwise, but decided against voicing her disagreement. 'What about Coireg?' she said. 'Are you going to admit him into the Order?'

'He would not wish it, and the discipline would not suit him. No, there is another way in which he can help us, and himself.'

Mazaret would say no more as they made their way to the Abbess's study where the War Council was to be held. Abbess Halimer of the Earthmother faith was waiting when they were showed in, an elderly, slightly built woman wearing a pale blue cassock. With her was Cheil Bardow, Archmage of the Rootpower, looking amiable and almost unremarkable in his customary brown and grey townsman's attire. Bardow rose from the study's great oval table in greeting.

'My Lord Commander – does the day find you well?'

'Well enough, Archmage, though I am saddened to hear that your patient will lose an arm.'

'Some lose much more, my lord.'

'Indeed,' Mazaret said stiffly, looking around him. 'I see that Captain Volyn is absent.'

'Delayed by pressing administrative problems, my lord,' said Abbess Halimer with a hint of amusement. 'His messenger assured me that he will not keep us waiting too long.'

'Very well. In the meantime, Abbess, tell me how the grain stocks are faring. I assume that you have spoken to the inimitable Gilly . . .'

As Mazaret and Halimer fell into discussion, Bardow came over to join Suviel.

'Ikarno appears a little cheerless,' he said.

Suviel told him about the death of Mazaret's father and the presence of his brother, and the Archmage became grave.

'This is disturbing news.' He frowned. 'This brother, Coireg, has a somewhat unsavoury history.'

'Ikarno has always said as much to me,' Suviel agreed. 'But he is certain that Coireg is a changed man. He even hinted at giving him some kind of task, but would say no more about it.'

Bardow shrugged. 'I may be flinching at shadows, but it seems coincidental that this news arrives mere hours after you ride into Krusivel with a lost heir to the Imperial throne. It is almost of a piece with this Byrnak matter.'

Earlier, the Archmage's reaction on hearing of her sorcerous encounter with the Honjir warlord had been one of alarm. Only after she had related the full tale had he revealed that there was another warlord, Grazaan of Northern Yularia, who was known to wield Wellsource powers openly.

'What is Ikarno going to do with his brother?' Bardow asked. 'Allow him into the Order?'

Suviel shook her head. 'He does have something in mind, but would not confide in me.'

'Perhaps he intends to discuss it here, should Volyn actually arrive.' Bardow gave a wry smile. 'No doubt the honoured captain will once more exhort us to include a siege of Besh-Darok in the battle plans,' he said with a dry chuckle. 'On the other hand, one of his rangers was present when we brought Tauric into the healer's chamber, so perhaps he has been considering the position of the Hunter's Children on the matter.'

'And if they decide to decamp over it,' said Suviel, 'where does that leave us?'

'In serious trouble.' Bardow glanced at her. 'But that's not going to happen. If Volyn was going to make the break, all two hundred of his men would be saddled and ready to leave now. I have been keeping an eye on their barracks and apart from some kind of minor brawl a few hours ago, everything is as it should be.'

'So why the delay?'

The Archmage was about to reply when there was a knock at the door and Suviel turned to see a temple sister entering ahead of two men dressed in sombre green.

'Reverence,' the sister said to Halimer. 'Captain Volyn and Sentinel Kodel.'

The first, Kodel, was slender and dark-skinned, his long black hair tied back in a queue, his hawkish eyes surveying everyone in the room. After him came Volyn who was shorter, barrel-chested and muscular, full of restless energy, like a wrestler always ready to wade into a fight. Curly fair hair and a dense but neatly trimmed beard added a roguish demeanour to his appearance. He and his subordinate inclined their heads to the Abbess and the Archmage and finally to Mazaret. Volyn grinned widely. Mazaret offered a thin smile.

Suviel watched the two war leaders carefully. The contrast between them went beyond differences in height and build, or in military methods. It was history that set them apart, a

weighty veil that neither could forget despite these past six years
of co-operation.

Nearly five hundred years ago, the Khatrimantine Empire's
ruling dynasty, House Tor-Cavarill, was deposed by another
branch of the Imperial family, House Tor-Galantai. The Emperor
Hasmeric Tor-Cavarill had died of a stroke just hours after his
wife's death from giving birth to their sole issue, a son. Hasmeric
himself had been an only child and with no immediate relations to
take up the role of regent, the responsibility for choosing a suitable
candidate fell to the Conclave of Rods. Under the influence of
House Tor-Galantai, the Conclave conferred the crown on Lord
Arravek Tor-Galantai, citing the need for a strong Imperium in
the face of the pirate princes whose fleets were threatening the
northern coast at that time.

Hasmeric's son, Coulabric, was brought up among the myriad
isles of western Dalbar, far from the capital, Besh-Darok. In
time he grew into a strong young man skilled in the arts of
the sword as well as the quill, and waiting for Arravek to pass
away so that the crown and throne would be returned to House
Tor-Cavarill. But on the day of Arravek's death, a crossbow
bolt found Coulabric's heart while he was out riding the hunt,
slaying him instantly. When Arravek's son was crowned Emperor,
Coulabric's supporters accused him of murder and conspiracy,
named themselves the Hunter's Children and declared eternal
enmity against House Tor-Galantai.

Considering this, Suviel felt a sense of foreboding as Mazaret
greeted Volyn. With a living descendant of Arravek here in
Krusivel, there was no telling what proposal Volyn would put
to the Council.

Their greetings done, everyone moved to sit at the oval table,
apart from Abbess Halimer who went over to unlock a plain
blackwood cabinet. From it she took three rolls of paper which
she brought over and unfurled. As wide as the table and half
as long, the maps were of heavy Anghatan paper and bordered
with grey-brown cotton. One showed the entirety of the former
Empire of Khatrimantine, another depicted in greater detail the

south-western provinces of Dalbar, Kejana, most of Honjir and southern Jefren, and the third was of the centre of the continent from Prekine to Besh-Darok and the Gulf of Brykon. All three maps showed signs of wear, small tears, an occasional scorch mark or wine stain, and were all that remained of the Order of the Fathertree's great archive of war.

The War Council began, and at once descended into disagreement. As Bardow had predicted, Volyn renewed his demand that Besh-Darok be included in the forthcoming campaign. Mazaret rejected the idea as unacceptably perilous, pointing out the small matter of the Warlord Yasgur's 14,000 troops. Volyn countered with the argument that with information from spies and sympathizers in Besh-Darok, their knowledge of the situation there was far more detailed than even six months ago. Suviel was surprised when, instead of dismissing this, Mazaret sat back and listened as Kodel revealed that the Hunter's Children now knew the location of troop barracks, the order of their defences, the pattern of the guard patrols, even the level of the city's war supplies. The Sentinel also produced maps of Besh-Darok, of its fortifications and of the docks, by which a small force of 200 would enter the city while the bulk of the allies' army assaulted the landward battlements.

'Our losses would be slight,' said Volyn. 'The main aim of the infiltrators is to capture all of Yasgur's senior officers, not to mention Yasgur himself. Without the head—' He made a chopping gesture '—the body is easy prey.'

The silence that followed was full of tense uncertainty as Mazaret gazed thoughtfully at the map of the entire continent of Toluveraz. Finally he spoke.

'Your plan has merit, captain. From what you say, it seems that it may indeed be possible to take Besh-Darok.'

Volyn almost managed to keep his surprise from showing, while Abbess Halimer was visibly taken aback. Bardow glanced at Suviel, smiling faintly as Mazaret went on. 'However, before deciding upon such a fundamental change to our strategy, there is another matter to be settled.'

'Ah yes,' Volyn said amiably. 'Korregan's bastard son.'

Halimer leaned forward in surprise. 'What's this?'

'Tauric, the young man who arrived with Suviel,' Bardow explained. 'He has the lineage birthmark and must therefore be the late Emperor's by-blow . . .'

'Rumours have been rife all night,' Volyn said, bending his head towards the Abbess. 'You see, the honoured Lord Commander harbours doubts about the Hunter's Children's willingness to fight on behalf of Korregan's heir. Let me assure everyone at this table that all we want is to deliver our land from tyranny. If, once that has been achieved, it is the will of the Council that this Tauric be crowned Emperor, then the Hunter's Children would not stand in his way.'

'Your words are most welcome, captain,' Mazaret said with a faint smile. 'In the light of such sentiments, I am sure you would be keen to see Korregan's heir properly prepared for the role he may be called upon to assume.'

'Of course,' Volyn said guardedly.

'Good, good. You see, young Tauric knows almost nothing of the responsibilties that the crown carries, whereas the Hunter's Children have a detailed knowledge of such matters. Also, it is a sad fact that Tauric will lose an arm due to the torture he underwent. However, even a one-armed man can hold a weapon and we all know that the Hunter's Children are skilled in the use of many weapons, as well as the Empty-Hand Pattern.'

'What are you suggesting?' said Bardow.

'Simply this – that the honourable captain takes Tauric under his custodianship and sends him to one of the Children's sanctuaries in Dalbar or Kejana where he will receive the tutelage and training that he lacks. Naturally, as Lord Commander of the Knights of the Fathertree, I would insist that several advisers accompany the boy, a mage or scholar nominated by Bardow, a sister from the Abbess's order, and another of my own choosing.'

His brother, Suviel realized. She regarded Mazaret in admiration: Volyn would have to accept this task or risk losing the opportunity of an assault on Besh-Darok, as well as stirring up the kind of fear and suspicion that could break the War Council.

Volyn sat back, stroking his beard and staring at Mazaret while Kodel whispered in his ear. Then he nodded sharply. 'This is an unusual request, my lord, but we shall not shirk it. This mild autumn will not last forever, and we must be ready to bare the knife before winter bares its teeth. If it pleases this Council, my deputy, Sentinel Kodel, will accompany the boy as custodian in my stead, and have responsibility for his safety and instruction. These advisers, however, must be prepared to accept the Sentinel's authority on all matters while within one of our sanctuaries.'

'I find that acceptable,' Mazaret said, looking at Bardow and Halimer who both nodded.

'And as for the proposed attack on Besh-Darok,' he continued. 'I will give it my cautious approval, provided that we commit no more than half our troops and that I command the infiltration force.'

For a brief moment Volyn said nothing, just stared at his hands which lay on the table, palms up. Then he clasped them together and looked up.

'Very well,' he said. 'Provided the command is held jointly with Sentinel Kodel.'

The two men regarded each other, their gazes unwavering till Mazaret gave a smile and a sharp nod. The tension in the room eased and Abbess Halimer sighed.

'Then it is agreed,' she said. 'New battle plans will have to be drawn up.'

'I would be willing to meet with the honoured Lord Commander and his senior officers on the morrow,' said Volyn. 'Or sooner, if necessary.'

'Tomorrow is timely enough,' Mazaret said. 'We have still to hear from Archmage Bardow. What he has to say could greatly influence our deliberations.'

Bardow leaned forward. 'You may be correct, my lord. All here must understand the gravity of what is being proposed, not least in the light of Gunderlek's ill-fated rebellion.'

'He did ask for our help,' Volyn said.

'And we were right to refuse,' Bardow retorted. 'For all his bravery, Gunderlek was a foolish man. We made it clear to him how perilous his undertaking would be. So understand – we shall be walking into a veritable drakken's mouth. But before I say any more, Shin Hantika has something to tell you.'

He nodded at Suviel and without adornment she related all that happened from the encounter at Wujad's Pool to her arrival at Krusivel in the early hours of that morning. Volyn was first startled then grave as she told of the incident involving Byrnak, while Halimer remained sombre throughout. When she had finished everyone was silent for a moment till Volyn spoke, addressing Bardow.

'So what is the meaning of Shin Hantika's tale?' he said. 'Are the Acolytes concocting some dark scheme?'

Bardow folded his arms. 'I fear that is the case, honoured captain. It is too early to be certain, but it may be that the Acolytes have found a way to confer Wellsource powers upon selected persons. We strongly suspect that one such is the warlord Grazaan – at the siege at Rauthaz he played a decisive role, accompanied by certain senior Acolytes.'

Volyn shook his head, face dark and brooding. 'So what are you saying? That we will be facing an invincible enemy?'

'I repeat, it is as yet too early to be sure, despite Suviel's account of this Byrnak's abilities. Thankfully there has been neither sight nor sign of the Daemonkind, but that does not lessen the danger of the Acolytes and their agents acting against us in the coming war.'

'Can your mages protect us?' Volyn said restlessly. 'This is what we need to be certain of.'

Bardow regarded him. 'While the Wellsource is significantly more potent than the Lesser Power, there has since the War of Invasion been little evidence of anyone employing it to its full measure, till recently.' He spread his hands. 'Captain, I could offer you bland and comforting assurances about our abilities and preparations but that would be doing us all a disservice.

The truth is that we do not know enough about the Acolytes' strengths and weaknesses.' He looked from face to face. 'Which is why I ask leave of this Council to send someone to Trevada to spy on the Acolytes in their fastness and try to discern something of their plans.'

Everyone was uneasily quiet for a moment.

'Prekine is a desolation,' Abbess Halimer said grimly. 'And Trevada has become a deadly trap. We have never sent any scouts there.'

'Nor have the Hunter's Children,' echoed Volyn.

Suviel watched Bardow nod at each comment, his eyes studying the map on the table. 'My intention was to send not a scout, but a mage.'

There was a murmur of approval. Then Mazaret spoke, his voice low, controlled. 'Who will it be?'

'Shin Hantika,' the Archmage said. 'Her mastery of the Lesser Power will allow her to penetrate the web of illusions that surround Trevada, while her skills in disguise and stealth will enable her to deal with more mundane difficulties.'

Astonished, Suviel stared at Bardow, who smiled apologetically. 'There was no time to talk with you before now. It will be dangerous, but I know you are more than equal to the task.' He turned back to the others. 'Does the War Council give its consent?'

Volyn nodded and after a slight hesitation Abbess Halimer did so too. Suviel looked across at Mazaret, hoping to see something like concern in his face, but her heart sank a little at the cool distance she saw there. Then he gave a slow, sombre nod and it was sealed.

'How long till Shin Hantika returns?' Volyn said.

'Four, maybe five weeks,' Bardow said. 'Contrary to what the Lord Commander said, do not be influenced in your plans by what I have told you. The arrangements previously made for the Mage Order will suffice.'

'You cannot take back your words, Archmage,' Mazaret said with a wry smile. 'How can we help but worry over them?' He looked over at Halimer. 'Your reverence, could we have some more applewater? This listening is thirsty business!'

The remaining matters – an appraisal of Krusivel's supplies of provisions and weapons, and reports on recruitment and training – were soon dealt with. Volyn and Kodel were the first to leave and as Bardow went over to speak to the Abbess who was rolling up the maps, Mazaret drew Suviel off to one side.

'Prekine is a dread place,' he said. 'You cannot imagine the dangers you will face. Will you not reconsider this undertaking?'

By the light of the chamber's wall lamps his long thin face looked suddenly careworn, his soft brown eyes full of anxiety. Her hand sought his.

'How could I?' she said quietly. 'Bardow was my mentor and now he is the leader of my order. I cannot refuse his bidding, Ikarno, any more than you could have refused the Emperor's command.'

She felt his hand tighten around hers. 'My heart . . . aches for you,' he whispered. A wave of love and sorrow passed through her and she fought to stave off the tears.

'Tonight,' she murmured. 'I shall not leave till the morning, I promise.'

He nodded, then released her hand and drew back slightly as Bardow came over. The Archmage regarded her with a raised eyebrow to which she gave a slight shake of the head, then said: 'The honoured Lord Commander was just remarking that the way to Trevada passes through very dangerous territory.'

'Danger lies all about us,' Bardow said evenly. 'All that differs is the degree of its malice.' He looked at Mazaret. 'Have you decided upon whom to send with young Tauric, my lord?'

'Yes, my brother, Coireg Mazaret.'

'Ah, the man who arrived with an old servant this morning.'

Suviel bit her lip as Bardow went on in a voice of calm amusement, 'I understand he has something of a mixed past, but clearly you are satisfied with him.'

'I trust him implicitly, Archmage,' Mazaret said coolly. 'Now, you must excuse me – I have arrangements for tomorrow to attend to.'

He gave Bardow a polite nod, and a slower bow to Suviel, who watched him turn and leave. Bardow waited till he was out of sight before crossing to close the door. When he sat at the table, Suviel did likewise and regarded him nervously for a moment before speaking.

'Weren't you understating the power of the Wellsource?' she said.

'Of course. If the others really knew how perilous our situation is, then we would truly be lost.' His eyes seemed to contemplate something beyond her sight, dark eyes which now held none of the warmth others were used to seeing. Suviel shivered inwardly as he turned that hard, focused gaze on her.

'Suviel,' he said, 'your real task is far more vital than gathering information. Once you reach Trevada, I want you to find a way inside what used to be the High Basilica and retrieve the Crystal Eye.'

The enormity of his words struck hard. Suviel felt as if she were suddenly hanging over a vast, empty gulf instead of sitting on a solid chair with one arm on the smooth table top. There was no fear, just a hollowness in her chest where her heart should have been. Foreboding, she told herself, suppressing an odd impulse to laugh out loud. When the danger is so great and so far away, the mind cannot encompass it.

'I thought the Eye was destroyed,' she said.

Bardow smiled bleakly. 'The Acolytes would never allow such a glittering trophy to be damaged.' He met her worried gaze with a touch of his old humour. 'Suffice to say that I know it's still intact and being kept in the Basilica.

'We have to have it, Suviel. If the Lord of Twilight's agents are growing in strength mere months before our rebellion begins, we will be forced to rely more heavily on the Lesser Power than we thought.'

'And the Crystal Eye magnifies it, lends force to its effects,' Suviel murmured.

'Exactly,' Bardow said, reaching out to take her hand. 'I am sorry to have to lay this terrible burden on you but there is almost no-one else I can trust. Guldamar and Terzis are stronger in the Lesser Power, but neither is able to move among ordinary folk with your ease.'

'There are no ordinary folk in Prekine,' she said, remembering the white-eyed Acolyte at Wujad's Pool.

Bardow sighed. 'Jeopardy and evil hazards abound where peace and harmony once held sway. If Besh-Darok and the Rootpower were the heart and soul of the Empire, Trevada was its mind, its calm, assessing regard. The Acolytes knew what they were doing when they took our towers and halls for their own. They know how to corrupt everything, even symbols.'

'They cannot corrupt everything,' Suviel said, 'because they cannot reach everything.'

The Archmage gave a rueful smile then straightened in his chair, as if putting remembrances and regret aside. 'Now, go and rest, prepare for the morning. Yes, I'm not asking you to leave before then. I wish it could be longer but time is against us.'

Suviel stood, laid a hand on his shoulder and said, 'I shall not fail.'

Bardow looked up at her. 'I hope not, Suviel, I hope not. For all our sakes.'

In another part of the temple, a man in a brown cloak came to a door at the end of a corridor and was about to knock when a voice came from within. 'Enter!'

With a shrug he entered, closed the door behind him and leaned against it, weariness making him feel suddenly weak. The room was small with two low cots, a crude trunk and a plain square table at which a short, grey-haired elderly man sat, wrinkled hands cupping a small bowl of water glinting with pinpoints from the candles placed around the walls. The elderly man turned in his seat and fixed him with a frowning look. 'Well?'

Coireg Mazaret gave a shaky laugh. 'The boy is being sent to one of Volyn's refuges, and I am to go with him.'

'And I will accompany you?'

'I insisted.'

The older man's frown relaxed. 'Excellent. Events are moving in our favour. Lord Ystregul will be greatly pleased.'

At that name, Coireg felt nausea ripple through his innards and he had to grit his teeth to subdue a wave of dizziness. Ystregul, the Black Priest of the Fiery Tree. A face came to mind, a man with pronounced cheekbones, long black hair hanging in braids, and eyes like daggers. Then he remembered his own hands and arms and chest covered in blood all those months ago, the blood of his father. He shuddered.

The man pushed the other chair away from the table with his foot. 'Sit,' he said.

Gratefully, Coireg went over and sat down heavily. 'Seftal, I'm sorry, I—'

Seftal silenced him with an upraised hand. 'The weaving of the Wellsource brings burdens to all its servants, and it takes time to find the strength to bear it. You will be strong soon.'

Coireg almost felt like weeping. The memory of waking to discover that he had murdered his own father was a collar of thorns that choked his every waking hour. It was Seftal, friend and fellow smuggler, who had spirited him away from Casall and, in an abandoned farmhouse, revealed his allegiance to the Wellsource and promised him redemption. Their later meeting with Ystregul had filled him with terror: the Black Priest had also promised him deliverance, but it was Seftal he listened to.

'Tell me what you know,' Seftal said.

Coireg related all that had taken place, both between himself and his brother, and during the brief meeting they had had after the War Council.

'The boy will be guarded by three score of the Hunter's Children, as well as the advisers. An ambush would have to be planned carefully.'

'It will,' Seftal said. 'We shall be in the enemy's camp and able to seize the boy at the right moment.' He smiled. 'You have done well, Coireg. Your place in the realm to come is assured.'

'And my dreams?'

'They will become calm and untroubled,' Seftal said soothingly. 'All things will be new and sweet, and great power shall be yours to command.'

Coireg breathed in deep as tears welled in his eyes. He covered them with a trembling hand. 'When I spoke to him the first time . . . when he said what he would do, I almost ran. But I faced him, I really did.' He shook his head. 'Without the clawseed draught you gave me, I don't think I could have gone through with it. I can feel it starting to wane now. Perhaps I could have another draught, just for the rest of the day.'

Seftal was silent a moment as he stared down at the bowl of water, and Coireg's heart seemed to beat in his chest like a slow, heavy hammer. Then he felt a wave of relief as the older man nodded.

'Yes,' Seftal said thoughtfully, without raising his gaze. 'Later.'

Chapter Seven

No sanctuary in the house of pain,
No life on a tree of fire.

Avalti, *Foreseeings*

Half a day's ride and seven leagues north of Krusivel, Suviel reined in her horse under a tree near the brow of a hill, and waited for the others to catch up.

It was in the early morning, as she was dressing, that Ikarno had revealed how the previous night he had pressured Bardow into allowing him to send two companions with her. She had kept any dismay from showing till she was outside the temple and on her way to the Mage Order's lodge where Bardow had met her on the steps.

'It changes nothing,' he had said in a low voice, drawing her aside.

'But when we reach Trevada—'

'Then you tell them.' He had spread his hands. 'What will they do? Try to stop you? No, they'll offer to help and you will have to decide if they can.'

Shaking her head she stroked her horse's neck as it cropped contentedly at a clump of grass. It was all because of Ikarno worrying about her safety. Yet she was the one who had travelled far and wide while he had stayed in Krusivel. Her expression softened as she remembered last night. Neither of them were youthful any more, but there had been an intensity to their lovemaking that recalled the beginnings of their relationship five years ago. By the way Ikarno had delighted and aroused every part of her, she knew that he feared for her and wanted to have a perfect memory of her, just as she felt about him. Last night she had been all that he wanted, as he had been for her.

There was the thud of trotting hooves and she looked up to see Keren approach on a dappled grey. From her face Suviel noticed that she was in a black mood, just as the trader Gilly Cordale came into view further back along the bushy defile. The stocky trader was smiling ruefully, his gaze fixed on Keren, and Suviel frowned.

'Is there a problem?' she said to Keren as she drew up beside her.

The swordswoman glanced back at the trader and sighed. 'Nothing I can't deal with,' she said evenly.

'Ride on ahead,' Suviel said. 'Stay within sight, though.'

Keren nodded and urged her mount on down the other side of the rise. Suviel waited till Gilly arrived and continued along beside him.

'I don't think she's interested, Gilly.'

'I think you're right,' he said. 'For now.'

She gave him an ironic look. 'You anticipate a change in her attitude?'

The trader rocked his head judiciously. 'The opening stages of a negotiation do usually seem unproductive. At the moment, she thinks that I'm an ill-mannered boor, but as the days pass I shall inadvertently reveal my more sensitive qualities – courage, understanding, warm-heartedness and a loving nature. Gradually, she will become intrigued by these glimpses and eventually,' he grinned, 'the negotiations will be concluded.'

She stared at him. Since first meeting him nearly two years ago, Gilly Cordale had never failed to appal her. 'I think you underestimate her ability to see through your little performance.'

Theatrically, he put a hand to his chest. 'Truly, I am wounded. How do you know that beneath this crass exterior does not lie a noble soul?'

'Oh, you mean there really *is* more to you than meets the eye?'

He laughed quietly and wagged an admonishing finger. 'Lady, be careful. You might be taken in by my little performance, too.' And he moved ahead a short distance, leaving her to stare after him in bemusement.

With the jagged heights of the Rukang Mountains at their backs and the foothills becoming thick with woods, they rode the main wagon track till it dipped towards a narrow gorge. Instead of continuing that way, though, Suviel led them along an overgrown side trail heading north-east, parallel with Gronanvel, the great valley which lay beyond the gorge. After several hours' slow progress they emerged at the bank of the Errain, one of the rivers that linked together the lakes which ran the length of Gronanvel. The waters there were shallow and easily forded, and by the time they were across and safely under cover, the day was almost done. Suviel proposed finding a place to camp and the others wearily agreed.

It was dusk when they came to a small clearing in a grove of tassel trees, their hanging litrilu blooms filling the air with a light fragrance. Unseen creatures scurried away at their approach and when Gilly dismounted and lit a torch a pair of tiny bull-lizards abandoned their meal of moss atop a large boulder and vanished into the undergrowth. Suviel and Keren were about to dismount too when a small figure jumped up from behind the boulder and darted across the clearing, past Gilly. But the trader was quick on his feet and caught the stranger by the arm. It was a child, a young boy. He cried out and clawed for release, then turned and tried to bite his captor. Gilly uttered an oath, dropped the torch and wrapped his other arm round the boy's chest, holding him immobile.

'You little brat!'

'Let me . . . let me go . . .'

Suviel hurried across while Keren picked up the torch. The boy froze, his eyes wide with fear, as Suviel went down on one knee, facing him.

'Ease your grip, Gilly, you're hurting him. Now, it's all right, you're safe.' She raised her hands in a calming manner but the boy averted his eyes and began to tremble. He wore rough shirt and trews, both torn and grubby. The shirt had a wet-looking patch of blood on one of the arms but she was sure that it wasn't his. Frowning, she lowered her hands. 'What's your name, boy?' she said softly.

Without meeting her gaze he muttered, 'Gevran.'

'Gevran, you've seen sorcery tonight, haven't you? What village are you from? Is that where it happened?'

Suviel ignored Gilly's look of surprise as the boy moved his lips. For a moment there was no sound. Then: 'They burned everything. They burned our house . . . and . . . they said the Mother was evil and the singer was evil . . .' His voice wavered into sobbing. 'My da, they burned him too . . .'

'Where, Gevran?'

'Hanlo . . .'

Suviel straightened and looked at Gilly and Keren. 'That's less than an hour's ride away.'

'What about the boy?' said Keren. 'Should one of us stay here with him?'

Suviel shook her head, surprised at how calm she was. 'He'll have to come with us. There's no knowing what is abroad tonight.'

Gilly released his hold on the boy and stared down at him with a kind of intense compassion. Then he looked up and Suviel saw a cold anger in his eyes.

'The boy will travel with me,' she said. 'You and Keren will ride before us and keep alert.'

Keren and Gilly glanced at one another, then nodded and hurried to remount their horses. Suviel reached out a hand to the boy. 'Come, Gevran. You'll be safe with me.'

Hesitantly, he took her hand.

They smelled the fires long before they saw them.

They were weaving a slow, fitful way through the enclosing

forest darkness, with only the faint radiance of a hooded tallow lamp to keep them from getting lost. The odour of burnt wood was growing stronger, an acrid sharpness that smothered the smells of wet soil and growth.

The boy Gevran made no sound as he sat behind her with his arms about her waist. It reminded her of her sister's son, Huranach, at that age and how he used to sing a simple little song about horses in time with their mount's gait. The memory was painful and she realized that she had not thought about that part of the past for a long time. But Huranach was dead and no matter how much she wished to bear a child, Ikarno's child, the truth was that her age was against her. Her role now was to play her part in this struggle and hope that the nameless high powers favoured them with good fortune so that the world became a better place for children to be born into.

Still, she treasured the weight of Gevran against her back and the trust which it implied. I will not let you down, she promised silently.

Before long a yellow glow could be seen through the trees, made faint and hazy by smoke. Keren doused the lamp and as they approached slowly Suviel commenced the thought-canto of Vigilance. As they drew near she could see a cluster of huts and small barns, some smouldering shells, others still burning furiously. In the middle of the village bodies lay scattered around a half-demolished square stone temple from which a column of smoke rose. The village appeared deserted but from within the Vigilance canto Suviel sensed several strange, flickering presences.

'Someone's still there,' she muttered to the others. 'We'd better circle round, see if we can find them.'

'Can't wait to break up their little party,' said Gilly, slipping a small buckler onto his left arm.

On horseback they slowly skirted the village, eyes scrutinizing every shadow, every doorway and window, every huddled, motionless body. Suviel could smell scorched flesh in the air, and heard Gevran sniffle at her back. They were halfway round and just starting to get a view of the temple's collapsed rear wall when three men in loose-fitting red garments emerged from it and came purposefully towards them. Each one wore a leather mask across the nose and eyes, and carried a short bow with an arrow already fitted and drawn. They halted a dozen or more paces away, between two smoking huts.

'Have you come here to pray,' said the one in the middle, 'or to die?'

'Pray to whom?' said Suviel, silently preparing another thought-canto.

'We are the disciples of the great Ystregul, Prophet and Shadowking of the Fiery Tree, he who was betrayed by his consort, abandoned at the Plateau of Arengia. Abase yourselves before its flames—' the man indicated the temple, still emitting a funnel of smoke, '—and you will be admitted to the ranks of the chosen. Denial is blasphemy.'

'And these villagers?' said Gilly. 'Did they deny your god?'

'They were dancing to a song praising the Whore Mother when we arrived. There is no redemption for the servants of evil. Their spirits have been harvested unto the Tree of Fire.'

'You know,' Gilly said. 'For a murderer, you talk very prettily.'

A knife-thin smile creased the spokesman's face as he and his companions raised their bows and took aim. 'Your spirits will feed the Fire of the Ages,' he said, and the three arrows burst into flame and were released as one.

Suviel was ready, the canto of Astray whirling in her mind, and she reached out to push, slow and lure. The arrows veered off in smooth curves, vanishing in the dark wood.

'Keren! . . . Gilly! Wait—'

But they had already rolled from their saddles and were on their feet, swords ready, heedless of her cry. The masked disciples tossed the bows aside, drew their own weapons and advanced. Suviel felt an edge of panic as she saw hot green fire glitter along those three blades and hurriedly began another thought-canto, praying she would be in time.

Gilly leaped forward to engage the nearest enemy and there was a flash as their swords clashed and red and green sparks flew. The trader cried out as some of the sparks landed on his hands and clothing. He backed away, trying to protect himself with his shield but was forced to parry some blows, causing more showers of deadly sparks. Keren was in similar difficulties, her clothes smouldering in several places as she struggled to defend herself against the other two.

Watching the deadly fight, Suviel strove to keep her mind clear and calm as the canto of Cadence reached its full potential and the Lesser Power murmured and surged within her. But Gilly and Keren were too close to their opponents to use the Cadence canto as a shield so Suviel reached for the Lesser Power, directing, focusing, gathering it in her chest, filling her lungs till they seemed ready to burst. She felt like a torch, burning with a silver flame that streamed up her spine and into her head. Then she opened her mouth, jaws stretching and released it all in a single, thunderous shout.

As her horse reared in fright, Gilly and Keren dropped their weapons and fell to their knees, hands covering their ears. Two of the disciples collapsed writhing on the ground but their leader just staggered, mouth gaping in agony, blood trickling from ears and mouth. Then he regained his balance, jaw moving jerkily as he swallowed blood, then he raised his sword and started towards Suviel, who had dismounted with the boy and was struggling to control her horse.

Suviel was unaware of the disciple leader until Keren shouted a warning. Panic threatened when she looked round and saw him running lightly towards her, his blade exuding a sickly green power. Next to her, Gevran gave a wordless cry of fear and clung to her. Facing that leather-masked killer, she knew she had no time to prepare another thought-canto and was fumbling in her pockets for anything which might aid them when a blackened figure came running and stumbling from a nearby burned-out hut, a spear clutched in his hands.

The disciple was mere feet away, bright blade swinging back, when the spear caught him in the side, and ripped bloodily up through his lower chest. The disciple bellowed in torment as the crazed charge flung him to the ground. His attacker, a man in ragged, scorched garments, made noises deep in his throat as he pulled out a long dagger and half-fell to his knees. Incredibly, the disciple was still conscious. His mask had become dislodged, revealing burning green eyes which he turned on the blackened man.

'Die, child of earth!'

The glowing blade was rammed into the man's side. He made a choking sound, seared head trembling, wide eyes staring down at the laughing disciple. Then he brought the long dagger down in one, smooth, hammering cut that severed the green-eyed head and silenced that tongue. The man released the dagger, and stared down at his hands for a second before sprawling limply on the ground.

'Da!' Gevran cried out behind Suviel, and suddenly he was running over.

'The others!' Suviel shouted. 'Gilly, quick, take their heads!'

The trader shook his head, snatched up his sword and swung at the exposed neck of the nearest disciple as he was getting to his feet. Keren forced herself upright, and staggered after the third disciple who was slowly crawling towards the forest. With a two-handed grip on her blade, she finished the grisly task.

Suviel ran over to Gevran, grabbing his hand just as it was about to close on the hilt of the sword buried in his father's side.

'No! Its bane would poison you, child.'

'But it's in him!' the boy wept. 'Da . . .'

'Gev . . .' whispered his father. 'Gev, don't . . .' He coughed, then stared at Suviel. 'Are they . . . ?'

She nodded. 'How did you know how to kill them?'

'My brother—' he grimaced with pain '— was with Gunderlek, escaped the siege of Rauthaz. He told me before he died. Took an arrow in the shoulder, arrow like this . . . hellblade.' He reached out to clasp the boy's arm. 'I've cousins in Beharis, lady. See him safely to them, I beg of you in the Mother's name.' His other hand dug hard into the ground at his side and his eyes looked into the distance. 'His songs were so beautiful, made us so . . . happy . . .'

Then his hand relaxed and his head sank back, eyes lifeless. Gevran held on to the other hand, weeping. Suviel let out her breath in a long sorrowful sigh then noticed Keren standing nearby, still unsteady on her feet and rubbing her ears.

'Can you hear me?' Suviel said, getting up.

Keren nodded. 'A little.'

'Watch over the boy for a moment,' she said. 'Don't let him touch that sword hilt, and don't you either.'

The swordswoman nodded and Suviel walked towards the temple, beckoning Gilly to follow her. By the red glow of its burning huts the village seemed to be drenched in blood, as if for a while it had become the personal realm of some god of torment, a domain of pain. There was little doubt in her mind that the three red-clad disciples had derived their powers from the Wellsource, but when their leader had talked of this Ystregul she had sensed nothing but utter, single-minded conviction.

She frowned. What had he said, about the Fiery Tree being the one who was betrayed at the Plateau of Arengia? Was this some perversion of the Fathertree faith, created by this Ystregul to feed off the despair of ordinary people? Prophet, the disciple said, and Shadowking. What did that mean?

Then the inside of the smouldering temple came into view and all thoughts fled at what she saw and heard.

'They come, Fate's performers.'

She heard a sharp intake of breath from Gilly who whispered a name: 'Avalti!'

'No more, Cordale's scion. An eye in the inferno, and what things I see!'

A man had been bound neck, chest and legs to a wooden spar jammed into the cracked centre of the domed Earthmother altar at the rear of the temple. But the altar was being steadily consumed, its stone dissolving into the flames which swathed the man called Avalti in a flickering emerald veil. His form seemed unharmed, his garments untouched, but his eyes were unblinking orbs that swam with bright colours. As he stared out at them, Suviel could not be sure if he was in agony or ecstasy.

'Yes, I . . . I see a snake with two heads in deadly conflict. I see a beast chained, I see a hollow Lord waiting to be filled, I see . . .' The many-coloured gaze sought out Gilly, 'I see an iron fox, eyeless to the hunt,' then moved to Suviel, 'a frozen bird, trapped under ice,' then looked past them, 'and a broken sword discarded.'

Without looking Suviel knew that Keren was standing behind her. Shaken and filled with dread, she raised her hand. 'Be silent! We do not wish to hear you—'

'I must speak!' An unanswerable anguish filled his voice. The altar was almost gone and as his clothes began to scorch and smoke, his mouth widened in pain. 'I see five become one, I see the triumph of power, I see a growing desolation, I see one become two . . .' The wooden pole was black and eroded and the raging fire was eating at the body of the man called Avalti, with everything below his chest already gone.

'I see the world, sunk in eternal night . . .'

Then flames rushed into his open mouth and he screamed. In seconds all that remained of him was a shapeless blazing mass that dwindled away to nothing. Green flames shrank, guttered and went out, and the wooden pole disintegrated, ash falling on the charred temple floor. Suviel shuddered and turned away to see Keren standing a few feet away, the boy Gevran huddled close to her.

'What did he say?' Keren said. 'He looked straight at me and spoke, but all I heard was a strange roaring sound, like a river far off.'

'Nothing of importance,' Suviel said, as if she believed it. 'He was driven mad by evil sorcery.' Ignoring the swordswoman's sceptical expression, she went over to Gilly, who sat on a staved-in barrel, staring at the darkened, gutted temple.

'Was that really Avalti?' she said quietly.

He nodded. 'I heard him sing at the High Day of the Orders

in Adnagaur, about a year before the sword fell upon us all. I thought he was dead.' He uttered a bleak laugh and rubbed his face. '"An iron fox, eyeless to the hunt" – what does that mean?' There was a desperate note in his voice. 'The fox is my family's emblem. What was he trying to say?'

All around them, the last of the fires were going out. In the smoky silence the village seemed almost asleep.

'Put his words out of your mind,' Suviel said. 'He was in the grip of the Wellsource and it gives forth nothing but lies.'

But the worst lie she knew was the one that was half a truth. *A frozen bird, trapped under ice.* Wujad's Pool.

So which half was true, and which half was a lie?

Chapter Eight

The chains of the King,
Make of us all an empire.

The Book of Parodies

The meeting took place in the Realm of Dusk, beneath a sulphurous sky, in a sunken dusty depression filled with sleeping armies. Wearing the suit of bright, spine-adorned armour once more, Byrnak rode along a wide aisle past ranks of wains and war machines, cavalry and chariots, soldiers and beasts, a panoply of warriors in their scores of thousands, all standing motionless and facing inwards. A faint, warm breeze made banners and flags sway limply and brought odours of leather and iron to Byrnak's nose. Beyond the edge of the bowl-like depression loomed a huge, tower-ringed citadel; a second one was just visible as a grey silhouette in the far distance. A deadening silence hung over the bowl, broken only by the sound of his mount's hooves and the desultory flapping of small pennons.

As he rode, a sense of recognition hung at the back of his mind, just beyond recollection. He saw brutal, fur-clad savages armed with clubs and spears; creatures like huge wolves rigged with leather harnesses; tall, black-maned warriors carrying red iron longswords; mounted soldiers with hooded warbirds on their shoulders; knights with horned helms and jewelled battleaxes; regiment upon regiment of men and women caparisoned for war, a poised and waiting host. It was all familiar, he knew, familiar to that part of himself that had once been a god. He pushed the familiarity away. *I am myself*, he thought angrily, *not the shard of a hungry ghost.*

For a second, Byrnak imagined that he heard distant, brittle laughter, then realized it was just horse harnesses swaying gently in the wind. Still, he shuddered.

Four figures on horseback waited at the centre of the great array of hosts, four Shadowkings. Three wore enclosing armour, while the fourth was swathed head to foot in black and red robes.

'He is the Black Priest,' said his steed.

Byrnak smiled humourlessly. This was only the second time he had joined with the Acolyte Obax in order to enter the Realm of Dusk, and while the invasive nature of it was no longer repellent, it still made him uneasy. While he could now command the kind of sorcerous power spoken of in stories and legends, that same power had taken something away from him. He could spread fire among his enemies, he could send spikes of ice raining down on their heads, he could turn foes into servants, alter flesh and minds and purposes, yet he himself no longer felt invincible. The ignorance that had given him certainty was being steadily dismantled by fate, by power, and by the undying knowledge buried within him.

Eight heads, four in helms and hood, four horselike, turned to watch his arrival. Byrnak guided Obax to a halt before them, leaned back and regarded them through the eye-slits of his own helmet, then indicated the surrounding motionless hosts with a sweep of his gauntleted hand.

'What is this?' he said.

'A god dreams,' said the Black Priest.

'Our dream,' added one of the others with a chuckle.

'Not my dream,' Byrnak said curtly, then on impulse unfastened his heavy, ornate helm and lifted it off. Free of the stuffy darkness, he shook his black hair loose and blinked against the sudden yellow glare of the sky.

'What do your dreams show you?'

From within the red folds concealing his face, the Black Priest's voice was deep and rough, full of restrained animal savagery. Byrnak grinned.

'Death,' he said. 'Everywhere.'

'Enough,' said one of the others. 'There are decisions to be made.'

Byrnak recognized the voice. This was the one who had done most of the talking during that first shattering encounter. According to Obax, he called himself the Hidden One, while the other two armoured riders were named Thraelor and Grazaan. And now that he was this close, he could see subtle differences in the armour that they wore. The Hidden One's helm was engraved with serpents and lizards. Another bore images of tentacular sea creatures (Thraelor, whispered Obax in his thoughts), while the third was decorated with spiders and scorpions (Grazaan). Byrnak glanced down at his own, resting on the saddle – fangs and talons, horned beasts, snarling.

'Death will be everywhere,' murmured the Black Priest. 'My disciples have already begun—'

'Yes, begun spreading useless terror,' interrupted the Hidden One. 'Drawing unwelcome attention to our strategy.'

'The Whore Mother's influence must be eradicated,' said the Black Priest.

'In time,' the Hidden One said. 'Once our army has fulfilled its purpose.' He turned to Thraelor. 'Stir that mount of yours, brother. What progress has been made in gathering the ones we want?'

Thraelor dug his heels into his grey steed's flanks. 'Answer!'

The horse's head swayed slightly from side to side for a moment before coming up, corpse-white eyes staring at nothing, open mouth drooling.

'Lordzzz . . . the Acolytes have delivered the commands and all, almost all of the warchiefs obey and are marching to northern Khatris—'

'*Almost* all?'

'Oscarg, a mountain warlord in Anghatan, refused the command.'

'Oscarg is powerful,' muttered Thraelor. 'He's been a thorn in my side for years. What has been done to correct this upstart?'

The horse made a rhythmic grating sound which Byrnak suddenly realized was laughter. 'Even as I speak, a flock of nighthunters are converging on his stronghold. We anticipate that his son shall depart for Khatris with a sizeable force before the next day is done.'

'Excellent,' said Thraelor. 'It is time the chieftains were reminded of the power of their god.'

'What of the Daemonkind?' Byrnak said suddenly.

Four heads tilted his way. The Hidden One chuckled quietly within his helm.

'The Acolytes, these half-blind servants of ours, have on our behalf tried to attract the Daemonkind's attention.' He prodded his mount in the neck. 'But with mixed results, eh?'

'The lair of the Daemonkind lies deep in the Realm of Ruin,' droned the horse. 'Of the ten Acolytes who undertook the mind-journey, only three returned with their faculties intact. Four did not return at all.'

'And was there a reply?'

'Yesss, there was a . . . reply: "We serve – we do not serve the ones who serve."'

'Did none of you think of making the mind-journey your-selves?' Byrnak sneered. 'Or were you afraid of getting the same answer?'

There was a tense moment of silence, then the Hidden One said, 'You have the right of it. The Daemonkind will only respond to the command of the Lord of Twilight, and none of us have that power or even that strength of will.'

'The Daemonkind are not necessary for our immediate pur-poses,' said the Black Priest. 'The Mogaun tribes will be sufficient for the battle to come. And my disciples.'

'However,' Grazaan added, facing Byrnak, 'we need a general to command our army. You would be the ideal choice.'

'Why not you?' Byrnak said warily.

'Thraelor and I have commitments in the north, while our

priestly brother will be fully occupied in dealing with the accursed Rootpower mages.'

Byrnak looked at the Hidden One. 'And you?'

'I have a delicate task to perform which requires my undivided attention.'

The Black Priest uttered a guttural laugh. 'When will we discover who and where you are, brother? Will we gasp in delight, or curse our foolish trust?'

'Trust is all,' the Hidden One said evenly. 'Together we shall have everything; apart, we would gain little more than scraps of greatness. Your trust in me is not misplaced, brothers, I swear.'

The Black Priest grunted noncommittally, while the others nodded. The Hidden One turned back to Byrnak.

'So,' he said. 'Will you be our general?'

Byrnak stared at the serpent-adorned helm then smiled. 'What forces am I to command, and what is our purpose?'

The serpent helm nodded in satisfaction. 'Our army will be several times that of our enemy, but our purpose is quite unique. Now, brother, listen . . .'

Awakening from the Realm of Dusk was a descent into suffocation. On that plain of hosts, existence had a quality that was at once dreamlike and pure; here, sitting at this long, heavy table before a crude, massive hearth, he could feel the squalor of everything around him, the dust in the air, the dried mud on his boots, the smells of wood and damp tapestries, even the odour of stale sweat from Obax who sat opposite, head resting on his arms. The filth of it all was engulfing, yet somehow pleasing.

Byrnak smiled. Chair legs scraped on flagstones as he stood and went over to the huge arched window overlooking Choroya's Court of Muster. From behind him came a quiet rustling as Obax stirred.

'Lord, are you well?'

Byrnak gazed impassively down at the lifeless bodies strewn about the court, and the lone weeping figures stumbling among them. A stench of smoke and blood rose to him.

'You may go,' he said. 'Send in my captains.'

As Obax walked unsteadily from the great hall, Byrnak turned from the window, crossed to the dais and kicked a ragged shape that lay beside the throne.

'Get up.'

The former warlord of Choroya and southern Honjir, levered himself to his knees then stood slowly before his conqueror. Azurech was a tall man but he cringed before Byrnak, his once-proud features marred by a broken nose and slack with dread. For a second he met Byrnak's gaze then, trembling, looked down at the floor.

An agonizing scream came from out in the court and reverberated around the great hall. Byrnak cocked his head and smiled.

'Are you ready to serve me, Azurech?'

Head bowed, Azurech moved his mouth as if struggling to frame words. Then: 'What . . . do you want of me, lord?'

Byrnak leaned in close, grasped the defeated warlord's chin and forced him to look up.

'Everything,' he said.

He stared into Azurech's eyes, thrusting his own awareness into the other's mind. Ruin and despair grew there like black jungles on a swamp of fear, fear of Byrnak and his power. How easy it was to turn the fear into loyalty, and the dark tangles into determination and purpose that grew strong and true towards the bright, life-giving light that was Byrnak, warlord and Shadowking.

He released his grip on Azurech who now stood straighter, his shoulders level, his eyes fixed devotedly on his master. Then the doors of the great hall swung open and three leather-armoured men entered, harnesses clinking and bootheels echoing noisily as they approached. Byrnak turned to regard them.

'I am leaving very soon,' he said. 'In my absence, your commander will be Azurech. I may be gone for several weeks but my hand will be upon you all – Azurech's will is my will, his eyes are my eyes, so you will remain vigilant and obedient.'

The three captains glanced nervously at each other, then

nodded. Byrnak let a sneer curl his mouth. These three displayed more volition than he cared for, but then he had bound them to him five days ago when his power to dominate was unpractised and crude. For a moment he considered tightening the bonds, then decided against it, curious to find out how they and Azurech would work together.

'These are my orders,' he said to the former warlord. 'Secure this city, root out any agitators and execute them, draft seven in every ten males over sixteen into a new city militia, have all traders register with a single merchants guild, and begin repairs to the walls and fortifications. Oh yes, and keep supplying rations to the refugees for another week then round them up and drive them south into Kejana. Then have those shanty towns demolished. Execute anyone who resists.'

'As you will it, lord,' said Azurech with a bow.

'Now get out,' Byrnak muttered. 'And find yourself garments suitable to your new station.'

He waited till Azurech and the three captains were gone then walked round behind the throne, through a curtained arch to a large room dominated by a long table and adorned with banners, spears and shields. To the right a stair led upwards, wide and winding, its blue and grey stones carved with leaves and vines. At the top he came to a large, circular tower room. There was only one window, its shutters firmly closed, its walls hung with rich tapestries depicting scenes out of battle and legend.

At the centre of the room stood the woman Nerek, clasped hands outstretched, with a huge four-poster bed lying half-wrecked and smoking before her, sheets twisted and strewn on the floor. Gleams, no, drops of brightness began to leak from between her fingers. Then her hands parted quickly and a knot of dazzling brightness streaked out to smash into the thick mattress. Canvas burst, wadded horsehair flared, and Byrnak watched in fascination as the bright knot traced a burning zig-zag trail across and through the mattress. After a few seconds it slowed, darkened to an angry red then spiralled in on itself, a flickering nub of flames that soon guttered out.

'Impressive,' Byrnak said.

Nerek spun, eyes wild with fear, a hot glow blossoming in her hands. Then she saw it was him and the glow died. 'I was ... teaching the fire to move,' she said, letting her arms fall to her sides.

'Sourcefire is a risky weapon for the untutored.'

'Then teach me more.'

Byrnak smiled. 'You already know enough for the task ahead.'

An eager hope lit up Nerek's features. 'Good. How do I find her?'

He regarded her thoughtfully. In her emotions she was utterly different from the others, with her fear and desire for him warring on the surface of an unpredictable anger. But it was her ability to tap the Wellsource that truly set her apart – none of the others he had bound to his will had displayed so much as a glimmer of lore talent. For that reason he was loath to tamper with her mind – that and the fact that she was created by that shadowed part of himself whose purposes yet eluded him.

Then there was the matter of the swordswoman. *Why would this ancient shadow, this fragment of a god that he carried, remake a young man into the form of that particular woman?* Was Nerek's pursuit of her some kind of test? He was unsure, but the compulsion was upon her and he knew she would have to pursue it.

Byrnak looked about him, spotted a tapestry near the doorway and went over to it, beckoning Nerek to follow. Being almost as high as the room, the tapestry was an elaborate affair edged with gold and silver vines and bordered with a sequence of panels depicting the progress of a king and his knights through adventures, predicaments and tragedies. The main portion showed the king hacking the last head from a many-headed monster against a background of burning trees and a boiling lake.

'An exaggerated account,' Byrnak said sardonically, touching the border with his fingers.

At once the central panel flared into a mass of pale green fire. The eldritch blaze took on a coiling appearance as if a whirlpool were drawing all the tongues of flame into the centre. Then, in an eyeblink, the gyring green fire changed into a slow-moving swirl of mist. Images began to emerge and grow clear, a village nestling among wooded hills with a stream running by. Three riders crossed a low log bridge, the first a man that Byrnak did not know, while the second one he recognized as the female mage who had frustrated his crude attack at the gorge. The third was Keren. Beside him, Nerek just audibly caught her breath.

A young boy climbed down from behind the mage, ran to a nearby cabin and banged his fists on the door. Adults and children, and a few dogs, came out and the riders dismounted to stretch their limbs and exchange greetings. Byrnak then directed the far-seen view up high and swung it round to show lowland woods and fields sweeping down westwards to a wide river mouth and the sea beyond. Nerek let out a sigh.

'They are still west of the Rukangs, at the south-western end of Gronanvel,' Byrnak said, 'but they will almost certainly seek a way through the mountain passes. I want you to head north to my garrison in the Nagira Mountains – I'll give you written orders for the commander there, ordering him to provide you with ten of his best riders.'

Alarm crossed her face. 'If I am to go without you, how will I know how to hunt for them?'

'The Wellsource will guide you. Touch it, breathe it, taste it and it will lead you to your destiny.'

She breathed in deeply, still staring at the images in the tapestry, and nodded.

'And when can I leave?'

'Soon,' he said, reaching for her. 'Very soon.'

Behind him the tapestry fell apart in a cascade of ash as fine as dust.

Chapter Nine

King Orosiada: Monster, you have laid my cities to waste, slain thousands of my people, and poisoned the very land. Before I carry out my judgement, tell me why you have done this?

The Beast Orgraaleshenoth: O blind and witless king! Because only the strongest weapons are worth breaking.

Tales of Yularia, book 3, 37

The abandoned mill was a square-built, two-storey building with thick stone walls and a small tower. Once it had been a fort guarding against raids by mountain bandits; the walls still had their arrow slits and a low parapet. At some point it had been converted into a mill, but now it was a dark and empty shell, its outbuildings gone to overgrown debris and the great mill wheel lying a short way downstream, entwined with weeds, rotting slowly into the muddy bank. Only the stream remained, pouring endlessly out of the Bachruz Mountains, carrying reflections of the night sky's stars down to empty them into the long depths of Lake Audagal.

Sentinel Kodel was quick to move everyone and the horses inside the mill, for which Tauric was truly grateful. The cold night air was causing the stump of his arm to ache in a way that made his head spin and his stomach rebel.

Inside torches were lit, revealing a wide, empty room with a low wooden roof held up by heavy wooden pillars. Off to one side was the big millstone and its driving axle, thick as a man's thigh, once attached to the waterwheel but now dislodged and lying on the millstone, its rust staining the granite. The floor was littered with rubbish and animal droppings which Kodel had one of his men sweep out of the main door. A fire was lit in a crumbling hearth, supplies were unwrapped from the pack horses, bedrolls were laid on the flagstones and soon the odours of cooking began to fill the room.

Tauric unpacked his own bedroll from his horse, aware of glances from others but not really caring. He took it over to an alcove near the doors, away from the rest, laid it on the floor and sat down heavily. He felt bleak, burdened by loss and by his thoughts. The initial shock of the amputation of his lower right arm had lessened, but the anguish remained. He was continually finding himself reaching for horse reins or plates or buttons with the hand that was gone, lied to by sensations that insisted it was still there. He stared down at his truncated limb, wrapped in cloth bound with leather ties, cradled it with his good hand and squeezed his eyes shut against tears as he thought of his father, the Duke of Patrein.

Flashes of memory came to him – running with his old dog, Holdfast, or riding out on the moors of southern Khatris, a trained crownhawk swooping to alight on his father's outstretched arm. He remembered visiting Tobrosa for the yearly horse races, and cheering on the duchy's finest riders. He remembered his mother, the Lady Illian, teaching him to write poems and how to play the four-stringed kulesti. He also remembered catching a glimpse of his father shedding silent tears at her bedside when life left her after a long illness. Then later, seeing him carrying her out to the fountain garden under a dusky sky and singing sadly for her.

Later there were lessons in swordcraft and archery, and duty and reponsibility, all against the background of growing tension between the Duke of Patrein and various Mogaun chiefs. Once, his father had sat him down and told him how he wished that he had aped his peers after the fall of the Empire and fled across the sea to Keremenchool. But he had chosen to stay, to stand between the ordinary folk and the Mogaun, and somehow protect them from the worst of what was to come.

His father. Tears stung his eyes, fell on his cradled half-arm. Yet even that had been lost to him after the Archmage Bardow and Shin Hantika told him of his real father and the awful responsibility that was now his alone.

Someone came over and sat cross-legged beside him. It was Earthsister Pirica, Abbess Halimer's adviser, a round-faced woman in her middle years, attired in a short grey habit and heavy cotton leggings. She offered him a wooden bowl of stew and a spoon, which he accepted gratefully, balanced on one knee and began to eat. He was almost finished when she said, 'Enjoying it?'

Mouth full, he nodded.

'Good. Now – who was king of Mantinor when the League of Jefren was founded?'

Tauric suppressed a groan. Ever since leaving Krusivel four days ago, Pirica and Himber, Bardow's adviser, had subjected him to a never-ending string of lectures and questions on the history and cultures of the Khatrimantine Empire and its predecessors. Some of it he knew well, especially that to do with Khatris and the southern kingdoms; on the northern realms his knowledge was patchy.

Pirica was smiling her waiting smile.

'Um, Tavalir the . . . Second.'

'The Third. And his High Counsellor was?'

Tauric could feel sweat prickle on his scalp. 'Akroom?'

'Okroom of Bhanav – who sent which army to their doom at the Pass of Rahl?'

He knew that one. 'The Golden Phalanx.'

The Earthsister nodded in satisfaction, and he scooped up the last of the now-cool stew and set the bowl aside.

'Some of these names and places may be unfamiliar to you,' Pirica said. 'But for all the peoples of the kingdoms they are part of life, strong threads in the tapestry of past and present.' She smiled thoughtfully. 'You're doing well.'

'Thank you, Earthsister,' Tauric said. 'Will Shin Himber want to question me tonight?'

'No. His back is bothering him again so he has retired early to rest.' She indicated a blanket-wrapped form lying over in a shadowy corner. 'But it could be advisable to study the manuscript he gave you, in preparation for the morning.' She gathered her short robe and stood. 'You might like to read mine over again, too.'

He waited till she was across the other side of the room before sighing. He reached for the small brown pack that held his few possessions and took out a thin book of frayed pages bound between hard torwood covers, their varnished surfaces worn and scratched with use. Resting it on his knees, he traced the words carved into the front cover – *The Roots Of Empire: Being a Discourse Upon Those Monarchs Relevant to the Formation of the Khatrimantine Empire* – then opened it at the chapter on the clans of Kejana.

But before long he had turned back to the beginning to reread the story of Orosiada of Ebro'Heth, the legendary king who united the kingdoms against the Daemonkind. Orosiada lost his left hand to one of those terrible monsters in battle when they descended upon his realm, yet he lived to rally first his own people then all the other kings to his standard, eventually defeating the invaders in the uplands of Prekine, forcing them to return to the Realm of Ruin. The mages and loreweavers who had been so vital to the victory were granted the province of Prekine as a permanent sanctuary and home, on condition that they would found colleges for the investigation and teaching of the Rootpower and the Lesser Power.

The empire that Orosiada created split into warring fragments in the reign of his grandson, Allutra, but Prekine remained, inviolate and impregnable, a point of stability down the millennia.

At the end of the chapter was a woodcut showing Orosiada attired for war, a longsword in his right hand, its point resting in the ground, and a long oval shield bound to his left arm. Tauric looked down at the stump of his own arm, trying to imagine something similar, then leaned his head back against the wall, eyes closed.

What's the use, he thought. *Orosiada was at least an adept of the Lesser Power, but I don't have any ability at all. Why should anyone see me as a king?*

There was the creak of hinges and he glanced over to see the Lord Commander's brother, Coireg Mazaret, enter by the main door. The man noticed Tauric watching him, gave a nervous smile and a nod then hurried over to his bedding near the hearth. Tauric frowned, turning away. Coireg Mazaret was a strange man of shifting moods, caution and uncertainty turning an hour later into optimistic bravado, so different from the Lord Commander. Coireg had spoken to Tauric a few times on the trail, pointing out animal tracks and other spoor, identifying some wood calls and bird cries, but he was no tutor. He seemed more interested in tending to Seftal, his old servitor.

Tauric returned to his book and was halfway through the chapter on the Empire of the Generals when a torch-cast shadow fell across him. He was surprised and apprehensive to see Kodel, Sentinel of the Hunter's Children, lowering himself into a cross-legged position beside him. Since setting out from Krusivel, Kodel had exchanged barely a dozen words with him, leaving Tauric feeling that he was the focus of resentment because of his ancestry. He knew of how House Tor-Galantai had supplanted House Tor-Cavarill generations ago, and how the supporters of the Tor-Cavarill line named themselves the Hunter's Children and vowed to see House Tor-Galantai removed from the throne. Now here he was, descendant of that house, sitting face to face with someone sworn to deny him the Imperial crown.

And part of him would be happy for that to happen.

Kodel's angular face was expressionless. 'How old are you?'

'I have seen seventeen summers, my lord.'

'You will call me Kodel, not lord. So – seventeen. Slept with a woman yet?'

Tauric shook his head, feeling suddenly flushed.

'Killed anyone?'

'No.'

'At least you can ride. What weapons have you used?'

'Shortsword, sabre and bow.'

Kodel regarded him for a long still moment, then said: 'Show me your arm.'

Out of the corner of his eye Tauric noticed Pirica watching from across the room as, trembling, he extended his cloth-wrapped left arm. Kodel unfastened the leather ties and unwound the bindings. 'Good. Only two layers and loose enough to breathe.'

He exposed the still-puckered, lividly scarred stump. Tauric felt oddly fearful as the man's rough fingers probed the healed wound, yet there was something both grimly practical and compassionate in his actions.

After the brief examination, Kodel began replacing the bindings. 'Where we're going there is a smith skilled in making false limbs in wood and steel. We'll have him make you several, one for holding a shield, another for a bow, and so forth.' Finished, he stood. 'Once you get your balance back, we can find out what you really know about fighting.'

'Thank you,' Tauric said.

Kodel grunted, then walked back to the fire in the hearth.

Tauric read for a little while longer before tiredness persuaded him to turn in for the night. Dousing the torch he'd wedged in the floorboards nearby, he lay down and pulled the blanket up to cover his head. Sleep's irresistible tide swept in over him soon after.

He dreamed that he stood before a tree burning in the night, its every flame a face contorted with pain. From one side a voice said, *Save them, save them!* He turned to see in a tall standing mirror the image of his father, the Duke of Patrein. *How can I?* Tauric cried. *I have no power.* The Duke shook his head, pointing at him. Tauric looked down to see that both his arms were whole, and of shining metal. Then a host of faceless iron warriors marched out from behind the tree and rushed him. As they attacked Tauric struck them with his shining hands and they fell apart, tumbling pieces of empty, rusting armour. Yet still they came, crowding in close till he was fighting them hand to hand. *Save them, save them!* came the Duke's voice once more, but Tauric had his hands around the neck of one of his attackers and in one violent motion wrenched away the helm to reveal a woman of unearthly beauty, long golden hair spilling forth, and eyes of icy starlight whose gaze struck him to the core as she said, *Save us, save us!* But something had him by the shoulder . . .

He was shaken gently awake to see Coireg's sallow features. The scout put a finger to his lips before Tauric could speak aloud.

'What?' His voice was a whisper.

The man glanced about the room lit by the faint glow of the burned-down fire and a couple of guttering torches. Only snores broke the quiet.

'There's something you should know about Kodel and the Hunter's Children,' he murmured. 'Wanted to tell you earlier, but I had to wait till my turn for the watch came round.'

'So what is it?'

'Tell you outside,' Coireg said, straightening. 'Make sure no one overhears us.'

Shivering, he followed Coireg outside. The night sky was a solid canopy of cloud and the air was icy cold. The scout beckoned and Tauric trudged after him along the side of the fort on a path of broken slabs, brushing past thick tangles of bushy growth. At the corner of the old fort, a figure stepped out of the shadows to meet them. It was Coireg's manservant, Seftal.

'It is good that you are here, young sir,' the servant said. 'All is as it should be.'

There was a blinding pain as something struck him on the back of the head and his legs gave way. Everything swung around him, then dissolved into grey nothingness.

Awareness returned in jolts of pain. There was a taste of blood in his mouth and a roaring in his head which swayed limply in time with his arms. Someone was carrying him over their shoulder, he realized. Then he began to hear a pair of voices.

'. . . are they? We should have met them long before now!'

'Curb your whining.' It was the old man, Seftal. 'We're far

enough away from the fort now to halt – here, by that tree will
do. They will find us, never fear.'

Half a dozen steps later Tauric felt himself being lowered onto
lumpy ground, all the time keeping his eyes closed. For a moment
or two there were only the sounds of his captors settling down
nearby, then Coireg spoke again.

'I'd have thought some of the others would be with us by now.
It sounded like a fierce fight as we left.'

'They will stay as long as it takes to finish the task.' Seftal
sounded unconcerned. 'At the very least, none of the heretics
will have the time to wonder about the whereabouts of our
young guest here. Who, if I'm very much mistaken—' a sharp
slap stung Tauric's face, making him yelp, '—is awake. Sit up!'

Tauric levered himself upright, edging away till his back was
against the tree. In the weak light of predawn the old man's thin
face looked cadaverous, his eyes full of a gleeful darkness.

'I am pleased to see that my associate's oafish blow has not
completely addled your wits. My master would have little use for
a mental cripple.'

Tauric shuddered. 'What do you want with me?'

'What you want – the Empire returned to its former glory
with the Emperor and the power of the Tree united. Only my
master, the Father of Flames, can give you this. Even now, a great
army is mustering in Khatris, preparing to destroy the southern
renegades and sweep away the last of the Earthmother vermin.
With you at its head, carrying the banner of the Fiery Tree, none
shall withstand you.'

'But what if that's not what *I* want?'

Seftal shook his head in mock pity. 'You misunderstand. For
you, there is no choice involved.'

Coireg shifted to his knees and moved closer to the old man.
'Seftal, I'm feeling tired, a bit dizzy . . .' Tauric heard a vague
thickness in his speech. 'If we're going to be on horseback
again soon, I could do with something to wake me up, refresh
me . . .'

Seftal made no reply and Coireg leaned forward on one hand,

his head drooping slightly. 'I don't need very much, just a sip.' He was pleading now. 'I did all you asked, did I not? Do I not deserve a little—'

'Very well,' said Seftal, taking a small phial from within his leather surcoat. 'But after this, there will be no more till we reach our destination.'

Nodding hurriedly, Coireg took the phial, unstoppered it and swiftly tipped the contents down his throat. He coughed, gave a shuddery intake of breath, then handed the phial back. Tauric observed the transaction with sick fascination, then noticed Seftal watching him out of the corner of his eye. The old man gave a calmly malign smile, as if to say, This is how you will be.

Coireg began to laugh softly, throwing his head back to breathe in deeply and stare at the sky. Then he pushed himself to his feet in a lithe motion. 'Ah, now that is much better. You know, friend Seftal, if you brought more of the draught you wouldn't have to be so miserly with it.'

'True, but then you would have to take more and more of it to get the same benefit. Inadvisable, considering how expensive it is.' His voice took on a steely edge. 'And not so loud.'

Coireg leaned a shoulder against the tree with exaggerated ease. 'It is a big forest. Perhaps my talking will help our friends find us—'

'Not likely,' came a voice. 'I killed them all.'

Startled, Tauric looked round to see Kodel emerge, sword in hand, from behind a dense screen of creeper and weeds. He was breathing heavily, and bleeding from a score of wounds on face, arms and hands, while his quilted armour was torn in several places. His features smouldered with hatred and his sabre gleamed dully.

'Hand the boy over to me and I'll see you both receive fair judgement,' he growled.

'Such optimism,' said Seftal, getting to his feet, one hand grasping Tauric's jerkin by the neck and hauling him up with astonishing strength. 'None of you are fit to judge the likes of us. Coireg – dispose of him.'

'Gladly.'

Kodel started across the clearing, glittering eyes fixed on Seftal. Coireg was advancing to cut him off, making small feinting moves with his sword, a straight, slender rapier. When he made a sweeping head cut Tauric thought the Sentinel was about to die. Kodel neatly dodged the blow, then suddenly stepped in close to grab the younger Mazaret by an upper arm and spun him off-balance, simultaneously kicking the legs from under him. As Coireg crashed to the ground, Kodel struck his head with the hilt of his sword, then straightened to face the old man.

'Release the boy, you wizened dog!'

Seftal just laughed and flung out his free arm. Harsh emerald light burst from his fingertips in a jagged web that leaped across the clearing and enfolded Kodel. Staggering back, he uttered a shriek of agony and fell to his knees. The livid tracery made a quiet tearing sound as it spread itself across Kodel's skin and clothing. Tauric could see bright and sickly green edging his staring eyes, his gaping, soundless mouth, and the creases and joints of his hand as it spasmed to let his blade fall. He slumped backward across the insensible Coireg, hands struggling for purchase on the ground, the green web covering his face and neck in a close weave.

Held by Seftal's implacable grip, Tauric sobbed in fear and terror. 'Let him go! Please . . .'

Seftal glanced round with blazing eyes, and he turned away.

'When you strike, strike with passion as well as might. Watch closely, boy. This is your first lesson in retribution—'

The old man's voice cut off suddenly with a brief, wet sound. Tauric felt the grip on his collar tighten and he looked back and cried out. Seftal's other hand now scrabbled and tugged at a rapier impaled through his neck. Emerald fire raged fitfully in his eyes and a grotesque wheezing came from his open mouth. Tauric tried to pull free but Seftal held on, now using the boy for support. Finding himself borne back by the man's weight, Tauric tore and hammered at the bony hand that was starting to choke him. Seftal's other hand was fluttering weakly at the rapier's hilt and his head was jerking and lolling, but his grip on Tauric remained unbreakable.

Then Tauric's foot caught a root and he toppled backwards, twisting away as he fell. A horrible, strangled scream came from Seftal as he struck the ground, driving the blade deeper into his neck. The eyes and mouth were full of venomous green fire. The hand at Tauric's neck finally loosened, went to the sideways-lying face and hesitantly fingered around one eye, then poked deeply into the socket where viridian flames seemed to ripple and burn within a head scoured hollow.

Backing away, Tauric saw the sorcerous fire gutter and die. Seftal went limp and lifeless, thin vapour rising from eyes and mouth. Kodel approached on stumbling feet till he stood over the corpse. He laughed and cursed, spat on the body and began to kick it in a furious rage across the narrow clearing. Then he tripped on a protruding rock and fell to his knees a foot or two from the prone Coireg Mazaret.

'How you deserve to die,' Kodel said to the unconscious man in a voice full of hungry hate. 'But alive you could serve our purpose.' So saying, he forced himself to his feet, looked round at Tauric with a cold gaze, and started across the clearing.

'Come on,' he said hoarsely. 'Get up.'

Tauric stared in fright. 'What are you going to do to me?'

Kodel frowned. 'Do to you?' He shook his head, reached down and hauled Tauric onto his feet. 'Boy, I'm going see you crowned Emperor if it's the last thing I do!'

Chapter Ten

The worst terrors take root only in the wreck of
nations.

Ivaduin Govur, *Epigrams*

From the shadows between a ruined wall and an immense fallen
pillar, Keren watched a gang of ragged youths beating two elderly,
well-clothed men. Fearful faces peered out from nearby tents as
blows rained down on the pair, and men hunched around cooking
fires huddled a little closer to the warmth, pretending to ignore
the sounds of violence and pain.

The beating stopped and after looting their victims, the youths
departed, laughing and jostling, sneering at the men by the fires.
As they left, Keren shifted her gaze back to the forms that lay
on the hard, stony ground, moaning and making weak motions.
Minutes passed and no one moved to help. Her feelings of anger
grew, yet she held back, sensing a certain fearful tension from all
the onlookers.

Then she noticed a line of hooded figures approaching through
the disorderly maze of tents and lean-tos. Keren withdrew further
into the shadows, recognizing the red attire of Fiery Tree priests.
They were all over this vast refugee camp like some deadly vermin,
hauling people away for interrogation, tithing money and food or
dispensing their own brand of summary justice.

They were not the only ones trying to assert authority. Keren
had seen gangs of youths and beggars, and the occasional squad

of mercenaries. The territories they had staked out made a hazy patchwork of the camp and skirmishes were a regular occurrence. But the Fiery Tree priesthood was clearly in the ascendant, mainly due to the supplies of grain and vegetables which they brought in by wagon from who knew where and distributed with ruthless purpose.

Their appearance at this time seemed too coincidental and Keren was sure that they were in league with the Mogaun. Previously, the yearly Blood Gathering at Arengia had been an occasion of rituals for the tribal shamans and those representatives sent by the chiefs, usually the second or third son. This year, however, whole kvals of warriors were converging on the northern forests of Khatris, ransacking all along the way. That was where most of these refugees were from, the razed towns and villages of central Khatris.

She watched the priests drag the two old men away then headed back along the ruined wall, clambering over heaps of grassy rubble, skirting large groups of refugees, and trying to keep to the shadows. But she still attracted suspicious looks whenever she stopped to ask the way to the healers' tent. One ageing beldame squatting in the lee of an overturned wain listened, then glanced at Keren's patched, grubby jerkin and worn-down boots, and grinned toothlessly.

'Tha's good shoes, soldier lady. Do me feet no end of good, they would.'

'Aye, old mother, and they're the only ones I have.' Keren crouched, lowering her voice. 'But when did you last taste cheese?'

The old woman's face went slack with yearning. 'Not since . . .' Then she frowned. 'You're just having cruel giggles with me.'

Keren shook her head, took a small wax paper parcel from a pocket and offered it. The woman took it, unwrapped a morsel of muddy yellow cheese no bigger than her thumb and daintily nibbled at it. Pleasure lit up her wrinkled features and she swayed very slightly from side to side.

'Ah yes, ah yes! Cabringan, from . . . the north-west steadings, I reckon.'

Keren smiled. 'You say so, do you?'

'I once owned me own tavern on the High Yular Road, girly,' she said with narrowed eyes. 'Back before those Mogarn invaded. Oh, but we served them all, great lords, merchant princes . . .'

'I've got a honeystick here, too, mother—' the old woman put out a hand, but Keren kept the delicacy out of reach, '—but I need to know where the healer's tents are.'

'Oh, them. Well, it's a ways down the sloping road, the west one. You'll not get down the east one, past those Fire priests, curse them.' She nibbled a bit more cheese. 'Most of the healers and herbgrinders are down on the bottom step, where the mercenaries and sellswords set up their dens.'

Keren nodded and held out the honeystick which was snatched immediately.

'Mmm, sweet, so sweet. We sold these in my tavern, and mintbuds from Jefren, and freshly baked pocket breads, and Honjir longapples, and . . .' The aged woman stopped, staring at the mouth-wet honeystick. After a second it fell from her grasp and she buried her face in her hands and wept. 'Gone, all gone. All the lovely food, my men, my children. Curse the Mogarn and their Blood Gathering! And curse you for making me remember. Get away, go . . .'

Torn with guilt and pity, Keren stood quickly and made her way off to the west, pausing for a single backward glance at the woman crying quietly over the lost beauties of the past. For a moment she wanted to strike out at something, anything, to exact some kind of retribution for the old woman's pain, to atone for what she had done. Then the moment passed and she stumbled on, heading along a rubbish-strewn walkway between the knee-high remains of what had been walls and the close-packed tents and meagre canopies pitched against them. The way soon turned to the right and after a second's hesitation she went on and found herself at a low, crumbling battlement overlooking the entire refugee camp. Thousands of campfires filled the wide shelf of ruins below, and the one below that, a carpet of lights that spilled over onto the open ground at the very foot of the mountainside. For this was

Alvergost, the greatest citadel of the ages-gone Brusartan kings, last great dynasty of the Jefren League.

Keren remembered that morning when she, Suviel and Gilly had ridden wearily to the top of a saddle ridge and found themselves gazing down at the huge, monolithic ruins. Alvergost had been built at the southernmost corner of the Khatris Plains, where the forbidding Honjir Range met the Rukang Mountains. Three immense levels were carved into the face of the mountain, each with its own inner walls, ramparts and towers, gates and sallyports. The ground level had been the mightiest, with three inner walls in addition to the main bulwark, and heavily fortified battlements following the line of the mountains to north and east.

But the Brusartan kings, like others before them, had held to the familiar path of dynastic decline. Vigorous, inspired leaders were followed by less competent ones whose offspring turned out to be indolent or insane. At the end of their century-long reign the League collapsed into civil war and fabulously intricate Alvergost was abandoned. Now the huge dusty ruin, ground down by the centuries, had fallen to an army of the dispossessed and the desperate. Earlier, in the morning's cold, clear light, Keren had seen hundreds of refugees stumbling in to join the thousands already here, farmers and townsfolk from Tobrosa whose pillaging by the Mogaun five or more days ago still marred the horizon with a black column of smoke. Alvergost by day was a heart-wrenching spectacle; by night it took on a strange beauty, three great steps of lights hazed by campfire smoke.

Suviel was down there somewhere, ministering to the sick and the wounded. When they had ridden down from the ridge earlier, an old midwife had recognized the mage's herbwoman attire and begged her to go to the healer tents and help. Suviel had agreed immediately, told Keren and Gilly to make camp near friendly people and wait for her return in the late afternoon. But dusk had come and brought the evening in its wake with no sign of Suviel. Worried over the mage's safety, Keren had decided that she would go and search for her. She had stood up, announced her intent and dashed off into the

night before Gilly could do more than utter a string of colour-
ful oaths.

She continued her westward progress along the ruined vestiges
of the battlements, soon reaching a stairway that the ravages of
time had reduced to a rocky incline. Descending, it met another
wider downward slope flanked by rounded nubs of columns
and etched with long branching grooves made by centuries
of rainwater. People were everywhere, sitting listlessly by fires,
arguing with each other, sleeping in mean tents, or begging as
she passed, their hands outstretched. Keren ignored them and
hurried on.

A short time later she came to a barrier of rubble and earthslide
and was gingerly following a crude path up it when a figure rose
up from behind a chunk of masonry.

'No further. Lay down any weapons you bear.'

Someone nearby uncovered a lamp and Keren backed off,
drawing her sword as quietly as she could.

'I mean to cause no trouble or offence,' she said. 'I seek a
friend . . .'

'It's a woman,' said an eager voice off to the side.

The man in front of her laughed, shifting a spear from one
hand to the other and moving down towards her. 'Risky for a
woman to be out alone in this camp, day or night. Why don't
you come along with me, now? I'll see no harm befalls you.'

'Come any closer and you'll see how risky it is for a man,'
Keren snarled. 'If that's what you are.'

'Hey, bit of a she-cat, this one!'

'What about it, Barew? Watch out for those claws!'

The man with the spear came into the light – a narrow face,
a balding head, and eyes full of hate while his mouth grinned.
'First,' he said conversationally to her, 'I'll cut you, then I'm going
to gut you.'

Whoops of approval came from the others as he went into
a crouch with the spear held two-handed across his chest. Not
good, Keren thought. The man had the look of an experienced
staffman. Barew feinted at her feet with the haft, causing her

to dodge, and was about to jab at her head when a voice rang out.

'Hold there! What goes on?'

'Caught us a brigand, major.'

'Just questioning her, like.'

'So I see. Barew, put up your spear.'

The newcomer stepped up to Keren's opponent, who ignored him, just staring at her for a moment before straightening to lean on his spear, face gone expressionless. A couple of torches were lit and when the major turned to her he uttered a surprised oath.

'So Byrnak didn't get you after all.'

By the light she saw it was Domas.

'Well met, Domas,' she said, sheathing her sword.

The former rider captain nodded, then glanced at Barew and the others. 'Get back to your posts. Any other intruders are to be brought to me, is that clear?'

There were mutters of agreement, apart from Barew, who pointed wordlessly at Keren with an outstretched arm before walking back to the barrier. Domas, now holding a torch, glared at him for a moment then beckoned Keren to follow him the same way. Warily, she did. Domas said nothing till they were on the other side and a score of paces down the slope.

'Barew is scum,' he said. 'But he's not the worst. At least he can keep his squad in line and doesn't rob everyone who comes within reach.'

'He's certainly taken a liking to me,' Keren said wryly.

Domas curled his lip in contempt. 'He's just another Byrnak, only smaller and weaker.' He glanced at her. 'So how did you and that young priest escape our former lord and master? And what brings you here?'

She shrugged. 'We were lucky enough to encounter someone willing to help, the same person I'm here looking for. Perhaps you've seen her – a tall, grey-haired herbwoman who would have ridden in on her own horse this morning?'

Domas frowned. 'I think I did see such a woman this afternoon, near the healers' tents.'

'Will you take me there?'

'Once you've seen the General. It's a standing order – all visitors bearing arms are to be brought before him immediately. No exceptions.'

The general was an imposing man, black-haired, tall and burly, not obese yet not in the prime of fitness. A patch covered his right eye and twin parallel scars marred the flesh from above the same eye down the cheek. He had a bushy moustache and several days' worth of stubble. Seated behind a trestle covered with papers, he regarded her with level scrutiny while toying with an empty dagger sheath.

'So, Keren Asherol,' he said. His voice was deep and husky, with a harsh undertone that suggested either strength or threat. 'Major Domas tells me that you were formerly a lieutenant in the Imperial army. Fought at the Battle of Wolf's Gate, escaped and worked as a sellsword ever since. That is a lot of experience, and all clearly well learned. I could use another veteran in the company, Keren. It would mean a captain's commission were you to accept.'

She thought for a moment. In these uncertain times, with Mogaun chieftains, merchants and even cities hiring mercenaries, it was a tempting offer. But she knew she could not break the promise she had given to the Lord Commander to protect Shin Hantika. It was a duty, a path of honour she was suddenly determined to follow.

'It is a generous proposal, general, but I have other obligations to fulfil. Sadly, I must decline.'

The General looked thoughtful, fingers rubbing the plain, use-darkened leather of the dagger scabbard. 'We live in a dangerous age, Keren. This would be your chance to ensure that you're always on the winning side.'

'My thanks, sir, but my decision stands.'

'As you wish. Domas will guide you to the healers' tents.'

Once Domas and the woman were gone, a short man in a long tattered townsman's cloak stepped from behind a flap at the rear of the tent and moved to stand beside the General.

'Well?'

The General said nothing as he reached down into a knapsack at his feet and pulled out a notched, rusty dagger. He slid it into the sheath and held it out. Smiling, the tattered man took it from his hand, replacing it with a small bag that chinked softly. As he hid the sheathed dagger within his cloak, there was a flash of red cloth from beneath the sleeve at his wrist. Then it was gone and he left without another word. The General turned back to the table, took up a quill pen and began to write out a set of orders.

The healers' tents were pitched well away from the mass of refugees, among trees by a stream which originated somewhere in the mountainside ravines north of Alvergost. As Domas escorted her there, he related something of his own experiences since the night she had escaped with Tauric. It seemed that her harsh words to him away from the camp that night had forced him to reconsider any plan of deposing Byrnak. Then later, when the guards discovered what she had done, he was spurred into decisive action.

'I told my rider serjeants I was leaving, and asked who was with me.' He laughed. 'All three voted to join me, and a handful of the men, the most trustworthy ones. Once Byrnak and his company left in pursuit of you, we deserters mounted up and rode off, "hunting boar" we told the rest.'

'Then?'

'We thought of riding north to Casall or Rauthaz, but we were low on provisions so we headed east through one of the mountain passes, thinking to try our luck in Tobrosa. On the other side we met the General and his men – they were part of a host of refugees fleeing the sack of Tobrosa, and when he invited us to join the company we accepted. That was a week ago and we've been here these last five days.'

He paused. 'The General is a canny soldier, Keren. You could do a lot worse than take him up on his offer.'

'I can't, Domas. I have other tasks to carry out.'

'Know what I think? I think that you've joined one of those

rebel bands we've been hearing about. There's supposedly a big one holed up in the Bachruz Mountains.' He stroked his chin. 'Would it take about a week to travel there, then turn around and ride here, do you reckon?'

Keren's felt unease at his speculation and the shadowy dimness of the trees where they stood, away from the light of campfires and torches, took on an air of menace. She loosened her sabre in its scabbard and forced a quiet laugh.

'I think that you're building castles out of grass, Domas,' she said. 'You've been listening to too much refugee ragtalk.'

Domas regarded her calmly for a brief moment, then shook his head, grinning.

'Ah, Keren, Keren – whatever your secret is, it's safe with me.' He pointed out a long, low tent through the trees. 'That's where the sick are tended so your friend should be thereabouts. When you're ready to leave, seek me out near the general's tent, but I recommend you wait till morning.'

She nodded, letting herself relax a little. 'Thank you, Domas.'

He made a batting motion with his hand. 'Nothing.' He turned to leave, then said; 'And Keren – try to come up with a convincingly detailed story next time, eh?'

Chuckling, he strode off back the way they had come.

Keren was self-reproachful as she threaded a way through the trees. Domas was right. She should have thought of a plausible explanation, some string of falsehoods to counter any scrutiny. She sighed. For some, like Gilly, concocting deceits and petty tales out of nothing was an effortless, natural ability. Had he been in her shoes, he would doubtless have fabricated a heart-rending story of destitute refugees, complete with names, ages and family histories, looking to him for succour, ending with Domas and the General drying tears from their eyes and sending him on his way with gold and food. The image amused her as she approached the tent.

Her smile faded when she saw a woman sitting weeping by the entrance. With a shock she realized it was Suviel. Keren hurried over, crouched beside the mage and murmured her name. Suviel raised her head and Keren saw utter exhaustion etched in her features, her eyes red-rimmed, her face pale, almost grey in the light from a nearby campfire.

'They die and I can't save them,' she said hoarsely. 'Some don't want to live, they're so weak and sick and empty . . . empty of hope.' She coughed. 'I've spent myself, Keren, and I'm all used up. Raal sent me out here to rest.'

Keren reached out to steady her but Suviel caught her hand in a trembling grip and stared at her.

'Listen, this Raal Haidar is a sorcerer. He uses a power I've not seen before, like ghostly braids and nets . . .'

'You should rest, try and sleep.'

Suviel went on. 'He says he is from an island kingdom far to the west of Keremenchool. If only we can persuade him to join us. I've asked him but he insists he cannot . . . I must go back inside and help.'

She tried to stand but fell to her knees and began to weep again. Appalled and shaken, Keren half-carried her over to the fire and made her lie down, ignoring her protestations as she wrapped her in blankets and folded one for her head. In a short while, she was sleeping deeply. Keren gently brushed strands of grey and brown hair away from Suviel's face, then rose to go to the tent. But she stopped, startled to see a tall man in a dark green robe standing a few feet away, methodically wiping long-fingered hands on a blood-stained cloth.

'Are you—' she began.

'I am Raal Haidar.' His voice was deep, melodious, and rang with authority. 'You are Keren Asherol, the swordswoman. Where is your companion, the trader?'

He had a narrow face and a high forehead, an imperious blade of a nose and eyes that were dark and powerful and cold.

'He is with our horses, camped on the topmost level.'

'That is unfortunate. There is much danger abroad tonight.' He turned back to the tent. 'Come – I require your assistance.'

'You require—' She bit back on the angry retort that rose to her lips and followed. Inside, small hanging lamps cast light on three rows of cots. Iron burners on pedestals filled the air with incense, an attempt to keep away insects and mask the smells of illness. But beneath the perfume she could still detect a fetid bitterness and the pungency of stale sweat. There were another two people ministering to the sick, a man and a woman, both of whom appeared weighed down by weariness.

The man called Raal Haidar indicated a crude table crowded with bowls, sacks and torn cloth.

'Wash your hands then bring me bandages,' he said, then walked up one of the rows and stopped by one cot. Keren glanced back out at the slumbering form by the fire, sighed and went over to the table. Some of the sacks there she recognized as Suviel's, most lying open, their contents laid out in neat groups around a mortar and pestle and other scholarly implements. Hands washed, she sorted through the scraps of cloth for long strips, tore up some clean-looking rags into more and took a good bundle over to Raal Haidar.

The tall man was examining a young boy whose arm, bare of its dressings, was a mass of sores. As Keren saw him, a panicky tremor passed through her.

'That's . . . that's the black yaws,' she said.

'Hmm. It is usually completely fatal.'

'Usually? But there's no cure! By the Mother, we're all at risk—'

He straightened and fixed her with a withering look. 'The dressings, if you please.'

Wordlessly, she gave him a handful of bandages and watched him take a small blue glass jar from his robe which he uncorked to reveal a rosy paste. Three bandages were smeared with the paste, then more were wound on to hold them in place. When he was finished, Raal Haidar washed his hands and went on to the next patient, gesturing Keren to attend him.

They worked on for at least an hour by Keren's reckoning, and throughout the tall sorcerer – which was how she thought of him – never once showed a glimmering of sympathy or pity for those he tended. His gaze was cold, his every motion efficient and full of certainty and Keren began to wonder if he saw the sick and injured as people at all. Only once had she attempted conversation with him and that he had cut short with a small gesture without even looking her way. Yet when he finally straightened and said, 'Enough' she wanted to continue.

'Why?' she demanded as he strode over to wash his hands at the table.

He shook water from his long, pale hands, dried them and said, 'Because our time here is at an end.'

Almost at once she heard voices from outside, among them that of Suviel. Keren tossed the last of the bandages on the table and dashed past the impassive Raal.

Two mercenaries with drawn swords held a dazed, half-awake Suviel between them while another four approached the sick tent. With them was the General and an uncomfortable-looking Domas. Keren glared at him as the General halted a few feet away.

'Give up your weapons and you will come to no harm,' he said.

She ignored the command and grinned wolfishly, hand resting on the hilt of her sword. 'Release my companion and you will likewise be unharmed.'

The General responded with a smile of his own. 'Surely you can see the futility of pitting yourself against us, woman. The terms of my compact require only that I deliver the herbwoman. If we have to kill you, it is no matter.'

'Keren,' said Suviel. 'Don't fight. There are other ways . . .'

Keren's gaze never left the General's face. 'Who have you sold us to, mercenary?' She put venom into the word. 'Those priests, yes? Then come, for I will not surrender to them or you.'

Her sword sang a metallic hiss as she drew it forth. The General shook his head.

'Impetuous, yet spirited. You could have been a valuable asset to my company, Keren Asherol. That can still be so, if you exercise a little prudence. Give me your sword and you will be safe, I swear it.'

Keren spat on the ground. 'Come and take it, lackey.'

The General's composure dissolved into anger. 'Take them,' he told his men.

Before they could move, a voice spoke from behind Keren.

'Halt! There will be no fighting.'

Raal Haidar was standing to her right, hands linked across his chest and concealed by the sleeves of his dark green robe.

'Unless you have a weapon, stay out of this,' Keren muttered.

The tall man ignored her and said to the General, 'You have made a grave mistake, for I fear you will have to return your fee.'

The General unsheathed his own blade, a plain broadsword with a battered basket hilt. 'And why would that be?'

'Because you will have no one to deliver, foolish warrior.' Haidar's hands parted and he raised one of them, forefinger pointing up, thumb-tip pressed against the others. He paused for an instant, staring straight at the General, who seemed to shrink slightly under the impact of that regard. 'Be fortunate in your journey.'

Then he spoke a long, single word and the world changed.

The word reverberated through her. Her skin crawled and her bones rang and the air in her lungs buzzed like a thing alive. One arm she wrapped across her chest, while the other quivered to the brazen sound of her sword, tightly grasped yet still somehow slowly slipping out of her fist. She could feel her hair writhing on her scalp and her eyes vibrating in their sockets. Then, with a fading undertone, the word ended and Keren straightened to look about her.

The General, Domas and their men were still visible, but only as horror-struck, tenuous wraiths searching in and around the tent. Night's darkness was gone, replaced by an all-pervasive white radiance that leached the colour from their surroundings – the tent, the trees, the grass, the flickering flames of the campfire. To Keren's eyes everything was in shades of crystalline white and grey, except for her companions.

Suviel stumbled across to Raal Haidar. 'What have you done?' she said in amazement. 'Where are we?'

Haidar, hand still upraised, looked around him as if in scrutiny for a brief moment before answering. 'This place is known to the arcana of my masters as Kekrahan. It is one of several spectral domains which closely overlap our own plane of existence.'

'We call them the Realms,' said Suviel.

Haidar shrugged. 'I do not know if we are speaking of the same things. As I understand it, the Realms are seperate planes of existence in their own right. This—' he gestured about him '—is but a ghostly half-world.'

'And how long can you keep us here?' Keren said impatiently.

'Not indefinitely, so it would be wise if we set out to find your other fellow-traveller who, I believe, is keeping watch over your remaining horses up on the topmost level.'

'How did you know that?'

'When we were tending the sick, your mind continually returned to this man, Gilly. My people are sensitive to fleeting thought-emanations and with you it was akin to hearing someone muttering under their breath.'

'Shall we go?' said Suviel. 'I have no desire to find myself back in our erstwhile captors' hands.'

Together they made their way through the trees to the pathway that led up the mountainside. It was like walking through a community of apparitions; although it was the middle of the night, there were still many refugees awake, huddled round fires or stealing among the tents and lean-tos on obscure errands. As they came to the earthslide and masonry barrier, where Barew and his fellows tossed dice by torchlight, a scrawny dog leaped to its feet and began barking madly at their passing. One of the guards hurled stones at it and the poor animal ran off yelping.

The same thing happened twice more, once with a bony cat which abandoned its meal of dead rat and scurried away, and again with a tethered goat which ran in a panicky circle till they had passed by.

Gilly and Keren had pitched their tent under a jutting rock. The trader was sitting on a boulder when they arrived, feeding a fire with scraps of tinder. Keren smiled at the moody look on his face and turned to the sorcerer.

'You can bring us back now.'

'Not here,' Suviel said. 'We might be seen.'

Keren pointed to a gap between the overhanging rock and the side of the tent right behind Gilly. 'There?'

The mage gave her a reproachful look. 'Trying to exact some petty revenge, Keren?'

'He deserves it,' Keren said.

Raal Haidar drew himself straighter. 'This is quite tiresome.' He uttered two quick, harsh syllables, and Keren felt an icy wave pass through her, leaving her shivering cold in its wake, with shadowy night once more shrouding all she saw.

Before them, Gilly had jumped to his feet and half-drawn his blade when recognition stayed his hand. Suviel hurried over to rub her hands in the heat of the fire and was joined by Keren. The trader quickly assumed an air of relaxed ease and sat back down.

'It would appear that I've missed all the excitement,' he said.

'There is no time for explanations, Gilly,' said Suviel. 'We had best break camp immediately before anyone comes looking for us. And we've only two horses between the three of us so the sooner we leave the safer I'll feel.'

'There will be four of us.'

Keren turned with Suviel to regard Raal Haidar. The tall man met the mage's cool gaze for a moment before a ghost of a smile crossed his face.

'Fate decrees that we be fellow travellers, Shin Hantika,' he said. 'Like you, my destination lies to the north, in Prekine.' He bowed his head very slightly, as if acknowledging her authority. 'I am sure that I can be of service to you.'

Suviel was silent and Keren felt a haze of unease at the suspicion, the certainty, that the only way Raal Haidar could know of their travel plans would be if he had picked it from among Suviel's own thoughts.

Then the mage nodded. 'Very well. We would be glad to have you journey with us.'

'And will we be travelling from here to there in the blinking of an eye?' said Gilly as he stood. 'Or can I look forward to days spent traversing mountains and fording rushing streams?'

'I fear we shall be confined to this plane of existence,' said Haidar.

Gilly frowned. 'I can scarcely contain my joy.'

Chapter Eleven

Whilst a half-truth and a half-lie,
Are perilous horrors to the unwary eye,
The unvarnished truth,
Is more terrible still.

Contemplations, 27

Incomplete, the spell hovered a foot above Bardow's table, a glittering, twisting knot of broken colours. A couple of thin-wicked candles in niches by the door gave off yellow halos of light, but the spell's luminescence was quite different. It sent weak rainbow flickers over the table's dusty clutter of books, withered plant stalks, grotesque figurines, pincers, files, quills and empty inkpots, and a couple of plates bearing the quarter-eaten, dried-out remnants of food. The mage sat in a tall chair, elbow resting on the chair arm, chin cupped in hand, his face looking tired and lined in the spell's radiance.

Bardow felt tired. If he had been shaping an ordinary scrying spell, it would have taken him a matter of minutes and demanded only a modicum of concentration and alertness. This scrying spell, however, was different. In effect, he was trying to recreate the farseeing aspect of the Crystal Eye by pitting several Lesser Power thought-cantos against each other. Already his head was ringing with the effort of maintaining the cantos of Behold and Veil, and Impel and Lure, balancing their open forces, keeping them focused on the same point.

At that point darkness enfolded light, red birthed black, white became silver became leaf green became jewelled blue became perfect circular ripples of oily shimmer. Bardow whispered the syllable which joined the beginning and the end of his fifth thought-canto, that of Binding. Opaque strands looped and looped around the composite spell, caging it.

He sighed with relief and sagged in his chair. As the thought-cantos slipped from his mind, a fading carnival of sounds and textures and emotions, he wiped his face with a trembling hand, and rubbed the smarting ache from his eyes. Once, back before the Mogaun invasion, he had attended a conclave where this very task was performed by Archmage Agatil; it had taken him but a few moments and fatigued him not at all. But Argatil had died with the Emperor at Arengia and the Rootpower was shattered and gone, leaving only the inelegant methods of the Lesser Power with which to achieve the impossible.

Sticks and mud to withstand the storm, he thought. *And even with the Crystal Eye, it may not be enough.*

Above his table the spell was now a small, pale orb, its face disturbed by tiny swirls of darkness that came and went. For now it was stable, but the antagonistic forces he had bound together would after a while begin to oscillate, then it was a matter of bringing those forces into resonance with each other. Thus would he achieve his goal.

Bardow gripped the arms of his chair and stood. But his legs felt frail and he staggered slightly to the side. Laughing weakly, he steadied himself for a brief moment then retrieved a tinderwheel from beneath a sheaf of parchments, lit a tallow lamp then walked gingerly over to the window. A heavy grey blanket attached to a pole and crosspiece hung like a banner across the shutters, and when he moved it to one side a tall, dazzling shaft of sunlight abruptly dispelled the gloom. Plumes of dust from the blanket sparkled in the brightness. Bardow tugged open the shutters, pushed wide the outer ones and leaned on the windowsill, resting his palms flat on the heated stone.

Krusivel was bathed in the bright gold of a noon sun, an

unexpected glory in this grey autumn. From the tower he could see people taking advantage of the uninterrupted warmth – washing was being hung out, roofs were being repaired, an extension to the barracks was under construction, and the horses were out in the upper fields, being run and raced by the ostlers and several of the knights. He breathed in deep and smelled grass and a hint of woodsmoke and suddenly found himself remembering . . .

He remembered leaning out of a high window very like this, with sunlight in his face and the cold sharpness of mountain air in his lungs. And gazing down at a narrow, sloping street that wound its way through the town, past college halls, lodging houses and inns, with alleys leading off to taverns and stalls selling herbs or odd curios, tailors, flowersellers, scryers' booths, a bakery whose delicacies were shipped to all the great cities, and an odd little shop which specialized in climbing paraphernalia. And looking up at the greenwings that dashed around the sky in great flocks, more often than not in flight from a predatory crownhawk . . .

Bardow closed his eyes, trying to hold the memory in place. Fifty years on and he could still recall his first days as a student in Trevada. His last visit had been a year before the invasion, since when he had heard only rumours and fourth-hand accounts of the awful havoc and slaughter visited upon the mage-town by the Acolytes after the dissolution of the Rootpower. If Suviel survived and returned with the Eye, he would finally know what, if anything, remained of the dear places of his youth.

The sounds of children's singing voices reached him. Peering down, he spied a group of six or seven boys and girls sitting beside a clump of catear blooms. One lad was half-singing, half-giggling the old nonsense verse about the pig and the pigeon. When he finished, two girls with long, braided fair hair stood up, clasped their hands before them and began to sing:

> Little seed become a shoot,
> Little shoot become a twig,
> Little twig become a leaf,
> Little leaf become a shrub,
> Little shrub become a tree,
> Little tree grow tall and strong.

As they sang, they acted out the words with their hands and finished with their arms raised above their heads and happy smiles on their faces. Bardow listened and watched with tears in his eyes. Although a simple child's verse, it contained, in a greatly abbreviated form, all the main elements of the Great Rite of the Fathertree which used to be conducted twice a year, at the height of summer and in the depths of winter.

We are all in winter now, he thought sombrely. *Yet our children still have the faith that we lost. Their innocence shields them from truth.*

Behind him there was a knock at the door.

'I'm busy,' he said over his shoulder.

'No, you're not,' said a woman's voice.

He turned to stare. 'I'm hard at work on a matter of great importance.'

'Not according to young Jeffi. He says you're sitting at the window and talking to the birds.'

Muttering, 'Mother preserve me!', he went over to the table and set a tall open book in front of the hovering spell, hiding it from view. Then he crossed to the door, unbarred it and returned to the window, saying, 'Come in!'

A pretty young woman entered with a tray bearing some small bowls, a beaker and a jug. She smiled brightly as she brought it over and set it in a small recess under the window ledge, then gave him an expectant look.

'I have been eating, you know.'

'True, Shin Bardow, but bread and cheese are entirely unsuitable for someone of your position and responsibility.'

Fionn had waist-length red hair and wore a brown dress and

yellow shawl. Some of the time she was Guldamar's assistant, but otherwise she seemed to have taken it upon herself to look after his day-to-day needs, bringing him food or having his clothes washed and mended. Bardow suspected that Suviel was behind this in some way.

As he sampled some of the bowls' contents – cooked vegetables, a salad sprinkled with nuts, and hot biscuits – Fionn went to stand at the window. Bardow heard some of the children call her name and she waved back.

'Congratulating your spies, hmm?' he said.

She looked round, and sniffed. 'I call them my little knights. I set them duties and tasks like brushing the paths or tidying the flowerbeds, and teach them some of the songs I knew at their age.' She paused. 'Till I began doing this, I hadn't realized how great a part of my life the Rootpower faith was, even as a child.'

'How old were you when the Fathertree was destroyed?'

'Just seven,' she said. 'Mother cried for days and Father wouldn't say a thing. Our village priest left to join the defence of the Fathertree temple in Adnagaur. And after all the priests died, there was no one to conduct the rites and speak the prayers, or teach the children or perform all the small duties that bound the village together. All that was left for us was to learn how to survive.

'When Guldamar brought me here a year ago, I was still learning about the Lesser Power. It was Shin Hantika, when she was here the time before last, who introduced me to the children. I felt that I had to tell them all the things I knew as a child.'

Bardow felt a pang of shame at his earlier remarks. 'So it was you who taught them "Little Seed".'

Fionn bit her lip. 'Was I wrong to do so?'

'No . . . I just wonder if such innocence is a help or a hindrance in this unforgiving age.'

She smiled. 'The Earthmother priestesses are most thorough in their teaching of history, Shin Bardow – the children do know what happened sixteen years ago. I just felt that a certain joy was missing.' She glanced back outside. 'I'm surprised that the mages did not sense it long before now.'

Bardow laughed gently and she looked at him. He filled a beaker from the jug and offered it to her, then poured one for himself. 'There you touch upon the dilemma at the heart of the Mage Order, such as it is. You see, before the invasion all the senior priests of the Order of the Fathertree were also members of the Mage Order, but not all mages were Rootpower priests. Yet when it came to the highest mysteries of the Rootpower, all mages studied at the Earthmother Temple in Trevada. It was not as complicated as it sounds, rather it was a joining of the mystical and the practical, a loving dance, balanced and harmonious.' He sipped at his drink. 'So when the Rootpower was destroyed, and Besh-Darok fell, and the priests died defending the temples, none of the few surviving mages were priests. Bereft of their powers, some took their own lives while others went into hiding. With the Archmage dead, it was left to me to gather the stronger, more resolute ones and bring them here, where we work to increase our abilities in the Lesser Power and prepare for the coming struggle.

'Occasionally, someone emerges and decides to join us, but most of the newer pupils are youngsters brought here by friends and allies.' He smiled faintly. 'All of them keen to learn and unafraid of highlighting their teachers' shortcomings.'

Fionn looked down. 'I am sorry if I have been disrespectful.'

He shook his head. 'What we do here is too important to allow respect to cloud the truth. Fionn . . .'

Hesitantly, she met his gaze.

'Continue teaching rhymes and stories to your "little knights",' he said. 'Bring joy into their days and their dreams.'

She nodded. 'Thank you, Shin Bardow. Perhaps you might care to come out and meet them.'

Bardow thought for a moment. 'Yes, I think I'd like that . . .' His voice trailed off as his ears caught a faint buzzing sound. Quickly he stood.

'But not at the moment,' he continued, guiding a surprised

Fionn back to the door. 'My apologies for hurrying you out like this, but there is something I have to attend to immediately.'

'Can I help in any way?' she said, pausing on the threshold.

He shook his head. 'There is some risk involved and I would not wish to expose you to it.'

'I understand. Till later, Shin Bardow.'

'Till later.'

As she left, he closed and barred the door, dashed back to the window and sealed the shutters, then went to the candle-lit table and snatched away the concealing book. The orb of the spell was visibly pulsing, its pale surface marred by criss-cross patterns of vibration. In his mind Bardow began the thought-canto of Binding once more in preparation for when the confined forces burst apart his first Binding.

Seconds crept by. Wax from the candle on his table gleamed and dripped down the encrusted stem of its holder. Bardow licked dry lips and blinked eyes that began to ache with the intense, unmoving stare. Then the candle flame wavered as the pale orb cracked. Silver turbulence shimmered within, expanded. Instantly he cast the new Binding at the unravelling spell and after a moment the orb – now the size of his head – ceased growing. Its surface was a shifting, mirrored mosaic and he saw his own face reflected in it a thousand times over before the myriad facets dissolved into a perfect blackness.

At last it was ready. Holding the Binding steady, he began the thought-canto Spiritwing. He tightened his concentration, focused his being on an imaginary point on the orb's featureless surface. Details of the surrounding room started to fade as the Spiritwing strengthened its hold on his senses. Everything melted into the black orb and suddenly he was flying into its funereal emptiness, endless gulfs of night through which he fell. There was a coldness here in the Void Between, a coldness that tried to coil itself around the awareness and sap the will. But Bardow resisted it, drawing on the warmth of all his memories.

Tauric, he thought clearly amid the exultation of flight. *I want to see Tauric.*

The Spiritwing wheeled and dived and the darkness brightened to a threatening grey. He descended through a stormy sky, great rafts of cloud and veils of mist and rain. The clouds parted and he saw a long range of tree-covered mountains stretching away before him, grey and hazy in the downpour. It took him a moment to recognize it as the northern spur of the Bachruz Mountains which extended to the Great Valley near Sejeend in Roharka. Then the Spiritwing banked to the right, sweeping him past the uppermost peaks of several mountains and south towards the vast forest of Falador.

Slowing, he came in low over the treetops near the forest's southern edge where it met the shores of Lake Ornim. Then the Spiritwing took him down among the branches, gliding gracefully through the trees. Water dripped from above but he heard nothing and felt nothing, only a heightened tranquillity and the sharp purpose of his search.

The light of torches and a campfire emerged through the gloom, the shapes of tents in a clearing, tethered horses cropping grass, and figures of men sat round the fire. Closer he moved, floating under tree limbs and over masses of foliage, and caught sight of Tauric off to one side, sitting opposite Kodel. With his good arm the boy was catching small stones tossed to him by Kodel. The stones came from the right or the left, low or high or with a spin, faster and faster till eventually Tauric missed one and burst out laughing. Kodel laughed with him, then paused, tilted his head as if listening and scanned the trees near Bardow's vantage point. Bardow smiled inwardly – Tauric might have none of the sorcerous potential of his Imperial forebears, but Kodel certainly seemed to possess some vestigial ability.

As if sensing that it had been detected, the Spiritwing retreated from the clearing. Bardow suddenly realized that there had been no sign of Himber, or Pirica, or the Lord Commander's brother, Coireg. However, a couple of Kodel's men bore bandages on head and hands – had there been a fight or an ambush? He pictured Himber's face, and when nothing happened he did the same with Pirica. The Spiritwing remained unchanged, which could only mean that both the advisers were dead.

Then he thought of Coireg and instantly his view of the clearing shifted in a blur of leaves and smoke and campfire flames and when the haziness came back into focus he was inside a tent looking down from its peak. Coireg Mazaret lay asleep on a grubby pallet, his hands and feet bound with rope, his face bruised and scratched. Bardow grew worried. What had Ikarno's brother done to deserve this?

At least the boy is unharmed, he thought. *And Kodel seems to have taken to him, which is no bad thing.*

He paused to gaze inward at the Binding and make sure it was holding. The canto still gyred steadily in his mind, although sooner or later the composite spell it embraced would inevitably fragment, by which time he would have to be back in his body. It would never do to be trapped in the Void Between for eternity.

Suviel Hantika, he thought clearly.

All sight dissolved and slipped sideways and the Spiritwing flew on through yawning dark emptiness, unerring and urgent. Iciness clamped itself around his essence, seeking to drain him through the faultlines of his anxieties and uncertainties. But he fanned the embers of all that he loved, people and places, the past and even the present, and endured. Soon the darkness parted to bright sunlight over mountains. The Spiritwing was carrying him north, low enough to see small white goats on the snowy upper slopes, digging for grass and roots. Then the mountains fell away to a short stretch of flat plain leading to an ancient ruined citadel.

He recognised Alvergost immediately and saw smoke trails rising from a crowded sea of tents. Refugees, he realized in dismay. Sweeping past overhead he just caught sight of some kind of riot at the foot of the great fortress. Then it passed out of view as the Spiritwing sped on over the mountains once more.

He was descending towards a barren, narrow-sided pass when the Spiritwing slowed. The pass dipped and widened to where a pool fed a cluster of meagre trees and bushes, and where more than a dozen riders milled about as if in confusion. The Spiritwing began to shift Bardow back to the Void but he said, Wait.

From above he watched the horsemen. Some were garbed in

mail or half-plate armour, others in studded leather, but all wore enclosing helms that hid their faces. These were Acolyte guards, he realized, notorious for their ability to track a quarry across the most difficult of terrain. Yet here they were, plainly frustrated in their hunt. If they had been chasing Suviel and the others, where were they now?

Suviel Hantika, he thought. *Find her.*

Again, the black touch of the Void Between, its deathly chill seeping deeper than before, a sure sign that the Binding was starting to weaken. But the Spiritwing seemed unsure of where to go – hazy images of mountains came and went, interspersed with glimpses of other places, a red chaos of shattered, drifting rock, a foggy green jungle, a sun-blasted plain. Instinctively he knew he was seeing snatches of the Realms, regions of primal power that were home to a host of spirits and entities both beneficent and malefic. He remembered undergoing the Rite of Tempering in a mountainside shrine above Trevada, and the ecstatic prolonged vision which had propelled him like a stormblown feather through the Realm of the Fathertree. That place had been vibrant with life. Flocks of indescribable creatures had carried or guided him on his journey, entire herds of animals had conversed with him in a single voice, and a majestic, towering tree – just one of a limitless forest – had spoken with many. He had awoken from the Rite a true mage, marked heart, mind and soul with the Rootpower.

A dead power, an empty throne. It was a bitter loss to know that these fleeting glimpses of the Realms were all that the Lesser Power would ever be able to show him. It was a wound that could never heal.

Still the Spiritwing wavered between places, only now one in particular began reappearing more often, the fog-swathed jungle. For a moment Bardow felt a spark of hope, then disquiet as he realized that it was either following the Spiritwing or drawing it closer. The darkness of the Void shaded into the misty murk, yet remained at the back of his awareness, holding him at the threshold. Bardow saw a dense tangle of growth, thick trunks whose bark glittered in a myriad shades of green, twisting viney branches bursting with great translucent teardrop leaves which shone with an inner radiance. Dew gleamed, collected, brimmed and splashed, and not even the tiniest creature was visible.

Bardow —

A shock ran through him. The voice was low and quiet, a degree above a whisper, yet there was power in it and something womanly . . .

Bardow, son of my daughters, custodian of the embers of the fire that was, hear me, I implore you. The dangers are greater than you know, greater than you can imagine. The Lord of Twilight's dark plans are working themselves into the flesh of the world like poison barbs. If you are not wary, your plans will become as his and all of life will be in danger.

Do not fail me. He took my beloved from me and I wander in my weeping sorrow and anger, hungering for retribution. I will have vengeance, son of my daughters. I will drive him to his knees before me and take his throat in my hand and cut it through. I will have it, but you must not fail.

The dark, veiled jungle blurred. Coldness tore at him with ragged talons and the blackness roared in his head as he spun away, falling, twisting . . .

He landed on his hands and knees on the floor as his tall chair clattered off to one side. The candles had burned out and the tower room was dim, weak light filtering in at the shuttered window. For a few moments Bardow just sat where he was, breathing heavily, trying to regain his senses and grasp the import of what had happened.

The Earthmother. He had been brought to the threshold of her Realm, and she had spoken to him, an event almost unheard of outside the Earthmother priesthood. Part of him hung between fear and awe, the feeling that such an experience was usually accounted as an act of divine blessing. That She would speak to him!

But his ceaseless need for understanding, for the cold knowledge of what is unspoken and unrevealed, reasserted itself, cutting through his confusion. There had been a warning. Somehow their aims were aligned with those of the Lord of Twilight or his creatures. What could it be? The planned uprisings? The decision to seize Besh-Darok? Cold anxiety stroked his skin as he thought of Tauric on his way to one of the Children's refuges. Or Suviel seeking the Crystal Eye . . .

He shivered. Why had the Spiritwing been unable to find her? He thought back, remembering how it had swept through the Void like an arrow swift to the target then lost its purpose and direction as if she had been suddenly snatched away . . . to where?

Grasping the edge of the table he got to his feet, fumbled in the darkness for his tinderwheel and lit a candle stub from among the table clutter. Some of his parchments were on the floor and there were scorch marks on the tabletop from the dissolution of his spell. He righted the chair and for a moment or two he stood there, leaning on the chair, wondering if the only thing he could do about Suviel was to wait and see.

No, he thought. *I must be able to do something . . .*

He was about to sort through several bundles of papers when something else came back to him: **I will drive him to his knees before me and take his throat in my hand and cut it through** . . .

He felt a deep unease. The Earthmother did have a darker aspect as guardian of the Gate of Spirits, a mournful yet stern face reflecting the twin responsibilities of tending the dead and bringing forth new life. That was the portrayal he had learned from initiates and abbesses of the Earthmother Temple, but it seemed that the death of the Fathertree had changed all that. Bardow sighed, rubbing his tired eyes – perhaps the most ominous thing he had learned was that their god had become vengeful.

Chapter Twelve

When my battle-hosts hunt you down,
And flights of arrows seek you out,
Ask not who comes against you.
For 'twas your hand,
That set it all in motion,
Your gorey, guilty hand.

The Saga of Prince Hachtek, 27, iii, traditional

The ridge they climbed was a grassless, pebbly slope, but every stone seemed formed from some opaque mineral, their surfaces dulled and scored. A pale, gritty dust rose to slowly permeate their garments. Suviel knew that this realm, which Haidar called Kekrahan, was truly dead – no movement, no life or colour other than themselves disturbed the desolation. The air was still and odourless, and the cold was more a bearable deadness of sensation than a biting iciness.

It was now over an hour since the relentless pursuit of a squad of Acolyte guards had forced Raal Haidar to shift them here once more; time enough for Suviel to observe their surroundings. And while this Kekrahan was clearly a forsaken wasteland, she knew that it had not always been so. She frequently saw the desiccated remains of trees poking up out of the ground, or lying half-exposed in the flanks of rubble and dust dunes.

Both she and the sorcerer were on horseback, while Gilly and Keren walked a few paces ahead as they climbed. The terrain seemed to follow that of the world they had left, but the far distance in all directions faded into a shifting greyness. Once or twice Suviel had noticed partings in that remote veil and glimpsed what appeared to be sheer, impossibly high cliffs. When she mentioned this to Raal Haidar he shook his head.

'Nothing but an echo of some other far-flung part of this continent,' he had said stiffly. 'This domain was wrought by sorcery and echoes of that power still remain, causing these mirages from time to time.'

'What else can we expect to see?' Gilly had drawled. 'Colossal cities? Dung heaps the size of mountains?'

The sorcerer had given him a blank look. 'Who can tell?'

As she rode Suviel glanced at Haidar and wondered. He was a curiously emotionless person, betraying scarcely a sign of anger or good humour, yet back at Alvergost he had worked tirelessly treating the ill and the wounded. Had that been no more than an exercise for him, or did his impassive exterior mask deeper, stronger motivations?

They came to the top of the ridge and gazed down. Ahead was a wide, steep-sided valley strewn with shattered boulders and gouged with long gullies that wound across to a deep depression over a mile away. Streams that once fed a lake, Suviel guessed. But she could see no water.

They were about to descend to the valley when Keren paused, hand upraised, and cocked her head. She looked at Suviel.

'Did you hear it?'

Before Suviel could speak, a faint, drawn-out howl came from the other end of the valley, and was answered by other howls.

'So there *are* creatures living here,' she said to Raal Haidar.

'Dangerous, cunning beasts,' he said calmly. 'They hunt in packs and clearly have our scent, so it would be prudent to return to our own domain. Our pursuers should be some distance away by now, but it might be advantageous to reach lower ground first.'

With everyone in agreement, they hurried down into the valley. The eerie howls continued to sound in the distance and to Suviel they seemed mournful rather than menacing. The horses, though, were nervous and growing skittish. Then, as they drew near one of the river-like gullies, Suviel spotted movement far off, just beyond the empty lake: a small dark form, smaller than a horse or a cow, running on four legs like a dog, dashing frantically this way and that but all the time coming closer. Others appeared, following the first, then a harsh and shivering cry rose up from nearby. Keren backed away from the edge of the river-gully where she had been standing, sword at the ready.

'We've got company.'

Suviel looked meaningfully at Raal Haidar who, unperturbed, nodded once and spread his hands.

Braids of light enfolded her, a patterned web which darkened the surroundings and began filling the valley with colours and shapes. There was a smell, a taste, of hot stone. And just before the last bleak traces of that domain faded she saw something haul itself up out of the gully and lope towards her. Then she was in a bushy glade, trying to calm her horse, speaking soothingly to it and stroking its neck. Gilly and Keren stepped back in case the mare reared but Suviel soon had her under control. Across the glade Raal Haidar regarded her difficulties with unconcern from his own placid steed.

Suviel dismounted, indicating to Keren to take her place.

'What kind of creature could exist in that place?' Suviel said to Haidar. 'What would it feed on?'

'Nourishment invisible to our eyes.'

Suviel frowned. 'Is it some kind of plant, or a fluid? Are there any other animals—'

The sorcerer halted her with a shake of the head. 'I am already weary from my efforts on your behalf and your questioning tires me. I would rather devote my remaining strength to our journey.'

Suviel felt resentment at this haughty rebuke, but knew that he was right. Swallowing her irritation, she inclined her head. 'Forgive me, honoured Haidar. Natural curiosity overcame my manners. There are several villages along this valley and at one of them we will surely find shelter and food, and perhaps more horses.' She turned to Keren. 'Am I correct in this?'

The swordswoman shrugged. 'This is Ubanye Dale. It leads to another two valleys that open out at the northern plains. They're all very fertile, many farms and villages, all controlled by a pair of Mogaun chiefs, Azbular and Droshal. But if the tribes are sending their fighters east, it might be safer.'

'I think we should assume that there will be Mogaun patrols on the road,' said Suviel. 'Therefore we must be cautious and alert.'

'Shouldn't be too difficult,' said Gilly. 'We'll probably smell them before we see them.'

'Well, that should even things up a little,' Keren said acidly. 'Because they'll certainly hear your flapping mouth before they see you.'

The trader was speechless for a moment, then a slow smile came over his face. Suviel could almost see the thoughts working their way through his mind, about how Keren was masking her true feelings for him with sarcasm. She sighed and walked on ahead with the others following.

A broad, worn path brought them out of the shadowed glade into the brightness of mid-afternoon. High, broken clouds raced across the sky, periodically obscuring the sun, but Suviel felt barely a breath of wind on her face as she looked north. There were several differences between here and the bleak domain of Kekrahan, besides the presence of life and growth in abundance. The glade was higher than that desolate valley's stony floor, and from here Ubanye Dale seemed much wider and longer. A low mountain spur cloaked in thick forest jutted across, dividing the long flat plain of farmland and hiding a great stretch of it from sight.

From here the trail would be easier than the passage through the mountains, at least for three or four days until they reached the steep hills that marked the border of Prekine. There, she would have to either leave Gilly and Keren behind while she went on to Trevada or confide to them her quest for the Crystal Eye. As for Raal Haidar, his purpose remained an enigma, but Suviel resolved to tease it out of him somehow before they arrived at Prekine.

As she walked on, aware of Gilly trudging along nearby, she thought about the journey to come. The last time she had travelled this way was one summer nineteen years ago, three years before the invasion, when she took her sister's son from Tobrosa to Trevada, then on to Casall and Rauthaz and eastwards through northern Khatris to Besh-Darok. It had been an aunt's gift to her only nephew before he went off to become a junior officer in the Imperial army.

She tried to picture the road to the north, but her thoughts kept returning to the awful creature that had clambered out of the gully and dashed towards them. Its limbs had seemed badly arranged, almost lop-sided, and possessed more than two joints. Its hide was hairless, smooth and ashen grey, looking more like stone than skin, and the head had been narrow, its muzzle long with jaws agape. But Suviel remembered no tongue, no teeth of any kind, and eyes full of a desperate agony. It hardly matched Raal Haidar's portrayal of a dangerous and cunning beast.

The rest of that day and the next saw them reach the other end of Ubanye Dale without incident. There were Mogaun in the valley, but no more than two dozen under a minor chief who sent them out on occasional, lax patrols that Suviel and the others avoided with ease. That night they slept in a small tavern built beneath the overarching canopies of two massive agathons whose enormous roots had shouldered their way into the taproom. In the morning Suviel bought a pair of hardy ponies from the keeper and they continued north. But by the early afternoon, torrential rain forced them to seek shelter and after a miserable trudge down a barren hill road they found a wide, bush-fringed cave with a short tunnel at the rear.

The tunnel led to a low-roofed inner cave, its rough floor charred from an old fire and its walls scored with crudely charcoaled remarks and profane designs. Gilly and Haidar tied the horses at the outer cave while the two women led the ponies into the inner one. By the light of a torch, and an oil lamp Keren produced from her saddlebag, Suviel saw two carven recesses that had once been shrines. Both had been desecrated, shattered by hammers or axes, but she knew from a few untouched symbols that one had been dedicated to the Earthmother. The other was less obliterated than the Earthmother shrine, but appeared far older.

'It's some kind of creature, standing,' Suviel said, rubbing encrusted filth from a relief carving within the recess, 'and holding something in each hand.'

Keren bent down to gain a better view while Suviel examined the shrine's interior. At last she had to admit defeat.

'Well, it is old, very old,' she said, straightening, wiping her hand on her robe. 'But I have no idea who or what it is for.'

Keren looked up, smiling faintly. 'I think it's a Nightbear shrine.'

'But the Nightbear is usually shown on all fours or curled up. I've never seen it standing with its arms in the air.'

'I have, in the north Honjir mountains.' Keren's smile turned sour. 'I was on a patrol for Byrnak, searching for one of his many enemies, when I happened across an ancient, half-abandoned village. The few inhabitants were elderly, not a child to be seen. But there was a giant agathon tree with a huge boulder embedded in the trunk near the base, and hewn into the face of the boulder was a kind of fane with a carving of a standing bear. The people told me it was the Nightbear but claimed they worshipped the Earthmother. I did notice fresh offerings by the bear's feet, though.'

Looking at the carving again, Suviel saw that the feet and hands did seem more like paws. Some mentors of the Earthmother priesthood believed that the Nightbear and the Skyhorse were, for their savage ancestors, an early manifestation of the Earthmother and the Fathertree. Others insisted that such deities were illusory figments for a primitive people desperate for certainty in a chaotic world which remained so until the advent of Wujad's vision and other portents.

Keren glanced momentarily at the way out then, in a low voice, said, 'Shin Hantika, there is something I wanted to ask you.'

Suviel sighed. 'I'll tell Gilly to behave—'

'No, no, not that. It's Raal Haidar – can we trust him?'

'Trust?' she murmured, and shrugged. 'All I can say is that he has proved a valuable travelling companion thus far. Wouldn't you say?'

The swordswoman looked sceptical. 'Something about him makes my blood run cold. I just look at him and . . .' She shook her head.

Suviel frowned, wondering. What if she was right? Could this Haidar be an Acolyte priest, or a created Wellsource mage like the Warlord Grazaan? But they had all been acted upon by Haidar's sorcerous shapings, and Suviel was sure that the tall man's power did not derive from the Wellsource. She remembered the feel of it, the hot-stone smell, the texture.

'I don't know what his purpose is,' Suviel said, trying to sound assured. 'But I don't believe that he's a danger to us.'

Keren shrugged, a gesture eloquent with doubt, and slipped out past the ponies. After fixing the torch in a cleft in the cave wall, Suviel followed her.

By the time the rain eased off, the day was showing signs of dimming, the iron grey of the sky darkening towards the east. No one was eager to spend the night in a cold cave though, so out into the cold and the damp they went, continuing north. The rain lessened to a sparse shower but the wind picked up, a true autumnal blast driving icy droplets into their faces. Suviel tugged the hood of her tattered cloak tighter and rubbed her cheeks and nose to bring warmth and feeling back. Through her own shivering she could feel her pony tremble and knew they would have to find refuge soon.

A copse of tall trees emerged from the darkness ahead and they came to a fork in the trail. Keren reined in her mount and pointed to the track leading off.

'I remember there being a holding behind those trees,' she said. 'We could ask them for shelter.'

A holding there was but there were no lights to welcome them, only the abandoned shell of a farmhouse and a few huts. They found one with a mostly intact roof and after lighting a fire in the crude hearth and wringing out their wettest clothing, they settled down for the night with Gilly taking the first watch.

They rose early to the sound of wind gusting in the trees and sighing through the gaps in their dilapidated hut. Outside the sky was a vista of thunderheads and dark rafts of cloud hurrying north on the wings of a gale. Riding away from the wrecked steading, it seemed that the wind which had opposed their progress yesterday was now urging them onwards.

Before long they entered Ilonye Dale, the valley that led to the border of Prekine. It was narrower than Ubanye Dale, the ground more uneven, the mountainsides steeper and more densely forested. Mist hazed the distance and shrouded the heights as they left the main way for the concealment of the woods, picking their way along disued tracks. Whenever the vegetation thinned Suviel caught glimpses of the farmlands below, small neat fields, herds of cattle and goats. So peaceful and normal, she thought bitterly, almost as if the invasion and all its pain and destruction had not been felt here. Then shame touched her with the certainty that most of those below would have lost some loved one either in the invasion or as a result of the mad folly of Gunderlek's rebellion.

It was near noon when they cleared the trees. The valuable cover of dense wood lay on the other side of a hummocky incline thick with grass, fallen leaves and unseen mudholes. They were barely halfway across when a group of riders emerged onto the slope further down. Keren cursed.

'Mogaun!'

'They have not seen us yet,' Suviel said. 'Just stay calm and head for that gap.' She pointed to where the trees stopped before a sheer rocky outcrop that rose to join a great shattered ridge. Then angry cries went up behind them and as one they urged their mounts into a gallop.

'Honoured Haidar,' said Gilly above the drumming of their hooves. 'A demonstration of your powers might be most useful.'

'If we encounter genuine difficulty, I will give your request serious consideration.'

'I am comforted,' Gilly said. 'Truly, I am.'

They raced for the gap, slowing as they approached and in single file passed through at a swift canter. Beyond was a high-sided gorge with a stream that poured down to the valley. Upstream was a boulder-strewn slope and a jutting rock ledge. Without pause they turned away from the valley and rode along the shallow stream. Their pursuers were in the gorge by the time they reached the ledge and arrows clattered on the rocks as they dashed away over the rise – and found themselves riding into a small Mogaun camp.

Startled warriors shouted and leaped aside as they galloped through, scattering sparks from the campfire and knocking over a crude tent. Gilly was out in front and he glanced back with a wild look on his face as he pointed to a copse off to the right from which more spear-wielding riders had appeared.

'Is this dangerous enough for you?' Gilly said, glaring at Haidar. 'Or has your courage failed you?'

The sorcerer gave him a venomous look. 'We are in the shadow of the Acolytes, child. Any use of my powers here would be as a blazing beacon in the night to their eyes. Now hold your tongue.'

Gilly flushed at this and Suviel spoke before he could reply.

'We do not have time for such pleasantries,' she said. 'This way – follow!'

She led them at a gallop away from the oncoming riders, down a bushy defile to where it joined a pass she was certain would bring them out near the edge of Prekine. She was right. The high, narrow walls widened to reveal sparsely wooded hills and a group of mountainous peaks beyond. There were also dozens of Mogaun on foot and on horse converging on the mouth of the pass, their whoops answered by others from above. Suviel slowed her horse to a trot and looked round to see more of the enemy up on either side of the pass. In despair she wheeled to confront Raal Haidar.

'Help us,' she said. 'What else can we do?'

When he refused to meet her gaze, she held back her anger, gathered what sense of inner calm she had and began the thought-canto of Cadence. She brought the elements together one by one, imagining it as a sequence of beads on a string, while constantly aware of the Mogaun coming nearer, their cries full of glee. She caught Gilly's eye.

'Cover your ears,' she said as she felt the canto gyre in her thoughts and the Lesser Power respond, an ebbing, a flowing, a pendulum surge mounting higher and higher. Her breathing slowed, deepened, the air chilling her mouth, nostrils and chest.

'Now,' she heard Keren whisper. 'Now . . .'

The Lesser Power swirled up through her, caressing her spine, enfolding her senses, rising to her throat as she opened her mouth, lungs full to bursting, ready to release it all in a single, shattering, unstoppable—

And the power died within her.

In horror she regarded the oncoming savages, then snapped her head round to stare at Raal Haidar. The sorcerer had his head bowed, hands held slightly away from his body, palms downward. One Mogaun warrior was ahead of the rest and as he came running towards them, grinning madly, spear cocked to throw, Haidar suddenly flung his hands upwards and the ground around them erupted. Suviel saw the Mogaun torn apart by the torrent of rock and soil as a fierce drone filled the air and made the breath in her throat rasp. Her eyes vibrated in their sockets, a stinging that brought tears.

Then the harsh sound was gone and a bone-white radiance bathed their surroundings. They were back in the desolate domain of Kekrahan, and the far-off immense cliffs Suviel had glimpsed before now towered above them, heights lost in cloud. Reining in her panicky horse, Suviel noticed Gilly riding towards her, down a barren slope, and heard howls in the distance.

'The black creatures!' he cried. 'There's scores of them heading this way.'

'Have you seen Keren and Haidar?'

'No, but I did see packs of those things converging on the other side of that hill.'

The howls were getting closer as they rode madly for the hilltop. Suviel saw Keren and the sorcerer halfway up the opposite slope, fighting off dozens of the creatures, one with sword and shield, the other with red bolts of fire. Then she looked over her shoulder and saw that a hundred or more were almost upon them. She began the thought-canto of Ember and drew the long dagger she seldom used.

'We'll have to make our stand here,' she told Gilly. White-faced, the trader nodded and readied his blade as the first wave of creatures crested the hill . . . and raced right past them.

'Why. . . ?' Gilly said in confusion.

Suviel stared in disbelief at the coursing mass of black forms, then across at where Haidar and Keren were hemmed in by scores of attackers scrambling over one and another. Then the sorcerer laughed, raised clenched fists above his head and hurled a wide scythe of fire at the nearest creatures. There was a crimson flash, a roar and smoke. When the smoke cleared, Suviel saw that the ground was covered in the mangled yet bloodless remains of the creatures. And at the centre of the dreadful carnage stood Raal Haidar, one hand holding Keren tightly by the neck, the other outstretched. For a moment Suviel thought the sorcerer was helping her stand till she saw the swordswoman's weak and futile attempts to break free. Then as more of the black dog-things arrived and moved closer, the sorcerer's form began to change.

Seams burst, garments ripped open and fell away in tatters. Shoulders widened and arms lengthened while the head grew large and reptilian. Muscles shifted beneath skin pebbled with scales of ebony and emerald. The hands became big and powerful, the fingers tipped with short, pointed talons. A pair of enormous, membranous wings spread from the great shoulders and an armoured tail lashed lazily to and fro.

For Suviel recognition was immediate.

'Daemonkind,' she whispered in horror.

The being tilted its head and warm golden eyes met her gaze across the intervening gap.

'How pleasing to be remembered.' Its voice was rich and deep.

'Why are you here?' Suviel cried in anger. 'Who called you?'

'Not so pleasing, however, is your disrespect.' Some of the black creatures ventured close to the Daemonkind who knocked them back with a sweep of one spiny wing. 'Know this, insect, that I am Orgraaleshenoth, Prince of the Israganthir, and that I will have my vengeance!' The Daemonkind reached out to point at Suviel. 'And I will have what you seek, woman. I had thought to make use of you all in my plans.' He looked down at Keren who hung limply in his grasp. 'But on closer inspection I see that this one will be enough.'

A group of the black creatures moved towards the Daemonkind and were blasted into ruin.

'So you're going to slay us,' Suviel said with forced calmness.

A dark grin came over that inhuman visage. 'Ah, no – there are other choices more pleasing.' He glanced up at the veiled heights of the cliffs. 'But my bringing you here has attracted some unwelcome attention, so allow me to convey you both from this place.' He looked at Gilly. 'First you. Enjoy what is to come.'

'No, wait! . . .' Gilly began.

Then his horse was empty. Suviel swallowed at the dryness in her throat, and wiped her perspiring hands on her cloak as she turned to face the Daemonkind prince. Keren was struggling against the fist that gripped her neck and Suviel's composure almost broke at the sight. *In the name of the Mother*, she thought in despair. *I've failed us all!*

The cruel grin widened. 'I know exactly where to send you.'

And suddenly she was plunged into darkness. For long, tormented moments Suviel thought that she had been blinded, then sight slowly came back. It was night and she was in a forest, sitting on wet leaves under a thick canopy of vegetation that cut off even the faintest starlight. She stood, brushed decaying leaves from her robe and tried to guess where she might be. Then she was weeping, face bowed into her hands as the shock and grief of what had happened sank in.

She drew a shuddering breath, held it for several seconds before releasing it in a long exhalation. She had to be in command of herself or she was truly lost. She leaned against a mossy tree, letting the calming silence of the forest imbue her thoughts with peace. Then she held her breath again, all motion frozen, her senses alert. There were voices, right at the edge of audibility.

Carefully feeling her way, she moved towards the sound. She slipped and fell several times but a vague glow appeared through the foliage and slowly grew. Soon she could see the flicker of a campfire in a clearing and figures sitting round it. Caution asserted itself and she studied them through the leafy branches – most seemed to be men, apart from one who looked female, with short fair hair and a rangy physique. Suviel could see only part of the woman's face since she was concentrating on the blade that was balanced on her knees, hands working its edge with a whetstone . . .

Exhilaration and relief coursed through her at the sight of that familiar motion. Dizzy with joy she pushed aside the springy foliage to enter the clearing.

Someone grabbed her from behind and kicked her feet from under her. Pain shot up her right arm when she hit the ground.

'Who is this?'

'I followed her, a spy maybe.'

'Please, no . . .' she gasped. 'Keren! It's me, Suviel . . .'

Hands seized her roughly and hauled her onto her back. A ring of men stared down at her, faces hard with suspicion, then another came into view, the woman, Keren . . .

But not Keren. She gazed at Suviel and recognition lit up her features, along with a smile of hungry satisfaction.

'You!' Suviel whispered.

Byrnak's creation, the mirrorchild Nerek, squatted beside her and said, 'Retribution has begun.'

*   *   *

Everything vanished with savage abruptness, and for an instant Gilly Cordale felt as if the very air was being sucked from his lungs. For one black, terrifying instant.

Then it was light and he was rolling down a steep slope of dry earth and pebbles, fighting to find a grip or even to slow his descent. To no avail. With his clothes covered in dirt, his mouth full of grit and his senses aspin, he came to a halt at the foot of the slope. Cursing, he spat out a few tiny rock fragments and lurched to his feet to discover that he was at the bottom of a dried flood gully.

He had to find Keren and Suviel. There was no telling what direction he should take, but that monster could not have sent him very far. So he hoped.

A low, rumbling sound caught his attention and as it grew louder he recognized the sound of horses' hooves at the gallop.

Could be riders, he thought. *Could be friendly, but my luck has been unreliable, lately . . .*

Then a close-packed group of riders appeared at a bend in the gully, and let out a chorus of gleeful howls as they spotted him.

They were Mogaun. Gilly took one look then leaped to scramble up the way he had come. But he was only a short way up when a stretch of pebbly soil slid away beneath and sent him back down in a cascade of earth.

The horses were very near. He could feel the vibration of thudding hooves in the ground and as he struggled to get up he could see them mere yards away, with the malicious grinning stares of their riders fixed only on him.

Then, seemingly out of nowhere, a bony, grey-haired man clad in furs stepped in front of the oncoming riders and threw up his arms with an accompanying shout. The horses shrieked in terror. Many reared and a few riders were thrown, while others lost their footing or were reined aside in time. All the while, the elderly man just stood there, untouched by the pandemonium he had caused.

As the Mogaun brought their mounts under control, the

man lowered his arms and turned to regard Gilly with sharp eyes.

'I am Atroc, Yasgur's eye-in-the-dark,' he said. 'And I have been waiting for you, Gilly Cordale.'

Part Two

Chapter Thirteen

Amid ancient glories overcast,
And treasures gone in fire and wrath
He scribes his lawless passage
Under skies veiled by ghosts.

Avalti, *Augronac's Lament*

With the towering massif of the Arengia Plateau at last within
sight, Byrnak let his mount walk a few more paces beyond the
treeline before reining in to sit and savour the view. Dense forest
clung all along the base of sheer, pitiless cliffs. Flocks of small
birds swirled and fluttered from treetop to treetop in pursuit of
insects or fruit. As Byrnak watched, a larger winged shape fell like
a stone out of the upper air and into the middle of one such flock,
seizing its prey and swooping away to devour it in some barren
higher perch.

Byrnak smiled grimly and turned his gaze eastwards, searching
for signs of the encampment which was his destination. He had
never been here before, yet everything he saw stirred recognition
in him. Had Hegroun played host to the spirit of his god before
and after the final battle? Byrnak thought that might account for
his certainty that this trail dipped down between low hills to a
fork, one branch curving north to join a road which came up from
central Yularia, while the other continued east to meet the March
Way, a wide track which linked the fishing towns of Mantinor
with Ebro'Heth. And there was an easily defensible small bluff

near the cliffs no more than half a day's ride from here, which would make an ideal camp.

He inhaled noisily, irritated by a sense of familiarity he could not share. It had begun to be wearing during the trip north through Khatris, the immense open skies of the central plains, the huge weathered natural stone columns of Pillar Moor, the ancient quarries of the Ogairn Mountains gaping like black wounds – everything held the resonance of old, old memories lingering just beyond recall. Occasionally, visions would impress themselves upon him, complete with smell, taste, and the feel of rain or sun or wind on his skin. And as he sat there on his horse, staring moodily across at the plateau, one such vision struck him like a blow, filling his eyes and skull, entrancing his mind for a passing instant.

Swaying in his saddle, head lowered as he rubbed one hand across his face, he heard the thud of hooves behind him, another rider approaching at a walk.

Byrnak straightened, gaze smouldering with a low anger. 'Obax,' he said. 'Look out at all this and tell me what you see.'

'I see the plateau, lord.'

'Yes. And?'

'Trees, a wide forest, hills, a stream . . .'

'And living things, Obax?'

'Why, there would be creatures, lord, birds, foxes, mice, fish—'

'I'll tell you what I have seen,' Byrnak said. 'Endless fields of mud and bloodied stone, a wrecked, ruined land, gouged and poisoned, a livid plain of filth where people writhe like worms amid decay.' He let out a single harsh bark of laughter. 'The realm of obliteration!'

And so saying he dug his heels into his horse's flanks and rode furiously down the trail, lashing it faster, as if he could escape that glimpse of desolation. For in his mind it was as if he had been shown all that would be left of himself, the self that was Byrnak, when all the Shadowkings were gathered together and the Lord of Twilight was made whole again.

He could sense that nebulous presence hanging at the back of his thoughts now. His taut, harried mind often gave it fleeting, changeable forms, sometimes a hulking, simian shape without a face, or other times a shadowy carrion bird, watching, waiting. But always it was leaking deranged notions into his thoughts, like a black rivulet of something beyond evil which now and then burst forth in elaborate visions.

His horse had slowed of its own accord in its headlong rush and he brought it to a halt beneath an overarching tree where he waited for Obax to rejoin him. He watched the Acolyte's approach, discerning a look of satisfaction on that long, white-eyed face. Byrnak knew that his fits and fugues gave Obax great pleasure, being harbingers of the Great Prince's steady emergence and eventual triumph, and he revealed as little of his inner torment as possible. Usually.

'Are you well, lord?'

Byrnak's stare glittered with anger. 'Seeking weakness, Obax? Delusions? Wanderings of the mind, perhaps? There is nothing for you to find.'

The Acolyte gave a gracious bow of the head which some-how failed to display subservience. 'On the contrary, lord, your continued good health is most gratifying. It serves our common goal.'

The milky orbs of his eyes seemed to look through him, and Byrnak toyed with the idea of striking this withered old snake down with a look of despite. But that would make him appear foolish and uncontrolled to his brothers, the four other Shadowkings. No, now was not the time. Besides, it might not be easy to find another Acolyte capable of carrying him into the Realm of Dusk.

'Do not presume to lecture me, Obax,' he said with the right amount of soft malice in his voice. 'Keep your life simple and free from harm.'

Then he urged his horse back onto the trail at a light canter, thinking: *Let destruction come and take it all, let desolation reign everywhere but in my mind.*

And a dark form shifted across the backdrop of his thoughts, a shadow among shadows, silent and watching.

The eastward trail widened to a stony cart road which ran through acres of wild woodland where fingerthorn vied with dog-ivy for mastery of the undergrowth. Then the way rose and fell across a succession of bushy ridges, from which they had glimpses of mile upon mile of forest with the occasional rocky outcrop or clear width of a lakelet interrupting the undulating dark green.

It was late afternoon when they saw the first signs of the encampment, tails of campfire smoke rising above the trees. As they drew nearer, open and undisguised along the road, a Mogaun patrol emerged from a mass of foliage, spears levelled, bows at the ready. When they got a closer look at Obax and Byrnak, the warriors forgot their challenge and knelt to press their foreheads into the dust of the road.

'Hasten before us to your camp,' said Obax sternly. 'Tell your chiefs that the Great Lord Byrnak has arrived.'

The patrol's leader raised his head. 'I hear and obey, high ones!' He urged his warriors to their feet, sent one scampering off towards the camp, then gave the newcomers a crisp bow before taking his men back into the forest cover.

It took another half hour to reach the encampment, and Byrnak frowned as he surveyed it. There was indeed a low bluff, part of a spur jutting from the plateau cliffs which loomed over all. Fast streams fed by waterfalls ran either side and came together in a wider watercourse which flowed away into the forest. However, the main body of Mogaun tents, many hundreds of them, had been pitched on the ground around the bluff, protected on the south by a partial stockade wall. On the bluff itself sat a large tent clearly made from several canopies, and surrounded by a handful of smaller ones. A single huge banner hung motionless over the entrance, the device that of a green flame on a red background.

Byrnak smiled in disdain. Ystregul, Shadowking and self-styled Father of Flames, was in residence.

The stockade gates swung open as they approached and a great roar went up from the thousands of warriors gathered to either side. Obax ignored the welcome, but Byrnak grinned and nodded, noting the clan and tribe totems that were raised and shaken as he passed by. A stench of unwashed bodies assailed his senses but he maintained an iron control over his features, and simply looked from side to side, sizing up these savage fighters. Sixteen years of overlordship had not made them soft and fat – their chiefs and shamans had seen to that, ensuring that no tribe or family forsook their traditional semi-nomadic way of life for the comfort of the cities. The petty rivalries and enmities that existed among the major and minor chiefs had served to keep their fighting edge, and had never been allowed to get out of hand.

Yet as he rode along, Byrnak noticed shrewder, less jubilant eyes watching and taking his measure, and recalled what his Shadowking brother Thraelor had said about certain chiefs who had been reluctant to attend this year's Blood Gathering.

I will take my measure of you, my friends, he thought, *and there shall be a winnowing in the battles to come.*

The great crowd of warriors drew back as the two riders progressed, and a knot of more imposing Mogaun advanced to meet them. These were the senior chieftains, some tall and bearlike, others barrel-chested, and all attired in a gaudy, eye-challenging motley of furs and pieces of shining armour, here a breastplate, there shoulderguards, or a long leather cloak with a high collar. There were ornate shields and swords – trophies from the war, crudely redecorated – and ancient tribal standards from which the shrivelled heads of vanquished enemies dangled. Most had more grey than black in their beards and manes, and would undoubtedly have ridden with Yasgur's father, the great Hegroun, when he led his vast hosts against the Khatrimantine Empire.

Yasgur. Byrnak almost laughed as the reason for the first phase of the Shadowkings' dark strategy came to mind. Then his mood turned grim as he contemplated what was to follow, once Hegroun's traitorous offspring had been dealt with.

The two parties came to a halt a few paces apart and one of the chieftains, a tall, brawny man with a long moustache and a forked beard – both silvery grey with the tips dyed blue – stepped forward and with a single motion thrust a two-handed sword into the ground. Byrnak knew that tradition expected him to descend from his horse and set his own blade in the foot-flattened earth as well. Instead he urged his mount forward a couple of steps, reached down and wrenched the great sword free to audible angry mutters, then held it point upwards above his head while staring directly at the cluster of tents atop the bluff.

The murmurs of outrage faded away, replaced by quiet laughter and gleeful nods. Byrnak dextrously slipped his grip down to the upper half of the blade and returned the weapon hilt-first to its owner, whose expression had remained stern throughout. Now, a bare-toothed smile showed as the ageing chieftain resheathed the sword and tossed it to a nearby servant who staggered under the impact.

'Greetings, Great Lord Shadowking. I am Welgarak of the Black Moon clan,' said the chieftain. 'Your blood is hot and your bones are iron.'

'And your army must be vast for you to challenge the Black Priest,' said one of the other chiefs, a stout man wearing a horned helm over lank hair braided in long tails dotted with fragments of gold and precious stones. He exchanged grins with his companions. 'And, if I'm not mistaken, it's invisible as well!'

There was laughter at this but Byrnak remained sitting on his horse, a sharp smile upon his lips. 'Why should I challenge one that I call brother?'

Laughter and grins faded. 'Forgive my cousin Gordag,' said Welgarak, directing a black glance at the stout chief. 'Fortunately for the Redclaw clan, he is as swift with his blade as he is with his mouth.'

Gordag shook his head, braids clicking. 'It is for the sake of our clans that I say these things,' he told Welgarak. 'And for our sake, too, cousin. We should know what the Acolytes and these Shadowkings intend for us, and why they insist on all the chiefs, high and low, attending the Gathering.'

Eyes turned to regard Byrnak, but he was surveying the

now-dispersing crowds of warriors. 'I see no Firespear banners or shields,' he said.

Welgarak spat in the dust. Hegroun had been chief of the Firespear Clan, as Yasgur now was.

'The boy has not arrived,' he said. 'Nor has he even sent word to say if he will.'

'Were he my son,' Gordag snarled, 'he would be flayed and hung. If I were—'

'Hold your tongue!' Welgarak was suddenly tense, looking up at Byrnak. 'Our loyalty to the Acolytes and the Shadowkings is without question. Whatever is asked of us, we shall do.'

Byrnak nodded. 'I know. There has not been a High Chieftain since Hegroun's death, am I right? But you are the chiefs of your people, and would know all there is to know about your warriors, yes?' He pointed at one, a lantern-jawed elder with a black bear pelt hanging from his shoulders, the animal's head covering his own. 'How many warriors do you have on foot, and how many mounted?'

The chief almost sneered, then remembered to whom he was speaking. 'On foot? Why, none. All Doubleknives fight from horseback, more than seven hundred of us.'

Byrnak looked next at Gordag, who met his gaze sullenly for a long moment before replying. 'Like Shestrol, all my men are riders and they total four hundred and seventy. A few have been training with the staff, though.'

Next was Welgarak. 'Six hundred and forty riders,' he said, thoughtfully fingering his forked beard. 'And another score and ten who are my personal guard.'

'Interesting,' said Byrnak.

'How so, my lord?' asked Welgarak.

'Only this, that in sixteen years you have learned nothing from the people you have conquered, whereas they have been watching and learning from you.'

'You mean the uprising led by that vermin, Gunderlek.' Gordag gave a derisive snort. 'Thraelor and Grazaan crushed him utterly at Rauthaz.'

'Yes, after a week-long siege,' Welgarak said. 'And then only because the Acolytes sent a horde of eaterbeasts and nighthunters into the city.' He shuddered visibly.

'You miss the point,' Byrnak said, staring at Gordag, who paled pleasingly. 'Gunderlek trained a cadre of well-armed and armoured foot soldiers, but instead of using the old Imperial way of massed ranks in frontal charges, he copied the Mogaun manner of small, fast-moving groups drilled to raid or fight on their own or as part of a larger formation.'

He straightened in his saddle, suddenly struck by a dizzy spell. The knowledge seemed to come from the air, yet he instinctively knew otherwise. He had discussed the Gunderlek rebellion with Grazaan, but not down to such military detail. Could it be that somehow he was sharing knowledge with the other Shadowkings? When he concentrated, he caught glimpses of the siege at Rauthaz, the flames of burning buildings, the grey haze of smoke . . . all of it Grazaan's memories, perhaps Thraelor's too.

The Mogaun chieftains were watching him now, frowns on their faces.

'Lord Shadowking,' Obax said. 'An emissary approaches.'

A rider was descending from the bluff, a man garbed in red and carrying a banner with the green flame sigil, its haft fixed to his right stirrup. Byrnak smiled. The Father of Flames had at last deigned to recognize his presence.

'Great Lord Shadowking . . .'

He turned back to see Gordag regarding him with a mixture of fear and determination. He nodded for the chief to go on.

'Lord, it is said that you . . . and your brothers . . . are the sons of the Lord of Twilight—'

'And you want to know if this is so?' Byrnak laughed. 'Such insolence. Don't you realize that I could strike you dead where you stand, or burn your heart in your chest, or cleave you in two and keep one half alive in utter torment?' He let his voice grow quiet and deadly and Gordag took a step back. 'But not this time. I believe that you can learn how to abase yourself before us, we who are his sons . . .'

He grinned at their confusion for a moment then looked to Welgarak. 'Have a full accounting of the strengths of each tribe and clan drawn up by one of your servant scribes. If I am to be your general, I must know everything.'

The herald was approaching, his mouth open and about to speak, but Byrnak cut him off with a gesture. 'You are here at your master's behest to invite us into his presence, are you not? Then say nothing, and lead the way.'

Chastened, the herald turned his horse's head back the way he had come and rode off at a canter. Byrnak nodded sharply to Welgarak and the other chiefs, then followed with Obax at his side.

The tents up on the bluff seemed formal, like a camp separate from the one below. Shades of red predominated, mostly dark and arterial. Strangely shaped flags bearing unfamiliar symbols hung from thin laths of wood which protruded from every canopy. A gust of wind made them sway and bend, and sent smoke from the few campfires swirling among the tents. Byrnak caught odours of burnt torwood and overcooked meat as their guide brought them to the awning-sheltered entrance to Ystregul's great tent. A score of warriors wearing bulky leather armour and steel gauntlets stood guard outside, all holding in their hands heavy edged weapons, longswords and battleaxes mainly. Only after Byrnak had surrendered his own weapons were they allowed to pass.

The interior was like a single large chamber, its ceiling made to seem lower than the tent's height by great swathes of patterned silk draped across a cane framework. Lamps burned above the silken ceiling, casting a diffuse, many-coloured glow on the hides which carpeted the floor. Long flaps of material hanging along either side formed small alcoves in which men dressed in loose-fitting green garments sat cross-legged, heads bowed, hands resting palm upward on the floor. Not one of them looked up or so much as stirred as the newcomers passed by, and when Byrnak tried to peer into their minds there seemed to be nothing there, no presence, no intellect, a void.

Several people, some Acolytes, others clearly servants and

scribes, were gathered around a couple of tables at the other side of the chamber. As the group of three drew near, a low voice spoke and all the subordinates stepped aside or left, revealing their master. Byrnak had thus far only encountered Ystregul in the dream-heavy environs of the Realm of Dusk, and then only a mere handful of times, during which he had appeared equal to the other Shadowkings in physique and aura.

Now, even though Ystregul was sitting in a massively-carved ironwood chair, Byrnak could tell that he was the taller by at least a foot and a half. His head was larger and heavier around the jowls with a long black beard that narrowed to a point and a long mane of hair carefully arranged in a fan across his shoulders. Dark, mesmerizing eyes gazed from beneath powerful brows and full, wide, sensual lips twitched with the ghost of a smile. Without looking, Byrnak knew that Obax and the herald were on their knees in obeisance, such was the overwhelming impact of Ystregul's presence.

'Greetings, brother, and welcome to this most humble abode.' The voice was deep and rich, full of authority.

Byrnak gave a bleak smile of his own. 'Greetings,' he said, glancing at the opulent surroundings. 'Yes, adequate. Though I will understand if you want to retain most of the furnishings when you remove to wherever your new . . . abode will be. Which I hope will be soon, brother, since I have a great deal of work to do—'

Byrnak broke off as Ystregul threw back his head and burst out laughing.

'Honoured brother,' he said, face bright with malign glee. 'I have no need to move anywhere. Here I sit and here I remain.'

'It was my understanding that command of the Gathering was to be mine.'

Ystregul raised a languid hand and snapped his fingers. At once, utter silence fell about them so that only they could hear each other, at which Byrnak arched an eyebrow in wry appreciation.

'You misunderstood,' said the Black Priest. 'You are to be general of the army, of its plans and its deployment when we march forth from this place. All else is under my hand, *my* direction.'

'You intrigue me, brother. What else occupies your attention? On what matters do you busy yourself?' Byrnak strolled easily over to a hanging tapestry of silk and gold thread. 'I'm just curious.'

'My disciples have much work to do,' Ystregul said, leaning back in the great chair. 'Despite sixteen years of occupation, the Acolytes and their agents have utterly failed to root out and eradicate the verminous Earthmother creed. Even as I sit here talking to you, my will reaches out to my senior disciples, guiding and advising, all by means of the loyal servants you see seated to either side.'

'They are soulbound?'

'That, and more.'

For a moment Byrnak saw Nerek's face in his mind's eye, but pushed it aside. 'These disciples,' he said. 'Are they garbed like these thralls of yours?'

'Quite similar, only in red.'

'And have you provided them with various trappings, symbols, images, holy texts, litanies?'

'Everything that they may need.'

Byrnak nodded slightly. 'It must be most tasking,' he said, ignoring the other's cold, unwavering stare. 'Shaping a fake creed then going to great lengths to supplant a dying one. Such dedication. I'm almost surprised not to see your face on the banners and shields.'

'It maintains the sense of mystery,' Ystregul said thoughtfully. 'But if you think that this is elaborate, you should see what domains of worship Thraelor and Grazaan have created in Anghatan and Yularia.'

'Such serves its purpose,' Byrnak said. 'And when the last of those feeble mages are in our hands, and the Great Prince assumes his rightful manifestation—' he made a sweeping, encompassing gesture, '—all this will be swept away.'

Ystregul stared with cold amber eyes and a secret smile. 'As will you, dear brother, as will you.'

In that moment Byrnak suddenly realized a truth: the Black Priest was just as reluctant as Byrnak to give up his individual existence and embrace obliteration. The pleasure he took in his surroundings and in the exercise of power made that abundantly clear.

And there was something else. Byrnak felt hatred for him, instinctively and completely, and without the slightest shred of misgiving. And he knew that this hatred came from that dark shadow at the back of his mind.

I have got to get out of this place, he thought to himself. With a slight gesture he cancelled the blanket of silence, then spun to face Ystregul with a bright smile.

'Brother, this has been a most instructive discussion but I have much to accomplish in a short space of time.' He crooked a finger at Obax who rose to his feet. 'We must prepare for whatever Yasgur may have in store for us, thus I must take my leave—'

'Ah, yes – Yasgur.' Ystregul stood to his full impressive height. 'There is news, which you would not be aware of since it came to me only moments before you yourself.'

Byrnak paused and half-turned as the Black Priest went on.

'The son of Hegroun has sent word – he and his retinue shall be arriving by tomorrow evening.' A grin widened in the bearded face. 'He intends to play a full part in the Blood Gathering. It seems that you will have to make new plans.'

Byrnak said nothing, just tilted his head in the slightest of bows then left with Obax at his side, full of the indefinable feeling that somehow he had been outmanoeuvred.

Chapter Fourteen

Cold wind brings a fine rain.
A branch trembles.
Withered leaves fall on the pool.
Tiny birds squabble nearby,
Scattering feathers in the grass.
While the far-away storm gathers its strength.

Eshen Karedu, untitled fragment

Dow Korren, speaker for the Northern Cabal, stood at the tall window, one foot resting on the low sill, and sipped his wine while looking out at Krusivel. Overhead, broken clouds raced across the sky, letting patches and shafts of midday sun through to the high valley. The main road along the edge of the lake was busy with squads of knights returning from patrol or drill, stableboys exercising mounts, women hauling laundry to and from the water's edge, and knots of townsfolk out enjoying a gossip under the fitful sun.

'Rest assured, Lord Commander, I am impressed with your enclavement,' he said. 'I just thought it would be ... well, bigger. Busier.'

He offered a smile that was almost apologetic and Ikarno Mazaret found himself warming to the man. The earlier informal meeting with all eight members of the Northern Cabal's delegation had tested his patience to the limit. Some of the older delegates had been blunt to the point of insult about Krusivel, something that Gilly had warned him of before leaving with Suviel and Keren.

'They'll probably send the likes of Raboul, or Frinok, or Vuruag, boorish toads all of them. But their speaker will be a different matter, Dow Korren most likely. Now there's a negotiator, face like a brawler, mind like a Dalbari usurer.'

To Mazaret, Dow Korren seemed more a wrestler than a common brawler. The man was barrel-chested, tall enough to look him in the eye and, as Gilly had implied, not the most handsome of men. A block of a head, bald and smooth, combined with a broken nose and heavy jawline to give an impression of stolidity, even brutishness. But the eyes were full of intelligence and humour, and his garments – grey trews, ochre shirt, and brown, pocketed tabard – were of the highest quality. The tabard was plain, lacking any insignia, and the only piece of jewellery he wore was a finger ring of fine silver mesh without stone or device. Mazaret, in his second-best ceremonial hauberk, felt at once garish and shabby.

Filling a bronze goblet with wine, he went over to join the northener. 'You're most tactful, Master Korren,' he said. 'Others in your delegation seem to think that Krusivel is deserted.'

'An understandable conclusion, given your lack of new recruits,' Korren said pointedly. 'Some of my companions might go so far as to say that the Redoubt is open and undefended.'

Mazaret laughed softly and shook his head. 'Not at all, sir, not at all. Krusivel is ringed with watchposts, and squads of scouts regularly patrol the less visible approaches. Neither friend nor foe can advance upon us unseen and the permanent garrison of sixty veteran knights is more than enough to repulse an attack in these narrow ravines and passes.'

Privately, though, he wished he had delayed yesterday's departure of the two new companies. Krusivel felt uncomfortably vulnerable, and the presence of 250 knights would have greatly strengthened his negotiating position. But the Northern Cabal's delegation had arrived three days early, catching Mazaret unprepared.

'Tell me, Lord Commander,' Korren said. 'How would you describe your dealings with Captain Volyn and the Hunter's Children?'

Mazaret swirled the roseate wine in his goblet thoughtfully. It was no secret that a certain animosity existed between the Hunter's Children and several northern traders. 'Amicable,' he said. 'We work well together.'

'How vital would you say they are to the forthcoming campaign?'

He smiled. 'Their importance cannot be underestimated.'

Korren nodded judiciously, and sipped at his wine. 'An appraisal you would presumably say applies also to your own troops.'

'Without hesitation.'

The northerner regarded him levelly.

'What would you say, Lord Commander, if I were to offer you a thousand experienced and well-armed warriors?'

Mazaret masked his surprise and merely raised his eyebrows. 'I would say – what are your conditions?'

'Few and straightforward,' Korren said. 'Simply put, we would ask you to delay the onset of your campaign by a month—'

'Till the end of the Farewell Harvest.'

'Indeed. And we would respectfully urge you to reconsider any assault on Besh-Darok which you may have planned.'

Mazaret looked at him with new respect, impressed that he already knew. 'Attacking the strongest Mogaun warlord? An interesting notion, Master Korren. What makes you think that we intend such a risky action?'

'An appraisal of the supplies requested by yourselves and the Hunter's Children in the past year, as well as the reports from our observers in northern Khatris and Besh-Darok itself.' The man shrugged. 'They clearly reveal that your allies are more numerous in that region than you stated earlier today. They could only be there for some military reason, like an attack on Besh-Darok.'

The Lord Commander weighed his empty goblet in his hand. 'You will, of course, allow me to see the reports you speak of.'

Korren smiled. 'Sadly, I was not permitted to bring them with me, given how perilous long journeys have become in these degenerate days.'

'I understand. But be assured, Master Korren, if our plans do include any such incursion north of the Great Valley, it would only be considered in the light of a dramatically swift and successful campaign to the south. And even then . . .'

He left the sentence unfinished, and Korren tilted his head in acknowledgement.

'However,' Mazaret went on, 'I am unable to put back the campaign in the way you suggest. The plans have already been set in motion and cannot be easily reversed.'

'I see.' Dow Korren drained off the last of his wine, savouring the taste. 'Then I feel there is little more we can discuss at the moment, Lord Commander. This has been a most pleasant interlude, and I look forward to our negotiations later today. In the meantime, there are several matters which I must discuss with my companions.'

Watching the man carefully place his goblet on a small round table nearby, Mazaret knew that there was a fundamental distrust between them which could never be bridged. Korren saw him, not as a leader but as a difficult obstacle to overcome in pursuit of the Northern Cabal's self-interest. It reminded Mazaret of the day-to-day intrigue of the Imperial court so many years ago, where mere words were often more effective than an assassin's dagger.

Dow Korren paused on the threshold of the open door and produced a small scroll case from his tabard. 'How foolish of me, Lord Commander. I almost forgot to give you this.'

Mazaret accepted it, twisted off the cap and shook out the parchment.

'It is a detailed manifest of our next supply shipment,' Korren went on. 'It should arrive off the Dalbar coast in a few days.'

Mazaret read a few lines then looked up, struggling to maintain his composure. 'But this can't be right. Most of the amounts listed here are for less than half of our requirements. Hides, cloth bolts, bar steel, hand tools, horsefeed . . . the horsefeed is less than a quarter of what we asked for.'

Korren nodded, his face a picture of sympathy. 'Sadly, several of our overland caravans were raided by the Mogaun, and since the ships could not be delayed we decided to send what remained in the hope that your other allies would be able to make up the shortfall.' He smiled. 'Which I am sure they will. So, my lord, till later?'

'I could have throttled him then and there, the snake,' Mazaret said acidly.

'Not the most diplomatic of responses,' Bardow replied as he applied a layer of redherb butter to a thick slice of bread then reached for a large chunk of cheese. 'But understandable.'

'He wants to drive a wedge between ourselves and the Hunter's Children, that's plain. But where's the advantage?' Mazaret drummed his fingers on the table. 'Why should they support us and the Children so willingly for nearly four years, then suddenly, when all our plans are about to come to fruition, begin these evasions and underhand ploys?'

They were sitting at a square table in a small archive room off the temple's central cloister. Tiny candles set into metal sconces on the table cast an even yellow glow on the walls, which were packed from floor to ceiling with scrolls, books, bundles of parchments, caskets and cases of every kind. There were smells of dust and leather and a smoky tang from the fire burning behind an iron grate in the corner.

'Dow Korren could be telling the truth, my lord,' Bardow said through a mouthful of food.

Mazaret regarded the Archmage for a moment. 'You think that he is?'

Bardow raised an eyebrow. 'Not in the least. However, in our dealings with him it would be to our advantage to appear to believe him. Thus we put him a little off-balance, such that he is not sure whether we are gullible or devious. Where he has but one game to play, we have two.'

Mazaret sat back, frowning. Negotiation and persuasion had become part and parcel of his duties since the retreat to Krusivel, yet still he loathed all the second-guessing, the deceit, the self-interest masquerading as high purpose. He was fortunate to have had the help and advice of Gilly and Bardow over the years; they understood dark motives and duplicity far better than he.

War and battle were where his own talents lay, the pitting of limited forces against the enemy, the details of tactics, the small day-to-day miracles of making do with meagre supplies. Which was why Gilly's news about the strength of the Mogaun tribes had been such a body-blow; together with Dow Korren's halving of the shipments, it made the forthcoming campaign look increasingly uncertain. Mazaret could almost picture in his mind the knights and the Hunter's Children riding out in columns and wedges, the places which had been chosen to engage the Mogaun, and all the possible outcomes. And he knew in his heart of hearts that they would be in the hands of fate from the moment the campaign began, living from day to day at swordspoint.

Such fears, though, he kept to himself. If the others could see the lie of the land as he did, the struggle would be over before it had begun.

He suddenly became aware of Bardow's steady gaze.

'She is safe,' the Archmage said. 'I'm sure of it.'

Mazaret was confused for a second then realized that his silence had been taken for brooding over Suviel and the others. Bardow had told him of his spirit journey, how he had seen Tauric alive and well, and Coireg bound and gagged. On hearing this Mazaret had felt exasperation, wondering if his brother had deserved such treatment, or whether Kodel had acted with malice, questions that would soon be answered. But such thoughts had fled when Bardow admitted that he could not find Suviel.

Now he felt a pang of guilt that his worries for most of the day had been about supplies and the availability of wagons, and not her. He longed for her company and counsel, yet knew that he could not dwell on her; with so much weighing on his judgement he dare not.

'I believe you,' he said, then straightened in his chair. 'What of our friends in the Southern Cabal?'

Bardow gave a lopsided smile. 'It appears that some of them have had businesses and property confiscated and given to Mogaun placemen. So, unlike Dow Korren, they are urging us to move faster and begin the liberation sooner.'

Mazaret laughed wryly and shook his head. 'What is to be done with these people?'

The Archmage was silent for a moment or two as he ate slivers of cheese pared from the wedge before him with a tiny, bronze-handled knife. Then he said: 'Seduction, my lord.'

Mazaret frowned, leaning closer as the Archmage began to explain.

More than two hours later, in a torchlit grove near the lake, Mazaret was savouring the rich, dark flavour of Hethu Valley ale while watching Bardow's scheme unfold before his eyes.

Members of both cabals stood talking, or gathered in groups to listen to a mandol player, or watch three of their number moving pieces on an improvised Waylay board, or gaze intently at a man who was juggling cups and rings, making them vanish and reappear. Beneath the crooked branches of a drael tree, four small casks sat on wooden frames tended by a tapsman who had been hurriedly recruited from the main barracks earlier. The evening was pleasantly cool, the nightflies were hardly to be seen, the atmosphere was relaxed, even jovial, and through it all moved Bardow, feeding the air of goodwill with a compliment here, a witticism there, or joining a conversation and steering it down a new direction with a shrewd observation or question.

It was a masterful endeavour. Mazaret marvelled as Dow Korren smiled at something the Archmage was saying, then, astonishingly, laughed out loud along with Bardow. Others nearby chimed in and a moment later Bardow made some excuse and came over to join Mazaret.

'My compliments,' Mazaret said. 'No raised voices, angry faces or poisonous looks.'

'There will be at some point, my lord,' the Archmage said acidly. 'When I finally tire of my role as performing monkey.'

He sighed. 'At least your men are satisfyingly entertaining – I'm glad you were able to persuade them to donate their services.'

'Little persuasion was needed,' Mazaret said, pointing to the mandol player, a red-haired, slender man who smiled and glanced around him as he played. 'Annsil there won several musical contests in Western Dalbar before deciding to join us, while Brac—' he indicated the juggler, a short, bearded youth seemingly oblivious to his audience '—was raised by Ovolni travellers, until his kintribe were massacred by the Mogaun.'

Bardow nodded thoughtfully. 'They provide a useful diversion while I joke and flatter and conciliate and entice. Dancing my little dance.'

Mazaret regarded the older man with concern. 'And what of other means?'

A wry smile came to the Archmage's lips and he glanced at the Lord Commander. 'I had considered it, my lord. But then I discovered that our northern friends are not without a degree of protection.'

'What . . . charms and amulets?'

'No, no, not that. Dow Korren has brought his own tame magicker. See the short man in a long coat, standing quite close to Korren? Although he has no great ability with the Lesser Power, he does have just enough to know if anyone else nearby attempts its use.'

'Hmm, thus Korren would be forewarned and very probably annoyed,' Mazaret said as he let his gaze drift slowly around the glade, searching the faces. Then he frowned. 'Captain Volyn did receive our invitation, did he not?'

'Ah. You've noticed his absence, my lord.'

'Like a bad tooth suddenly gone missing,' Mazaret said. 'But it appears he has sent some eyes and ears in his stead.'

Bardow nodded, eyes staring down into his drink. 'Over by the kegs, two men in shabby quilted jerkins?'

'The very same.' Mazaret glanced at the archmage. 'Is the honoured captain making a point by sending his underlings?'

'Who can be sure?' Bardow said testily. 'When not accompanied by Kodel, Volyn tends towards the erratic in his negotiations. Perhaps he feels he is insufficiently near the centre of attention.' He tapped a hollow note from his wooden beaker, an elegantly carved vessel with a inward-curving lip. 'Time for a little more ale and a lot more prattling. Or should that be the other way round?'

With a smile and the sketch of a bow, he moved away. Mazaret watched him stride over to the ale kegs where he engaged Volyn's men in light conversation while refilling his beaker. The Lord Commander shook his head in admiration when, moments later, they were laughing at one of Bardow's off-colour jests, its punchline delivered after the familiar mock-furtive glance to one side and the head leaning closer.

The evening wore on, darkening and cooling yet remaining comfortably mild. Twice Mazaret allowed himself to be drawn into a conversation, but was careful to keep his comments brief and noncommittal when the topic came round to the negotiations. His role in this little masque was to be the grave, unspeaking presence of authority. Therefore he maintained a reserved and aloof air, except when he found himself discussing with Peilon, the Southern Cabal's leader, the relative merits and demerits of hunting boar in the forests of southern Cabringa.

Occasionally he caught sight of Bardow moving from group to group, still talking, regaling and beguiling. Then, at one point, he looked up and saw one of Volyn's men across the other side of the grove, leaning on the tree stump that stood near the temple pathway. He was alone and seemingly ill at ease, hands gripping an empty tankard, eyes flicking from crowded grove to temple path and back. Mazaret excused himself from the three merchants who had been boring him with their trading tales, and moved clockwise round the grove, seeking to approach the man from his blind side. Then a surprising sight snared his attention.

At the centre of the grove, Bardow stood between the leaders of the Northern and Southern Cabals, Korren's bland smile more than matched by Peilon's ale-flushed grin as the Archmage spoke to them both. Mazaret glanced quickly over at his quarry, and cursed – Volyn's man was gone.

Bardow, meanwhile, was still talking, watched by a now silent audience. Mazaret heard the Archmage speak of 'consensus' and 'concord', but his gaze was searching the trees all around them. What was Volyn up to? Those two men of his had been posted here for a reason, to watch the gathering and report back, that much was clear.

Then he saw movement along the pathway from the temple, five forms coming towards the grove. Mazaret tossed aside his nearly empty mug and went to meet them. Cabal members drew back to allow him through and Bardow spoke to him but he gave no reply, just walked a straight line that led to the tree stump near the temple path where he came face to face with Captain Volyn.

Like his men, Volyn was attired for horseback travel – a dark green cloak over leather harness with heavy woollen leggings and sturdy boots. His four companions kept their cloaks closed, succeeding in only partly concealing the loaded crossbows that they carried. Mazaret stared at each in turn, and lastly Volyn.

'You risk a great deal coming here in this manner,' he said calmly.

Volyn said nothing as he reached inside his cloak and produced a small rolled-up parchment which Mazaret recognized immediately: it was the formal treaty of alliance he and Volyn had signed years before. With his angry gaze fixed on Mazaret, Volyn tore the parchment into four pieces then took a dagger from a sheath at his waist.

There were gasps, and a small commotion. Bardow pushed his way to the front and one of Volyn's men raised his crossbow, aiming it at the Archmage. Mazaret shook his head at Bardow and turned back to see Captain Volyn place the pieces of torn parchment on the tree stump and raise the dagger above his head. There was a thud as the blade struck the parchment fragments, impaling them on the stump, and Volyn stood back.

'It is done,' he said. 'It is over.'

'In the Mother's name, why?' said Mazaret. 'When we are on the brink of war, why do you do this?'

'I am not blind, nor deaf to the agreements you arrange in secret. A thousand northern soldiers, am I not correct?' Volyn's mouth contorted with rage. 'And a halving of the supplies from our northern friends, too, eh?' He levelled a trembling finger at Mazaret. 'Are such actions trustworthy or treacherous?'

'You have been grossly misled, captain—'

'I think not. This is but the culminating enormity in a series of affronts that we have endured since joining our cause with yours, and will be the last. This is now ended.' Volyn made a slashing gesture with one outstretched hand and turned to leave.

'Hear me out, captain! You have not yet heard the truth—'

'I am no longer interested in anything you have to say! My warriors await me at the gates of Krusivel – I go now to join them.'

Bardow stepped forward. 'And what of the boy Tauric, captain? You vowed he would be safe.'

Volyn glowered at him. 'I have despatched a message bird, mage. Your cripple-prince will be returned unharmed in a few days.' He looked back at Mazaret. 'Our paths diverge from here on. We have our own purpose and destiny to pursue and you would be well advised not to interfere.'

Mazaret fought to control his anger and remain silent. A furious outburst would be pointless, he knew, and would diminish what dignity remained to him. As Volyn's broad cloaked form receded into the darkness, flanked by his guards, Mazaret turned to face Bardow. His face was pale and angry, one hand clutching a thick-stemmed bronze goblet so tightly Mazaret thought it might snap.

'We were outmanoeuvred,' the Archmage said in a thoughtful, almost amused tone utterly at odds with his demeanour. 'Quite expertly, too. Dow Korren must have used some intermediary to poison Volyn against us, one of his trusted aides, perhaps.'

Dow Korren. Mazaret looked around the grove for him, but the Northern Cabal and its leader were already on the path back to the temple grounds. For a second he thought he saw Korren glance back over his shoulder, then the northerners were indistinct forms fading into the night.

'My lords?'

Mazaret turned to see one of the southerners, his expression downcast and nervous as his gaze flicked between them.

'Master Peilon asked me to present our apologies as we must return to make ready our departure in the morning. An account of these events will have to be given to the Cabal council before any further decisions can be taken.' He paused, shook his head. 'Such a pity, my lords, a very great pity.'

Mazaret's thoughts raced as he spoke. 'Good sir, thank Master Peilon for his noble sentiments and inform him that I would speak with him before he leaves tomorrow.'

'As you wish, my lord,' and the southerner bowed and left.

Frowning, Bardow opened his mouth to speak but Mazaret cut him off with a sign for silence. When the last southerner had slipped off down the murky path, the Archmage said, 'Why? What is to be gained?'

Mazaret paused to marshall his thoughts and frame an answer. 'The sorcerous search for Suviel you undertook . . . can you perform another?'

Bardow's shoulders sagged visibly and he sighed heavily. 'Yes, my lord, if you so command me, I can invoke the Spiritwing once more. For whom will I be searching?'

Mazaret took in the sight of the now-deserted grove, an overturned stool, abandoned mugs and beakers clustered on the trestles, one vessel lying on its side in a pool of ale gleaming in the fading light of the pole lanterns. It was growing cold now and he shivered slightly.

'You recall Volyn's mention of destiny?' he said. 'The Hunter's Children's destiny, which can only be—'

'Placing a living descendant of House Tor-Cavarill on the Imperial throne.' Bardow looked straight at Mazaret. 'That's who you want me to find, a man—'

'Or woman—'

'—or child, whose appearance we do not know, whose name is a complete mystery, and who could be anywhere.'

'Nevertheless, I want you to try. If I can convince Peilon and his companions that we may be able to . . . persuade the Hunter's Children to stay with us, then success is yet within our grasp. But I have to know who and where this heir is.'

Bardow's gaze grew steady and penetrating. 'And if I find him for you, what are you going to do with him? Take him hostage?'

'Yes, to use as a bargaining piece.'

'Very well, my lord. I shall retire to my chambers and begin at once.'

A moment passed, two, and he was alone. A chill breeze filtered through the trees and the torches wavered and lessened slightly. He took a step in the dimness, which brought him right up to the tree stump, laid hold of the dagger and with a wrench tugged it free of the wounded wood, ripped parchment leaves still stuck to the blade. A nearby torch guttered lower and the tree stump seemed to bleed shadows into the encroaching gloom as Mazaret stumbled back along the path to a firelit bedchamber and a sleepless night.

Chapter Fifteen

A stream wears and widens a crevice.
A seed grows in a crack in a wall.
A hot spark flies into dust-dry tinder.

Suffering, anger and revolt,
Bind the people to fate's wheel.

Anchal Gunderlek, *Letters To Cabringa*

With a junction of the ruined labyrinth just ahead, Tauric paused to regain his breath. Blood thundered in his head, and he felt swathed in sweat and body heat. The hilt of the practice sword was slick in the palm of his good hand so he dried it on a fistful of grubby shirt held in his other hand, his new right hand.

Jointed steel fingers glinted in the muted morning light that came in through the tunnel's caved-in ceiling. Each finger had been meticulously engraved with the likeness of fingernail and skin creases, but time and the wear of combat had added innumerable scratches and pits to the metal surfaces. And now dust and grime streaked the metal limb up to below the elbow where a tight leather band hid the joining of steel and skin. It was easily cleaned – the Armourer had shown him how to use running water and brushes, then how to put on the full leather sleeve that would afford it some protection during battle.

It had been a wonder, that moment when he looked down and saw this new limb for the first time, and in that moment he had believed that he would never again have to remember what Byrnak had done. But his dreams offered up a betrayal of that hope, and sleep seldom came easily.

Tauric held up the metal hand and moved the fingers, clenching them in a fist. His control was still uncertain, even he could see it was so, which was why the Armourer insisted that he use his left hand as often as possible.

Then he heard someone say, 'I can hear the breath slowing in your mouth, and that means you've stopped. Too many of these mistakes and I'll have you.'

Suddenly alert and with the wooden practice sword held ready, Tauric began creeping away from the voice and towards the junction. Dust hung in the air like a veil. These corridors were as wide as a cart and walled with rough planking now split and rotten. Sometimes he had to step over piles of rubble and earth beneath a grass-fringed hole in the ceiling, or beside a collapsed wall. He ignored the turn-off, a narrow opening stretching off into utter blackness, and continued along the main passage.

In places the gloom was almost smothering and he swallowed hard as his thoughts grew fearful. A long time before, the Armourer had told him, long centuries before the rise of even the League of Jefren, followers of the long-dead Nightbear faith had built the underground maze as part of their mysterious rituals, perhaps as a place where trapped bears ate living sacrifices . . .

After a few paces he paused, held his breath and with a quivering alertness listened. Nothing, no footsteps, nor creaks or the like, except for a faint hollow tapping.

There was a massive crash and the wall next to him gave way in a cascade of earth, roots and rotten planking. Tauric leaped backwards in fright as a tall figure came towards him through the billowing dust clouds. Swiftly, Tauric regained his balance then turned and made a run at a nearby cave-in, jumped for the sagging edge of the gap in the ceiling and hauled himself up and out. Rolling across long grass soaked with morning dew, he scrambled to his feet, scurried over to another hole in the ground and slid back down into the dimness.

Crouched in the half-light, he listened to the hissing, clicking sounds of earth and stones trickling down after him. After a moment there was stillness with only the sound of his heart beating faintly in his ears. Then he heard the Armourer's voice, low and muffled as if from a distance: 'An interesting tactic, boy. Instead of taking advantage of my momentary confusion, you fled. Be reminded that we are here to practise conflict rather than avoidance. Next time I expect you to stand your ground. Remember, the first to land a blow is the victor.'

Tauric nodded in weary agreement. Then he frowned – his father – no, the Duke of Patrein – would not have decried his impulse to retreat. He could almost imagine the duke saying something like 'Experience counters the advantage of surprise', while regarding him with those piercing blue eyes and prodding the palm of his hand with a rigid forefinger.

A sudden sense of sorrow and loss cut through him, sharp and irresistible. Sighing, he forced his mind back to the moment, burying his feelings under thoughts of combat, his strengths and his weaknesses. Deliberately, he hefted the practice sword in his flesh-and-blood hand, a bundle of yard-long cut rods bound to a heavier wooden shaft. While not at all lethal, it made a loud rattling bang when it connected and left throbbing bruises or welts on the skin, especially when wielded by the Armourer.

He almost laughed out loud. The Armourer (who seemed to have no other name) was taller, heavier and faster than he, not to mention the man's experience with weapons of all kinds. When all the combat advantages lay with the enemy, what was left?

The duke's voice came back to him from memory – *Guile, and ingenuity.*

Tauric leaned back against the wall planking, hearing it creak as he thought for some moments. Then he went over to a nearby heap of cave-in debris and dug and scooped aside handfuls of stony dirt until he came up with two lengths of wood not too ravaged by rot. One he shortened, snapping it with the use of two rocks, and with a narrow strip of cloth torn from the bottom of his shirt he tied it to the other as a kind of crosspiece. Then he took off his shirt, tugged it over the rudimentary frame, propped it against the wall and stepped back. His spirits sagged – to even the least discerning eye it would look like the contrivance it was.

He shook his head. It doesn't have to be convincing, he thought. Just distracting for long enough.

A scrape and a footfall disturbed the quiet, coming from the darkness beyond the grey patch of light below the ceiling hole. Tauric snatched up the shirt on its sticks and crept away with steady, careful footing till he came to where the passage ended in a T-junction. Then he scuffed his foot once in the dirt, loud enough to be heard, then crouched behind the corner and fumbled on the floor for a small pebble while peering round. It was not long before he saw a darker shadow move within the darkness, taking on form and detail as it approached – Tauric recognized the tall frame and broad shoulders of the Armourer, pale light picking out the metallic studs of his leather jerkin, one of his big hands gripping a practice sword.

Tauric tossed the pebble across the junction into the lightless murk of the other passageway where it made a brief but audible noise. The Armourer went into a crouch, facing the direction of the sound, moving back to the wall and sidling along to the corner where Tauric waited.

Gripping the frame and shirt, he stepped out, threw the decoy at the Armourer's head and dropped to his knees. He thought he felt cold air on the top of his head and heard the rattling impact of a practice sword hitting the wall as he swept his own round at the Armourer's legs.

It struck home with a bang. The Armourer uttered an oath as Tauric rolled away. Clambering to his feet, he saw the man bent over, rubbing a reddening patch on his shin. For a moment there was a gleam of anger in his eyes, then he looked down and picked up the shirt on its sticks. He examined it for a moment, then gave a rueful chuckle and tossed it across to Tauric.

'A decoy – I like that,' he said, dusting his hands on his leggings. 'But decoys seldom work twice.'

Tauric disentangled his now-filthy shirt and pulled it back on. 'What if it's a better decoy? What if there's two?'

The Armourer nodded. 'This is what you will learn when you begin training with the troop.' He held up his hand as Tauric opened his mouth. 'Which will be soon, I promise. For now, we shall return to the holding and get your arm and the rest of you cleaned up for your tutors.'

Above ground the air was icy and damp with the promise of rain. Tauric followed the Armourer through long, dewy grass up a gentle slope towards Barinok Stronghold, their breaths making pale clouds in the cold. The stronghold had once been a monastery dedicated to the Order of the Fathertree, which accounted for its heavily fortified appearance, sheer stone walls that encircled two adjacent hilltops and blocked the vale which passed between them. A long, high-sided building lay within the walls, a rambling, untidy-looking structure which had at some point in the past clearly been a keep and several other buildings, until something forced the occupants to rebuild it.

The Fathertree monks must have felt at great risk of attack to go to such trouble, Tauric thought. Perhaps it was just after the collapse of the League of Jefren; that period was full of bitter wars and factional power struggles.

Tauric could feel the first spots of rain when they reached the postern gate, a low, narrow door made from a single, foot-thick piece of blackwood fixed between iron plates and so heavy it took three men to crank the winch that lifted it out of the way. Once through, there was a rattle of chains and cogs and a thud that Tauric felt through his boots as the gate fell back into place. They climbed a flight of stone steps to a small room where three waiting guards bowed (but only to the Armourer, Tauric noticed).

'Sire,' said one, 'I was instructed to inform you that Sentinel Kodel has returned, and that Steward Eskridan requires the immediate attendance of both yourself and the ward Tauric.'

The Armourer frowned. 'I and my companion are not permitted to make ourselves presentable?'

The guard looked uncomfortable, and Tauric began to feel uneasy.

'Sire, the message was quite specific – you are to see him immediately upon your return to the holding.'

'Very well, we shall do the steward's bidding.' He looked at Tauric. 'Follow me and stay close.'

They encountered few people on the way to the steward's chambers, which lay near the top of the old keep. Most were servants but occasionally they met some of the Hunter's Children in ones or twos, who saluted the Armourer as they passed yet left Tauric with the feeling that they were looking at him. Despite knowing that his imagination was to blame, his uneasiness grew as they progressed through the lamplit, cold stone quiet of the stronghold. His mind turned to thoughts of the Lord Commander's brother. On their arrival here, the last he had seen of Coireg Mazaret was a bound, hobbled figure being roughly led down to a lower level, 'the cages' as Tauric heard one guard call them. Since then, there had been neither word nor sign of the man.

When they at last came to a tall, iron-banded door at the end of a passage, the Armourer seemed to pause for a moment before knocking. A voice bade them enter and the Armourer lifted the latch, leading the way in.

The chamber was well furnished with wall hangings, patterned mats, cabinets and a polished, oval table, but what caught Tauric's eye was the debris scattered to one side of the hearth, splintered pieces of a chair and something else, a small stand perhaps. There were also two men in the room, one waiting nervously next to the table, eyes flicking down at a small scrap of paper on the unmarred, shiny surface while a taller man stood over by the high window, leaning on its sill. It was Sentinel Kodel. Without turning, he said: 'My thanks for your prompt arrival, Armourer.' His voice was level and relaxed, in stark contrast to the palpable tension in the room. 'Matters have arisen which demand our loyalty and recognition of duty. Steward Eskridan, recite the message again.'

The steward carefully picked up the scrap of paper and began to read.

Eskridan,
Know that our alliance with the knights of the usurper is at an end. Never again shall our destiny and purpose be sullied by the deceits of odious plotters. I require you to order the immediate halt of all collaboration and the recall of those warriors involved thus. Employ whatever means you deem swiftest to communicate these commands. Also, the ward Tauric is to be escorted with all haste to Oumetra by Sentinel Kodel and a dozen riders. I shall be there to meet them on their arrival.

These orders by my hand, this the 16th day of the Gather Moon in the 1109th year of the Empire.
                                                    Captain Volyn.

The steward let the paper fall to the table and in the silence that followed, Tauric's uneasiness turned slowly to fear. They were sending him to Oumetra, not back to Krusivel. There was a threat in the message – 'I shall be there to meet them on their arrival'. Volyn he knew regarded him with suspicion if not dislike, so what was the man's intent in this? His mouth was dry, his new arm felt heavy at his side and his legs trembled under him, but he made himself stand steadily and betray no anxiety.

'Events,' said Kodel from the end of the room, 'seldom happen as one expects.' He turned from the window and approached the table. Tauric saw scratches and smears of blood on his hands and a smouldering fury in his eyes, and realized who had smashed the furniture.

'I can have a troop of riders made ready whenever you wish, Sentinel,' the steward said.

'That will not be necessary,' said Kodel.

'But the captain's orders—'

'The Captain's orders will be carried out,' Kodel snapped. 'I will escort the boy to Oumetra and the Armourer shall accompany me. No others are necessary – I am confident that our ward will follow my commands without question.' He looked at Tauric. 'Do I have your bond on this, as you have mine?'

Tauric remembered the incident at the mill and Kodel's words after slaying the old man – 'I'm going to see you crowned Emperor if it's the last thing I do.'

'Yes,' he said hoarsely.

'Good. Sir steward, have three of your hardiest mounts harnessed and provisioned within the half hour.'

'As you wish, Sentinel.' The steward bowed and left, and Kodel turned to Tauric.

'Go to the bath house and get washed and dressed in journey clothes. When you return here, we shall have armour for you and perhaps even a blade?' He looked at the Armourer who glanced at Tauric and gave a half smile and a nod.

'Yes. He's ready.'

As he left Tauric wondered how much danger he was getting into, now that Kodel seemed to have set himself against his own leader. He flexed his metal hand, trying to imagine a sword held tight in its cold grasp, but felt only a hollowness in his stomach as he hurried down the main stairs of the keep.

Chapter Sixteen

Beyond this tract of dream and fancy,
Beyond the wrack of hate and death,
Lies a far, sweet land,
Where once I was a prince.

Jedhessa Gant, *The Lords Desolate*, Act 1, ii, 9

The birdloft was warm, the air heavy with the combined odours of seed and droppings. Blade-thin shafts of noon sunlight slipped in through cracks between the timbers, piercing the gloom, outlining rows of wickerwork coops and the hunched-over figure who muttered to himself as he peered in at his charges.

Bardow waited by the trapdoor entrance, fanning himself with one long sleeve, enjoying the occasional wafts of fresh air that came up from below. No matter how often he came here, the Archmage always felt as if his nose were under assault, and it took some moments for his senses to accustom themselves.

'What was them places again, laddie?'

Bardow allowed himself a small smile. Mecadri was from the Ogucharn Isles and never had been one for respectful terms of address.

'Oumetra, Scallow, Oskimul and Scarbarig,' he said.

'Scarbarig . . . hmm, that's that mining town south of Sejeend, is it not?'

'The very same.'

Mecadri the pigeon keeper nodded and came over. He was a

short burly man with a straggly beard and was wearing several layers of grubby clothing liberally decorated with food stains and fragments of bird seed. On his head sat an ancient hat gone shapeless and floppy with age, its wide brim frayed and notched and bearing other stains unlikely to be food.

He held out one hand, gloved in an old black leather gauntlet whose finger and thumb had been cut away, and Bardow gave him a little sheaf of slips, two of each except for the Oumetra message which had three copies. Mecadri *tsk-tsked* and shook his head.

'Sending three birds is a waste, ser. There won't be another delivery from Oumetra for at least a week.'

'That particular message has to get through,' Bardow said. 'Time is against us and I cannot risk losing one of your birds to a hawk or a hunter, and it being the only one with the message.'

'As you say,' the keeper said. He returned to the coops at the other end of the loft and began busying himself with the slips and the birds he had chosen while humming a tavern song.

Bardow stood watching but his thoughts were going back over what he had discovered a day and a night ago. That invocation of the Spiritwing canto was far more exhausting than the time before and had taken him to the very limits of his endurance. He'd had barely enough strength to scrawl a note to Ikarno Mazaret before slipping into unconsciousness and a sleep he did not wake from until early this morning.

His note to Mazaret had been only a few words – *Oumetra, a square with two fountains, house of sheep, flowers in the window* – and his recollection of their exact meaning was hazy at best. He could remember the sheer effort needed to make the Spiritwing look for any of the heirs of House Tor-Cavarill, no matter how far removed, and then to trace the bloodline through the gulfs and veils of the Void, leading to Oumetra.

What the note did not contain were the other things he had discovered. Upon picturing the swordswoman Keren in his thoughts, the Spiritwing had made not the slightest movement, which implied that she was dead. And when he tried the same with the trader Gilly, all he could discern was that he was somewhere far to the north-east, perhaps in central or northern Khatris. Tauric he had seen soundly asleep in the fortified monastery of Grinok, not yet aware of Volyn's message winging its way towards him.

But it was Suviel who was the focus of his worries. The Spiritwing had swept him through the Void and brought him out south of Prekine to a narrow trail which threaded along a ravine choked with thorny bushes, leading to a clearing where a group of travellers were making camp beneath a dusk sky empty of clouds. Suviel was a robed and hooded figure sat bound and gagged in the back of a small cart, while one of the others was standing nearby, saying something to her. Then the stranger's face had come into view and Bardow had been astonished to recognize Keren. It took him a moment or two to discern the subtle differences and realize that this had to be the mirrorchild Nerek, Byrnak's abomination.

Suviel sat still in the cart, despair starkly apparent in her bowed head, her tired features. She looked so helpless and pitiful yet still not defeated – twice Bardow saw her slowly shake her head in response to something Nerek said. His heart went out to her and almost involuntarily he found himself moving closer, seeking to let her know that she was not forgotten.

It had almost been his undoing. The mirrorchild had spun to face him, her hands already full of a shimmering emerald glow which cast a lurid light across her features. Bardow barely had time to withdraw as that deadly fire leaped towards him, widening to engulf him. There had been a moment, an instant of stinging pain when it almost had him, then the Spiritwing broke away and he was hurled back into the fathomless deeps of the Void, free to begin the search for the Hunter's heir.

In the loft, Bardow watched Mecadri whisper an endless stream of soothing noises to his birds as he fastened tiny message cases to their legs and one by one took them to the open, slanted casement and flung them skyward. Each message gave specific orders to their secret rebels, commanding them to avoid any conflict with Hunter's Children agents or sympathizers for the next few days. The ones bound for Oumetra included notice of

Mazaret's imminent arrival, and were the last to be dispatched. Yet as the pigeon keeper released the first of the three birds, Bardow felt a dark foreboding steal over him. While he had been in the smothering grip of exhausted sleep, Mazaret had persuaded the leaders of the Southern Cabal not to make any far-reaching decisions, assuring them that he would be able to return the Hunter's Children to the alliance. Then he had taken one of the best horses, a grey Yularian stallion known for its endurance, and left in the middle of the night.

What was Mazaret's purpose? He could think of only two possiblities – either the Lord Commander was going to try and kidnap the boy (Bardow was nine-tenths sure that the heir of Tor-Cavarill was male), or he was going to kill him.

No, he thought. *Ikarno would never do such a thing.*

But a shiver passed through him as he pondered the situation, his thoughts growing darker, drawing together what he knew and what he felt and other less certain shreds of chance. And Oumetra began to loom large in his mind. Many threads were gathering there, forces and destinies twisting together in a knot of dread consequences.

And try as he might, Bardow could not unravel it.

Unnoticed at the other end of the loft, Mecadri the pigeon keeper carefully carried the bird bearing the third and last message for Oumetra to the slanting casement and the sunshine. He lifted the little creature to his face, met its beady regard for a moment, then murmured a farewell before tossing it up and out of the loft in a flurried flapping of wings.

Ikarno Mazaret rode hard beneath an ill and leaden sky, his face masked with a swathe of cloth against the chill rain coming wind-driven from the north. It was late morning and the trail he followed was little more than a ribbon of hoof-hammered turf winding through the wooded hills and downs west of Lake Audagal, a route on which he was unlikely to encounter a Mogaun patrol. After leaving Krusivel the previous day, he had rested half the following night in a shabby hostelry on the Redway, the wood-and-brick road that ran northwards arrow-straight through central Kejana. But true sleep had evaded him and he rose, resaddled the grey and left at a gallop with the predawn light.

Now Mazaret's mood was as grim as the weather. What would he do when he found the scion of House Tor-Cavarill? Hold him hostage, thus risking everything on his safety and wellbeing, as well as Volyn's willingness to comply? Would it not be better to secretly spirit the boy away and then have him killed?

He shuddered. Till now his plans and purpose had been clear and straightforward, his enemies the savage Mogaun and their sorcerous allies, his tactics plain and direct. But this predicament burdened him with a choice of poisonous gambits and shrank the world to a dark and narrow path.

I don't know, he wanted to cry out. *I don't know what to do!* And when he wondered what Suviel would have said, he could almost see and hear her say, *You cannot . . . you must not . . .*

With a prayer to the Earthmother on his lips and a blast of cold wind at his back, he rode on.

Soon after noon, he had crossed the Oungal Downs and was heading towards the shores of Lake Audagal. This was a country of moist pastures and water meadows and while he came within sight of several villages and steadings, he was careful to skirt every one. Before leaving Krusivel he had exchanged his polished hauberk for a scarred leather harness and the battered trappings of a down-at-heel soldier-of-fortune. It was a disguise he hoped would never be put to the test.

By mid-afternoon, he took shelter in a glade full of nesting clatterbeaks with the wind tossing the heads of the trees overhead and a heavy rain soaking the long grass all around. Once rested, he remounted the grey, turned its head south and was on the move again. Unfortunately, his progress along the lake shore became fitful, forced into diversions and hastily sought hiding places when patrols of Mogaun cavalry, the mounts as barbarically adorned as their riders, passed by. Their banners and shields bore the snarling dog device of Begrajic, the Mogaun chieftain who held sway over this part of Kejana and whose warriors had repeatedly attempted to reach Krusivel, only to come to grief in the deep valleys of the Bachruz Mountains.

Eventually he left the road altogether, choosing instead the rutted cart-tracks and grassy footpaths that linked the farms and tiny hamlets which were scattered among the wildwood-cloaked slopes east of the lake. It was nearly sundown by the time he emerged from a mire of clawbush and lugweed and found himself not far from a wide stone bridge spanning a rain-swollen river called the Nolvik. Across the river, blurred by poor light and a persistent drizzle, were the grey outlines of Oumetra and beyond it the dark expanse of the sea.

The coast road and an offshoot of the Redway met here, bringing a few travellers, mostly afoot, who were hurrying to be within the city walls before nightfall. Mazaret urged his mount up from the muddy hollow and over to the bridge, slowed to a walk to cross it, then spurred it into a swift canter again and rode for the city gates.

As he neared, his eyes took in the details of the outer wall, seeing where some parts of the battlements had been strengthened and others heightened since he was last here almost six years ago. Then he noticed a knot of people outside the arched gates and off to one side, one or two hand-held torches brightening the dim surroundings. As he came closer someone lurched away from the others to be sick against the city wall. Another in a long cloak and a hat went after him while the guards at the gate guffawed and mimicked the unfortunate. Mazaret grimaced in contempt then brought his mount to a halt to look over the heads of the onlookers.

Hammered into the ground near the wall was a crude stake and tied to it was the body of a Mogaun male. From the five red rings piercing the skin along one side of the jawbone, Mazaret knew that this had been one of Begrajic's warchiefs, perhaps even one of his sons. The armour suggested as much, being a sleeveless leather harness stained a dark brown and strengthened with close rows of rough bronze discs rivetted in place. To Mogaun eyes it would previously have appeared magnificent, a token of power and authority; now it was slashed and grimy, stained with blood and mud, and with many discs missing or half-ripped out. Whoever had done this had gone out of their way to deliberately wreck the armour along with its owner, in order to make some kind of point.

The worst of it, though, was the manner of execution. The Mogaun had suffered death by amputation, joint by joint till all that remained of him was the torso and most of one arm. It was a particularly cruel and agonising way to die, and Mazaret had a notion about who was responsible, if not why.

With mouth closed against the stench of death, he dismounted and led his horse towards the gate. There were five guards in heavy leather corslets, their idle gazes scarcely noticing the travellers who passed through the gate. One of them did stare at Mazaret with a kind of ill-natured, grinning interest but he made no move to stop him. Mazaret knew from reports that the warlord Begrajic had hired mercenaries to occupy Oumetra and maintain order. He wondered who their commander was. Many so-called free companies roamed the lands of the former Empire, all of them full of brutal toughs and thugs and all of them in the pay of either the Mogaun or the Acolytes.

There was a deep wooden creak as the gates swung shut behind him, followed by a heavy thud as the bar came down. Mazaret led the grey away, glancing about him as he tried to gain his bearings. The city of Oumetra was built largely of a dark, almost blue stone mined half a millennium ago in Dalbar. The city's founders had wrought their walls and halls and towers on a heroic scale, the streets and squares likewise. The intervening centuries, and the demands of a growing population, had seen those spacious public areas narrowed or entirely filled by cheaper buildings of wood or brick, or (occasionally) stone salvaged from the ruined towns of the Easterly Hills.

The streets were dim, narrow canyons, their gloom broken by the lamplight of windows or the porch lantern of a barrelhouse or those stables still open. The stench of sewage was everywhere and Mazaret kept away from the gutters as he walked along a main street leading into the city. He was looking for an inn called the Moon and Anvil where he was to meet one of the Earthmother Order's agents. After following directions given by a couple of surly townsmen, he found himself standing before a low doorway over which hung a weathered sign carved with a quarter moon and an Armourer's anvil.

Down a short alley beside the inn was a stable where he left his horse to be watered and fed. With his saddlebags over one shoulder he entered by the back door and made his way along a low passage to the taproom. The noise and the beery warmth enfolded him as he squeezed through to the counter. After a shouted exchange with the barkeep, during which he paid for the stabling, a room for the night, and a jack of dark ale, he went to stand in a corner of the room near a shuttered window, slowly drinking.

As he waited, he surveyed the crowd and realized that the loudest laughter was coming from a group of soldiers and their doxies camped over by the door. Whenever one of the mercenaries bellowed some coarse remark or provoked a burst of giggles from their female companions, the background conversations of the other customers always died down for a moment or two. A few heads shook and murderous looks flitted across faces turned away from the source of the racket, then the general hubbub of voices returned. There was an air of smouldering anger in the room, Mazaret thought, restless and unpleasant. If the soldiers stayed, there would be a fight here before the night was done.

As he lifted the jack for another swallow of ale, a man passing by on his way to the jakes paused to stare swayingly at something on the floor. He bent down to pick up something and held it out to Mazaret on a distinctly grimy palm.

'Heh . . . this yours, good ser?'

It was a coin, an old Roharkan penny with the ox-head side face up. Mazaret kept any reaction from showing in his face – ox was the password or signal he had told Bardow to include in his message to Oumetra.

'Why yes, thank you.'

'No bother,' the man said, then whispered as he turned

away, 'The back door. Finish your drink first.' Then he was gone.

The ale, flavoured with some kind of spice to mask the sourness, seemed to take an age to finish. When he was down to the dregs he left the jack on the floor, shouldered his saddlebags and went out the way he had come in. He paused on the threshold of the back door until a figure detached itself from the shadows across the alley and came into the weak light of the stable lamp. It was the same man, only without the drunken disguise.

'This way,' he said, heading for the end of the alley.

Mazaret glanced around. The stable boy was nowhere to be seen so he hurried after the stranger, who had pushed open a decrepit-looking door in the wall of the adjacent building. Mazaret followed him into a dim, dank room smelling of mildew and lit by a candle on a shelf. His guide produced an oil lamp from somewhere, lit it from the candle then led him from the room and further into the apparently deserted building, along a narrow corridor, through a succession of small rooms, and up a spiral stairway, finally pushing through damp, moth-eaten curtains to arrive in a large shadowy chamber. Mazaret could just make out benches arranged in a semicircle around a raised platform against one wall. The wall had once been hung with tapestries and carvings but now there were only scorch marks and charred fragments of wood.

A group of men stood to one side of the platform, a few holding lanterns which cast forth yellow auras of light. Two of them came forward to meet him, one a slightly built man in what looked like labourer's clothing, the other tall and distinguished in expensive attire and carrying a large, thin book under one arm.

For a moment they stood regarding one another in silence. Then the aristocratic one opened his book at a marked page and gazed intently at its contents.

'Is it him?' said his slender companion, taking a dagger from within his shirt.

As the intent gaze went from book to Mazaret's face and back, Mazaret became aware of more than one pair of feet moving softly in the darkness behind him, and he strove to remain relaxed. At length the well-dressed man nodded and closed the book.

'The hair is longer and greyer,' he said. 'And the face is thinner. But it is him, certainly.'

'I think he means that I'm older,' Mazaret said.

'Courtesy forbids,' said the other man drily as he put away the dagger. 'I am Geraine, my lord, leader of these rebellious rogues. This—' he placed a hand on the shoulder of the man with the book, '—is Havall . . .'

Havall gave a gracious tilt of the head.

'And your escort is Kammer.' Kammer nodded sharply, his face unreadable. 'My apologies for all this furtive skulking, but a party of Mogaun shamans arrived last night and the whole city has been on edge since. We dare not go out on the streets, even at night. We even sent one of our number, a lad with only a trace of the Lesser Power, away from Oumetra lest the Mogaun warlocks sniff him out.'

He paused, regarding Mazaret for a moment. 'My lord, the message from the Redoubt said something about our alliance with the Hunter's Children being at an end.'

Mazaret nodded. 'Captain Volyn and his advisers decided to go their own way and were not to be persuaded otherwise.'

'This will make things far more difficult.'

'But not impossible,' Mazaret said. He laid a hand on Geraine's shoulder and the two men began walking towards the rear wall. 'Now, tell me more of these shamans. Were they responsible for the little spectacle outside the gates?'

'That was Achaj, one of Begrajic's brood, as brutal a savage as the rest, yet he began lusting after a woman from the town and had her taken to his camp north of the city. Her brother made a public outcry about it and Achaj was ready to have him drawn and quartered, until the woman begged for his pardon. Which Achaj gave.' Geraine uttered a dry chuckle as they halted beside the platform. 'Then the shamans appeared a few days later, questioned him about this unforgivable lapse into mercy and decided that such weakness had to be expunged. Hence the remains you saw outside.' He glanced at the others. 'Oh, how we wept.'

Quiet laughter went round the others, a hard sound for all its muteness, hard with a need for vengeance.

Mazaret offered only a neutral smile. 'So how much of a danger are the shamans, ser Geraine? I've an important task to carry out and I'd like to know of any little difficulties we might encounter.'

'What is the nature of this task, my lord?'

'I want a certain person taken captive, unharmed, and out of the city and heading north with me directly afterwards.'

'And where is this person to be found?' Geraine said.

'Somewhere in Oumetra there is a square with two fountains, yes?'

'The old Imperial Square,' said Kammer. 'That's over in the merchants' quarter, right near the Tasna canal.'

Mazaret looked at the straight-faced man. 'What of the phrase "house of sheep"? Does that mean anything to you?'

Frowning, Kammer thought for a moment or two then looked at Geraine. 'Bilar, the draper's, it has to be.'

'Interesting,' said Geraine turning to Mazaret, 'seeing as it's also a safe house for the Hunter's Children.'

'Does this present some difficulty for you?' Mazaret said evenly.

Geraine grinned. 'Not at all. In fact, one of our refuges just happens to be right across the canal at the back of Bilar's.'

'Astonishing.'

'In truth, such fortunate coincidences are surely the Earthmother's apology for life's other little difficulties.' Everyone laughed and Mazaret could not help but join them.

The way to the refuge led along lightless alleys, across dim back courts and through cellars and deserted passages strewn with rubbish. Mazaret smelled the canal before they came to it, and was able to look down at its inky blackness cutting between the close-packed buildings as he followed Geraine and the others up a narrow staircase fixed somewhat loosely to the side of a warehouse. A door at the top opened into a loft reeking of bird droppings. Part of the roof had fallen in and the rustling of unseen vermin accompanied their footsteps as they hurried across to another door, beyond which was an enclosed catwalk. Mazaret tried not to think of the long fall waiting below as aged planks creaked underfoot.

At the other end, they entered the attic of a large townhouse. The wooden walls were unadorned and a battered table and six chairs sat on a surprisingly thick carpet. Two of Geraine's men used their small lamps to light a pair of hooded lanterns which sat on the floor, while Geraine went over to the single shuttered window and with a small object held to his eye peered through the slats. Mazaret went over to join him and saw the rear of a long, ramshackle building some six storeys tall in places. Many windows seemed boarded over, with only a few lit from within.

'That is the draper's,' Geraine said, pointing directly across. He then offered the object he had been squinting through. 'Care to see? Have you seen one of these before, my lord?'

Mazaret frowned. The object was a stubby leather cylinder with a glass disc in either end. Taking it, he realized that it was actually made of two tubes of leather, one slightly smaller and able to slip in and out of the other.

'A near-eye device,' Mazaret said, putting it to his right eye. 'I have heard of them but never used one.'

Geraine showed him how to twist the larger piece in or out, and the dark blur of the building opposite suddenly coalesced into a sharp, detailed image. Mazaret uttered an oath and snatched the device away, then smiled and raised it again. In the encroaching night the rear of the draper's was a mass of darkness, apart from those windows lit from within. He surveyed every one but saw no flowers as Bardow had mentioned, only a very large woman down in the back court soaking yards of cloth in a trough, and a servant girl sewing at a fourth-floor window.

Mazaret sighed and returned the near-eye. Geraine gave him a questioning look, then shrugged and resumed his own scrutiny of the draper's.

'So what are we looking for?' he murmured.

Mazaret considered telling him about Bardow's vision, but wondered if it would sound improbable. It had also occurred to him that this window with flowers might be at the front of the building, or even that it might be a window with flowers carved in the stonework around it and how would they see that in this darkness?

'Hmm, she certainly is pretty,' Geraine said. 'Can't say she's familiar, though. Maybe she . . .' He went still and silent for an instant, then gave a low whistle. 'Well now, who is this?'

Smiling, he straightened and passed the near-eye to Mazaret who quickly adjusted it till he could see the fourth-floor window clearly again. The girl had put aside her sewing and was talking to a burly man dressed in the plain brown garments of a town trader. It was Volyn.

Then the second shock came when the girl, upset about something, stood and moved away from the window, revealing a few yellow flowers in a small white vase. He lowered the near-eye and handed it back to Geraine.

'Who is it?' said one of the others.

'Why, none other than the honourable Captain Volyn,' said Geraine.

There was a stir of surprise and exchanged mutters in the attic.

A girl, Mazaret was thinking madly. *The heir of House Tor-Cavarill is a girl.*

'It's her, isn't it, my lord?' Geraine was giving him a penetrating look. 'She's the one you want taken, and you're none to happy about it, I wager.'

He ignored the last comment. 'Yes, she is the one I must take back to Krusivel.' And his words sounded hollow to his own ears.

'When is it to be done?'

'This very night. Volyn may be planning to move her, so we move first.' Mazaret met Geraine's hard gaze. 'We move now.'

Chapter Seventeen

Revenge begets ruin,
And dreams grow solid,
In the sundered light,
Of the tyrant's night.

Calabos, *Beneath the Towers*, act 2, iv.20

The barge-train moved slowly along the canal towards Oumetra's lock gate, hauled by four well-muscled men. The three barges were laden with sacks of grain, vegetables and fruit, a farewell harvest from the fertile fields of north-east Kejana. A single long tarpaulin covered all three vessels, protecting the cargo from the elements, and in the night gloom the barge-train resembled some huge serpentine creature, the pilot's lamps like oddly askew glowing eyes.

Tauric, Sentinel Kodel and the Armourer were huddled together in a small round boat tied to the heavy hawser that linked the second and third barges. Loosened flaps of tarpaulin hid them from view on either side, but through holes made in the canvas with sharp dagger points they were able to see something of the outside. Kodel and the Armourer were braced against the stern before and the prow behind in an attempt to keep their boat from thumping against the barge hulls.

Tauric could hardly see a thing in the darkness beneath the canopy, and was constantly fighting the nausea brought on by the stench of over-ripe food and the appalling odour of fish-rot rising from the bottom of their boat. The Armourer had acquired it from an unwatched jetty several miles along the riverbank from the northern bridge earlier that day, and it had been a good couple of hours since managing to steal this ride into Oumetra. Tauric was relieved that they were about to enter the city, and looking forward to smelling anything other than cabbages and fishguts.

The barges slowed and Tauric heard voices outside, the pilot exchanging greetings and ribald banter with the lock wardens before the gates opened and they were under way again. Through one of the holes in the tarpaulin he could see the cobbled towpath and the high side of the canal sliding slowly past, lit by an occasional wall lamp. Dark moss and lichen, gleaming with moisture, covered the huge stone blocks of the canal wall, while pale fungal growths sprouted here and there like malformed hands.

Kodel whispered something to the Armourer, then leaned closer to Tauric.

'The barges will be turning into one of the private wharfs very soon,' he said. 'Be ready to push away when I signal.'

Tauric nodded, and watched the two men carefully lift the tarpaulin at one side up and over their heads. Then the Armourer unfastened the rope that bound them to the barge hawser as they heard the pilot's voice again and the creaking of ropes as the barges began to slow. Kodel looked back along the towpath then up ahead for a little longer, then gestured them to push. Momentum took their boat towards the towpath, then strenuous paddling carried them to the foot of stone steps out of sight of the private wharf.

The boat was tied to a rusting iron stanchion and as they climbed up to the towpath Tauric began to hear the muffled sound of many voices shouting somewhere on the other side. At the top of the steps Kodel paused to look around him, sniffing the air.

'Rioters,' he said. 'Armourer, you will remain here and guard the boy while I meet Volyn and decide what our next step shall be.'

'As you say, Sentinel.'

'Use that alcove there. If anyone presents any threat, deal with them as you see fit.' He looked at Tauric. 'We've given you a blade, but you are only to use it if the Armourer tells you to. Otherwise, keep it sheathed and do as you are bid. Is that clear?'

'Yes, sir,' Tauric said nervously.

Kodel gazed at him for a moment, then gave a thin smile. 'It is only my concern for you that makes me direct you thus. Your safety is vital, and once our business here is concluded we can be safely away.'

He nodded sharply to the Armourer, then turned and hurried off into the darkness.

Tauric and the Armourer went over to the alcove, found a couple of discarded crates and were about to settle down to wait when Tauric paused to stare at a big yellow glow coming from behind a large warehouse on the other side of the canal.

'It's a fire,' said the Armourer. 'Someone's house or shop is burning. The riot won't last, however. The Mogaun will be in the city soon, and that will be an end of it. Which is why you should sit and look like you're not involved.'

Pulling his cloak tight about himself, Tauric sat on the crate and waited, trying to imagine what was happening across the canal.

The top floor was deserted. Thick tallow candles in wall niches lit the main corridor along which Mazaret and Havall crept, careful to avoid creaking floorboards as they peered in room after room. But there was not a soul to be found, just a few overturned chairs, half-sewn garments lying draped on benches and tables, and in one room a large unfinished tapestry of a joust on a frame, coloured threads trailing on the floor.

In the rooms at the front of the building they could hear the angry sounds of the crowd in the square outside. News of the unrest had come just as Mazaret and Geraine and his men were reaching the abandoned upper floors of the warehouse next door to the draper's. Geraine had listened to the messenger tell of how a taphouse brawl had spilled into a street off the merchants' quarter then turned into a riot.

'Most of the dog soldiers are over in the Beggar District, having running fights with bands of rogues and outcasts,' the messenger had said, still gasping for breath. 'The other apprentices are heading here to join in. Some are saying they'll put the custom houses to the torch.'

'What about Vaush?' Geraine had said. 'What is he doing?'

Vaush was the commander of the mercenary company.

'No one's seen him, but there's been ragtalk that he left the keep with nearly half his company and he's somewhere in the city.' The messenger coughed. 'Them Mogaun warlocks are still up at the keep, though.'

Geraine had nodded then begun to give orders. He and his men would descend to the square and try to talk some sense into the apprentices, while Havall accompanied Mazaret and Kammer guarded their escape route through the loft.

Mazaret paused on the threshold of the room nearest the landing and the main stairs and sniffed the air. Woodsmoke.

'The fools have set a lumber yard alight,' Havall said quietly from across the corridor. 'The Mogaun can't fail to see it from their camp.'

'If Vaush asks Begrajic to intervene,' Mazaret said, 'how long before they're at the square?'

Havall shrugged. 'Less than a quarter of an hour.' He seemed to come to a decision. 'May I suggest, my lord, that you go down to the next floor by the servants' stairs while I take the main stairway and scout for any guards?'

Mazaret raised an eyebrow. 'Why do I feel that I have little say about such a course of action?'

'Actually, it is none at all,' Havall said cheerily, then he stepped warily out onto the landing and out of sight. Mazaret shook his head and moved off in the other direction.

Down on the fourth floor he strove to be even quieter than before, while seized by a heightened tension between hope that the girl would still be there and fear for the same reason. The discovery that the scion of House Tor-Cavarill was female had struck deep, adding further to the weight of indecision he carried. He felt sick at heart at the thought of killing a young woman purely on the basis of her bloodline, yet he clung to it despite the burning of his shame.

He had listened at and looked in three chambers at the rear of the building and was softly approaching the fourth when he froze, hearing a girl's voice humming a simple tune. Almost at once the humming stopped and swiftly he pushed open the door and stepped inside. The young woman was over in the opposite corner, hands gripping a long, carved tapestry pole, her stance full of readiness and determination.

'I know why you are here,' she said.

She was of a slight physique, slender, almost willowy, her well-proportioned narrow face framed by long, straight golden hair. She could not have seen many more than sixteen summers, yet she had a presence and a dignity beyond her years. And her eyes, so clear and steady, were strangely unsettling.

She tried to strike Mazaret with the pole as he moved towards her, but he caught it effortlessly in one gauntleted hand and wrenched it from her grasp. She flinched but did not cower, and with a trembling stillness stared him in the eye, and for an instant it was as if Suviel was standing there before him, her sad disapproving gaze looking into his inner spirit and seeing the shame there.

And he knew he could not do it. Any vestige of intent to violence evaporated under that courageous regard. He opened his mouth to say something reassuring, to calm her, but the sound of running feet made him turn.

Havall appeared in the doorway, panting for breath, one hand leaning against the frame. 'There were guards down at the front doors, but rioters are getting in through the windows. And I met Kammer on my way back – says he spotted some of Vaush's mercenaries creeping through the warehouse next door, so he's gone down to the back court to find another way out.' He glanced at the girl, and sketched a half bow. 'Milady . . .'

'Havall, we have no time for introductions,' Mazaret said. 'If the situation is as grave as you say, we must leave now.' He held out a hand to the young woman. 'Come with us. I give you my word that no harm will come to you—'

There was a thud and a cry and Mazaret spun round to see Volyn standing over a sprawled and groaning Havall, a club in one hand and a small metal crossbow held in the other, outstretched and pointing straight at Mazaret.

'That I doubt very much.' Volyn regarded Mazaret with a burning stare. 'Drop your blade, my lord. Good. Alael, my dear, we must be gone with all speed. Come to my side, quickly.'

Powerless, Mazaret watched the young woman go over to stand behind the captain.

'Turn around, my lord,' said Volyn, levelling the crossbow at Mazaret's face. 'Now, if you please.'

He did so, the wild impulse to lash out curbed by thoughts of a steel quarrel burying itself in the back of his head. He heard Volyn move closer and say: 'I leave you with the gift of your life. If I see you again, I may take it back.'

Mazaret was listening not to the captain's words but to the sounds of his movements, the creak of his leather boots, the faint clink of a buckle, and the swift rustle of a swinging arm. He bent forward in an attempt to duck, but the club glanced off his head and struck his shield-arm shoulder, throwing him against the wall near the window. Stunned, he slumped to the floor with agony in his shoulder and a sickening nausea surging in his head, and fought to remain conscious.

He heard Volyn mutter something, then footsteps receded. The room swum before him as he opened his eyes and struggled to his feet. He gingerly probed his shoulder and was sure it was not broken despite the painful swelling that was already forming above the shoulder-blade. He went to Havall, still prone in the doorway, but he was out cold so Mazaret recovered his sword from the floor, winced at the stabbing pain in his left temple, and staggered out of the room in pursuit.

*   *   *

Arogal Volyn first felt the touch of destiny at the age of twenty-three as a serjeant in the Seventh Roharkan Echelion, then garrisoned in Sejeend. During an Imperial visit to the city one summer, he had been patrolling a pallisade down by the docks when he saw a dripping form haul itself out of the water almost directly below him. The Emperor and his entourage were alighting with all due ceremony and fanfare and at first Volyn had been seized with panic. Then an astonishing thrill had passed through him as the figure raised a bow and took aim at the very person of the Emperor as he strode across the gantry between his ship and the quayside.

Volyn acted without hesitation, snatched a weighted dagger from his belt and hurled it at the assassin. The dagger caught him between neck and shoulder-blade and the arrow shot off to one side, fell into the water and sank out of sight. And afterwards, after all the confusion and hearty congratulations and bestowing of honours by the city fathers, it was the thrill of that moment that stayed with him, that moment when everything – *everything* – had been in his hands.

The second time was in the terrible dark days just after the Emperor had died at Arengia. The southern provinces had not yet fallen, but with all the Imperial armies of any consequence broken by the Mogaun and their sorcerous allies it was only a matter of time. Arogal Volyn had been in Adnagaur, close to exhaustion after a three-day ride from the battle of Baspur Vale where the Roharkan militias had been crushed by a Mogaun host and flocks of winged horrors called down by the Acolytes of Twilight. In despair he had fled east, back to Cabringa and the provincial capital, and to his family, only to find his brother, Keraun, struck down by sickness and hovering on the brink of death.

There in that room, Volyn learned how the woman his brother had married two years before was a direct descendant of Coulabric Tor-Cavarill, and thus also their child, Alael. With his fading strength, Keraun showed his brother several brittle, yellowed parchments which proved the claim, then begged him to help his wife and child. With the male scions of House Tor-Galantai slain, Keraun asserted that only the line of Tor-Cavarill could now provide a fitting monarch for Khatrimantine. Through his weary sorrow Volyn felt the bright, invigorating touch of destiny once more and vowed to protect his brother's wife and the infant Alael, and to work towards the goal Keraun believed in.

It had all been going so well, the alliance with the Knights of the Fathertree, the growing ties, the detailed planning of the uprising. Then at the eleventh hour came the unexpected, Korregan's bastard son by the Duchess of Patrein. Volyn's support for Tauric was intended to allay any suspicions of ill intent, an apparent burying of the hatchet. So that when Tauric fell into his hands, he was finally free to act according to the fundamental purpose of the Hunter's Children. Once the uprising had begun, the Fathertree Knights would be forced to lend their aid, and if the boy Tauric had to die . . . well, tragic accidents happen in times of war.

These thoughts and others came to his mind as he led Coulabric's girl-heir by her hand out of the draper's back door and across the lightless yard. He shuddered inwardly to think how close he had been to losing the most precious person in all of Khatrimantine. Mazaret's intent could only have been that of murder, and if he had been permitted just a few more seconds with Alael she would be dead and the future would have belonged to a crippled, untutored boy.

All life is a struggle against corruption, Arogal Volyn thought grimly.

There was an acrid taint of smoke in the air and he could hear cries and shouts coming from the square and a clash of swords from the darkened building next door. Volyn felt his smouldering anger flare up at having to abandon one of the Children's most valuable safe houses. The idiot townsmen and Vaush's paid thugs had between them turned Oumetra into a cauldron of malice and resentment, but it was Mazaret and his allies who had almost taken advantage of the situation.

'Have courage, Alael,' he murmured over his shoulder. 'Once across the canal we shall be safe with other friends.'

In the poor light her features were unreadable but the weakness of her grip on his hand and the way she trailed behind him made plain her reluctance. He curbed his annoyance and kept it from showing as he led her across the yard to the corner furthest from the back door. There were a couple of planks missing from the heavy wooden fence and through the gap Volyn was just able to make out the form of one of Geraine's men standing nearby. Gesturing Alael to be silent and still, Volyn flattened himself against the fence and made a hissing sound. After a moment the man's head and shoulders appeared, and Volyn struck a savage blow to his throat. The man gave a choking gasp and collapsed in the opening, half in the yard, half out on the walkway.

'Quickly,' he said to Alael, steering her through the gap. He then bent and dragged the insensible man into the shadowy yard before following her.

Beyond the break Volyn paused to survey their surroundings, the nearby footbridge and the path on the other side of the canal. All seemed to be safely deserted for now. He looked at Alael and beckoned.

'Come – friends await us.'

But she did not move, just stood half turned away from him, her head lowered. He felt his irritation rise again and forced his voice to remain calm as he spoke.

'Alael, right now time is our foe and haste our only ally. We must be gone else our enemies corner us—'

'But what if I do not wish to go, Uncle Volyn? What if I do not wish to become a great queen? Have you never thought to ask me whether that is what I want?'

There was an anguish and a strength in her voice that Volyn had never heard before and while he was angered by her words, part of him was pleased.

'What we want and what we must do are not always the same,' he said in low tones. 'You know who your forebears are, what blood flows in your veins, and what destiny has gifted to you and yours—'

'Yes, I know because you and mother told me.' She gazed out

at the canal, her long hair pale in the darkness. 'You both think you know so much about me,' she said bitterly. 'But you don't. There are things I have which are mine alone. Things which are not destiny's toys!'

Volyn stared at his niece with cold fury in his eyes. She glanced up to see his expression and backed away a step or two.

'*Destiny*? What do *you* know of destiny? You think it to be some grand force, arranging and moving us all like pieces on a game board, like a puppet master pulling a myriad strings?' He shook his head. 'No, no. Destiny is like a mote, or a seed of glory floating across the lands, touching this life or that, drifting here and there like a feather on an endless journey. When it comes to us we have to be ready to grasp it with all our strength, harness it to our will and commit ourselves to the path of greatness . . .' His voice softened. 'When the moment comes, choices become stark and some things, precious things, have to be discarded so that the seed of destiny can grow unhindered. I wish you could see that . . .'

She had not altered her stance but there was a hint of uncertainty in the way she bit her lower lip. Volyn sighed, spread his hands and stepped closer.

'But perhaps you are right. I'm getting old, and sometimes I forget what it is to be young and at the start of life.' He laid a gentle but firm hand on her shoulder and turned her to face him. 'I only have one thing to ask of you.'

'What is it, Uncle?'

'Forgive me,' he said and with his other hand in a fist quickly struck her on the jaw, just heavily enough to stun her. As she went limp he caught her and lifted her onto his shoulder, then hurried along to the footbridge.

Startled by sounds of fighting, several birds darted from the eaves of the building next door in a burst of fluttering wings, like shadow rags flitting and wheeling among greater shadows. Volyn was almost at the other side of the bridge with his burden when he heard soft, swift footsteps come up behind him. Turning, he fumbled for the crossbow with his free hand,

then went still as he looked round at the point of a sword raised
to his face.

'Carefully place the girl on the walk,' said Ikarno Mazaret, pale
eyes cold and angry beneath dishevelled grey hair.

Volyn did so, bending with Alael cradled so that her head did
not strike the wooden fencing. She moaned, eyes fluttering open.
Volyn straightened and, with his gaze still on her, took a half
step sideways towards Mazaret then brought his elbow round in
a sharp arc, knocking the sword aside. With a growl of triumph,
he swung his other fist with his full weight. Mazaret sidestepped
the oncoming blow, grabbed Volyn's upper arm and pushed him
across the bridge. Volyn struck the bridge's wooden handrail, it
broke under the impact and he fell through the air, plunging into
the freezing canal.

The water seemed to suck the warmth from his bones as he
struggled to the surface. Shaking drops from his head, he heard
footsteps receding and his rage filled him as he shucked off his
cloak and swam over to a rusty iron ladder near the bridge.
Uttering a string of curses, he began to climb. He pictured in
his mind all the agonies and indignities he would inflict upon
Mazaret, alongside his fear for Alael. He was almost at the top of
the ladder when a hand came down, grasped his arm and pulled
him up. Back on the canalside he squeezed water from his eyes
and looked into the grim visage of his lieutenant, Kodel.

Relief surged through him. 'Sentinel! I cannot express my savage
joy at the sight of you here. Coulabric's heir is in gravest danger,
taken from me by the leader of those petty knights. Now there
are two of us and if we are quick we can yet retrieve what is—'

He stepped forward but Kodel put out a hand and shoved him
backwards. Volyn was astonished then furious.

'What is the meaning of this?'

Kodel gave a sneer of contempt. 'What a blustering, blundering
oaf you have been, you and that clanking relic Mazaret. Now
neither of you have the girl – she was up and off like the wind
before he could lay a hand on her.'

'I don't believe you.'

Kodel shrugged. 'I care not. For you are a fool, captain, and you will die a fool's death.'

Volyn tore his heavy broadsword from its sheath with a metallic hiss, and spat on the stone flags. 'Treacherous dog! I'll split your face like a rotten cabbage!'

Kodel's only reply was a slight smile as, in a single leisurely movement, he unsheathed his narrower blade and attacked. Instantly Volyn knew that he was staring at his death, and was barely able to parry the cascade of lightning-fast thrusts and cuts. Kodel hardly seemed under strain at all, his every blow and feint seemingly effortless while Volyn was fighting with everything he had.

He could not outfight Kodel, or outrun him along this canal, so his only chance of survival was to make a break for the bridge in the hope that he could get back to the draper's and out among the crowd. Then the opening came – he beat Kodel's sword back with a flurry of furious blows then spun on his heel and dashed towards the bridge, heart hammering in his chest, and grabbed the wooden rail to swing himself round onto the span.

He was just a few steps across when he felt the sword enter his back low down and to one side, a flare of agony and the sense of deep, terrible damage. He staggered then slumped to his knees, sword hilt slipping from weak fingers, his other hand barely able to hold himself up. There were steps nearby and a figure standing over him. He felt something hot pouring down his side then his arm gave way and he was aware of being pushed between the posts of the railing.

Great Father forgive me . . . Alael forgive me, he thought as he fell from the bridge. *Who will protect you . . . ?*

And for the second time he was engulfed by the canal's dark and icy waters.

Chapter Eighteen

Thus the Nytebear prowls and roars,
'Neath fullest moon and blackest nyte,
Whilst the Skyhorse stalks in stealth,
Hiding her wings and greatest might.

Temple carving from northern Khatris, trans. Antil Fehris

Tauric shivered in the cold and coughed quietly, trying to clear his throat of the irritating reek of burning. In the quarter-hour since Kodel's departure, the fires Tauric had seen earlier seemed to have spread and a haze of smoke now blanketed the area. Gauzy light haloed a scattering of canalside lamps and the reflected glow from the square behind the high buildings across the canal was a dull, sullen orange.

He and the Armourer sat within the alcove in silence. He knew from past experience how fruitless it was to try and engage the big, impassive man in anything resembling pleasant conversation. Instead he rested as best he could with his damp cape held closed across his chest and stared into the dark shadows further along the canal towards the centre of Oumetra, the direction in which Kodel had gone.

But after their long journey from the forest of Falador, it was not easy to stay alert and he found himself having to stifle yawn after yawn. He dozed a moment or two, and then the massed sound of wings, mingled with a shrill piping, startled him fully awake and he jerked in surprise as a small cloud of birds sped past, some only feet away. In wonder Tauric leaned out of the alcove and watched them wheel in unison like a single creature, climbing higher above the city, with other birds joining the flock as it rose still higher till they were lost to sight. He smiled as he looked back at the Armourer, who had apparently missed the entire spectacle. That was when he first spotted the girl running towards them along the side of the canal.

Her long hair flew like a banner as she came on, hair so pale it was almost white. Tauric found himself staring as she neared, as her features grew more distinct in the weak light. A taut feeling uncoiled within him, like the hollow panic brought on by teetering over an abyss, except there was more – expectation, fascination and recognition.

He recalled the abandoned mill and the vision that had assailed him in his sleep, the armoured warriors who fell apart when he struck them and the one whose helm he wrenched away to reveal a woman with long white hair and eyes like starpoints . . .

The girl caught sight of him and slowed, staring directly at him. Her hair, he saw, was very light brown and her eyes were quite normal. But it was her, he was certain. He stepped out of the alcove towards her, ignoring the Armourer's grunt of disapproval, and her expression became fearful, her mouth gaping, one hand outstretched in denial.

'No,' she whispered. Then louder: 'No!' And she broke into a run again, rushing past Tauric and off down the canal towards a footbridge.

Seized by a nameless need Tauric looked back at the Armourer, who was now on his feet, beckoning him to return to his side. Then another figure emerged from the darkness at a run – the Lord Commander Mazaret.

'After her, boy! Stop her! *Help* her . . .'

'No!' said the Armourer. 'You must stay here.' And he seemed about to draw his own blade when he recognized the Lord Commander. Tauric shrugged at him, and dashed off in pursuit of the girl with his own sword at the ready.

Up ahead, the girl tripped and fell and he heard her cry out in pain. But she got to her feet and ran to the footbridge, paused for an instant to look back at him then ran across. Tauric could hear the Lord Commander's own labouring pace behind him as he reached the bridge, feet hammering on the heavy wooden planks.

On the other side the girl ran straight on, up a sloping alley which curved to the right and away, Tauric hoped, from the square. Perhaps she thought to lose him in the maze of back ways, but she was visibly tiring and he was rapidly closing.

Then she turned the curve into the shadows between high walls and vanished from view. He pushed himself faster, hand grasping the brickwork at the corner for purchase as he hurtled round in time to see her dart into an archway on the left. Panting for breath he got there a second or two later and plunged on, leaping down a row of stone steps, through an ivy-choked opening and out to a dim alley, only to be confronted by a calamitous sight. The girl was sprawled in the mud, her legs trapped by a tanglenet while a man in black leather armour, maybe a city guard, was walking towards her, raising a spear to strike.

Without pause, Tauric threw himself at the guard. The guard saw movement and started to turn, but Tauric slammed into his shoulder and both crashed to the ground. He had his blade ready, holding it like a dagger, and in rage and fear he drove it between the man's shoulders. The guard let out a bellow of agony that reverberated around them, convulsed in agony.

Tauric let go the hilt of his blade and scrambled over to the girl. The guard's death throes, a horrible writhing accompanied by a gasping for breath, lasted a few seconds before he slumped into immobility. There was a roaring and a cheering and only then did Tauric realize that the fight had had scores of witnesses.

He and the girl were at the end of the alleyway, where it opened into the corner of the square. Fires were burning at the other side of the square, and crowds of townspeople armed with poles and axes were gathered around a large dais improvised from crates and furniture upon which was a pile of bodies, nearly all wearing a heavy black leather armour.

Rioters danced over the corpses, or spat on them from the sides.

As Tauric worked to help free his companion from the tanglenet, a couple of slatternly market women came over.

'Are you well, dearie? That's a nasty cut, that is . . .'

'I'll – I am in good shape,' he said, confused by their looks of awe, then looked down to see that the leather sleeve had come adrift and his steel arm was showing. He started to pull it back up, but resumed cutting at the tanglenet's fine fibres.

'You should have stayed away,' the girl said sullenly. 'I was in no danger.'

For a moment Tauric was speechless, then inexplicably angry. 'No danger? Then what was he about to do with that spear – go rat hunting?'

She shook her head, and Tauric thought he saw a little of the strange fear from before creep back into her eyes.

'Please,' she said. 'Leave me alone. Take care of yourself instead—'

An awful scream cut through the din, and voices began shouting: 'The Mogaun are in the city! They're in the square!' In seconds, utter pandemonium ensued, mobs of people running away to the main thoroughfares leading out of the square, or into buildings which offered some safety, however meagre. Some stayed to construct hasty barricades in street entrances or doorways from upturned carts and any looted furniture, while a handful dashed by Tauric and down the alley. Then a column of riders entered the far side of the square at a canter. After a moment or two, the Mogaun split into several groups and attacked the strongest pockets of resistance first.

'We have to get away from here,' Tauric said to the girl, but she gave no reply, instead looking behind them along the alleyway. He glanced over his shoulder and saw three figures coming slowly towards them out of the darkness at the end of the alley. They were dragging their feet as they walked, heads hung low, and as they emerged from the shadows he recognized them as some of the townsfolk who had fled past them just moments before.

Then they looked up and Tauric gasped in horror – each face had black pits where eyes had once been, empty sockets which sought out Tauric and the girl and guided their deathly owners onward. The market women shrieked and fled, long skirts lifted clear of their feet.

The girl tugged Tauric wordlessly by the arm, but first he retrieved his blade then backed away with her. He glanced at the opening he had come through just moments before and saw the Armourer and the Lord Commander battling another five living corpses armed with clubs. Who could have done this, he thought, brought these unfortunates to life and sent them to fight? Tauric could almost taste his own fear, and found himself trembling all the way from his stomach to his extremities, all except his metal arm, its cold and still hand holding his sword in a level, unwavering grip. It became his anchor as they retreated up the alley towards the square and the awful screaming clamour of the battle.

'The square is too dangerous. We'll have to run past them,' whispered the girl as the three eyeless townspeople came nearer and nearer. 'They don't look able to keep up with us . . .'

'I wish I could be that sure,' Tauric said, teeth on edge.

'Then I'll distract them while you attack them from the side.' And she darted back along the alley, snatched up the spear dropped by the guard earlier and managed to dance away from grasping hands that lunged for her. And, Tauric saw in disbelief, she was grinning as she fended off her attackers. *Mad*, he thought wildly, *she is completely mad*. And raised his sword and rushed to the attack.

But there seemed to be little they could do to harm those who were already dead. Hacked and slashed by blade, or pierced and bludgeoned by spear, they still lumbered back into the fray, forcing the two youngsters away from the alley entrance and out into the square. Tauric could now heard the racket of fighting coming clearly from all around, and feared the sound of approaching hooves. Every joint ached and it seemed that he was covered in a multitude of scrapes, cuts and bruises. Their opponents looked worse with deep gashes, missing fingers, and the other terrible mutilations Tauric and his companion had been forced to inflict in self-defence.

Then the girl's spear broke. She stepped back, lost her footing and fell. At once, one of the dead leaped at her. Instinctively, Tauric brought his blade down on the attacker's exposed neck and severed the head. Bloodless, the body collapsed in the dust and Tauric grabbed the girl by the hand and dragged her along the side of a building, searching for an open door. The other two took a few steps in pursuit, then stopped. Confusion passed over their ruined features for second before each let out a single, soul-wrenching howl and fell to the ground.

And behind them, just emerging from the alley's shadows, were three Mogaun warriors. They were smaller and older than others Tauric had seen, and wore strings of bones and feathers over shapeless fur garments. Long grey braids framed wizened faces full of bright hate, and eyes that were trained on Tauric.

'The Mogaun shamans,' whispered the girl as Tauric helped her to her feet. 'Oh no, they musn't—'

Three pairs of leathery hands rose chest high, long-nailed fingers crooked as if grasping something unseen. The shamans moved their lips in unison, muttering a continual stream of guttural syllables. Tauric felt the hairs on his neck and head prickle as he pushed and hammered madly on a door he had found, to no avail. Then the shamans stamped the ground and threw their hands outwards in Tauric's direction.

Tauric was engulfed in a ghastly emanation of power. Strength drained from his limbs and he sank to his knees, his mind racked by a pulling and a tugging as if by claws that searched his very thoughts. This was a horror beyond imagining, in a way worse than the tortures he had suffered at the hands of Byrnak. He wanted to cry out, to somehow let his pain pour out but he was helpless and senseless, crushed beneath a torrent, an ocean of lead and stone . . .

Suddenly, light penetrated the grey veil, the torment fell away and he felt himself being lifted to his feet. A hand on his arm,

his steel arm. The girl. A peculiar radiance cloaked her, and he
heard her sob as she raised his metal arm and pointed it at the
three startled shamans. Through her quiet weeping she began to
whisper a series of strange words over and over and over till he
began hearing them in his own mind like a single bell chiming.
In one instant he was staring at the Mogaun, blinking the sweat
from his eyes, and in the next a pure white fire erupted from his
hand and spewed across the intervening space.

The shamans burned. Writhing and screaming, they tried to
struggle free of their furs but the fire wrapped itself around their
forms, hungrily devouring them.

'I'm sorry, I'm so sorry,' the girl was babbling. 'I didn't want
this, and I don't want to be . . .' She paused, both hands pulling
him closer. 'I'm sorry, but I have to do this . . .'

He tried to turn towards her but she was whispering again and
the words were like tiny silver birds which entered his head, their
wings striking against the inside of his skull, making it ring like
a cave of glass. Tauric was staring into her reddened, tear-wet
eyes when a blinding light filled his head and wiped her from
his sight.

The next thing he saw was a dozen Mogaun riders galloping
straight for him across the square, feathers fluttering from the
points of spears couched at him. The night seemed like day, and
the riders wavered as if seen through water, yet Tauric felt as if
his body was strong and heavy, his feet planted solidly on the
ground. He could see such details, such a vividness in everything,
individual hairs of soft rich brown and deep iron black in the
furs the warriors wore, or the sheen of firelight reflected from the
hammered texture of the crude leaf mail they wore. The blinding
light shifted within him and his metal arm sang. Suddenly the
riders let go their spears and weapons, some toppling to the ground
to scrape and claw at their scalps, while the rest of the horses halted
in their charge and began leaping and bucking wildly to dislodge
those still hanging on.

A demented joy filled Tauric as he strode around the square,
giving himself over to the whispering light, letting it do its

work, and staring in fascination at what he wrought. Groups of warriors rushed him and were thrust back dead or wounded, blood jewelling their limbs or the ground. Hard-pressed defenders in the barricaded positions around the square hoarsely cheered him as he dispensed retribution with the hot white power which blazed around his steel arm. One heedlessly brave Mogaun climbed the outside of a shop front to leap on him from above, but the light in his head saw it before he did, caught the assailant and hurled him across the square and through the shutters of an upper storey window.

'You cannot harm me!' he shouted.

This is not you, screamed a voice inside himself. *You are not doing this – this is being done to you . . .*

The light began to dim. The words in his mind grew slower and deeper. Then he saw some of the defenders clambering over their barricades and was confused for a moment or two before he saw the surviving Mogaun horsemen regrouping at the other side. It seemed that they were preparing for another charge, then they turned and rode from the square. Cheers and triumphant shouting went up all around, but Tauric felt as though everything was falling away from him. The light in his head was guttering now and the vividness of things was blurred, losing all presence and beauty. He had been filled beyond his limits and was now emptying to the dregs of his spirit.

Tauric's legs gave way and he slumped to a sprawled sitting position. He heard someone calling his name, the broken word only making sense after being repeated several times. The words in his head were grave and stately now, tones of finality, of resolution. A man in leather armour crouched down before him, a slender, middle-aged man with grey hair and blood oozing from cuts on his brow and cheek. The Lord Commander Mazaret, he realized dully. Then he began wondering about the girl – he still didn't know her name, yet she was important somehow . . .

Then his grasp of his surroundings dissolved and blackness took him down into nothingness.

*   *   *

While the physician attended to the arrow wound in his shoulder, Mazaret sat in a heavily ornate chair by the audience chamber's window, gazing out at the city of Oumetra. It had been raining, and noon sunlight was edging through breaks in the cloud, making the city shine. The audience chamber was high up in the Great Keep and from where he sat Mazaret could see the massive structures of the city's founders and the lesser, frailer buildings which clustered around them. And if he leaned forward a little he could see the crowds still gathered in the courtyard below, all hoping for a glimpse of the youth who had performed wonders at what was becoming known as the Battle of Imperial Square.

Frowning, he sat back, provoking an agonizing twinge in his shoulder.

'My lord,' said the physician in exasperation. 'I cannot work if you keep moving thus—'

'Good ser, you have been burrowing in my arm for half the morning. What do you hope to find?'

The physician was a slender, ascetic man with a neatly trimmed grey beard and moustache, and he wore a long, rich yellow robe embroidered in red at the collar and cuffs. He gave the Lord Commander a vaguely disappointed look. 'With respect, my lord, the arrow head shattered on piercing your armour but the shaft drove tiny shards of flint deep into the flesh. I have extracted several fragments but still have others to recover. May I advise another mouthful or two of the fraol?'

Mazaret scowled and raised to his lips a silver flask chased with hunting scenes and took a swallow. The powerful Dalbari liquor coursed down into his stomach and a pleasant warmth spread through him.

'A fine vintage.'

'Our former lord, the esteemed Vaush, thought so too,' the physician murmured drily. 'How sad that he remains missing.'

'Not any longer,' said another voice. 'We found a gang of beggar boys playing kick-and-catch with his head a hour ago.'

The last time Mazaret had seen Kodel had been in the early hours of the morning, shortly after the Mogaun made their final, half-hearted assault on the main gate. Then, he had been wearing gashed, blood-stained leather armour and the torn remnants of a rider's cape, and his hair had been wild and dishevelled. Now he wore finer clothing, an armless black jerkin over a pale yellow shirt with dark brown leggings tucked into high boots. His long black hair was oiled and tied back in a warrior's topknot, accentuating his long face and hawkish features. A cavalry sabre hung on his left hip and a simple dagger was strapped to the right calf.

'And the whereabouts of this trophy?' Mazaret said, offering him the flask.

Kodel grinned. 'Hanging over the main gates, right next to Begrajic's ugly head.'

'What of the rest of Begrajic's warband? Do we know where they are going?'

'Geraine's scouts say that they rode north along the shore of Lake Audagal, as if heading for their northern encampment, then doubled back along the Redway. They were last seen riding full tilt towards Hargas.'

Mazaret nodded. Hargas was an important fishing port whose Mogaun overlord was Vasegd, half-brother to Begrajic. Vasegd would be sure to be enraged at the death of his brother and would hurry to move against Oumetra.

At his side the physician made a satisfied sound, and when Mazaret glanced round he saw the man folding away a small white pad of cloth on which lay a cluster of tiny black slivers.

'That is the last of it, my lord,' he said, wrapping a dainty pair of silver tongs and other instruments away in waxed velvet. He applied an ash-grey salve to the wound, bandaged the area with strips of fine linen, then packed all his impedimenta away in the pockets of his long ochre coat.

'I would advise rest for at least a week, my lord,' he said. 'And the dressings to be changed twice a day. If pain returns after a week, or the wound begins to weep or smell malodorous, call me at once.' And with a grave bow, he left.

There was silence for a short while. Mazaret watched Kodel

sample the fraol, sluicing it around in his mouth before swallowing it and regarding the flask with an approving nod.

'Clothing belonging to the honoured Captain Volyn has just been recovered from the canal,' Kodel said after a moment. 'No body has yet been found, nor have there been any reports or sightings of him from elsewhere in the city. Until his remains are found, or he reappears safe and well, I am forced to assume his responsibilities.'

'I understand,' Mazaret said, uncomfortably reminded of the struggle he had had with Volyn on the footbridge the previous night, but also recalling a glimpse of the man paddling towards the canal bank. 'I share your concern. In the meantime I think we should talk about the girl – her name is Alael, am I correct, of House Tor-Caverill? And she can use the Lesser Power in a way I have never heard of before.'

Kodel seemed not to have heard, just stood looking out of the window for a moment. Then: 'Has Tauric Tor-Galantai remembered anything more about what occurred at the square?'

'No. He can recall very little from when the girl Alael began using him as some kind of vessel for her talent.' Mazaret regarded the other man with a frown. 'However, he did tell me how you helped and protected him since leaving Krusivel. Why would you do all that for a boy who has no mage ability when the Hunter's Children have been hiding a girl who has?'

A gleam of something close to anger came into Kodel's eyes. 'For the simple reason that I knew nothing of it. Whenever Volyn spoke of her to his senior officers it was in the broadest terms and he made no mention of such powers. But I believe that not even he knew – he and I had many private discussions and while he told me a great deal about Alael and her past, he never so much as hinted at anything to do with the Lesser Power.'

'There has been no sign of her anywhere?'

'Nothing, no witnesses or rumours. I visited our sanctuaries across the canal and had them all searched, to no avail.'

Mazaret listened closely, and something in the words sent doubt threading through him despite the steady sincerity in the man's words. 'How convenient, careless even, for you to be afflicted by two disappearances. You don't think it possible that someone in your faction is concealing her from us?'

Kodel gave him a savage look. 'The stench of your suspicions is overwhelming, my lord, yet I will not be provoked by sneering words. Know that the loyalty and obedience of all of the Children's attendants and agents is unquestioned. If you have any genuine challenges to make then speak out. But before you do, remind yourself of where you were when the honoured captain fell into the canal.'

Stung by the scarcely veiled accusation, Mazaret was on his feet in a second and about to reply when a burst of loud cheering came from outside. Both men turned to stare down at the thousands of townspeople now crammed into the Great Keep's courtyard and the figure who stood on the wide balcony overlooking them all.

It was Geraine. The slender man raised his hands and gestured for quiet, and the mass of voices died away to nothing.

'My friends – for a decade and a half we have suffered invasion and the torments of barbaric oppression. How many of us have lost those dear to us in these long years of darkness? Who has not been touched by grief and loss? Who among us did not feel despair when brave Gunderlek fell in Yularia, and ached with the desire to fight back, to somehow even the scales of justice?' His voice lowered. 'We have waited for such a long time for something, a ray of hope, a sign, any kind of victory. And in a single night all of that came to pass! For that which we thought gone forever has returned, the bloodline which the Mogaun and their foul allies tried to extinguish at Arengia has come blazing back to life!' A buzz of excitement rose from the crowd and Geraine smiled. 'I can say no more. Let him speak for himself.'

Geraine strode over to a broad curtained archway at the rear of the balcony and stood to one side. Horns sounded from upper windows, three short blasts, and two attendants emerged from the curtain, each carrying a large banner bearing a white tree on a dark blue background. Mazaret felt a thrill of joyful recognition, and heard astonished mutters ripple through the crowd, some of disbelief, others of ecstatic anticipation. It was the symbol of the Khatrimantine emperors, its depiction forbidden on pain of death these sixteen years. Then the horns sounded again, the archway curtains parted and Tauric stepped into view. He looked at Geraine who bowed his head, and a thunderous roar erupted from the crowd. Hats were tossed in the air, people cheered and sang and hugged each other as Tauric walked up to the balcony railing. He wore a simple tunic and trews of pure sky blue, the attire of a priest of the Fathertree. The tunic's short sleeves left his arms bare and his metal one lacked the leather covering so that it gleamed in the sun.

He raised his other hand for silence and slowly the clamour subsided. An utter peace held sway for some brief moments during which he stood and surveyed the sea of hopeful faces before him. Mazaret began to fear that the lad's confidence had broken, then Tauric spoke in a voice trembling with emotion.

'My father would have been so proud of you!'

The roar of cheers and stamping and shouts was tumultuous and died down only after several moments.

'The battle we fought yesterday is only the beginning, and once word of it travels outwards from Oumetra then others will know that the time of freedom is at hand. From the mountains of Dalbar to the plains of Roharka, people will rise up and throw off the chains that have bound them for so long. You will need leaders, great leaders like Geraine, whom you all know so well, and Lord Mazaret, commander of the Knights of the Fathertree, a man who fought at my father's side at Arengia and who is among us this day.' He broke off as shouts went up naming himself, hands outstretched and pointing up at him, and he shook his head. 'I am but a youth and only recently come into the full knowledge of my heritage—'

The shouts grew more vociferous, demands and pleas that he lead them. Watching, Mazaret muttered: 'Accept the role, lad.'

'He will, my lord,' said Kodel at his side. 'He must.'

Tauric bowed his head a little, raised his hand and spoke over the noise. 'If it is your will that I play a leading part, then so be it. But others shall direct the strategy of our rebellion and ensure victory. Together we shall become the Mogaun bane, and their vicious grasp shall be cast off forever . . .'

A small group near the foot of the balcony began chanting 'Emperor Tauric! Emperor Tauric!' Tauric shook his head impatiently, gesturing sharply at them with his real hand.

'No! I am not the Emperor,' he said fiercely. 'Nor will I lay claim to such a title until all our lands are free and the enemy has been vanquished.'

Mazaret stared in amazement, seeing in the youth the same commanding nobility that his father had possessed, and seeing belief and bright hope kindling in the faces of all those below. There was something almost dreamlike about the scene, as if the entire throng of Oumetrans was entranced by Tauric's straightforward honesty and direct words.

'Now,' Tauric said, suddenly seeming to tire, 'return to your homes and your hearths, rest, and offer prayers to the Earthmother. The days ahead will be hard and full of struggle.' He paused, gazing slowly from side to side and out across the great crowd. 'But we shall prevail. Be ready.' He raised one hand, his metal one, almost in a half-salute, and as the crowd roared his name he walked away from the balcony and went back inside the keep. Mazaret shook his head, simultaneously amazed and delighted and even a little unsettled.

'An astounding speech,' he said. 'I would not have thought Geraine able to frame such words.'

'It wasn't Geraine,' Kodel said.

Mazaret stared at him and the Sentinel met his gaze with one eyebrow arched. 'You seem surprised, my lord.'

'I cannot deny it – I am.'

'There is no mystery. My parents were well educated and greatly fond of masques, plays and other forms of stagecraft, so it was inevitable that I gained certain skills.'

Both men still stood at the window, one at either side. Below, some parts of the crowd were still chanting while others began to disperse. From this vantage Mazaret could see right across the roofs of Oumetra to the far-off Rukang Mountains. Their peaks were veiled in low cloud and a wall of rain which was darkening by the minute.

'Tauric told me how you rescued him from my brother and the old man,' Mazaret said quietly, eyes fixed on the approaching downpour. 'Did you question Coireg about the incident before you came here? I want to know why he did such a thing.'

'There is little to tell,' said Kodel. 'The man who played his servant was an agent of this Ystregul, the one who calls himself Shadowking. He drew your brother into petty smuggling near Casall, then enslaved him with vile potions like clawseed. Such drugs affect the mind and cause the growth of dark obsessions – in his case he believes that he is responsible for your father's death. I know nothing of his past, but he is now a broken reed.' There was a pause. 'He is under constant guard at our holding at Grinok, but if you wish him taken to Krusivel . . .'

Mazaret tiredly rubbed his chin, then shook his head. 'It would be better to leave him in your charge for now, while we deal with other more pressing matters. The Mogaun warlords will not let our challenge go unanswered, despite the gathering at Arengia. It is time to move swiftly.'

'I agree, and to that end I have already dispatched messenger birds to the stewards of the Children's strongholds, countermanding the orders they recently received.'

'And the matter of the honoured Captain Volyn?'

Kodel shrugged. 'He has not been found, nor has he come forward. However, we have yet to undertake a thorough search of the canal itself – it is possible that he may be lying wounded somewhere. But I fear the worst.'

'So it is your wish to reinstate the alliance between the Hunter's Children and the Knights of the Fathertree?'

'I see no prospect of victory otherwise, my lord.'

'It gladdens my heart to hear your words, honoured captain.' He put out his hand and the two leaders shook hands with a warrior's grasp. A feeling of elation came over Mazaret, chasing away his sombreness, and he turned to stare out at the far lands once more.

'We will topple these bandits from power,' he said. 'The spirit of the Earthmother will be felt again, and those dog-sorcerers will hear our battle-cry and tremble!'

Then the moment was past and the ache of his shoulder wound brought him back to present necessities.

'For now, however, I too will have to despatch messages, to Krusivel and other places. The first will be to our agents in and near Hargas.' He grinned. 'I think that Vasegd will become too busy to devote much time to us. So, where is the birdloft you used?'

'There is one here in the keep, my lord. Follow me – I know the way.'

Part Three

Chapter Nineteen

Power amid the darkness
Can tear souls asunder
And reforge them anew.

The Book of Earth and Stone

Keren Asherol felt as if she had been climbing the steep hill-path for most of her life, yet there was still strength in her legs and breath in her chest. It was the rhythm of it, the regular foot-by-foot progress, which seemed to sustain her. The path ran between a stream running swift below a sheer mass of rock to her left and dark, impenetrable woods to her right. The pure smells of the hillside filled her nose and mouth, and roused a dormant hunger and thirst. She was about to pause and suggest a brief rest when a pack of Wellbeasts emerged from the trees up ahead.

'Let them cover three-quarters of the distance then move aside,' came Orgraaleshenoth's voice from behind her.

There was a feeling of tightening pressure around her throat, and with teeth gritted she nodded. In the four days since Suviel's and Gilly's sorcerous banishment, the Daemonkind prince had never missed an opportunity to remind her, with his invisible tether, who was the master and who was the slave. After the first few instances of punishment by pain or choking, she had quickly learned not to antagonize her captor by word or deed. *Stay alive*, was the thought she harboured. *Survive.*

She set her feet apart and readied her blade as the Wellbeasts loped and scuttled and galloped towards her. There was no brandishing of spears or knives, for these monsters were animal in origin. Keren shuddered to recall some of the twisted and formerly human horrors they had encountered since crossing into Prekine.

The fear and elation of battle alertness gripped her as the beasts came on. When they were just yards away she dived to one side, right to the stream's edge. A couple of the creatures swerved towards her in their blundering rush, and the nearest, a grotesque amalgam of dog and crow, howled as it leaped at her. In the next instant it fell screaming and writhing, innards spilling from its cloven underside. Keren uttered a snarl of satisfaction as she wheeled to face the other attacker, a cadaverous wolf from whose shoulders sprang the upper torso of a wildcat. Spitting and shrieking, it charged. Keren twisted away, meaning to behead the wolf-thing, but lost her balance as her boots slid over wet stones in the stream. She staggered back and the beast would have been upon her if it too had not slipped. As it struggled to regain its feet, Keren moved in closer with one lightning-fast slash to its throat and it collapsed in quickly fading convulsions, its blood mingling with the waters.

Chest heaving, she turned to see Orgraaleshenoth in human form, tall and robed to the ankles, mouth wearing a savage grin as he fended off half a dozen attackers with another handful lying dead at his feet. The beasts swarmed about him, snapping and caterwauling, then fell back as the Daemonkind prince made a wide and deadly sweep with his blade, a long, straight two-handed sword. Keren hacked at one, a boar with snake heads sprouting from its back, and when it went down in a ghastly welter of blood and brains the others recoiled in panic.

A bloodlust came over her and she found herself laughing and shouting as she slashed at the retreating creatures. She cut one down with a single disembowelling thrust, hacked the legs from under another and was about to dash after the rest when suddenly she was gasping for breath. The grip around her throat tightened, her vision grew hazy, her lungs cried out for air. She fell to her knees, mouthing silent pleas.

'Self-control, child of earth,' came the Daemonkind's voice. He was standing over her, wiping gore from his longsword with a handful of grass. 'Even in the heat of battle, your obedience to me must be total. Indiscipline does not serve my purpose.'

Then the terrible grip eased and blessed air surged in. Tears sprang to her eyes as she coughed and choked on a rawness in her throat. Deep, rough breaths shuddered through her and she swallowed to make saliva in her mouth. Aware of Orgraaleshenoth walking away, she angrily wiped the wetness from her eyes then lurched to her feet, snatched up her fallen blade and followed.

Under a murky afternoon sky, they trod the path as it twisted deeper into Prekine. Rain fell in furious bursts that lashed and buffeted them then passed, leaving a bitter odour in the air. Once, they sheltered beneath an overgrown spiraleaf tree and while waiting for the deluge to ease off Keren spotted a nest among the foliage. It held two eggs, both smashed, and a dead chick, and it was then that she realized that she had not heard a single birdcall for two, maybe three days. But then, perhaps she had been too engulfed by despair to notice.

The hills steepened around them, slopes smothered in gorse and thorny vines. Ahead, their destination grew ever nearer, the Oshang Dahkal, a rough semicircle of peaks and ridges rising from low, rounded hills in the north to a cluster of crags and jagged heights in the south. It was there nearly two thousand years ago that Orosiada had ordered the founding of the communities and academies which became the mage stronghold of Trevada. Keren had visited it only once at the age of twelve, accompanying her parents on a pilgrimage, and her memories were coloured by impressions of jostling crowds and a long road which curved all the way up to the spires and courts of the High Basilica.

But those were memories from a time of gladness and joy, of brightness and innocence. As she trudged along behind Orgraaleshenoth in the shadows between these empty hills it was as if all the darkness was becoming part of her, seeping

into her soul and allowing not a glimmer of hope. She wanted
to weep but would not let herself.

Stay alive. Show no weakness. Survive.

It was not until the dusk was settling like a veil across the land
that she noticed how cold it was becoming. She donned another
tunic over the one she already wore and pulled on a second pair
of breeks, and still she was shivering. Orgraaleshenoth seemed to
show not a hint of discomfort, but her breath was now a visible
plume of vapour and she could feel an unnatural iciness nipping
at her toes and fingers. She thought of the rumours and warnings
she had heard about Prekine in recent years, some of which she
had already verified with her own eyes. Some tales spoke of dread
spells of ice laid upon the earth, or dense, impenetrable tangles of
talonvine which choked the dales and hills and encircled Trevada
itself. She would have asked the Daemonkind but feared his
response.

It was nightfall when they happened upon a village tucked
away in a hollow between two hills, next to a small, marshy
lake. In the dimness, the lake was a flat stretch of blackness,
the cottages and barns no more than a cluster of silhouettes.
There were no signs of life, no lamplight or voices, no crying
of babes or sounds of barnyard animals. As they approached the
nearest cottage, Orgraaleshenoth held out his sword and made a
gesture over it. A pale blue radiance brightened around it and he
advanced towards the door, pushing it open.

Within, the air was so bitterly cold that Keren's teeth ached
with every breath and a deep shivering seized her. The ensorcelled
blade sent a feeble light into the single large room where still forms
lay huddled together under blankets before a dead hearth. The
body of a man lay curled up on the floor next to that of a dog,
and another sat at a crude table, head resting on one arm with
the other hand outstretched and grasping a dagger. Frost lay over
them all and everything else in the room, a glittering, preserving
mantle. Death was tangible here, and Keren backed away to the
door's threshold, watching Orgraaleshenoth bend to examine the
bodies, brushing frost from this face or that hand, pressing or

prodding the frozen flesh. And Keren remembered the healer tents at Alvergost and how the Daemonkind prince had tended to the sick and the wounded, and wondered at the reason for such a meticulously impersonal scrutiny.

The scene was repeated in several other cottages, Keren standing in the doorway blowing on her hands while Orgraaleshenoth moved among the dead. Her own vaporous breath floated around her in the still air like a grey aura, while the Daemonkind's exhalations came in long, heavy plumes. On their return from the spectral domain of Kekrahan, Orgraaleshenoth had resumed the human form Keren had known as Raal Haidar but now that outward appearance was like an ill-fitting costume, strained at the seams by the brute force of what lay beneath.

According to the sagas and the prayer songs, the Daemonkind were the Lord of Twilight's oldest and most powerful servants, creatures which emerged from the Great Lake of the Night in the wake of the birth of the world. The Lord of Twilight caught sight of them despite the engulfing darkness, perceived their potential and offered them a place at his side in exchange for a deep oath of eternal loyalty. Each and every one of them swore the oath, binding themselves and their descendants, blood and bone, body and soul into the service of the Lord of Twilight. Keren imagined that dark spirit, that dread god, waiting somewhere while its servants and thralls wrought havoc and evil all across the great continent of Toluveraz. And she shuddered as Orgraaleshenoth's words came back to her – 'I had thought to make use of you all in my plans . . . but on closer inspection I see that this one will be enough.'

Yet if the Daemonkind were the Lord of Twilight's servants, why was Orgraaleshenoth attempting to secretly enter the citadel of the Acolytes, who owed fealty to the same master?

She clenched her hands, trying to force some warmth into them, then noticed the Daemonkind prince straightening, his stance alert, his features intense and distracted.

'What is the—' she began.

He halted her with a gesture and for a moment or two there

was nothing but the faint sound of their breathing. Then, imperceptibly at first, Keren felt the dead silence begin to deepen, a creeping engulfment of her senses. The surroundings faded into hazy outlines and to Keren it was as if they stood on the abyssal floor of a vast ocean, intruders in depths of glimmering grey. She also noticed a dark thread linking her neck to Orgraaleshenoth, who was a shadowy figure standing with his back to her as he stared off at something in the murk.

Then she saw them. Spectral people, dozens of them, of all ages, men, women, children, sitting together, talking, eating, arguing, playing, walking, running, laughing, weeping. Was she seeing the ghosts of those who had lived in this house down the years, and their friends and relatives? They rushed about, passing through each other, a bustling weave of vitality and life, all oblivious to her, looking past her at someone else. Like the young man in robes who was staring straight at her with a wondering smile on his lips . . .

A blaze of light blotted out everything and at the centre of it she glimpsed a scene which made her catch her breath – it was Tauric, his right arm a thing of metal wreathed in hot white flame which lashed out at unseen adversaries. It only lasted an instant but she saw a raw confusion of emotions in his stare and was filled with dread for him. Then it all vanished, like a door closing, plunging her back into the cold dimness of the cottage.

Orgraaleshenoth was laughing, a soft, low sound of malice. 'How deliciously futile! Orosiada's true heir is forced to use her power, but tries to make it seem that the false heir is responsible.'

'I don't understand,' Keren said. 'Tauric's hand was on fire . . .'

'You saw?' The Daemonkind regarded her thoughtfully. 'Interesting, but not unexpected. The soulbound often catch fragments of their masters' experiences. You saw the boy and nothing more?'

Keren nodded, and he gave her a heavy-lidded look of satisfaction. 'The time will come when you will see more, much more.' He laid his glowing sword on a trestle table and sat on a nearby bench. 'Now you should rest, restore your strength as we shall be leaving at first light. Do not go far.'

She found a lean-to at the back of the house and, wrapped in blankets taken from inside, she settled down. But despair choked her thoughts like a black fog drifting and writhing through her mind, and true sleep was hard to come by. Spells of drowse came and went, bringing dreamlike recollections of some of the ghostly figures from earlier.

She woke to the familiar tug at her neck and the pale radiance of an ashen dawn filtering into the lean-to. Outside, the abandoned village looked sad in the light of day, its few buildings surrounded by encroaching waves of undergrowth. Then Keren turned and found herself looking up at the heights of the Oshang Dakhal, and was astonished at how close they had come the previous night. She shook her head, yawned and stretched, then groaned at aching muscles in her back. She was about to do a few stretching exercises when Orgraaleshenoth appeared from the front of the house and beckoned her to follow as he set off. She sighed, retrieved her backpack from the lean-to and hurried after him, rubbing gritty tiredness from her eyes and trying to finger her hair into a semblance of neatness.

From the village onward, the way grew steep, the ground stony and the green of growing things sparse and faded. A thin mist hazed the air. No breeze or creature intruded upon the cold calm of the path as it rose towards a ridge running between bare spurs of rock broken only by a hardy tree or clump of bushes. Occasionally the mist parted to reveal a long view of the lands below, a grey-green terrain made tiny by distance, still and undisturbed except by the gleam of a stream wandering among the foothills. Then either the mists would close up or there would be a pressure at the neck to get her hurrying on.

Her thoughts kept returning to that glimpse of Tauric, his arm strangely whole yet giving off that sorcerous corona, and the look in his eyes, fear conflicting with fury, astonishment with glee. It was the look of someone who was in the grip of another's will, or being dragged along by some inexorable force, and she felt a

sad sense of kinship with him for it. There had been several times
in her life when she had surrendered herself to either personal
impulse or to the will of others. Years past when she was just
seventeen (a world, an age ago, it seemed), she had been travelling
over a high pass in winter, returning to her parents' holding, when
heavy snows forced her to take refuge in a mountain wayhut. Only
there was a man already there, a mercenary by name of Ahamri.
He gallantly offered her the only cot and bedded down on the
stone floor.

And at some point in the middle of the night, some imp of need
woke her and spoke to her with her own body. Ahamri was in his
thirties, but fit and lean and not at all bad looking, and the imp
of need made him utterly desirable. Careless of caution, she had
flung the woollen blankets aside, crept across the floor and slipped
beneath his own covers. He had opened his eyes in surprise, then
a slow smile came over his lips, and after that she ceased to notice
the cold.

Then later, after the Mogaun invasion, in the aftermath of the
calamitous defeat at the Battle of Wolf's Gate, she had been with
the remnants of the Earl of Malvur's battalion as they retreated.
Leaderless and cut off from the south by the enemy's advance they
had had no choice but to head into the mountains of Prekine, and
it was in one of the deep valleys that they chanced across a
train of wagons, one of the Mogaun's supply convoys. In a fit of
vengeful rage they had attacked the thinly guarded wagons and
it was only afterwards that Keren discovered that they had held
Mogaun females and children, whom her fellow soldiers had slain
without hesitation.

Sickened by this, she had saddled a horse the following night
and galloped off into a rising storm, lashed by gale-driven rain as
she rode further north, not thinking where she was headed. At
some point in the early hours of the morning she had slowed to
rest in a hollow on a mountain path facing east. The storm was at
its height, and between two peaks she could make out the curve
of crags and ridges that was the Oshang Dakhal. Faint clusters
of lights were the only signs of the communities of Trevada and,

as Keren watched, lightning stabbed down at its highest point again and again, dazzling nets and webs that seemed to tear at the rock itself.

A veil of darkness had swept through the mountains of Prekine then, plunging all into a new night that did not fully lift for another two days, by which time Keren had buried her armour and anything else bearing the Imperial sigil, and was on her way north seeking work as a sellsword.

Now, as she climbed a steep path towards sheer cliffs, she remembered the old peasant name for the Oshang Dakhal – the Home of Lightnings, told to her by an aged scholar in Choraya a couple of years ago.

About a dozen paces ahead, the Daemonkind came to a halt and pointed at a cleft in the scrubby undergrowth lining the rocky path. 'This way,' he said, and with a couple of downward steps he disappeared from view. A sense of foreboding passed over her like a prickling shiver but she followed him without pause.

A narrow crevice, loose with pebbles, sloped down into a dim, stony ravine. Keren felt perspiration tingle all over her body as she descended in an undignified scramble that became a light run. She almost fell but used her hands to stay upright. Orgraaleshenoth was waiting at the bottom, a disdainful smile upon his lips.

'I hope you are not beginning to tire,' he said. 'We have much to accomplish this day.'

Keren dusted off her leggings and gauntlets. 'I appreciate your concern,' she said wryly. 'I am well and not yet wearied. However, I can't help wondering at our destination.'

The smile widened as he raised a hand and pointed straight up.

'But the only way into Trevada is at the other end of the Oshang—'

'I shall make another way.' And he turned and walked on, Keren following at a short distance, every footstep carrying her towards some unknown dread.

Although the ravine was dry and barren, there was evidence of long-gone plant growth along its sides, nets of frail, desiccated fibres stretched across the bare walls, and the exposed stumps of bush roots, grey, withered and dead. Bones there were, too, the tiny skulls of birds and rats, and just once, where the ravine became a short tunnel through solid rock, the remains of a human skeleton, skull and ribcage and one arm. It lay in a hollow between the ravine wall and a jutting slab, probably wedged there by a flash flood. Who could it have been, she wondered. An adventurer, a thief who sought to enter the High Basilica unseen? Or a soldier, perhaps even a Mogaun warrior? Unsure, she sketched a quick bow of respect and hurried on.

The Daemonkind prince had slowed his pace to a deliberate walk, pausing occasionally to study the rock wall, sometimes reaching out to touch it, then moving on. After a while he came to a halt.

'Prepare yourself. Whatever you see is only a glimpse into the Realm of Veils. Do not forget that we are still standing on solid ground.'

She nodded, and he raised his hands, fingers spread widely. His eyes stared up at the ravine wall with an intense burning gaze and for a second Keren thought she saw a huge, hulking beast shape waver about him. Then he swept his hands together in a single, sharp clap.

Keren gasped as their surroundings shimmered into gauzy transparency. Beneath her were pale depths falling away into smoky nothingness, and a sense of panic gripped her. She staggered but fought to regain her balance, forcing herself to feel the ravine's rocky surface under her boots. Then she looked up and gaped in astonishment. The rock wall, the entire upthrusting immensity of the Oshang Dakhal, had become like glass shot through with opaque planes and faint silvery wisps. Far above she could make out clusters of tiny shadowy shapes, the temples and other buildings of Trevada. But what caught her attention were the chains of glowing lights which began a short distance in front of her and extended all the way up to the summit. They were like mother-of-pearl, and each one was a different shape. It was almost as if a vast jewelled array hung within the highest peak of the Oshang Dakhal, directly below the High Basilica.

She was allowed to regard that perfect, enigmatic beauty for just a second or two more before Orgraaleshenoth made a small gesture and the grey reality of stone and dust returned. In the silence the Daemonkind stared into the sheer rocky wall for a brief moment, then strode off along the ravine. 'This way, swiftly now.'

He led the way to a fracture in the wall, a fissure that was taller than Orgraaleshenoth but no wider than two fingers. The Daemonkind placed his hands on either side of the crack, as if readying himself to pry it apart by brute force. Then Keren heard him mutter words and syllables that sounded ill-suited to human mouth and tongue. A faint glow surrounded his hands, then a web of tiny cracks radiated from them to cover an oval, head-high area of the wall. Hands lowered, Orgraaleshenoth stepped up to the tall fracture and began pushing his way into it. Keren saw the edges of the fissure distort to allow him passage, all those fragments of the wall moving against and over each other, as if the solid rock had become something alive and malleable. He was half concealed when he glanced back, reached out with his free hand to grasp Keren's wrist and pulled her after him.

She held her breath as rasping stone brushed over her face, pressing down on her head, squeezing her entire body but not to the point of pain. She also felt a tug on her sheathed sword and her backpack, but neither were torn away. Inching along through the vitals of the Oshang Dakhal, Keren wondered if this was what it felt like to be a mole or a mudmouse, burrowing into the ground with unthinkable tons of rock directly overhead . . .

It ended at last with Keren stumbling out of a rough wall into a tunnel dead-end that would have been lightless were it not for the radiant curtain which blocked the way. It shone with shifting polychromatic colours, like lampoil on water, and clung to every surface of the tunnel, forming a perfect barrier. This, she realized, was just one of those jewelled lights she had seen hanging within the Oshang Dakhal.

'The founders of Trevada discovered these tunnels soon after the walls of the High Basilica were raised.' Orgraaleshenoth walked past her to stand before the bright barrier, examining it. 'And they decided to make use of them, widening some, extending others, then putting into place a complex series of spells and wards. It was the Ordeal of Essences, meant to test those aspiring to the highest positions of magehood.' He laughed. 'But since the Acolytes of Twilight occupied the Basilica, some changes have been made. Some – not all – of these spell barriers were altered to provide a certain . . . entertainment? Captives and criminals are sent down into the Ordeal, and their downward progress is watched with amusement.

'You see, the Ordeal leads directly up into the Congruence, the temple of the High Basilica, where the Crystal Eye is kept. I cannot interfere with the spell barriers – that would set alarms sounding all over this pitiful continent, never mind Trevada.' The Daemonkind stepped over to her, dark glittering eyes staring into her own. 'No, I need to find another way through, and you will provide me with that way.'

Before she could react, he grabbed her by her jerkin, hoisted her off her feet and threw her bodily into the barrier. It seized her, held her motionless for the tiniest instant. Then lightning struck. She shrieked as agony coursed along every limb and exploded in her chest, a dazzling eruption of white fire that slammed into her head.

Through the devouring torment Keren was vaguely aware of her body being hurled into the tunnel on the other side. She had no eyes to see with, no ears, no feeling from limb, skin or bone, yet she saw Orgraaleshenoth in his true form, huge, pale and spectral, standing over her.

She felt a loosening within her and the place where she was seemed to drift sideways. She was able to see the sad, seared ruin of her body and would have wept if she could. Then the drifting halted and she was able to see an ashen thread joining her and the Daemonkind.

'Death has no claim on you,' he said. 'You are my key, my doorway.'

As she glided back towards her poor corpse, she could see it begin to change, the charred flesh falling away to be replaced by healthy skin, her eyes reforming from blackened scraps, her hair growing from her new scalp in a surge of brown. She felt herself being lured towards her flesh, like a leaf drawn from still shallows back into the surging stream . . .

Then she was tipping her head forward, forcing herself to her feet. A few burnt shreds of clothing fell onto the tunnel floor. She was naked, until Orgraaleshenoth, tall and gauntly human again, threw her a plain brown robe. As she slipped it on she noticed the charred remains of her backpack, and her sword, broken into two twisted, smoking pieces. And immediately she remembered the prophecies of the spell-tortured singer, Avalti, and the one he had directed at her – *a broken sword discarded*.

'There are another twenty-seven spells between us and the inner temple,' said her master. 'We have no time to lose.'

She nodded grimly to herself, and followed.

Chapter Twenty

Trace upon my ancient face,
My bold, black plan,
To break the siege of Time.

Calabos, *The City of Dreams*, Act 3, i.25

It was early evening when Byrnak, Warlord of Honjir and General of the Host of Clans, laid down his long white quill pen and carefully read over the new orders by the soft light of an oil lamp hanging from the ridgepole overhead. The parchment seemed pale and golden, almost translucent, and the letters of every word were scribed with a heavy black ink.

The orders decreed that the number of warriors being trained as foot soldiers be doubled to ten in every hundred, and that a full third of all stores of grain, livestock, arms and armour be turned over to his own quartermaster. Byrnak smiled, recalling the Mogaun youth he had appointed to the post – of the twenty-four tribesmen pledged into his service by the senior chiefs, Hogal was one of five sent as spies, as Byrnak and Obax discovered through sorcerous scrutiny. Now, of course, they were all loyal and true, though not soulbound – in their minds he had tied subtler knots of pride, honour and devotion. Somehow he found that far more satisfying than obedience founded on terror and pain.

Byrnak studied the parchment again, the confident pen strokes, the straight, unwavering lines of words, and the tangled characters of his signature. He frowned. When he had arrived at the Blood

251

Gathering encampment four days ago, all he had known of the Mogaun script were a few scattered words and phrases. Now it felt like second nature to him.

He almost laughed out loud. *My deepest thanks*, he thought sardonically, picturing himself delivering a mocking bow to the darkness at the back of his mind. *Yet more knowledge I never knew I possessed!*

There was movement outside the tent and the entrance curtains were pulled aside to reveal the white-eyed visage of the Acolyte Obax.

'Great lord,' he said. 'The honoured Chief Yasgur and his advisers have arrived. They await your pleasure.'

'Good. Bring chairs, and wine.'

Servants brought three chairs, then another entered carrying a tray with a squat green bottle and four bronze goblets which Obax scrutinized before allowing them to be placed on the table. Byrnak, meanwhile, finished studying the new orders and carefully laid the parchment on top of two small, wrinkled slips of paper already set before him, messages which had arrived on the wing earlier that day, then nodded sharply to Obax who clapped his hands twice.

The curtains parted and three men entered. Yasgur was broad-shouldered and handsome, clothed in a long black cloak over polished leather. The cloak bore an embroidered crossed-spears device near the throat, and a simple gold circlet rested upon his brow. With him was a burly Mogaun warrior with the hard, watchful eyes of a senior officer, and a stocky, bearded southerner whose relaxed smile faded under Byrnak's chilly gaze.

With hands resting on his waistbelt, Yasgur bowed, a carefully minimal gesture. 'Greetings, Great Lord Byrnak. I come in the name of the Firespears to make the traditional offerings at the place of our great victory, and to speak upon serious matters.'

Byrnak nodded slightly, silent for a moment. 'If I was your father,' he said, 'and you had ignored my requests for your attendance for three days, I would have dragged you from your tent and made you eat with the dogs.'

The officer snarled and took a step forward but Yasgur put out an arm to stop him. 'Ghazrek . . .'

Byrnak ignored the officer, instead keeping his gaze on Yasgur. There was fury in his face, tempered with a wariness lacking in his subordinate. Yes, he had the sharp pride of birth and achievement, along with self-discipline and the ease of command. Yasgur could prove useful, if he agreed to lead the army's vanguard as the other Shadowkings wanted. If not, he would have to be disposed of.

For a second Yasgur stared at Byrnak, then smiled a knife-thin smile.

'My obligations to the other chieftains kept me from heeding your request,' he said. 'As Hegroun's son, I have a number of duties to carry out. No insult to yourself was ever intended, lord.'

Noting the lack of an apology for the officer Ghazrek's outburst, Byrnak gestured for them to sit and directed a thought at the Acolyte: *Obax – the drinks.*

As they settled themselves in the low, rough-made seats, Obax poured out the wine, a dark red reputedly looted from Tobrosa. Byrnak took the first sip, then raised his goblet in a wordless toast to Yasgur who exchanged glances with his companions before following suit.

'I shall be brief,' Byrnak said. 'There are several nests of rebels throughout the south, particularly in Kejana and Cabringa, which the Acolytes and the Council of Chiefs have intended to move against for several months now. This year's Blood Gathering was deemed perfect for assembling again the Host of Clans with which we can obliterate the last dregs of the old Empire and remind our vassals and their people of our strength and our pitiless dominion.' He moved the newly written sheet of orders to one side, picked up one of the message slips, glanced at it and went on. 'The intention was for the Host to march south after the rites of the Gathering, but we received word from Kejana today which changes everything.'

Yasgur nodded. 'The uprising in Oumetra.'

'You know of it. How?'

'I have . . . associates in Hargas, in south Kejana. They tell me that there was revolt and fighting in Oumetra which led to the death of Begrajic, a lesser chief, and the defeat of his warriors and the mercenaries he had hired. The city is now in the hands of outlaws apparently led by a boy claiming to be Korregan's bastard son.'

Impressive, Byrnak thought. *He knows more of the details than I do.*

Yet dangerous, lord, Obax replied in mindspeech. *What else might he know?*

'Just so,' Byrnak said to Yasgur. 'The rebels will undoubtedly try to foment unrest throughout the south, therefore we must act before that happens. The rites of the Gathering will be postponed and the Host of Clans will ride forth tomorrow morning. I want you to command the vanguard.'

The officer Ghazrek grunted in surprise, and Byrnak decided that if the man objected aloud he would have him torn apart by horses. But he remained silent, as did Yasgur for a moment, his face sombre. The bearded southerner, however, smiled slightly and seemed to nod to himself.

'You accord me a great honour, lord,' Yasgur said carefully.

'Not so,' Byrnak said, picking up the second message slip. 'There are doubts about your loyalty to the clans and to the memory of your father. Leading the vanguard against the rebel vermin would demonstrate otherwise.'

'Doubts about my loyalty?' Yasgur leaned forward, anger quickening in his face again. 'Who has been spreading these poisonous lies? My honour is unmarred, and my allegiance to the cause of my father is unbroken. Who would deny it?'

'This does,' said Byrnak, holding up the second slip of paper. 'A message from our observers in your city of Besh-Darok, telling of great numbers of your troops, almost half of your entire army, riding out into the country this very morning.' He tossed the message onto the table. 'You came here with six hundred warriors of the Firespear clan, and omitted to mention the additional seven thousand which you also now have in the field.'

'Great Lord Byrnak,' Yasgur said. 'Before leaving, I gave my
generals the authority to act as they see fit in defence of my lands –
clearly, they also have received word of the revolt in Oumetra and
are taking steps to prevent any similar uprising in Khatris. There
is nothing more to that message than this, great lord, nothing, I
swear it. The soul of my father would rise up and strike me down
were I ever to take arms against my own people!'

A pretty speech, mused Obax. *He almost means it.*

'So, you will lead the vanguard?' Byrnak asked.

'I shall,' Yasgur said without hesitation. 'The Firespear warriors
would be proud to—'

'The vanguard will consist of Doubleknives and Bloodfists.
Your warriors will come under my personal command, but you
may keep a small personal guard, along with your disrespectful
underling and this other one.' And as Byrnak turned his gaze upon
the southerner, he felt something stir within him, a shifting in the
shadows in his mind, a presence focusing its attention, pushing its
way to the front of his thoughts –

A seed, this one. A seed of disaster and triumph . . .

Byrnak sat frozen, immobile in the grip of a dark will.

**Yet still he is prey. As you are prey. Submit, and you are
mine. Defy me and you will be consumed** . . .

Vision blurred into grey and blood red. He was vaguely aware
of voices raised in concern, saying his name over and over, then
heard Obax insisting that the audience was at an end. All whispers
in the background as that deathly voice spoke on as if to itself, now
like the rushing moan of a whirlwind, then harsh and resonant like
syllables of iron, rising to a screeching pitch, or falling to a deep,
bestial drone from which only snatches and fragments of words
emerged.

When at last the chaos subsided and his sight was restored, he
found he was lying on the floor of his tent, wrapped in a thick
woollen blanket. Weak candleglow came from the table, and the
figure seated there he recognized as Obax. The Acolyte noticed
his recovery and leaned over him.

'Are you well, Divine One? Can you speak?' The priest's face was full of a fearful eagerness. Pinpoints of reflected light gleamed in those grey-white eyes, and a faint patina of perspiration shone across the hollow-cheeked features. 'Can you understand me?'

Byrnak levered himself up on his elbows and smiled maliciously. 'Only too well, Obax.' An odd exhaustion filled him but he masked it with glee. 'How oppressed you must feel by the absence of divinity, by the way I hold on to myself.'

The Acolyte looked shaken. 'Lord, forgive me, but I heard the voice of the Bringer speak through you—'

'And what did you hear?'

Obax hesitated. 'It was in a very ancient language, a temple argot once spoken in the cold valleys north of Keremenchool. I was only able to understand a few words and phrases, but it was as if the Bringer was talking to himself, asking himself questions and answering them.' The Acolyte shuddered, but his features were full of the believer's fire.

Byrnak shifted his weight to lie propped on his right arm, gazing thoughtfully up at the candle. So Obax never heard what was said about Yasgur's companion, the southerner, or about Byrnak's own fate. *Defy me and you will be consumed . . .*

A curious urge to laugh rose in him but he suppressed it and instead tried to sense the inner terrain of his thought. But the shadows within were still and seemingly empty, unlike those in the tent around him. The guttering candle flame threw great flickering shapes of blackness across the patterned canvas and the long banners decorated with the many symbols of the Mogaun. The half-parted drapes at the tent entrance shifted in a light breeze and somewhere outside a flag was flapping. Through the drapes Byrnak could see a slice of the night, black as priest's ink, strewn with motes and glints, and he pictured the camp beyond, the thousand or more tents, the smouldering fires, the guards patrolling, the ostlers tending to the huge herd of horses penned to the north. He imagined seeing it all from above, then moving west across the raised-up flatness of the plateau of Arengia to the coast of Ebro'Heth and out to sea, to the ocean, its deep abyssal blackness reflecting the night with no horizon in sight at the far-off edge of the world . . .

He let out a long, muted sigh. 'I am weary,' he said to Obax. 'Help me up.'

Grasping his servant's arm, he got to his feet. A passing dizziness made him sway for a moment, then he shook off Obax's hand and walked unsteadily through the flaps to the rear of his tent, where he collapsed onto the fur-heaped pallet that was his bed. Obax brought the candle in and balanced it on a two-thirds empty weapon rack. Byrnak did not look round, but he could almost feel the Acolyte watching him for several moments. He heard a murmur, a benediction perhaps, or more likely an invocation, then the rustle of cloth and muffled footsteps receding.

Pale gold was the candle's light. It gleamed on the points of carelessly stacked spears and the blades of a matched pair of horse gaivals, and made the burnished face of a bronze shield glow. As he lay there on his side, he could see part of his face in the shield, his features lined, his beard untrimmed, his eyes heavy. Grey webs of sleep were starting to fall on his thoughts, but before he could enjoy that slow, gentle smothering, something pierced it, something familiar, a voice.

Lord, my lord, do you hear me?

He struggled to keep his eyes open, and thought he saw a faint shape in the polished shield, a wraith figure standing with arms held out, imploring.

My lord, your most faithful servant seeks your counsel . . .

'Nerek . . .' he whispered, and reached out his hand. But it was a hand made of dream, and it dissolved in sleep's incoming tide.

Gilly Cordale sat on a stool next to an iron brazier half-full of glowing embers, warming himself while Yasgur, prince of Besh-Darok and chieftain of the Firespear Clan, paced back and forth along the length of the tent.

'What they say is true after all!' Yasgur was saying. 'This great lord, this Byrnak, is a host of the Lord of Twilight. The way his face changed . . .' He shook his head in wonder. 'I have heard

others call him Shadowking, same as that Ystregul. Not ones to
make enemies of, eh?'

Gilly nodded, remembering how Byrnak had been staring at
him when that misty aura began to appear. The aura was pale
and wispy at first and clung to the man's form like a second
skin, then a tinge of amber and crimson had flowed into it
like a vapour of torchlight and blood. As Byrnak's features were
blurred, another face had emerged over his like a crimson mask
whose cold eyes seemed to look at things which were not there
while a cruel mouth spoke and smiled and laughed. Gilly had
heard almost nothing, just a muffled syllable or two, before the
priest Obax, clearly in a panic, unceremoniously bundled them
out of the tent.

It had been terrifying, Gilly realized, almost as much as
that moment when he and Suviel had beheld Raal Haidar's
transformation into one of the Daemonkind. Then there was
that sorcerous confrontation at the burnt-out village, and the
encounter with the tortured singer, Avalti, and those lines of
prophecy – *'an iron fox, eyeless to the hunt . . .'*

He shivered. *I am not a young man,* he thought. *I have survived
thirty-one summers and had my share of fights and seen sights both
terrible and glorious. But I have witnessed more dread sorceries in
the last week and a half than a gang of kings. What can ordinary
men do in the face of such power, except make jokes before they're
swept away by the storm?*

Then he grinned. *Well, why not? If the jokes are good enough,
perhaps the gods will laugh and be lenient.*

'You're amused, ser Cordale,' said Yasgur. 'What at?'

'The look on the Acolyte's face, lord,' he said, thinking
quickly. 'Never have I seen a man more unprepared for divine
intervention.'

Yasgur smirked at that, then began to laugh, his hilarity
growing till there were tears in his eyes. He pulled up a second
stool and sat down, shaking his head and wiping his eyes as Gilly
looked on in a kind of wonderment.

'Ah, you're a fine companion, Gilly. Now, while we wait for

Ghazrek to return with the food, I wish to hear your thoughts on our meeting with the great lord.'

The irony of it, Gilly thought. *After years as an advisor to Mazaret, I'm cast by sorcery into the very heart of our enemies, dispensing advice to one of their leaders. If this is Fate's idea of a joke, I'm dreading the punchline.*

'My lord,' he said, 'to be blunt, Byrnak wants you dead.'

Yasgur grew sombre, stroking his well-clipped black beard. 'You're certain about this?'

'By commanding the strongest army in this region, you pose the greatest immediate threat to Byrnak and Ystregul and whatever plans they're hatching. So he coerces you into leading the vanguard and has his spies wait for the first serious skirmish, then—' Gilly shrugged '—an unseen spear or sword thrust to the vitals, or an arrow gone astray, and it's done. You'll have a magnificent hero's burial, songs will be sung to soothe your spirit and battles will be fought in your name.'

'Among my people, the dead are chased away by the shrieks of the womenfolk,' Yasgur said matter-of-factly. 'Sadly, I do not intend to have them shriek for me too soon. Surely my personal guards will be able to shield me from any assassin.'

'In the heat of battle, lord?' Gilly shook his head, then an idea struck him. 'But what if you were not the only chief in the vanguard . . .' Animated, he turned to Yasgur. 'The Council of Chiefs are holding a battle rite of some kind tonight, am I right?'

'A feast of gorging and ale-guzzling, which I am expected to attend.'

'Excellent. If you were to announce to the assembled chiefs your new command and predict the great victories, spoils and battle honours that must inevitably come your way, is it not likely that some of them will volunteer to ride at your side?'

Yasgur frowned, and Gilly had to force himself from showing any impatience. 'No, they could not since their place is at the head of their own tribes.' His voice became bitter. 'A duty which is denied to me.'

'Then what of their sons and brothers?'

'Some might be tempted, certainly, but honour would compel them—'

He broke off as a figure carrying several cloth-wrapped bundles pushed aside the tent flaps and entered. It was Ghazrek, his grinning, bearded face bearing greasy signs of food already eaten, and his presence bringing a waft of beery fumes.

'At last – we eat!' he announced, kneeling down to unfold his bundles. Gilly felt his stomach rumble with a sudden hunger as pieces of roast fowl, stuffed iloba roots, baked pastries and other delicacies were laid bare. Some bottles of strong Rorgith wine were produced and uncorked, and as fingers dipped into the feast Ghazrek related what rumours and ragtalk he had come by concerning Byrnak.

'I've heard it said that he's raised the dead,' he said through a mouthful of meat, 'turned men into goats and swans into women, and caused a stream of fire to pour out of a mountainside. And when he invaded some city away in the west, he brought the defeated generals together and swapped their heads around!' He mimed with his hands, and Yasgur snorted in disbelief.

'Who told you that?'

'A Doubleknife from Jefren.'

'Hah! Doubleknives – horse-loving goat thieves. And where did you hear the one about the river of fire?'

'From a Bearclaw . . . I know, I know – goat-loving horse thieves!'

Both roared with laughter, and Gilly smiled politely. *Mogaun humour*, he thought. *I'll understand it eventually.*

Ghazrek bit on a leg of roast bird then gestured with it. 'I heard something which I know to be true, though.' He leaned in conspiratorially and went on in a quieter voice. 'A serving girl told me that the Great Lord Ystregul suffered a strange fit earlier this evening, right in the middle of a meeting with his various lackeys, and it sounded very much like what we saw in Byrnak's tent. Seems he had to be carried off to his sleeping chamber. Near unconscious, he was.'

'Perfect, lord,' Gilly said to Yasgur. 'There will be no interruptions if you attend the feast and announce your good fortune.'

Ghazrek looked puzzled and Gilly explained what had been discussed earlier. The officer nodded in vigorous agreement.

'The southerner is right, my lord. This accursed Byrnak will have you slain as soon as possible.'

'You speak of our commander with disrespect,' Yasgur said half-heartedly.

'Lord, you saw what I saw,' Ghazrek said. 'The man is hag-ridden, as is the other one, Ystregul. Who can tell what evil spirits are sitting in their heads, claiming to be the Lord of Twilight himself? You must survive so that we may survive, and ser Cordale's plan is a good one. And if you wait a while before speaking of your new role, I may be able to sow seeds here and there.'

Yasgur looked thoughtfully at Gilly, then Ghazrek and back again. Then he nodded, smiling. 'Your counsel is good, and I shall follow it. Old Atroc was right, Gilly – you are a good adviser as well as a good companion.'

Gilly inclined his head, acknowledging the praise and remembering his first encounter with Atroc, Yasgur's personal seer. When the Daemonkind Orgraaleshenoth had snatched him away from Suviel's side, he had found himself in the middle of a boar hunt, sprawled in the dust and rocks of a dried-up riverbed with a party of Mogaun warriors riding towards him. The only thing which had stopped them from hurling spears at him was a stooped, scrawny old man clad in furs and a loincloth who calmly stepped in front of the riders and held up his hands.

Then when Yasgur had arrived moments later, the old man had told him that Gilly was sent by the gods to be his companion on his journey to Arengia. To Gilly's amazement, the Mogaun pondered this proclamation for all of a few seconds before nodding and agreeing. The old man had then taken Gilly by the arm, steered him off to one side and said, 'You may call me Atroc, southman. I have been seeing your face in the stars, in the clouds, in the lines of my hand since I was a boy.'

After that, Gilly had been almost constantly in the company of Yasgur and Atroc for the few days before Yasgur was due to leave for the Blood Gathering. There had been many times when he could have murdered Yasgur with a good chance of escape, but he had found himself liking the man, a personal discovery nearly as profound as realizing that some Mogaun could be fairly civilized. At least those under Yasgur's command.

And as Yasgur and Ghazrek prepared to leave for the feast, his thoughts went back to his last sight of Suviel in that pale, eldritch realm the Daemonkind had called Kekrahan.

What happened to her? he wondered. *Was she as lucky as me?* He grinned and shook his head. *Assuming that this is lucky!*

Chapter Twenty-one

Wear masks, not mirrors,
In the Kingdom of the Dark.

The Litany of Magehood, prologue

The image of Byrnak hung over the fire, features sculpted in ensorcelled smoke. From where she sat, bound, gagged and propped against a pile of saddlebags, Suviel could feel the awesome power radiating from Nerek as she strove to gain her master's attention. The woman was standing with arms outstretched and a faint green aura shifting and twitching about her like a thing alive.

Everything in the clearing was cast into sharp focus, blades of grass, dry twigs among the dusty ash and charred pebbles of old fires, the stack of spears, knives and cleaning rags, the four masked guards sitting cowed and subdued to one side, the gleam of firelight on the studded leather they constantly wore. Suviel could see the utter concentration in Nerek's stance and her visibly trembling hands . . .

Then the eyes of the face in the smoke came to life and Nerek cried out: 'My lord, your faithful servant seeks your counsel!'

The eyes gazed down at her and for an instant the mouth seemed about to speak. But the intelligence went out of the face, which lost its shape, drifting apart and upwards as the spell broke. Suviel felt the accumulated tension of power in the clearing collapse and die away. The light from the fire lost its brilliance and the surrounding night closed in like a tightening noose of shadows as Nerek sank to her knees, mumbling and quietly sobbing. She looked defeated and exhausted, but a moment later she sprang to her feet, went round the fire and spoke rapidly to her guards. The words were spoken in an archaic dialect of the Mogaun tongue and Suviel caught just enough to understand mere guard duty orders.

Eyes closed, she sighed and let her head fall forward. Nerek's mood swings were becoming more pronounced the closer they came to the Oshang Dakhal and Trevada. In the four days since the Daemonkind pitched her into Nerek's hands, Suviel had found herself coming to pity Byrnak's creature as she was torn this way and that by raging, and sometimes conflicting, emotions. Suviel was sure that Nerek feared Byrnak while also being drawn to him, having seen a hunted look come into her eyes whenever his name was mentioned. Then there was the pursuit of Keren, this savage need to capture and slay her, which contrasted sharply with an obsessive interest in the swordswoman. Suviel had been repeatedly questioned about Keren, what she was like, her likes and dislikes, what she had done and why. Lacking personal knowledge of the woman (Keren had not been the most garrulous of companions), Suviel had found herself embroidering her recollections with deduction and guesswork in order to satisfy Nerek's hunger for detail.

There was the scrape of a footstep nearby and she looked up to see Nerek standing over her. With her hands she loosened the gag and removed it, and Suviel wondered what would happen next. More questions to do with Keren, perhaps, or Raal Haidar? She had kept silent about the Daemonkind, insisting that the man was a mysterious sorcerer from beyond Keremenchool who had turned on herself and the others for some unknown purpose.

It was her own purpose which had led to such guile. They were camped just an hour or two from the gates of Trevada, and were Nerek to know that a prince of the Daemonkind was intending to gain entrance to the Acolytes' citadel by stealth, she might see fit to alert the Acolytes, thus eradicating whatever slim chance Suviel might have of laying hands on the Crystal Eye.

Nerek regarded her neutrally, then pushed several strands of Suviel's hair back from her face. Suviel almost flinched but held herself steady as her captor tucked the stray hairs behind her ear in a surprisingly gentle manner.

'We shall enter Trevada in the morning,' Nerek said. 'Just you and I – the guards will wait here for our return. We will present ourselves as hunters seeking work as scouts or spies, or even just foragers, so consider how you can best play the part before you sleep tonight.'

'As you wish.'

A small smile came over Nerek's face. 'I will have your co-operation in this, Suviel Hantika. I know what to use to ensure it.'

She reached down to one of the saddlebags behind Suviel, tugged out a flat, cloth-wrapped object which she set to one side, then pulled a blanket from another bag and draped it carefully over Suviel. 'Now, think and sleep.'

She turned and went back to the fire, sat on the ground and unwrapped the small package. Suviel felt a ripple of uneasiness as Nerek produced a handmirror into which she stared, tilting her head this way and that, as if looking for something. The memory of that terrible transformation in the mountains of Honjir came back to Suviel and she wondered what had happened to the mind of the young man that Nerek had once been. Had he been wiped away, like footprints on a sandy beach at high tide, or did some fragment of him yet linger, haunting Nerek's thoughts?

She pushed aside the insoluble problem, and wriggled into a more comfortable position facing away from the fire. A short while later she became aware that fine rain was falling, little more than a heavy mist, but she was too tired to care. Quite soon she was too tired to stay awake.

She woke to a grey morning full of the sounds of packing and horses being harnessed. One of the guards brought her a cooling bowl of broth and a handful of berries then stood waiting as she ate hurriedly. The masked servants of the Acolytes remained a mystery – she had already suffered pursuit by the likes of these, and suspected from both their posture and their sharp musky odour that they were not entirely human.

When she had finished, another guard came over and hauled her to her feet while the first one used a dagger to sever the bonds on her feet and wrists. Once this was done, they stood either side of her as Nerek came over, halting several yards away. She had tied her pale hair back in a topknot and wore a long cloak of some heavy blue-grey material over her mailed jerkin and leggings. But it was the fire she was carrying which struck dread into Suviel's heart.

A bright knot of flames writhed in her cupped hands, tiny undying flames of carmine and amber that rippled and coiled around each other like a burning thread with no end. Nerek bent her head, moving her lips as if whispering to it, then glanced up at Suviel, smiling a secret smile. Without warning the two guards grabbed Suviel by the arms and Nerek lightly tossed the living fire at her.

She twisted uselessly against the guards' grip as the burning thing flew towards her face, tendrils spreading like wings. She fought the urge to close her eyes, staring with futile courage at the oncoming doom . . .

It blurred into opacity just feet from her, all the colour and detail draining from it as it flowed into nothing before her. Suviel felt a wave of warm air strike her face, smelling like the heat of a forge, hot stone and iron. The guards released her and Nerek came nearer.

'Do you know what I have done to you?'

Struggling against dizzy nausea, Suviel shook her head.

'And you call yourself a mage. Are you even able to name the fires of old?'

Suviel straightened in surprise. Nerek's question was part of the rote catechism of mage teaching, albeit a part that never seemed to be of any practical use. Nerek stood watching her with an expectant tilt of the head, so she dredged her memory and began to recite.

'Fire of the earth, fire of the sky, fire of the waters, never burning, fire of song, fire of learning, fire of night, fire of day . . .' She tried to remember. '. . . Fire that sleeps, fire that rages, fire that watches, fire that—'

There was a prickling sense of presence, and as she glanced quickly to one side she caught a glimpse of something hovering at her shoulder, a feathery form bright with flaming colours. Then there was nothing, only empty air.

'The fire that watches,' Nerek said with a kind of intense satisfaction. 'I have made a servant and set it over you. I gave it my breath and my word so I will know if you intend to become . . . troublesome.'

Suviel summoned her remaining dignity and met Nerek's gaze. 'Then since my fate is in your hands, I have no choice but to trust you. So be it.'

Nerek uttered a quiet, mocking laugh but Suviel saw the shadow of uncertainty in her eyes as she turned and walked away, passing out the final orders to break camp.

Fitful showers came and went as the party finally left the clearing on horseback. The air was mild and heavy with the moist odours of earth and foliage, yet there was a pervading taint of decay which Suviel could almost taste. There was the occasional howl and yip of some unseen beast, more mournful than menacing, and once Suviel saw a black furry creature the shape of a rat but the size of a dog dash across the trail ahead.

Not long after that, they came to the edge of the forest and paused for a moment or two as Nerek issued her final commands. The masked guards were heading north through the undergrowth while Nerek and Suviel, and her invisible watcher, continued towards Trevada.

The Oshang Dakhal loomed ahead, a 2-mile curve of rocky promontories and crags that rose steadily to the sheer cliffs and peaks upon which was the High Basilica and the academies of magecraft. Between it and the forest lay a wide valley divided by a river, a ruined terrain where clusters of charred tree stumps poked out of the weedy ground and rubbish floated on stagnant pools, and where only the broken traces of walls suggested that people had once lived here.

The bridge over the river was crudely made from large blocks of pale stone but only when they drew nearer did Suviel realize that they were columns and flagstones looted from an ancient Fathertree temple which had once stood near the riverbank. She had thought that her prior knowledge, gained from travellers and spies, had prepared her for this poisoned, ravaged scene, but the reality of it shook her. As she rode over the bridge and saw where countless other hooves and feet and cartwheels had chipped away at the beautiful relief carvings she found herself weeping.

Gone, she thought. All of it gone, all the gardens and the songbirds and the groves of ankeril, the homes of farmers and artisans, all the sweetness of Prekine, ground down and wiped away.

It was worse, far worse than anything told to her second or third hand. She brought her horse to a halt at the mid-point of the bridge and gazed down at the swollen waters of the river she once knew as the Aithel. With tears running down her face she stared at the ugly brown torrent and contemplated throwing herself into it. It would end this drawn-out spasm of pain and there would be no more need for grief and struggle and loss. But before she could dismount there was a flash of fiery amber near her shoulder, and a leaden lassitude settled over her.

'What is this? What were you going to do?'

Nerek came back alongside and angrily snatched the reins from Suviel's unresisting hands. Then she saw the tears and anger gave way to puzzlement. 'You wanted to kill yourself. Why?'

For the first time Suviel felt a flash of raw, unreasoning hatred towards the woman, and for an instant pictured herself with her hands round her throat. Then a kind of shame came over her and she shied away from the image. Bending her head, she wiped the wetness from her face.

'You do not know what this place was like before the invasion,' she said. 'And I cannot explain to you what I feel at seeing it now.'

Nerek shrugged. 'New things will grow here – is that not so? Others will come and build homes and farms, too.'

'Mogaun homes,' Suviel said bitterly. 'Mogaun farms.'

'I care not,' said Nerek, surveying the open stretches of land between them and the high, wide open gates of Trevada. 'There is no time for this. We must continue – now.'

With a jerk on the reins of Suviel's mount, she urged both horses into a gallop. On the other side of the bridge they followed a muddy track across uneven, waterlogged land. As the two women approached the city, Suviel saw riders and wagons coming and going at the high, wide gateway which had been divided in two by a thick wall of stakes, one side for entrance, the other for exit.

Nerek had by this time returned the reins to Suviel, and as they came up to the gates she said: 'There will be an Acolyte watching all who enter, so I have placed a spell over us to conceal our true natures. Just remember – we are hunters from the south, from Honjir, here to find work as foragers or spies.'

Suviel nodded morosely, and they rode into the long, dark entrance. There was a stench of horse manure and rotting garbage, mingled with the odours of human and horse sweat, and a constant hubbub of conversation, the creak of wheels and the clatter of hooves on the cobblestones. Most of those that they queued with were Yularians or Anghatanis on foot carrying great bundles or pushing carts, while the few riders were fur-clad Mogaun warriors. At the other end of the tunnel, a group of guards – mercenaries with company badges on their chests – gave their weapons and belongings a cursory inspection and waved them on. They were there, Suviel realized, to prevent disorder and catch any obvious troublemakers while relying on unseen help to pinpoint genuine threats.

Like us, she thought. Then she smiled thinly. *No, like Nerek. I hardly count next to the magnitude of her powers.*

Now dismounted, they led their horses away from the guard post and into a busy crowd of travellers and city dwellers on the edge of a square. Instinctively Suviel looked to the right and up at the balconies of the building immediately next to the gateway. But no students sat at the Five Moons anymore, sharing drinks and stories and singing songs. Now, only semi-naked prostitutes leaned on the rail, leering and beckoning to the men below.

Everywhere someone had something for sale. Sallow-faced traders sold weapons, clothes or food from the backs of wagons while footsore new arrivals offered what looked like loot from private houses, a pair of fine leather shoes, or a bronze figurine, or a handful of ornamented hairclips and pins.

This place was once called Journeyman Square and although the fountain with its back-to-back statues was still there at the centre, its limbs and heads were missing and blue paint was daubed on the marble. The four ancient agathons which once stood at the corners of the square were gone, some of the buildings were burned-out shells, and filth marred every surface. But in addition to all this degradation, there was something else wrong with the entire busy scene, some small detail which nagged away at the back of Suviel's mind without revealing itself.

Dodging the attentions of pickpockets and drunks, they made their way round the square past a succession of squalid taverns and grimy stalls selling boiled shellfish or dubious-looking sweetmeats. As they came to an alleyway between buildings, Nerek paused to make sure no one was close enough to overhear.

'My master's allies here have posted only one of their number in this part of Trevada, and since his attention is solely occupied by incomers I have let the veiling spell fade and lessened the strength of your constant companion.' There was a small smile. 'We must press on. The higher part of the city is walled off and my enemy is already there—'

'Suvi? Little Suvi? Is that really you . . . ?'

An old, grey-haired man in ragged garments, tottered towards them up the alley, one hand grasping a walking stick. Suviel stared at his face in amazement and joy.

'Master Babrel?'

But before another word could be spoken, Nerek had thrust her horse's reins into Suviel's hands and was moving towards the old man called Babrel with dagger drawn. Few eyes turned their way as she grabbed a handful of his grubby coat and dragged him back into the alley darkness. In horror, Suviel wound the horse reins about her hand and led them quickly in pursuit.

'Don't hurt him, Nerek. Please, I beg you!'

'He recognized you,' Nerek muttered, pressing the old man against the alley wall with an arm at his throat and the dagger at his chest. 'He spoke your name aloud—'

'He was a porter at one of the academies during my student days,' Suviel said hurriedly, reaching out to lay a hand on Nerek's shoulder. Nerek flinched, glancing sharply at her. 'Babrel will not endanger us, I swear. Look at him – how could he?'

Nerek shifted her glare to her captive and after a moment or two of unwavering scrutiny suddenly stepped away from him and snapped her dagger back in its waist sheath. 'You know this part of the city well, old man? Is there somewhere we can safely stable the horses?'

Breath wheezing in his bruised throat, Babrel nodded, braced his weight on his stick and began to hobble down the alley. Suviel flashed an angry glance at Nerek, tossed her horse traces to her, then went to Babrel's side, a helping arm about his shoulders. He felt shockingly bony.

'Master Babrel, why are you still here?'

Babrel gave her a sideways look with one eyebrow arched, a facial gesture she remembered so well.

'Why did I not abandon and flee with the others, you mean?' He gave a disapproving snort. 'Someone had to remain to bear witness, young Hantika, to keep watch and perhaps even save a little. Do you understand?'

'I do.'

'Good. And I hope you and your two accomplices have not been idle all these years. What were their names, again . . . ?'

Suviel sighed. 'Pelorn and Cavaxes.' They had been her closest friends during her time at Trevada, Pelorn with her waist-long hair and mock-haughtiness, and Cavaxes of the deadly wit. The three of them had stayed together long after attaining magehood, and for a time it had seemed that their friendship would remain unbroken. There was a sad ache as she realized that she had not thought of them for years.

Babrel seemed to notice her silence. 'Do they still live?'

'They both died at the fall of Besh-Darok.'

For a moment he was silent. 'Many good people gave their lives in those final days. Too many. Now only the brutal and the powerful survive,' he said, adding, '"As must I."'

Suviel smiled briefly, recalling the couplet of verse he had quoted from:

> A hundred monsters,
> And a thousand treacheries live on,
> As must I.

It was from the *Black Saga of Culri Moal*, a long story-song full of obscure allusions and grotesque imagery. She could imagine its unknown writer living through a period as calamitous as this one.

She eyed the lightless black hulks of buildings to either side as Babrel led them on. The grey afternoon light exposed the broken chimneys and collapsed eaves of the rooftops, but scarcely filtered down to narrow alleys littered with refuse and muddy from blocked drains. Before the invasion these buildings were student inns, and quarters for carpenters, papermakers, bookbinders and glassblowers as well as a bewildering variety of artisans producing everything from shoes and candles to kites and sail-driven carts.

'They're all empty, these houses,' Babrel said. 'Most are too dangerous even to step in through the front door, what with rotten floors and crumbling walls. All the mercenary scum and their parasites live around Journeyman Square and a few of the grander buildings along the Great Wynd, so they're the only places that get any kind of repairs.' They had rounded a corner and Babrel indicated a three-storey building which had been constructed against one of the many rocky crags which confined Trevada. 'Except for one or two others.'

As he started towards it Nerek paused, a hard suspicious expression on her face. 'We're being watched,' she said.

Babrel shrugged. 'Scavengers, beggars, drunks . . . outcasts,' he told Suviel. 'You have not said anything about your companion, and I know better than to ask. But anyone can see how dangerous she is.' He resumed his hobbling progress 'No one would interfere. Come.'

He led them down an alley to where a huge sheet of sailcloth, grey and stained from years of rain and mould, hung across a wide gap in the side of the building. The sharp rankness of damp, decrepit cloth filled Suviel's nostrils as Babrel pushed the sheet aside and gestured the women and their horses through. Suviel's mount jerked his head, reluctant to pass from dimness into pitch darkness, but while she calmed him Babrel went within and lit a lamp from a tinderbox.

The weak glow revealed a high-ceilinged room with a counter along one side and a dilapidated staircase leading up. Broken furniture was heaped in one corner but the floor appeared freshly swept. Suviel looked around with a growing sense of familiarity as she hitched her horse to a wooden pillar.

'This is the Steward's Tabard, isn't it?' There was a long empty recess behind the counter where the kegs had been, and vacant shelves and niches in the wall above where tankards and bottles had sat. This had been the taphouse set aside for the rod-serjeants and wardens of the various academies and libraries of Trevada. A refuge forbidden to students and masters alike, the Tabard had also played host to many famous poets and minstrels; it was a popular rumour back then that Avalti had written the bulk of his *Song of the Queen's Regard* within its walls.

'After the fall of Trevada,' the old man said, 'and after the sack and all the slaughter, I hid in this ruin for months, hating it yet having nowhere safer to go. But it eventually became my home.' He glanced upwards. 'I have a room up on the next floor, quite a comfortable one, too. There are other rooms you and your companion can use, if you so wish, and the only way up is by a concealed ladder. Those stairs are an impassable deathtrap.'

'Useful if you need to be warned of intruders,' Suviel said.

'But only if you have an escape route,' added Nerek.

She was standing at the bar, fingering the deep scores and gashes in the countertop while studying the empty pegs and ledges once adorned with tapestries, paintings and figurines. 'Do you have any treasure hidden away, old man? Any baubles and pennies?'

To Suviel's surprise, Babrel smiled. 'No, only worthless things. A few wooden carvings, poorly made by my own hands, and a meagre flower or two.' He looked at Suviel. 'Would you care to see?'

She turned to Nerek. 'By your leave?'

The sorceress gave a half-shrug. 'We must stay here till nightfall, so gawp over trinkets as you will. But keep out of sight, and have a care.'

It was an oblique reminder of Nerek's invisible watcher, and Suviel was silent as she followed Babrel out of the back of the taproom. A low passage led past doorless pantries and servant rooms to a larger room strewn with smashed barrels and crates. Babrel had lit a candle from the lamp in the taproom and by its light Suviel could make out dark stains on the dusty floorboards, old blood stains. But Babrel was already at one end of the barrelroom, clearing some rubbish away from a door which creaked as he opened it. Hurrying after him, she stepped through and found herself outside.

Except that it was outside in the narrowest sense. From where she stood on the threshold she could reach out and lay her palm flat on a sheer wall of rock, the jutting crag against which the Tabard had been built. Yet the original builders had contrived to create a tiny plot of ground, a secret garden that was the length of a four-wheeled cart and which widened from an arm's width near the door to no more than a couple of paces. Perhaps those long-gone, nameless founders had meant from the start for it to be a secret, since Suviel had never heard of such a thing in all her time in Trevada.

'The Tabard's walls do block off a lot of daylight,' Babrel said. 'But my little sprigs seem to gain nourishment despite the gloom.'

He was standing next to three sturdy-looking saplings, which Suviel gazed at in frowning puzzlement for a moment till she recognized the leaves.

'Agathons,' she said in amazement, going over to take a closer look.

Babrel nodded, pleased. 'During the sack, the Acolytes' beastmen cut down the four ancient ones in Journeyman Square, but afterwards I dug some seeds from the upper branches and this is the result.'

Gently, she stroked one of the small, bifurcated leaves between finger and thumb. The upper surface was dark and shiny, the lower paler and covered with a fine fuzz. 'I've never seen very young agathons before . . .'

She stopped, revelation striking home with a sudden force as the vague wrongness she had felt before revealed itself to her. Eyes wide and troubled, she turned to look at the old man.

'The children, Babrel. After sixteen years, why aren't there any children in Trevada?'

He met her gaze levelly. 'Before I answer, Suviel, I want to know why you are keeping the company of such malice.'

Black despair welled up in her on hearing his question but even as she contemplated telling him everything, she felt the presence of Nerek's watcher at her shoulder, felt the numbing tendrils of it touch the fringes of her mind.

'I cannot tell you,' she said. 'All I can do is ask you to trust me. I'm no danger to anyone at the moment, and certainly not to you.'

'It is not myself I'm worried about.' For a moment he said

nothing. Then he seemed to make up his mind, crooked a beckoning finger at her and went over to the grey, weathered wall of the tavern. Following, she watched him bend down and rap out a series of knocks on a low wooden panel. A second later, a waist-high section of the wall moved in a little, then with a scraping sound slid to one side.

'It's only me,' Babrel said. With some difficulty he kneeled beside the opening and gestured Suviel to do the same. 'And I've brought a friend.'

She sat next to him and saw beyond the dark gap the pale, rag-clad forms of almost a dozen small children. None appeared older than perhaps nine or ten, and nearly all regarded her out of faces that were hard with hunger and mistrust. There was also a little girl, perhaps two or three years of age, that she found herself playing the smile-and-look-away-and-back game with as the others looked on silently.

'They started rounding up orphans and beggar urchins about a year ago,' Babrel said softly. 'When other children began to go missing the few families moved away, and now no children are born here. But by then the Acolytes were having more brought in by wagon. Some are kidnapped, others bought outright from starving refugees, but they are all taken further up in the city, beyond a high wall they built along the terraces above the Hagradio Stairs.' He shook his head. 'They demolished the Arch Library for building material.'

Suviel felt a rising sense of dread. 'What do they want with these children?'

'I don't know. When I ask these ones about it, they all close up tight, or almost all of them. From what one or two told me, it appears that the Acolytes are using the Grand Orbicle for their foul experiments, and that they lock children into strange iron caskets decorated inside and out with symbols and words, then conduct rites upon them.' His voice wavered a little. 'They won't say anything about what happens after that.'

A few of the children within the wall shrank back as if trying not to hear, and Suviel regarded them with an appalled pity. She had read of the savagely cruel rituals carried out by followers of the Wellsource down the ages, but this was new to her. She wished she could gather these wounded innocents close and somehow take their hurt away, but she remained where she was and breathed in deeply to keep herself steady. 'How did the children escape?' she said.

'They were kept in the store vaults beneath the Grand Orbicle, in an area cleared of all those props and costumes. One of the children either found a fissure in the wall or widened a crack, squeezed through it and found a narrow passage.' He shrugged. 'The Oshang Dakhal was supposedly the site of a Skyhorse temple in ancient times – perhaps it dates from then. Perhaps it is just a fault in the rock.

'About a score of them had got into the passage when there was a rockfall. Some were crushed, while the rest followed the route till they emerged halfway up the sheer face of the Oshang Dakhal with the night all about them.' He smiled at one of the younger children and Suviel saw tears glint in his eyes. 'Can you imagine being just eight or nine years old, trying to edge your way along a ledge that is narrower than your foot? Somehow they traversed the crag to a wide fissure which they climbed. I found them in one of the carved galleries near here yesterday morning, exhausted and starving. If it had not been for one lad called Rovi I don't think they would have all survived – apparently he helped and encouraged them all the way.' He leaned forward to speak to a thin, dark-haired girl. 'Ils, would you ask Rovi to come out?'

Nervously, the girl glanced at the others and back. 'He . . . he's not here.'

Babrel was suddenly anxious. 'So where is he?'

'He went to meet his brother.'

'Rovi never said that one of the boys was his—'

Ils shook her head impatiently. 'Gawn wasn't with us when you came. He went to find a way out, but he's come back for us and spoke to Rovi with the long voice.'

Suviel listened with growing unease. Was this 'long voice' the

same as the Mage Order's mindspeech, and if so what did that
imply about the Acolytes' vile abuse of these children?

'We'll have to get the children away from here,' Babrel said.
'For all we know, Rovi is already in the hands of the guards and
telling them where we are . . .'

Suviel . . .

She held up a hand to silence him. 'Wait—'

*Suviel, we have visitors. Come quickly, and bring the old
man . . .*

She stood, helped Babrel to his feet and said, 'My companion
needs us back in the taproom.'

He frowned, but nodded and once the wooden panel was
back in place they hurried back indoors.

Suviel heard voices muttering as they retraced their steps along
the servant corridor, and as she entered the taproom from the side
of the old stairway she noticed that there was more light than
before. Then the entire room came into view and she slowed
to a halt.

Nerek was standing with her back against the long, bare
counter, with a feral smile on her face and a fiery nimbus
wreathing her right hand. Before her stood two small boys,
neither seemingly older than nine or ten, yet both faced her
with an air of eerie calm.

'Ah Suviel – so glad you could join us,' Nerek said. 'I was
just explaining to our visitors how inevitable their fates are. They
think they are rebelling—'

'You are the enemy's instrument,' said one of the boys.
'Not us.'

As he spoke, Suviel stared at him in surprise and growing
dread. For there were two voices, his own and another muted,
hoarse whisper which she heard in her thoughts rather than with
her ears.

'You know so little,' Nerek replied. 'Your shadows are my
masters' shadows, your words, your every breath is from their
mouths.' Both her hands were ablaze now. 'I can see what shares
your souls.'

'Gawn,' Babrel said quickly. 'You must go, you and Rovi—'

'Too late, old man,' said Nerek, clasping her burning hands before her. 'Their time has come.'

'No!'

Babrel tried to rush past Suviel but she grabbed him round the waist and held him back. 'Don't be a fool, Babrel. She'll—'

Hot amber fire blossomed from between Nerek's hands and streaked towards the boys. The one called Gawn made a small gesture and in the next moment the sorcerous fire split into a dozen threads which slowed and spread outwards, falling to the floor and hissing away to nothing. Nerek just smiled a little wider and the fire in her hands went from angry golden-red to a furious white.

Then the boy Gawn took a step forward, one hand outstretched and pointing at her, and in that ghastly double voice said: 'We also see what is hidden – we can see your soul.'

His face took on a look of malefic glee which made Suviel shudder, and with his extended index finger he scribed a circle in the air before him. And suddenly a black disc was hanging there, its surface shining and reflective. Nerek gasped and staggered back against the bar, its scarred wood smoking and charring where she held on for support as she stared in undisguised horror at what the black circle was showing her. Then with a shriek she swung away from it and fell to her knees, whimpering like a whipped dog, slowly slumping down onto the floor.

As Suviel rushed across the room towards her, Gawn swept his hand through the black mirror and it dissolved into tenuous grey wisps. The other boy, Rovi, said something to him and he nodded. Suviel took little notice and knelt beside the delirious Nerek, wondering why she felt this concern as she tried to tug the woman into a sitting position. Then she let out a muted cry of shock and recoiled when she saw Nerek's face.

One side was Nerek's, but on the other the flesh and even the bones beneath seemed to be in a state of flux as another set of features came and went. And Suviel remembered all too clearly those terrifying moments by that chasm in the Honjir mountains when Byrnak had taken a young man from his company and turned him into this woman. This half-glimpsed face she could see was masculine, but what did that say about Nerek? Was she truly nothing more than a fragile mask? – was that what she had seen in that black circle?

There was a sudden flare of heat at her shoulder, and a needling pain which came and went. Looking round she saw the boy Gawn, his small hands grappling and twisting an amorphous fiery shape, the watcher which Nerek had set over her. In mid-struggle, the thing lashed out with a blazing tendril and opened up a deep gash in Gawn's cheek. He never flinched, instead thrust a hand into the heart of the formless creation and tore it into embers and shadowy shreds. The wound on his face gave forth no blood and as Suviel watched it closed up and vanished.

Nerek curled up with her face in her hands, rocking back and forth, making childlike sobbing sounds. Gawn glanced at her for a cold moment, then turned to Babrel, who still stood by the old staircase, staring in wide-eyed fear.

'The Acolytes will be here soon,' he said. 'You must take the others and find somewhere safe for them.'

Babrel looked at the other boy. 'And you and Rovi?'

'They will be looking for us, so we shall lead them elsewhere.' He swung his gaze upon Suviel, and gestured at Nerek. 'They will know of her now, and they will find her in time. If you go with the old man you might evade them.'

She regarded the helpless woman by her side, and felt pity. 'I can't leave her like this,' she said. 'I have to help her somehow.'

'Then get her away from here, away from the other children. Now.'

Suviel sighed. Despite the frustration and anger which were crowding her thoughts, she knew he was right. Steeling herself, she stood over Nerek and gently coaxed her up onto her feet. The face seemed more like she had been, but shadowy ripples still came and went and her eyes were red with tears and unseeing with fear.

'May the Mother watch over you,' Babrel said in a hoarse voice.

Suviel just nodded, and with an arm round Nerek's waist guided her past the heavy sailcloth curtain and out into the darkening city.

Chapter Twenty-two

> **King Alobrin**: What are we to do? How can we
> survive this ghastly lingering night?
> **Grand-Steward**: If you do not use the darkness,
> Lord, the darkness will use you.

Gundal, *The Circle of Night*, act 1, i, 18

The northern reaches of Gronanvel, the Great Valley, were
shrouded in rain, a steady, fine rain which soaked every garment,
matted the hair and beaded the face. For the 250 men riding
north-west along the shores of Lake Unglin, it was a discomfort
to which most had become wearily accustomed.

For Archmage Bardow, however, it remained a source of
teeth-gritting irritation. For three days, all the way from Krusivel
to the hidden camp near Vanyon's Ford, then north-west along
Gronanvel, the weather had been unrelentingly cold and wet.
Now, riding with wet leather reins held in half-numb hands, and
with sodden clothes clinging to chest, arms and legs, he longed
for his warm, dry chambers back in Krusivel, and the comforting
smells of paper and candles and spell ingredients . . .

He sighed, and shook his head. *What a poor excuse for an
Archmage you have become*, he thought sourly. *Absorbed in your
own trivial woes while others are preparing to fight and bleed and
die. How pitiable and selfish. Surely Argatil would have been far
more resolute and self-possessed when he rode with the Emperor to
Arengia.*

Then the column slowed as the path narrowed to a defile between dense, unbroken forest and an outcrop of jagged rock which jutted into Lake Unglin. Bardow looked up at the crags and the treetops and the grey, grey sky and tasted the rain which trickled down his face to his lips.

It was clean and faintly sweet. He smiled, remembering Archmage Argatil's fondness for rich food, fine wine and conversation – perhaps that fateful journey north had been less dour than he imagined. After all, the Emperor was accompanied by the finest and bravest warriors of his realm, Mazaret included, as well as the Archmage and the Fathertree itself. Triumph must have seemed assured. It was only when they were in sight of the Arengia Plateau that news had come of the crushing defeat of the Northern Army at Pillar Moor. Korregan might have prayed for a victory by his Western Army, but he never lived to hear of its destruction at Wolf's Gate Pass.

We, on the other hand, are rushing towards a battle we are sure of winning, but only because the enemy has not yet put forth their greatest strength.

Sejeend was the destination. While these 250 knights rode along Gronanvel towards the Roharkan capital, Mazaret and Kodel were approaching from the south with a mixed force of irregulars from Oumetra and some 300 Hunter's Children. Oumetra had been left in the hands of a local rebel leader and his men, reinforced by a large band of fierce, bearded warriors newly arrived from the Ogucharn Isles.

It was something of a desperate gamble. The scattering of uprisings sparked by the Oumetra revolt had been savagely suppressed, despite help from sympathizers and clandestine agents, and only in eastern Kejana and parts of Cabringa was the rebellion making headway. So Mazaret and Kodel had decided to abandon the original plan of trying to hold everything south of the Great Valley and instead to consolidate in the lands east of a line joining Oumetra and Sejeend. Thus Sejeend had to be taken, and held.

Bardow uttered a quiet chuckle, drawing uncertain glances

from those riding nearby, but he kept his thoughts to himself and rode on.

As the unnerving narrowness of the defile widened, a slender, hooded rider came up past Bardow to trot beside his gifted pupil Guldamar, a tall, brown-haired man who rode ahead in the vanguard. A small hand bearing a blue ring pushed back the hood, revealing one of Medwin's best students, a young female mage called Terzis. She was a short, lithe woman with clear-eyed, beautiful features which seldom displayed anything resembling a smile. Close-cropped sandy hair served to emphasize her sombre demeanour. After losing her parents in the convulsions of the invasion, she had spent several years in a grim orphanage in Adnagaur before Medwin himself had discovered her abilities during a visit to the port.

Contemplating them, Bardow's mood grew dark. For all that Guldamar and Terzis were two of the most talented apprentices that they had, Bardow knew that he was taking a terrible risk in pitting them against Mogaun shamans. But the demands of the plan of attack were unavoidable and admitted few if any alternatives.

Not long after leaving the defile, the column of knights passed a sheltered glade where the commander, one Rul Yarram, called a halt.

'It will be a brief respite,' Yarram said to his senior officers. 'We are less than an hour's ride from Sejeend, so quarter-rations for both men and mounts. That's all.' He was a short, wiry man in his fifties possessed of a certain nervous energy and a dominating persona. When he glanced over at Bardow, the Archmage sighed and replied with a nod then watched a satisfied Yarram dismount and gather his lieutenants about him.

Bardow swung himself gingerly down to the ground, grimacing with the accumulated aches of three days on horseback. As he kneaded muscles in his lower back, he heard the slow hoof-thuds of a rider drawing near.

'Master, you should let Terzis or myself mindspeak with Medwin. Surely we can ill afford any weakening of your abilities.'

Bardow smiled. 'Ah, Guldamar,' he said without looking round. 'In some ways you are a credit to my teachings, but in others you still have progress to make.' Finished with his exercises, he regarded his student. Guldamar was a handsome young man, his long, dark-brown hair braided back in several tails after the fashion of Dalbari mountainmen. Looking concerned, he dismounted and stood beside his horse with the reins in his hand, mouth opening to speak. Bardow forestalled him.

'When you get to my age, you'll realize that self-sacrifice is not always a good thing. I mindspoke with Medwin and Mazaret when we reached Vanyon's Ford because it was too far for you, and I'm doing so now because I want you bright and alert when we arrive at the walls of Sejeend.'

Bardow paused a moment, noticing a plain blue ring on one of Guldamar's fingers, then he went on.

'Now, find Terzis and go over the elements of the Cadence thought-canto and its variants – make sure they're fresh in your mind. And with any luck you will live to be my age.'

Looking chastened, Guldamar bowed his head then led his mount away. Bardow watched him leave, then shook his head, wondering whether the rings signified friendship or something deeper. Then he hitched his horse in the shelter of a nearby eyeleaf tree and tipped a little feed on the ground before striding over to where Rul Yarram was patiently waiting.

The thought-canto of Inner Speech was similar to Spiritwing, though not as demanding, and after only a few moments he was speaking with Medwin, eldest of the three mages accompanying Mazaret. Once the Lord Commander learned of Yarram's whereabouts, his response was concise – *We shall attack Sejeend's southern battlements within the hour. You must proceed without delay.*

After that, the men were given a few minutes to finish whatever they were eating before being ordered back into their saddles. Back on the lakeside trail, now churning into mud beneath scores of hooves, Bardow paused off to the side for a final backward look.

Across Lake Unglin, lush flatlands, tilled fields and pastures stretched back less than a mile from the lake shore then rose abruptly into the upthrusting immensity of the Rukang Mountains. A great cataract spilled from a centuries-worn notch in a cliff-face directly opposite, grey-white falls which hazed the air, crashing torrents throwing up clouds of vapour from a boulder-strewn pool at the foot of the cliffs. Here, at the eastern throat of Gronanvel, the Rukangs were at their steepest, their grimmest, most trackless and impassable. Bardow thought of the plains of Khatris which lay beyond, a country once known as the Land of Swords for all the battles fought there in olden times. Then, the Rukangs had been a vast bulwark against invasion from the south – now, they forced anyone coming from the north to choose between Vanyon's Ford and Sejeend.

And when we take Sejeend, Bardow thought sombrely, *the enemy won't have a choice at all.*

The assault on Sejeend's lakeward defences began as planned. Rul Yarram arranged his cavalry in two wings with Bardow, Guldamar and Terzis in the front rank of the left. From there they would unleash a volley of Lesser Power spells and bring down part of the main wall and hopefully one of the three towers which guarded the approaches. Yarram's knights would then pour through the gap and take the defenders unprepared.

Battle standards were produced from saddlebags, snarling creatures of war on pale blue backgrounds. Banners flying, the knights cantered in formation from behind a long spur of forest and into full view of the ramparts of Sejeend. With exacting grace both wings wheeled to face the enemy and broke into a steady gallop. By now the rain had lifted and occasional shafts of sunshine lanced through the clouds, flashing on wet armour and unsheathed blades.

Bardow rode in the front rank flanked by Guldamar and Terzis. Each had begun the thought-canto of Cadence several minutes before, and Bardow could feel an aura of Lesser Power gathering about them as the walls grew nearer.

He glanced sideways past Terzis at the straight, glittering ranks of galloping riders and thought, *Soon, very soon . . .*

Then he looked back to scores upon scores of enemy troops streaming out of a couple of open gates and racing pell-mell towards the oncoming cavalry.

'What insanity is this?' Guldamar shouted above the din of the charge.

Bardow did not answer, fixing his gaze upon the approaching mob. Everyone seemed to be a 7-foot Mogaun savage roaring though a bristling beard and brandishing a club, a spear or a poleaxe. At first glance it was an unnerving sight but there was nothing co-ordinated about it. *Guldamar is right*, he thought. *This is madness. So what am I missing?*

He frowned, trying to block out all other sensation as he began a second thought-canto in his mind. Knifeye, seeing through to the truth . . .

The strain of maintaining both spells was like a burning burden in his head, but he maintained it. Off to the right, Yarram was gesturing the front ranks to level their spears as Bardow saw an onrushing knot of brutish warriors turn into terrified, rag-clad townsfolk. In horror, he wrenched his horse rightwards, trying to slow the impetus of those behind, trying to reach Yarram's wing of riders.

'Stop!' he cried. 'It's an illusion – don't attack!'

But it was too late. There was a mingled crash of screams as spears and swords struck down the blindly rushing, spell-disguised people. In a matter of seconds the open ground was a scene of slaughter. The carefully planned charge dissolved into confusion as some of Yarram's men dismounted and went to the aid of maimed and slain innocents. Bardow saw one young knight weeping over a dying woman he had speared only moments before, and another struggling to staunch a deep wound in the neck of an old man.

A hand grasped his shoulder roughly and he turned to see a dishevelled, blood-spattered Yarram.

'How could this happen, wizard?' he snarled. 'Tell me, by the Mother!'

Bardow glared at him out of a hard knot of cold rage. 'A Mogaun shaman is behind this abomination,' he said. 'Get your men back on their horses, commander. We have vengeance to exact.'

Yarram met his iron gaze for a moment, then gave a sharp nod and rode off to goad his knights into action. Bardow sought out Guldamar and Terzis, and saw them tending to the wounded. His call to them was wordless, imperative, and they were back astride their horses and riding to meet him in moments.

Terzis was pale and trembling, her eyes red from tears, hands holding the reins in a white-knuckled grip. She seemed unable to speak, unlike Guldamar.

'I have never . . . never seen such a barbarous . . .' The young man struggled for words. 'And I know where he is—'

'The middle tower,' Bardow said. 'He is watching us right now. I can feel his joy.'

As one they turned to face the town, the walls, the middle of the three squat towers. Savage chants and jeers were faintly audible over the cries and moans of the wounded. Bardow strove with his senses, shutting it all out, then with head bowed he focused on the thought-canto of Cadence, making its elements and gyring form the axis of his intent.

Like a song of his blood and bone, like a fire fuelled by heart and mind, it grew up from somewhere in his chest, up into his throat. He was vaguely aware of his companions enacting the same ritual as the spell burgeoned till he knew he could restrain it no longer. And all his anger erupted in a wordless roar out of which the Cadence sound was born. An instant later came Guldamar's, then Terzis'. The air itself distorted, grass tore and pebbles leaped with the passing of that three-fold shriek of power.

Invisible, it flew across the open ground. There was a moment of anticipation. Then it struck the tower. For a long instant the building held, powdered mortar puffing from between cracks, a few roof slates sent spinning. Then, like a child's toy of wooden blocks, it gave way, teetered and collapsed, clouds of dust billowing around crashing tons of timber and stone. A large piece of the tower toppled sideways onto a stretch of the ramparts, crushing dozens of the defending mercenaries and demolishing the wall. On the other side, a section of wall fell backwards into the town, tearing open a pair of heavy wooden gates. Yarram saw the opportunity and led his knights in a mad charge towards the unguarded gap.

But Bardow was already at the gates, urging his horse over the splintered wreckage, swinging his stave at the few remaining dazed mercenaries. With a harsh clattering of hooves he rode into the cobbled town street and stared about him with a piercing gaze. When the tower had first begun to totter, he had seen a scrawny figure leap from one of its lower windows and now that the Cadence canto was spent he knew from suddenly heightened senses that the Mogaun shaman was alive and heading towards the south of the town. Bardow followed, head full of the sight of dying innocents, heart full of vengeance.

The roads sloped up in the direction of the pale stone mass of Hojamar Keep and the low saddle-ridge it had been built to guard many centuries ago. As he rode the din of Yarram's battle receded, only to be replaced by other sounds of confusion. Gangs of townsfolk roamed the streets looking for Mogaun sympathizers or any mercenaries foolish enough to stray out alone. Smoke was rising from a dozen places across the town and from the battlements up on the ridge came the faint noise of fighting.

But Bardow was engaged in the hunt, tracing the hate-taste of the shaman through the streets of Sejeend. The bounds of his mind stretched as he shaped three thought-cantos, three separate and distinct braidings of smell, texture, form and sound, symbols both explicable and cryptic which were his personal links to the Lesser Power. The strain of it grew with each step, and although he could feel it starting to eat into his strength he was heedless, driven.

Few approached him as he rode through the smoky, twisting streets, and those who did he struck insensible with the thought-canto Lull. Before long he came to an imposing townhouse whose tall, narrow windows had been tightly shuttered and whose tall

doors of carved agathon were guarded by four Sentinels. Using
Lull he disposed of them from horseback then dismounted,
hitched his horse to a wall stanchion and climbed the steps to
the doors.

Inside was a long, dim hallway hung with heavy tapestries,
their details scarcely revealed by a couple of weak, flickering
tallow lamps. There were a few doors leading off, yet Bardow
made for the main staircase at the far end. He knew there were
prisoners behind those doors, their fear and despair seeping out
into the hall like a thin odour of agony. But they would have to
wait until he had dealt with their tormentors.

He climbed through four floors of darkness broken only by
grey slivers of daylight from a poorly fitting window shutter, and
the occasional lamp or guttering torch. All sounds were muted,
the murmurs of prisoners, or their weeping, the creak of steps
underfoot, faint shouts from outside, but no guards patrolling.
Bardow could feel the malicious expectancy of his waiting enemy,
and the towering arrogance.

Overconfident, he thought. *Good.*

At the top floor his senses drew him to a short passage and five
steps leading up to a door whose tree-and-bell carvings had been
defaced with an axe. He paused and looked down at the stave he
had brought with him – it was a two-foot-long piece of agathon
wood, its ends heeled with bands of rediron, its length incised with
symbols and intricate patterns. Although it was not sorcerous, and
held no power of its own, it was well made and satisfyingly heavy
in the hand. He nodded to himself – it would have to do.

Then, with forced calmness, he stepped up to the door and
pushed it open.

The hate was palpable as he entered the darkened room, a
hate as thick as smoke, engulfing, tainting. Light bloomed from
rushlights placed at either end of a long trestle, upon which a
hooded figure sat cross-legged. Glinting eyes regarded him amid
a deathly silence. There was a sharp, unsettling odour in the air
and his undersense told him of the complex symbols drawn in
blood upon the floor.

'*Ohosstu jun gyor sashdno maroi, yaspe?* – Have you come to burn me with your flames, o mighty candle?'

Bardow's reply to this mocking barb was the thought-canto Lull, hurling its pent-up power straight at the Mogaun. A blue-white nimbus flickered around the seated shaman, who grinned and uttered a low chuckle as the aura began to falter. Undaunted, Bardow released his second spell, the thought-canto Seethe, which he directed at the shaman's clothing and at the trestle beneath him.

Boiling steam erupted from the Mogaun's furs and likewise from the trestle's wooden planks. He shrieked in sudden pain and tore off his upper garments while scrambling bare-footed down onto the floor. Enraged, he flung out his arms towards Bardow, bony fingers hooked in claws, and spoke a string of barbaric words interspersed with clicks and other sounds.

Symbols appeared on the floor, glowing a hot, corrosive green. Simultaneously, the rushlights' weak radiance brightened and thickened, an eldritch sight in the steam-veiled room. Suddenly, the dense knots of light fountained towards the ceiling then swooped down at Bardow in the shape of huge fiery hands.

He reeled on his feet as they struck and enfolded him in an abominable grasp. Yet he stayed upright, eyes fixed on the wildly gesticulating shaman, and on his scrawny neck. The huge conjured hands were tightening their grip on his neck and chest, twisting, crushing. But he shut out the torment and instead used his third and final thought-canto, Trueflight, to enbind the stave he held in his free hand. With the last of his strength he drew back and hurled it at his foe.

All movement seemed to slow to a crawl. The Mogaun saw what Bardow had done and began to turn away but the enchanted stave altered the curvature of its flight accordingly. The panicking Mogaun held up a hand to fend off the attack, and the stave punched straight through it and the underside of the shaman's chin and lanced up into his brain.

Bardow fell to his knees, all vigour spent, even as his enemy staggered back against the wall, bloody mouth making ghastly wet sounds. But the eyes remained fixed on Bardow, who sprawled over on his side. From within the dreadful twin grasp of malign sorcery Bardow stared at floor level across at the shaman, now slumped against the wall, with his head tilted to one side and blood darkening his neck, and refusing to die. The eyes burned with hate, the lips silently mouthed and snarled, and to Bardow it seemed as if the Mogaun was feeding on his own agony.

And he despaired, knowing that all his strength and skill had not been enough, knowing that his death was upon him. As his sight began to fail, he wished he had hoped less . . .

Running footsteps clattered somewhere in the house, doors banged, voices spoke and wept. The footsteps came nearer and he was vaguely aware of newcomers in the room. Someone spoke his name, then uttered a curse. There was the hiss of a drawn blade followed by the sound of a sword striking flesh. And again. Suddenly the crushing pressure was gone and a blurry realness crept back into his vision. Someone had opened the shutters and natural light filled the room. He could just make out a figure standing over the shaman's still form, one hand lifting up something by long strands – the head, he realized.

Someone else crouched close by and stared worriedly at him.

'Archmage – do you hear me? The Mogaun scum is dead. Do you understand?'

The man was broad-shouldered, with cuts and bruises on his unlovely face and a fresh gash on one side of his smooth, hairless scalp. Recognition cut through the exhaustion.

'The Mother must surely have a sense of humour,' Bardow said hoarsely, 'to make you my rescuer, ser Korren.'

Dow Korren, chief negotiator for the Northern Cabal, gave an ironic smile. 'I and my associates were waylaid during our return journey, Archmage, which we did not find the least bit amusing. Still, it is good to find you well.'

'I'm a breathing ruin, as you can clearly see. Help me up, if you will.' As Dow Korren lifted him into a seated position, he went on. 'I'm a cup drained to the dregs, a log charred near the core, a river baked to the merest trickle . . .' He paused, suddenly aware of how he must sound. He sighed, rubbed at his eyes with trembling hands then focused on the other man in the room and was pleased to see who it was. 'Leave that cursed thing be, Guldamar, and come over and speak to me of the fight.'

The young mage had placed the shaman's severed head on the trestle and was squatting before it, frowning as he contemplated the grisly object.

'The last I saw of the fighting was Yarram leading some of his men in pursuit of a few Mogaun still on horseback and trying to escape. Terzis was helping a few of Yarram's captains to protect a captured Mogaun chieftain from a mob bent on revenge.' With the point of the sword he still held, he scraped at the black, flaking symbols on the floor. Then he raised it to indicate the blood-spattered head. 'Something is amiss here.'

'Explain,' Bardow said, suddenly uneasy.

Guldamar shook his head. 'Some kind of presence yet remains in the room, and the head is part of it. I think.'

'Then we chop it up and feed the pieces to the greenwings,' Dow Korren growled, pulling a long dagger from his waist.

'No, wait,' Bardow said, forcing himself shakily to his feet. He staggered with the effort but Korren lent a supporting arm. 'There is only one certain way of purging whatever lingers in this place – fire.'

'We burn the body?' said Korren.

'This room,' Bardow said. 'The entire house.'

'We would have to get everyone out,' Korren said.

Guldamar got to his feet and resheathed his blade. 'Then we should begin.'

Bardow nodded, glanced around the room then paused in wonder at what he saw through the open shutters.

The window faced south and from this height offered a view across clustered roofs to the keep and the battlements along the nearby cliff edge. There was fighting up there, knots of men struggling and charging, with the thick of it taking place on a wide stone bridge which joined the battlements to the keep. Heaving throngs of warriors from both sides were locked in deadly combat, and at its centre flew a banner, a great blue flag bearing the image of the Fathertree. Instinctively, Bardow knew that Tauric was near that banner and he felt a surge of conflicting emotions, a deep-seated joy at the proud flaunting of their long-oppressed emblem, and a biting anxiety over the boy's safety.

'Our comrades need our help,' Guldamar said urgently. 'Come, we shall clear out this foul place and put it to the torch.'

'I would gladly aid you,' Dow Korren said. 'But my colleagues were imprisoned in the lower town – I must discover their whereabouts and release those who yet live.'

With a hand still resting on Dow Korren's shoulder Bardow turned from the window. 'You shall have help in your search – I shall see to it.' He grimaced at the acrid odour of the room. 'For now, let us begone from here.'

To Tauric it seemed that he was clamped in a vice of bodies. Gathered all around him in a tight phalanx were the men who called themselves the White Companions, a dozen or so young men Kodel had selected from the hundreds who volunteered before they left Oumetra. On Tauric's left was tall Aygil, the muscles of his arms bulging as he strove to hold the great banner aloft, while on his right, ever-vigilant, was Kodel's nameless deputy, the Armourer.

It was frustrating. From the moment he and the others had climbed the scaling ladders up onto the cliff battlements, he had been surrounded and protected and never given the chance to swing his sword in anger. And now the Hunter's Children, who in their scores surrounded the White Companions, were driving forward along the bridge, forcing the mercenaries back towards the keep. Men were fighting and dying for him, Tauric knew, and he felt a helpless fury as he saw one of the Hunter's Children take a spear thrust in the shoulder which sent him toppling over the bridge's low parapet.

A hand gripped his shoulder and the Armourer spoke above the battle's din.

'You are already in enough danger,' he said. 'And still you accomplish much. See how they fight for you.'

Tauric nodded yet could not shake off the sense of frustration. He remembered something that Kodel had said to him in Oumetra just days ago – 'An emperor cannot be a mere symbol. To his subjects he is more than a mortal man wearing a crown, so he has a duty to do and to be more.'

He was about to say as much to the Armourer when a shout went up from the enemy troops. One of their number had clambered onto the shoulders of the second rank only yards away, and with a dagger in either hand he launched himself over the heads of attackers and defenders alike, straight towards Tauric.

Closed in on all sides, Tauric struggled to draw his sword. But the Armourer was swifter by far and with a savage accuracy brought his own blade round in a silver blur for the mercenary to impale himself as he came down. The dying man crashed into Tauric who reeled backwards, involuntarily grabbing Aygil the standard bearer and dragging him down too.

At this, the enemy let out a mass roar of triumph and retaliated in furious onslaught. Cries of 'He is fallen!' made the Hunter's Children at the front falter and glance back. The mercenaries seized the moment and made a disciplined rush in the direction of the wavering banner, even as some of the White Companions hauled a dazed Tauric from beneath the bleeding corpse of his assailant.

Then the enemy broke through, some four or five brawny soldiers wielding swords and maces and easily beating aside the few White Companions who stood against them. Without hesitation the Armourer shoved Tauric towards a knot of Hunter's Children already moving to his aid, then lunged at the nearest mercenary and felled him with a single blow.

Recovering his senses, Tauric saw Aygil struggling to lift the great blue banner, its pole snapped in half from the crush of bodies moments before. Kodel's words came back to him once more – *An emperor cannot be a mere symbol* – and he snatched the broken banner from a surprised Aygil and with a sudden surge of strength held it above his head. He cried out, 'In the name of the Fathertree!' and led a charge past the Armourer's mêlée and towards the open entrance of the keep.

Someone bellowed orders and panicking defenders leaped to close the gates, but too late – Tauric and his followers rushed up to the heavy wooden doors and shoved them wide open. Inside was a high, oval room with rich tapestries and drapes on the walls, heavy hide rugs scattered across the floor, and a fire burning in a massive hearth. Along the wall a stairway curved up to the rooftop battlements, and several teardrop-shaped lanterns hung from two tall wooden lamp-poles.

The few defenders near the doors retreated to the fire, where a larger group of mercenaries waited. Although armed and ready, they made no move to attack and instead glared at Tauric and his metal arm and the banner which he had balanced on one shoulder so that the flag hung about him like a cloak. Tauric thought he saw fear in the eyes of some of them and felt a certain satisfaction.

Then there were mutters, the mercenaries moved apart and a tall man stepped forward. He wore heavy leather armour, well tailored in ochre and carmine, a close-fitting bronze helm, and on his right arm a spiderclaw. The gauntlet-sword was a thing of deadly beauty, overlapping strips of metal covering from the wrist down a long glove of some reptilian hide, its pebbled surface gleaming grey and silver in the firelight. The gauntlet's palm and fingers were fitted to the hilt of a broadsword with stitching and straps, making it all of a single piece.

The spiderclaw came up, levelled straight at Tauric, and golden light flashed along its edges.

'I am Crolas, Governor of Sejeend,' said the tall man. 'Yield to me and lay down your weapons, and I will guarantee you all safe passage back to the south.'

For a long moment there was only the sound of fighting from outside and the hiss and crack of logs burning in the hearth. Then Tauric spoke.

'I am Tauric Tor-Galantai, heir to the throne of Besh-Darok, defender of life and land . . .' His voice shook but he had found the words and went on. 'If you and your men lay down your arms now, much of what has happened here will be overlooked. Make term with us, Crolas, and join us in this fight.'

Crolas regarded him levelly. 'You speak well, for a stripling—'

'Thank you, my lord. I expect to be much improved come the day of my coronation.'

At that, a crooked smile. 'I fear you do not understand what stands against you, the sheer number and terrible powers of your chosen enemy. No, ser Tauric, I shall not surrender to you, for the sea does not make terms with a sinking ship.' He turned to his men. 'Take them.'

But even as the words were out of his mouth, Tauric was dashing towards the stairway with the others hard on his heels. Crolas urged his guards after them and as swordfights broke out on the lower steps Tauric heard the mercenary chief call out his name. Slowing in his upward rush, he glanced down to see Crolas grinning and pointing to the head of the stairs.

More armed mercenaries were descending from the roof and edging down to meet Tauric and the vanguard of his outnumbered band. Fear and despair rose in him, threatening to overwhelm his reason. *Trapped*, he thought, *because of me . . .*

As the mercenaries came closer, Aygil spoke up. 'We are here to die for you, lord. Let us face them!'

'Fight and live, Aygil!' he cried as the standard-bearer and five others dashed past him and stood shoulder to shoulder. He watched as the first rank of mercenaries attacked, feeling angry and helpless. Then a movement to the side made him look round, and he gasped and jerked backwards as one of the tall lamp-poles came toppling towards the spot where he stood. The teardrop lamps swung wildly on their chains, one came loose and fell to the floor with a deep chiming sound, spraying burning oil onto nearby rugs.

The top of the lamp-pole struck the stair with a loud wooden bang, bounced once and for a moment was still. Then the end began to judder slightly, making faint scraping sounds on the stone. Tauric looked past the edge of the stairs and was aghast to see Crolas, with acrobatic grace and balance, running up the improvised ladder.

In the time it took Tauric to ready his sword with his metal hand, Crolas leaped the last few feet and knocked it from his grip. There was no hesitation in the mercenary's actions, only swift and brutal efficiency. But as he swung the spiderclaw blade down in a glittering arc, Tauric's desperation lent him speed enough to move his artificial hand in time.

Sparks flew as metal struck metal with a harsh clang. Hate spurred his strength, he closed his gleaming fingers about the blade, twisted and snapped it in half. Crolas' features betrayed a mixture of surprise and fury, but still he moved to the attack and lunged at Tauric with the broken blade, landing an awful blow to his shoulder. The leather armour he wore took the worst of it, but the pain was stunning. Semi-conscious, he crashed to the steps.

He did not hear the fearful shouts of his followers as they rushed to form a ring about him. His every sense was swamped by a shadowy numbness which somehow held him below the surface of the world but kept him from sinking into black nothingness. Yet he was not alone – another presence was here, a fleeting immensity, a pervasive nullity . . .

Oh, foolish son . . .

Sensation burst upon him, heavy smells of green growth—

. . . **Son of a foolish son** . . .

—tastes of earth and decay and roots, odours of forest and fen—

. . . **your haste serves nothing, your death serves nothing. Knowledge serves, devotion serves, preparation serves. Listen now, and learn** . . .

New impressions flooded into him, making him victim (hands tied behind his back, ankles bound, mouth gagged, and a heavy sheet lay over him), then observer (a horse and cart, a darkened alley, a weakly moving form in the cart, half-concealed, a grubby floral dress, long pale girl hair)

Tauric, help . . . please . . .

Alael! He could feel the texture of her thoughts, the closed-in terror and the narcotic weariness that deadened her limbs and dragged at her mind.

'Where are you? Who—'

They . . . outside Oumetra they trapped me . . . drugged me . . . remember this morning, saw a white keep, soldiers, riders . . .

But the effort was too much for her and he felt her thoughts drift apart and her presence fall away, even as he was plunged back into waking pain . . .

'No, wait – he yet lives!'

Through blurred sight he recognized Lord Commander Mazaret crouched next to him, one hand keeping him seated upright while the other lightly slapped his face. All the fighting seemed to be over, for there were only the moans of the wounded and dying to be heard. Tauric still felt the horrible pain of his shoulder, and his head was full of grey veils, but now he fought to stay conscious, to speak.

'She is here!'

'Don't tire yourself,' Mazaret said.

Then another squatted on the steps nearby – Kodel. 'Who is here?'

'Alael!' Tauric almost shouted. 'She is a prisoner, here in Sejeend. We must rescue her . . .'

Mazaret and Kodel glanced at each other, then listened carefully as Tauric related the events of his strange vision. The Lord Commander's gaze became oddly intense when he spoke of the first voice and the strong odours of the forest, while the chief of the Hunter's Children was a still, regarding presence throughout. When Tauric had finished, Mazaret got to his feet.

'If her captors intend to leave, it will be by the north or east gate. I will have patrols sent to both – no cart or wagon will pass unsearched, I promise.' With a sharp nod to Kodel, he hurried down the steps, shouting orders as he went.

'A good man,' Kodel said. 'If somewhat stiff-necked. He was not amused to learn that you and your followers had joined the assault with my approval. My friend the Armourer was similarly put out by your impulsive charge, although like me he sees that you have the essential qualities of a good commander – intuition and luck.'

'Kodel,' said Tauric. 'What happened to the mercenary chief, Crolas?'

Kodel reached behind him and dragged something into view – it was the spiderclaw, the reptile hide of its upper-arm covering torn and slick with blood. 'I heard of the offer you made him. It was more than he deserved – pity that he made such a poor choice.'

'He didn't seem like an evil man,' Tauric said, troubled. 'I almost found myself liking him, even though he was my enemy.'

'Of course,' said Kodel with a wintry smile. 'Your enemies cannot betray you – they can only kill you.'

Chapter Twenty-three

The standard has been raised,
And the dagger is blooded.
The enemy knows our names,
And the number of our arrows.
Driven by the blast of Time,
We rush towards the brink.

Vosada Boroal, *The Great House of Hallebron*, book iii, 1.27

Cloud-broken sunshine was brightening and darkening the court-yard outside when Mazaret emerged from Hojamar Keep. The first person he saw was Rul Yarram climbing the long main steps, so he descended to meet him partway.

'Commander,' Yarram said, saluting with open right hand against his chest. 'I can now report that the enemy's presence within Sejeend no longer presents a threat. Apart from those we have killed or captured, there are no more than a dozen Mogaun still at large, with about a handful of mercenaries holed up somewhere, perhaps hoping to pass themselves off as townsfolk or Roharkans from the country.'

Mazaret indicated the smoke trails rising from a number of places across the town. 'But it seems that our problems are not over.'

The Rul nodded. 'The mobs. We've been hard put to deal with some of them, especially when pursuing enemy stragglers – the looters attack us and the Mogaun without discrimination.'

'So – sixteen years of barbarian rule has finally borne its fruit,' Mazaret said, staring bleakly out at the town. 'Did you know that Sejeend was once a haven for master weavers and tapestry-makers, Yarram, a place of learning and beauty?'

'My grandfather was from here, ser,' Yarram said thoughtfully. 'I used to visit him twice a year until he died, almost a year before the invasion.'

Mazaret looked at him in faint surprise. *It must be hard for him to see the town brought so low,* he thought. *How might I feel to walk the streets of Besh-Darok again after sixteen years?*

For an awkward moment neither spoke, until Yarram broke the silence.

'When will the reinforcements arrive, ser?'

'Two hundred knights of the order are due by nightfall, and another hundred before the dawn. As for the Hunter's Children, Kodel tells me that a hundred bowmen will here by late evening, with smaller groups arriving throughout the night.' He gazed levelly at Yarram. 'But even if our forces grow, the Mogaun will inevitably move against us and when they do it will be a sore, hard fight.'

Yarram straightened. 'What are my orders, Lord Commander?'

'Place all your men, bar twenty, under your most trusted officer – by my order they are to seek out any grain or victuals store still intact and near the keep, make it secure and send a messenger to me here. In the meantime, Yarram, you will take your twenty men across the town, post ten at the east gate and the rest at the north gate where I want you to remain. All wagons and carts leaving the town must be searched for a young girl, perhaps bound and concealed. She seems sixteen summers of age, slender with long, fair hair and may be wearing a floral dress.'

'And if we discover her?'

'If it is safe and if she is fit to be moved, bring her to the keep with all despatch – otherwise, she is to be kept from harm at all costs.' He laid a hand on the man's shoulder. 'It will be dangerous, Yarram, but the girl must be found. She is an unschooled mage of great power and must not fall into the hands of the Acolytes.'

A steely determination came into Yarram's eyes. 'I understand, ser. By your leave.'

Mazaret nodded and watched the officer hurry away down the steps. *Would you be equally eager if I told you that she was Tauric's rival for the throne?* he thought, then smiled ruefully. *Yes, I think you would. You are an honourable man, Rul Yarram.*

Tauric. Thoughts of the young heir brought back with sharp clarity the wild alarm he had felt on seeing the Fathertree banner unfurl on the keep's high battlements. When he and scarcely a score of his knights broke through into that great chamber and saw the mercenary chief Crolas standing over the prone Tauric, Mazaret was certain that all was lost. Then Kodel had appeared out of nowhere and after a mad flurry of blows Crolas lay dying at his feet.

Which meant that Kodel had saved Tauric from looming death twice, and in turn Tauric was clearly coming to regard Kodel as a mentor. Mazaret, uncertain of Kodel's motives and uneasy at the possible consequences, now felt a vague resentment after hearing Tauric's account of his vision. Listening to the boy speak of a terrifying spiritlike voice and strange, intense smells of leaves and earth, he was privately amazed at the similarities to the reverie he'd had when his family died in Krusivel years ago.

Not for the first time, he found himself wondering what kind of presence truly lay behind such visitations. His own had suggested that of the Earthmother, but what could her purpose be, and was it good or evil, or neither? Once, while on a secret buying trip to Scallow, he had chanced upon a travelling Ogucha seer from the islands and queried him about a few details from his vision. The aged man, sitting cross-legged beneath a low canopy of cheap yellow silk, had fixed Mazaret with a doleful stare as he produced a little sack from within his grubby robe and tipped out the contents. After poking amongst the bones and pebbles and dusty feathers for several moments, the seer had muttered, 'You will have no wife, but many sons.'

At the time he had felt like striking the scrawny old man but the need for anonymity had stayed his hand, and now he smiled wryly at the memory.

One of Kodel's men, a flame-haired youth in the greys and browns of the Hunter's Children, approached with a message from the mage Medwin. At once Mazaret followed him down the steps, in through the great doors to the lower keep and along to a dining chamber hastily rearranged to hold meetings. For the next half hour he engaged in heated discussions with a handful of men who had been town stewards and wardens before the invasion, two administrators appointed by the Mogaun chieftains (and now co-operating rather than face the mobs), and several surviving nobles released from the dungeons.

With a combination of coercion and cajolery, Mazaret and Medwin persuaded them to work together in restoring order to Sejeend. Mazaret found himself playing the harsh disciplinarian to Medwin's reasonable negotiator, and thoroughly enjoying it. As the provisional town council began drafting its first decrees, the soldier and the mage walked back up to the courtyard.

'That was a fine performance, Lord Commander,' said Medwin, a grey-bearded, portly man whose dark brown robe was as spotless and undamaged as it was before the battle. 'I almost believed you when you proposed burning at the stake anyone guilty of supplying the Mogaun with harvests from seized lands.'

'If I didn't believe it,' Mazaret said, 'neither would they. Nor would a couple of the former collaborators have turned quite so gratifyingly pale.'

Medwin laughed. 'Then I should assure you that the flattery I employed in that room was far less sincere.'

'And where is your fellow-mage?' Mazaret said as they emerged into the courtyard. Uninterrupted sunshine was filling the walled-in parade ground with brightness, warming the stones and baking the dust out of the ground, and Mazaret felt a sudden prickle of perspiration across face and neck.

'Oh, Eshmor is talking to the town's Earthmother priestesses and initiates about opening healing rooms in the keep for the sick and wounded.'

Mazaret frowned. 'I thought the Earthmother orders in Sejeend were wiped out – the persecution and torture in this part of Roharka was especially savage.'

'They went to extraordinary lengths to maintain the offices of their chapter with initiates trained and ready to assume another's position if they were taken by the enemy.' Medwin shrugged. 'How such an arrangement would rest with the Abbess back at Krusivel is, ah, debatable . . .' His eyes widened and he waved to someone across the courtyard. 'Why, there's the Archmage – he would be able to shed more light on the question.'

Mazaret saw Bardow and the female mage Terzis entering through the tall courtyard gates, the former leaning on the latter's arm. Medwin raised his arm in greeting and strode on faster, drawing ahead of Mazaret. The mage was barely two paces in front when he stumbled, put both hands to his throat, let out a strangled cry and slumped to the ground, gasping. At the same time, over at the gates, Terzis had uttered an agonizing scream and was lying in the dust, writhing while Bardow crawled towards her.

Mazaret rushed to Medwin's side and found him with his hands clapped over his eyes, muttering: 'In the name of the Mother – he's dead . . . !'

A pair of Hunter's Children came over, offering help, but Mazaret waved them away. 'Who is dead, Medwin? Who?' he said.

His voice seemed to break through the hysteria and the mage lowered his hands and looked straight up at him.

'Guldamar is dead – betrayed by cruel sorcery, then throttled . . .' He touched his own throat with a trembling hand. 'I felt him try to reach us as the life . . . the life went out of him.' He breathed in sharply, and reached to clutch at Mazaret's surcoat. 'A shaman! My master dealt with one of them, but how could we know that another was hiding himself from us . . .' Medwin shuddered, and seemed on the point of tears. 'And poor Terzis . . . lend me your arm, my lord, I beg you. Let me see her and the Archmage.'

Sentries from the gate were trying to help Bardow and Terzis to their feet as Mazaret half-carried Medwin over to them. Terzis was sitting with her face buried in her hands, sobbing and refusing to stand.

'Medwin told me that Guldamar is dead,' Mazaret said to Bardow. 'Is this true?'

The Archmage looked ashen and weary. 'I exhausted myself in battle earlier and I only felt the edges of whatever happened to Guldamar, but yes . . . I think that he is gone.'

'How could this be, Bardow?' Medwin said.

Bardow seemed dazed. 'I'm not sure. He would have been with Dow Korren, helping him find—'

'Dow Korren?' Mazaret said abruptly.

Then Bardow quickly told him how he had tracked a shaman from the western walls to a townhouse where he engaged in a nightmarish struggle, and was saved by the intervention of Guldamar and Dow Korren.

'He claimed that he and his colleagues had been taken prisoner, and that he had to find and release them.' The Archmage rubbed the heel of his hand across his forehead. 'I insisted that he took Guldamar with him, and now—'

'Do not blame yourself for what that snake has done,' said a voice. It was Kodel, with Tauric at his side. 'His Northern Cabal has thwarted our stratagems on many occasions.'

Mazaret felt a surge of irritation at Kodel's presence, but concentrated on the urgency of the situation.

'How much of the murder do you recall?' he said to Medwin. 'Do you have the slightest idea where it took place? Was it inside the town or outside?'

'It is difficult, it was over so quickly . . .' The mage closed his eyes, put his hand to his chin and mouth. '. . . In the town, in shadows . . . shadows of a tall building—'

'In the shadows of trees,' said Terzis, and all eyes swung round to her. She now sat with head raised, her eyes staring into mid-air. 'Tall, old trees, near a high wall—'

'The north wall,' said Medwin.

'Excellent,' Mazaret said. 'We should find that with ease—'

'The shaman,' Terzis went on. Her voice had sunk to a low monotone, and she and Medwin had locked gazes. 'He is full of fear, everyone, the betrayer Korren, their hired rogues . . .'

'. . . Their prisoner, in a wagon . . .' Medwin murmured.

'. . . A young woman . . .'

'. . . bound, gagged, drugged—'

'Alael!' gasped Tauric.

'Then he was dead,' Terzis said, tears falling once again. Bardow came over and Medwin crouched next to her, and as Mazaret and Kodel shouted for horses to be readied and brought forth, the mages held hands in silent grief.

The ground outside the north wall of Sejeend sloped downhill to copses of wildapple trees and amberry bushes. A track followed the line of the ramshackle wall, forking before it reached the north-east corner, one branch continuing eastwards to join the main road to the north, the other dipping into a bushy gully before climbing into densely wooded hills and the cloaked mass of the Rukang Mountains beyond.

At a point not far from the fork in the trail, two riders waited, staring down at the mingling of footprints, hoofmarks and cartruts which had churned the damp ground some time before. All the footprints issued from a ragged-edged doorway in the town wall, the layers of mortar and stone that had blocked it now reduced to rubble.

A hooded figure emerged from the doorway, brushing away strands of climbing wallthorn. Bardow pushed back his hood, looked around and frowned.

'They've still not returned?'

Upon his horse, Medwin shook his head while next to him Tauric opened his mouth to speak, only to be forestalled by the sound of approaching hoofbeats. Bardow turned and saw Mazaret and Kodel riding up from the gully path. When the band of companions had first reached this place, Kodel had quickly seen the wagon tracks and traced them to the darker of the offshoot paths. Both Mazaret and Kodel had set off in pursuit, accompanied by more than a dozen mounted knights, yet now they were returning alone. Bardow let his concern show in his face as the two men reined in their horses before the others then dismounted.

'We almost had them,' Kodel said without preamble. 'They led us a merry chase up and round that hill to a wide bridge across a mountain river. From there, it was a steep climb up a mountainside—'

'There are a lot of old mines up there,' Mazaret added. 'Someone must be working some of them, as the cart road had been maintained recently.'

'The road goes high into the mountains,' Kodel went on, 'and is hewn from sheer walls of rock. We came round a sharp bend and found ourselves staring into a great gulf, as if a giant had torn a deep cleft in the mountainside. The cart road follows the curve of it all the way round – looking across, we could see horses and a wagon moving along, and their riders gazing back at us.'

'Then the mountainside above us broke away,' Mazaret said. 'It missed us by a matter of feet, but it crashed into the road and swept it away.'

'The shaman,' said Bardow.

'Just so,' Mazaret said. 'We descended with all speed to the bridge, where I sent my knights downstream to search for another crossing and to see if they could pick up Korren's trail again. Then we two returned.'

Bardow sighed, and ran his fingers through his thinning hair. 'So, is it fair to say that the girl will be taken to Besh-Darok? Ser Kodel, what say you?'

Bardow noted a slight frown on Mazaret's face, then was intrigued when Kodel looked uncomfortable for a moment before replying.

'It can be their only destination – the Acolytes there will be most eager to examine her.'

An unspoken horror filled the lengthening silence.

'We have to save her,' Tauric said suddenly, his face flushed with emotion. 'We can't let them harm her –'

'Lad,' Mazaret began. 'You don't know what you're saying—'

'We must stop them!' Tauric shouted down at him, now angry. 'We must go to Besh-Darok and take it by force!'

The youth held his mount's reins clenched before him in his metal fist while staring angrily at Mazaret, and Bardow felt a chill go through him at this sight. The older man seemed about to say something, but he visibly held himself back, for which Bardow was relieved. Then another spoke in composed, matter-of-fact tones.

'The heir is right. We must attack Besh-Darok and save the girl from the Acolytes. There is no alternative.'

Kodel was calmly feeding fragments of pocketbread to his horse as he said his piece, and affectionately stroking its muzzle. Next to him, Mazaret just stared, fury steadily showing in his features. Before Bardow could speak, the Lord Commander began to clap slowly.

'Congratulations, ser Kodel. You return to your obsession with immaculate timing. How unfortunate that the size of our combined armies would not suffice to breach one tower on the great battlements of Besh-Darok. Yet perhaps that is all that you require to satisfy your twisted honour – one final, glorious defeat!'

In the face of this outburst, Kodel remained curiously unperturbed, and regarded Mazaret soberly. 'I repeat – we have to seize Besh-Darok and keep Alael from falling into the hands of the Acolytes. You forget the plans we have long prepared, and our deep knowledge of the city's defences – we can do it. We must do it, because we have no choice.'

'There is always a choice,' Bardow murmured.

'And I choose "no",' said Mazaret.

'But why is this girl of such import?' said Medwin, glancing at Bardow. 'The Lord Commander told me that she is a powerful, if unschooled mage – is it worth risking everything we have gained this day to save a girl, even is she is a mage?'

'Medwin, there is much you are not aware of,' said Bardow. 'As well as possessing more than just a touch of the Lesser Power,

Alael also happens to be the direct descendant of Coulabric Tor-Caverill.'

Medwin's face paled. 'In the name of the Mother . . .'

'There is more,' Bardow said. 'There is another reason why the Acolytes want her in their power, one which I'm almost certain only ser Kodel is aware of.' Kodel offered a wordless, wry smile as Bardow continued. 'And that is the reason, Ikarno, why ser Kodel is right.'

Mazaret's stare was full of resentment, and the Archmage pushed on, knowing what had to be said. He had recovered some strength since the terrible sorcerous battle earlier, but not enough.

'Wait, let me explain. There was a secret at the very heart of the dynasty and kingship of the Empire – direct descent from the line of Orosiada conferred great potential and abilities—' He glanced at Tauric, almost apologetically, '—with a very few exceptions. But there was a secret rite, a blood ritual conducted after the coronation ceremonies which forged a link between the new emperor or empress and the realm of the Fathertree. Through this ritual the full majesty of the Rootpower was revealed and he or she took on a true, life-long affinity with all the lands of the empire.'

He paused, fingering a broken twig of wallthorn, then nodded to himself and went on. 'The blood ritual, the Vraoleach Dor, involved a sacred object called the Motherseed. I've never seen it, but my master, Argatil, described it as roughly egg-shaped, as long as the upper arm, with the look and texture of old, dark wood but the weight and coldness of solid stone.' He glanced at Kodel. 'Would you agree?'

'Our knowledge of it is less detailed, save that the Motherseed was said to be the size of a man's fist.'

Bardow shrugged, then faced Mazaret. 'The enemy went to a lot of trouble to capture Alael and get her out of Sejeend, and if we know about the Motherseed then the Acolytes will inevitably know as much if not more than us, given that Besh-Darok has been in Mogaun hands for sixteen years. Ikarno, who can tell what they are planning for Alael, but we can be sure that the consequences will not be good. So we must attempt to rescue her – it may not be necessary to seize Besh-Darok in its entirety, but we must do whatever is required. I am filled with dread for what might happen if we do not act, else I would not say what I have said.'

Mazaret stood stock still, his anger dissolved away by Bardow's words. Instead, he felt as if a great burden had been placed on his shoulders while trepidation hollowed him out. From the memory of a score of battles and half a hundred skirmishes, it came back to him, the recognition of that old wordless animal fear of chaos and death. And how much worse was it now, with the crushing finality of what they now faced. Thinking over all that had gone before, it seemed that a terrible inevitability had driven them to this place, this moment, this decision.

And still the full tide of evil is yet to come against us, he thought in private despair. *Can we hope to stem such a deluge? Have we the strength not to break before our weapons?*

He breathed in deeply, then one by one looked at all his companions.

'We must do what we must do,' he said simply. 'We will go to Besh-Darok.'

Part Four

Chapter Twenty-four

Now this accursed power stirs,
And not even death will bring peace.

Avalti, *The Song of Dreams*

'Tell me about the Realm of Ruin,' said Keren, sitting on the tunnel's sloped, uneven floor, staring coldly back at the shimmering barrier through which she had so recently passed. 'Tell me again.'

'Once it was the Daemonrealm, home to those that the Lord of Twilight first raised up from the Great Lake of the Night, a gift from his hands. A long world it was, majestic halls stretching away, towering columns and cambers in shining black and silver and glittering stone. There were chambers for birth and death, for talk and sleep, for eating and fighting. The air was pure, and the light came in red, amber and gold from living statues.' There was a pause. 'I saw none of this. Dissidents and schismatics among my ancestors opposed the Lord of Twilight's purpose here in the Realm Between and actively worked against him, aiding his enemies, the two apostates.

'On discovering this betrayal, the Lord of Twilight's response was swift, overwhelming punishment. Where his hand passed, only destruction remained and the glories of the Daemonrealm were shattered. I and my forebears were born amongst rubble and the fragments of splendour, yet our loyalty has never wavered, and our resolve to rebuild our realm remains undimmed.'

Keren felt cold to the core, as if her flesh and bones were made of things dragged from the bed of the ocean. *How many Wards of the Ordeal have I passed through*? she wondered. *How many times have I been remade*? She gazed down at the pale skin of her hands, examined them, tried to remember holding swords, spears, shields . . .

'Who are the Shadowkings?' she said. 'What do they want?'

'They are fragments of the Prince of Dusk, splinters of his greatness who plan and scheme with masks and swords and lies. Armies march for them, but antipathies exist – each wants to possess the might of the Lord of Twilight without giving up their petty selves. And yet they must, for a cup cannot contain an ocean. Till then, the Daemonkind shall withhold their aid because we do not serve those who are themselves servants.'

She laid her hands on the floor of the tunnel, pressed down on the rough stone. It seemed almost warm to the touch and she could feel the deep, intricate sorceries which permeated this part of the Oshang Dakhal. Old power, subverted by still older powers. 'Is the Rootpower completely dead?'

'All that remains is a broken dream. Kekrahan was how we named the Realm of the Fathertree; it is a near-lifeless desolation and will in time fade to a memory of a memory in the long, slow thoughts of the Void. Without the Fathertree and the Rootpower, opposition to the Lord of Twilight's unbridled might will never again be ordered or prevailing.'

'What do you know of the war?'

'It is scarcely worth the name. The Imperial remnants and their few allies stumble from one ill-conceived skirmish to the next, and now they intend to attack Besh-Darok and prevent the Acolytes there from carrying out the Vraoleach Dor upon the descendant of a long-past deposed emperor. Yet even if they do capture Yasgur's citadel, and rescue the girl, it will avail them nothing – the Shadowkings will come against them with a great army and the flock of nighthunters which the Acolytes are awakening far above us. Defeat shall be total, and there will be no quarter.'

Images came to her, dim chambers where masked servitors

watched over terrible winged shapes stirring fitfully from sleep. Was she seeing what he was seeing, or what he was imagining?

'What is the Crystal Eye?'

Hesitation. 'A gift to mortals, one of three donated in a long-forgotten age. From then it passed through the hands of those who knew little of its potential and those who knew too much. It has both aided kings and brought about their demise, and has been the downfall of more than one empire. Sometimes the Eye is venerated, other times loathed, but always it stirs fear, be that fear of its powers or the fear of not using it. In Orosiada they were well – balanced – after using the Eye to send me back to my own realm, he founded the mage communities of Trevada and passed it into their safekeeping. And when the Mogaun hosts invaded a thousand years later, the mages' fears sealed their fate.'

'Why do you want the Eye?'

She could feel the weight of his compelling gaze, but remained where she was, sitting, waiting.

'The Acolytes have little or no use for it, and the Shadowkings regard it as a mild nuisance held safely out of the reach of any mage. Yet it remains a source of the Lesser Power, which would be invaluable in rebuilding the glory of the Daemonrealm. When we emerge from the Ordeal, in the heart of the Basilica, the Eye shall be mine for the taking.'

'What of me – will I be alive or dead, or worse?'

'Do not mistake the destruction of flesh for the death of the spirit. I have strengthened your essence with my own, and repaired whatever damage your form suffers, sufficient at least for the purpose of passing through the wards.'

The flesh of her face was cold, her arms, her breasts, her midriff, everything, cold and unresponsive. She wanted to cry but could not.

'And when this is all over?' she said shakily. 'What then?'

'I shall remake your body exactly as it was, so you may better determine your fate. Then, if you desire, you could take on our form, become one of the Daemonkind and return with me to our realm. Your essence has already gained much from our alliance, so the potential is already there.'

Keren felt an echo of revulsion. 'If not, will I ever be rid of you?'

'Never.' Faint amusement in the voice.

She got to her feet and faced the Daemonkind prince. Orgraaleshenoth's spectral form almost filled the tunnel, even crouched as he was and leaning against the wall.

'Do you know what slavery is?' she said.

'Neither the word nor the idea exists among us. There is only strength and honour, and purpose and obedience.'

The cold amber eyes stared down at her and after a moment she looked away, despairing. *No one can save me from this, she thought. All I have is obedience . . .*

She sidled past the great form, and walked away up the tunnel towards the next ward. In a single movement she pulled her long shift over her head, tossed it aside and, naked, broke into a run. Dark laughter came after her, the ward's deadly, shining veil loomed and she threw herself into it.

After the steep climb up the gulley path, Bardow paused on the more level ground of the ridge to regain his breath and gaze down at the coastal town of Adranoth. It was a cold, cloudy night and the sea stretched away eastwards into a wide, engulfing darkness. There were a few glimmers of light from fisher steadings dotted along the coastline towards the rearing cliffs of Thoiranar Point where some dedicated soul yet maintained a ware beacon for mariners. Down in Adranoth torches and lamps were burning everywhere, especially in the taverns and taphouses, where heated discussions were taking place in reflection of the talks still going on in the town's great Guildhall.

Bardow shook his head, recalling some of the comments, curses and clichés which had been exchanged, and made his way further along the bushy ridge. A certain group of individuals had arrived earlier that evening and had been waiting impatiently upon him for nearly three hours.

A four-strong patrol, two knights and two Hunter's Children, passed him heading the other way, all of them bowing heads in respect. Annoyed but resigned, Bardow acknowledged them with a benign nod and murmured a blessing lifted from a dusty liturgy he had unearthed from the keep library just before the hasty departure from Sejeend. As the men resumed their patrol, Bardow sighed and was about to continue along the ridge when a voice spoke from the shadows.

'Paternal benevolence suits you, ser Bardow. Have you ever considered fatherhood?'

It was Kodel, leaning against a spiraleaf tree, his arms crossed. Split seed cases from the tree's last monthly outbudding still littered the surrounding grass and as Bardow approached he could detect a trace of the sweet odour which they exuded.

'Mages rarely marry,' he said. 'Most women, through misconception and market rumour, believe us to be menacing or cold, or merely not quite human. And women who become mages . . . well, they have usually suffered in some way and seldom make agreeable companions.'

'And those men who pursue the path of magecraft?'

Bardow smiled. 'Eccentrics and misfits, for the most part, wedded to their solitude with unshakeable fidelity.' He looked down at the town. 'Except for those burdened with responsibility.'

Kodel's gaze remained on the Archmage. 'Has there been any progress in your bargainings?'

'Indeed, yes. The town fathers have agreed to hand over half of your boats and all the crews—'

'Half?' Anger glittered in Kodel's eyes.

Bardow shrugged. 'There are claims that these vessels were stolen from Adranoth by those acting on your orders. But the Lord Commander and my colleague Medwin are still down at the Guildhall trying to resolve these details.'

Kodel's expression darkened. 'They lie. It was only a handful of boats which my people seized, boats which the Mogaun were using to patrol this part of the coast. It seems to me that the point of a sword could swiftly settle such sham details.'

Bardow regarded him thoughtfully. The twisting course of this man's moods was a constant source of fascination – he could by turns be considerate, witty, impassive and brutal. The announcement back in Sejeend that his agents in Roharka had a flotilla of boats hidden at a small island and ready to use in the assault on Besh-Darok earned him new respect from many of Mazaret's officers. Also, his shrewd, even-handed tutelage of the young Tauric allayed much of the suspicion harboured by those older hands who had grown up believing the Hunter's Children to be no more than dangerous fanatics. Against this was the undisguised savagery which occasionally leapt into view, sometimes without warning. Rumours persisted about cruelties perpetrated during the revolt in Oumetra, and more than one eyewitness told how Kodel, in a fit of berserk rage, had hacked the arms from the corpse of Crolas, the mercenary chief.

Yet there was no doubting his commitment to their cause. It was just that at times, like now, he seemed more like a force of nature than an ordinary man.

'The point of a sword would leave an enemy at our backs,' Bardow said. 'Do not forget, it has been only days since the townsfolk freed themselves from the local Mogaun chief, thus there is an issue of pride at stake. In any case, they know we have an army up here, so it is a matter of patience and prudence.'

'It is also a matter of time, which is growing shorter by the hour,' Kodel said, his gaze full of unwavering intensity. 'We must embark and sail for Besh-Darok very soon, ser Bardow. I have just had word from our agents there that the remainder of Yasgur's army has left the city. Except for the city militia and some foot-soldiers, Besh-Darok is almost undefended.'

Bardow's heart leapt. 'That's splendid news—'

'Yes, it would be so were it not that the departing army has turned south and is marching straight for Sejeend.'

For a moment Bardow was speechless as the sudden elation died, leaving an awful hollowness. 'When did you learn of this?' he said.

'In the last hour. One of my scouts is already on his way back to Sejeend with a message for the town's council, warning them to prepare.'

'That army must number in the thousands,' Bardow said, appalled. 'They cannot possibly withstand it.'

Kodel nodded sombrely. 'Their only true hope is for us to reach Besh-Darok and take control of it. Nothing else would force Yasgur's host to turn back.'

'You were right – time is against us.' Bardow let his gaze drift out to the distant, dark sea, and shivered. 'I must mindspeak with Medwin and appraise him of these developments.'

Kodel pushed away from the tree, took a pair of long rider's gauntlets from his waist and pulled them on. 'Be sure to stress the urgency of the situation. You might also care to mention my own lack of patience.' He gave a sharp nod. 'Till later.'

Bardow watched him walk away and down the other side of the ridge, down to where the bulk of the army was encamped. *How joyless he seems*, he thought. *And how thoroughly in tune with these grim days.*

Putting aside such reflections, he sat at the foot of the spiraleaf tree with the sweet tang of its seeds all around him, and with eyes closed let his thoughts settle. It took little time and effort to find Medwin, gain his attention and pass on Kodel's revelations.

Events harry us like dogs after prey, was Medwin's dismayed response. *While these quibblers pick apart our every utterance then pick apart the words themselves. I almost feel that they are daring us to move against them.*

'They fear that we shall be defeated,' Bardow said. 'You must convince them otherwise.'

I would sooner persuade rivers to flow uphill . . . Ah, we must speak later – food is being brought to the table, heroic amounts of it . . .

'How is Mazaret bearing up?'

The honourable Lord Commander provides a plausible counter-point of menace to my own very reasonable and affable approach. Sadly, it is not as effective as we would wish. Could you not postpone this meeting of yours and rejoin us?

'I must speak with our new colleagues,' Bardow said. 'They are here out of their own volition, and if I do not greet them they may decide to go their own way. We cannot afford to lose such a group of mages.'

I understand.

'I am sure there is a way to overcome our hosts' reluctance,' Bardow said thoughtfully. 'If they will not be persuaded, perhaps they may be seduced.'

Perhaps . . .

Medwin's presence faded, leaving Bardow poised between waking and the Void. Medwin was right – they were caught between pursuing their own strategy and reacting to the stratagems of others. They needed an advantage, like the Crystal Eye, but since his last search for Suviel, when he found her captured by Byrnak's mirrorchild, he had been unable to discover her whereabouts. She could be dead, he knew, or in thrall to the mirrorchild or worse. But he would have to try again. He had to know the truth.

Bardow was rested and recovered from the arduous struggles at Sejeend, and able to form the Spiritwing thought-canto in moments. He had only just pictured Suviel in his mind when the Spiritwing swept him off into the Void, down into the thronging nothingness, down through vast heights and soaring depths. An endless dissolving dream, endless, deathless, timeless.

And yet there was direction in the Spiritwing's progress, a path which drew him onward to a place where the walls of the Void thinned to a veil. Through it he saw a dim passageway, its smooth walls of stone bearing long bands of carvings whose hauntingly familiar intricacies were lost in the poor light. Two forms lay on the floor, one curled up to one side, the other sitting against the wall, head fallen forward as if in sleep. But even as Bardow was taking in the details of the scene, the seated figure came awake, head snapping up in sudden alarm, lips moving, hands forming a gesture of warding.

'No, wait!' he said.

Suviel Hantika froze in mid-invocation, a fearful suspicion visible in her features despite the gloom. But that waned as she got to her feet and edged a little closer, caution shading into relief, mouth adopting a weary smile.

'Bardow,' she whispered. 'I thought I would never see you again.'

'I've been trying to reach you, but you have been invisible to my every sense,' he said. 'And with no word from you, we have been fearing the worst.'

She shrugged tiredly. 'The power of others kept me from doing so, first as the mirrorchild Nerek's prisoner and now here in the Acolytes' domain.'

Realisation struck quickly along with long-buried memories. 'You're in Trevada, in one of the meditation galleries! Why, you can look across at the High Basilica from the inner balconies—'

But she was shaking her head. 'Most of the balconies are gone, and the galleries . . . well, there are few stretches as whole as this one. The rest are shattered rock, laid open to the elements, or have become the lairs of monsters.' She shuddered visibly. 'It's only by chance that we've progressed this far without being taken prisoner.'

'So who is your companion?'

Suviel sighed. 'It is Nerek, Byrnak's creation.' And Bardow listened to her tell of how Nerek put a fire guardian over her before they arrived at the gates of Trevada, how they encountered first Babrel, an old servant of the academies, then a group of escaped children, two of whom possessed powers sufficient to overwhelm Nerek and cast her into a torment of the mind. The Acolytes were already hunting for the children, and Suviel and the deranged Nerek had been lucky to evade capture.

'The children were all so scared of being caught again,' Suviel said. 'According to Babrel, they would say nothing of their experiences, except for some mention of being locked in iron caskets covered in symbols.'

'Strange,' Bardow said, masking a dread suspicion. 'Is that all?'

'No. When Nerek confronted the two boys, she told them she could see what shared their souls, and when they spoke I felt another voice speaking with them.' She rubbed her eyes wearily. 'I've never heard of such vile things being done to children, Bardow. Have you?'

'I'm not sure. I would have to consult the archives back in Krusivel.' *But that would be only to confirm details of a horror I am already certain of. Suviel cannot be burdened with such knowledge just now.*

'If you're not at Krusivel, where are you?' Suviel said, peering closer. 'Is that open sea behind you?'

'On a ridge overlooking Adranoth,' Bardow said, and briefly related the highlights of all that had transpired since Suviel left Krusivel – the rebellion in Oumetra, the appearance of a direct descendant of Coulabric Tor-Caverill, the siege and capture of Sejeend, the abduction of Coulabric's heir by a Mogaun shaman, and the fateful decision to attack Besh-Darok by sea.

Suviel looked shaken by this last piece of information. 'But how could we succeed against Yasgur and his army? And why go there in the first place?'

'I once read an old treatise on warfare which said that one should move quickly in unexpected directions and attack places the enemy cannot protect.'

'Well, both you and I are certainly doing just that,' Suviel said, sardonically. 'Although the reasons for my course of action appear the more rational of the two.'

'There are reasons . . . which I dare not speak of for now, but they are compelling, and they made it difficult for us to choose any other strategy.' He paused. 'But speaking of reasons, you have not yet explained why you are keeping Nerek with you.'

'I thought she might be of some use,' Suviel said, glancing down at the sleeping form, but Bardow saw pity soften her features.

'Is she not likely to put you in danger?'

Still watching her companion, she said, 'And what of using Spiritwing to speak to me here – is that not perilous?' Then she turned, eyes tearful. 'My apologies, master, I—'

'No, you are right.' He felt stung by self-recrimination. 'I must end this now.'

'How is Ikarno?' she said abruptly. 'Does he speak of me?'

'Not aloud,' he said. 'But he is well.'

She nodded, relaxing a little. 'Thoughts of him have kept my spirit warm when the nights were darkest. I will see him again, when I return with the Eye, I promise.'

'Do what you can, daughter. Our thoughts are with you. Farewell.'

And before she could say more, he released his mental hold on the Spiritwing canto. All its elements drifted apart in his mind, and the dim passageway faded from sight as his awareness toppled backwards through oceans of shadow, skies veiled in glittering black, deserts paved with snatching thorns . . .

He breathed in sharply, and blinked. All the night's smells, sounds and appearances came at him in a single leap. The tree against his back, the wet grass his hand lay upon, the sweetness of cracked seedcases, the darkness and a light sea-breeze, tang of salt . . .

Shouts came from nearby, a general hubbub of voices, along with the creak of wagons. For an instant, Bardow thought the camp was under attack then he noticed one of Mazaret's commanders, Yarram, hurrying along the ridge towards the gully path. Bardow called out to him while struggling to his feet.

'Ser Bardow,' the knight said as he approached. 'Have you taken ill?'

'I appreciate your concern, Captain, but I am in good health. I have just woken from a doze to all this activity – what is happening?'

'The tents are being struck, ser. Word has come that Adranoth's leaders have released all the boats and their crews, and even offered help with provisioning.'

Yarram looked as openly bemused as Bardow felt. 'What caused such a change of heart?'

Yarram rubbed his chin. 'I do not know for certain, but it is said that halfway through a feast earlier, the mage Medwin played a harp and sang a song of such surpassing valour and defiance that the town fathers were shamed into giving up their claims. Whatever the truth, we were ordered to break camp a short while ago.

'Now, ser, if you will pardon my haste, I must attend to my troops and mounts.'

'By all means.'

He gave a slight bow and as he left, Bardow allowed himself a wry grin. Medwin the bard – who would have thought that he harboured such a talent?

Then he remembered the volunteer mages he was supposed to have met by now, and with a sigh hurried along the ridge path. How much calming and flattery and persuasion will this take, he wondered morosely.

Then he laughed. *Maybe I could sing them a song . . .*

Chapter Twenty-five

Where the air is black,
Where frost burns and fire freezes,
Where the walls are cracked by screams,
Where hate drips from fang and talon.

The Lair of Monsters, 2, iv, trad

'Who am I?'

Suviel struggled with Nerek's weight as the woman's legs buckled. Keeping her own panic under control, she half-carried Nerek over to the wall and eased her down into a sitting position.

'Please tell me – who am I . . . ?'

In the engulfing gloom of the gallery Suviel could not quite see her companion's face but she knew that those features were twisting and altering. She had witnessed several of these transitions, where the two personas inhabiting the body fought to gain the upper hand, and she was almost thankful for the darkness.

Since speaking with Bardow a hour or two ago, the possibility of capture had haunted her, causing her to stay on the move, searching for a way through these ruined galleries. From memory she knew that some passages led to other collegiates and seminaries, such as the Cloister of Songs (being a school of history) or the Forge (a hall of debating), and then directly into the High Basilica itself.

All I have to do is get through this maze without being trapped by the Acolytes or their servants, without even attracting their attention, then slip into the Basilica and unnoticed spirit the Eye away.

Ah yes, and keep Nerek safely with me.

She rubbed her tired eyes. It was a mad, hopeless strategy but it was better than having no strategy at all.

She waited only a few more minutes before coaxing Nerek up on her feet again. The woman made weak noises of protest but allowed herself to be led away along a cold, high-walled corridor whose ceiling had been supported by slender columns, several of which lay toppled. The spectral radiance of the starry night slipped in through holes in the ceiling, serving to reveal the outlines of great carven faces on the walls, whose eyes were closed in tranquil smiles.

Presently, the corridor began to descend in a series of broad, shallow steps and Suviel knew that they would soon be near the entrance to the Forge. Thus far they had encountered no enemies and detected no evidence of anyone abroad in these broken galleries. Suviel had, however, sensed something in the air, a faint bitterness like refined minerals, the kind that Bardow occasionally employed in his spells. Perhaps it was just the smell of wrecked masonry and the old dust they were disturbing as they trudged along.

Roughly a dozen paces short of the foot of the steps was a place where part of the wall had either collapsed outwards or been torn away, leaving a tall, jagged gap which gave a breathtaking view of the lands west of Trevada. By night, the dense forests of Anghatan were a black cloak stretching north and south, and westward as far as the Druandag mountains. In the impenetrable darkness beyond was, she knew, the great inland sea of Birrdaelin, and beyond that the hilly domains of Jefren.

Sadness born of longing for what was past welled up in her. How beautiful it looked under the stars. She could not help recalling sweeter, happier times, summers spent in Jefren with her friends, Pelorn and Cavaxes, exploring ancient Nightbear tunnels in the southern hills, and paying respectful visits to the more hospitable of the witch-horse tribes.

Now brigands and bands of Mogaun roamed the hills and the witch-horses were no more, wiped out to the last by order of the Acolytes.

'I hate this place – why did you bring me here?'

At the sound of that petulant voice, Suviel's heart sank. It was Falin who had won out.

'To keep you from harm,' she said turning away from the gap. Her companion stood by the opposite wall, head bowed, one hand pressed to the stomach as if in discomfort, the other raised to the face.

'It is you they would harm,' was the reply in a voice growing louder. 'I am faithful to my master, who is also their master!'

Suviel crossed the passage in two swift steps and grabbed Falin/Nerek by the arm.

'Keep your voice down!' she hissed. 'Don't make me use a spell on you.'

The other turned his head slightly to glance at her. Starlight glinted in an eye full of malice.

'I hate this place . . . and I hate *you*!'

Without warning he lashed out with both hands, shoving her backwards. Suviel tried to turn as she fell and her left hand and hip struck the stone floor first. She gasped at the pain but bit back a savage oath as she scrambled to her feet in time to see a slender, wildly running form reach the bottom of the steps and bolt out of sight.

'Curse him for a fool!' she muttered, then dashed after him.

From the bottom step all her surroundings were swallowed by an inky darkness. Suviel paused a moment, then moved over to the wall and followed it round. This had been a students' meeting hall of sorts, with a higher floor reached by spiral stairs, and she recalled that there were several exits at both levels. Then she heard a noise, a scraping footfall, and she froze. A cold stone silence reigned in the blackness. Calming herself, she focused her awareness and reached out, striving for vision. At first there was nothing, then she began to distinguish tenuous outlines, the contours of pillars, seating alcoves, and doorways that were no more than shades of darkness amid the dark.

And there was movement, a figure stepping through an archway over on the right. She hurried as quietly as she could across the chamber and followed.

She felt her way along a passage till it turned left into a stretch where the murk was broken by a meagre illumination. The walls and the high, arched ceiling were marred by patches of glistening lichen which gave off a faint grey glow. But it was sufficient to reveal the corridor ahead and Suviel had just started along it when a cry of horror came from the shadow-veiled far end. Falin/Nerek appeared at a panicky run, saw Suviel, stumbled to a halt and darted up a side passage. Suviel lunged after him.

When a pair of half-open doors loomed before her she realized that this was one of the ways to the Forge, the great debating hall. There was another fearful cry from within and as she slipped between the doors she could smell the same bitter odour as before, only stronger and more acrid.

The Forge was a great oval chamber, nearly 100 yards across at its widest, with steep, surrounding tiers of seats and benches and heavy balconies which jutted out over the lower floor. Three podiums on broad plinths were arranged around the centre, one each for the opposing debaters and the third for the adjudicator. Falin was crouched whimpering at the foot of one of the plinths and staring off into the shadows. At the sound of Suviel's approaching footsteps he jerked round, looked at her for an instant then flung out a trembling, pointing hand.

'Kill her! She's the enemy—' Glancing back at the shadows he began shaking his head desperately. 'No, not me, her! She wants to destroy you! – I only want to help . . .'

Every instinct Suviel possessed shrieked retreat, but when she turned she found herself staring at a hulking shape so black it merged with the lightless murk beneath the balcony. Ice-blue eyes gazed pitilessly down at her from an indistinct head, and an unanswerable fear made her back away in Falin's direction.

The eyes moved after her a little way, as if examining her, and a sepulchral voice rang in her mind.

A mage, brothers and sisters. A mage!

A sussurus of eager malice came from all sides. Looking up at the tiers of seating, Suviel saw masses of shadowy forms shifting in the darkness and hundreds of eyes regarding her.

Our guest is a mage, the voice continued. *Be welcome, mortal, and behold.*

The amorphous shape before her suddenly gleamed with spreading light, metallic greens, blues, purples. It resolved into scaly haunches, a heavy torso that was two, three times the size of the biggest ox Suviel had ever seen, a long, fanlike tail, and wings folded along the upper flanks. A thick neck curved up to the head, wide blunt-snouted jaws parted to reveal a double-row of tearing teeth. A single horn grew up from behind the head, pointing forward over the eyes, and two similar protrusions jutted beneath the lower jaw, except these looked corroded, their tips broken and split.

We know you. We have not forgotten the sweetness of mage-flesh, the creature said as others emerged from the shadows, monstrous forms brightening. *Do you know us?*

Suviel knew. These were the nighthunters, the Acolytes' most feared servants. It was said that many years before the Mogaun invasion, the Acolytes had delved into the deepest, darkest pits of the earth and captured a multitude of vile beasts, survivors from a long-gone age. With this seed-stock, they bred new monsters for war and terror.

Hundreds of them, now revealed, watched her restlessly from the looming tiers of the chamber and from atop the podiums, an assembly of fanged menace. Suviel had come to a halt at the centre of the floor and could now see an alcove set into the seating directly above a broad entrance. Dark ruby light came from the too-red flames which burned and flickered around a carved figure seated there in a high-backed throne of stone.

An image of the lord of us all, a shrine that burns with the force of our relentless devotion.

Down on the floor, the nighthunters began pacing round, circling Suviel and Falin who lay curled up, keening quietly to himself. And other voices spoke in Suviel's mind, heavy and intrusive.

Drain them, pain them . . .

I can taste their pride and fear . . .

Drink their power . . .

Old woman, young woman, yet the older one is stronger . . .

Are we not the ones who broke their temples and feasted on their spirits . . . ?

Sacrifice them to the shrine . . .

Crack their bones, eat and dance and fly . . .

Suviel stood with one hand pressed against her head as the voices drove into her thoughts. Then her fear changed and became anger, her raised hand she clenched into a fist and lowered to her waist as she glared straight at the nighthunter who had spoken to her first. When there was no hope of reprieve or rescue, all that was left was defiance, loud defiance.

'When you are defeated, as you will be,' she began, 'my voice will rejoice from the Void, and when you are broken and dead, my spirit will dance on your bones.' With the toe of her boot she scraped a line in the dust on the floor and backed away till she was near Falin. 'Now, enough talking – unless you intend to brag me to death.'

The creature parted its jaws in a semblance of a grin and its voice sounded in her head once more. *My claw-name is Avorst. Prepare to die.*

As Avorst drew back his head, Suviel let the Cadence thought-canto she had readied unfold from her thoughts. The nighthunter made a deep coughing sound, its head jerked forward and from the broken-off horns beneath its jaws twin streams of dazzling flame jetted forth.

Suviel flinched as they struck the shield of her spell. Dense flames raged against the Cadence barrier, rivulets and tendrils clawing for purchase, but it held. Suviel could feel heat in her face and the thudding of her heart from the strain. Perspiration tingled on her scalp and neck, yet her mouth was dry.

As the fiery onslaught died away Avorst looked closely at her for a moment before launching another assault, then a third and a fourth. After each, the monster paused to examine Suviel who, by the fourth attack, was remaining upright by sheer force of will. Beside her Falin crouched with hands pressed tightly against his eyes. I had hoped that this spell would be enough to save us, she thought. Sadly, it seems not . . .

Just then, Avorst gestured to the other nighthunters as they circled – three paused, turned their heads towards Suviel and unleashed their fire. As the barrier was engulfed Suviel felt her last strength start to drain away, feeding the Cadence thought-canto. Her legs gave way and she fell to her knees, and harsh words rang in her mind.

You cannot withstand us forever.

Avorst had come nearer and Suviel watched helplessly as he raised a foreclaw and began to slowly push it through the Cadence barrier. A faint drone emerged from somewhere, and Suviel could see pain and fury in Avorst's eyes as the Cadence spell took its toll on his limb. Talons lost their shine, callused pads were scoured and chafed, scales chipped and split, scores of tiny gashes rasped by the barrier. The drone was now a howl and still Avorst persisted, the clawed forelimb bleeding from a multitude of wounds, trembling as it came closer and closer to Suviel's face . . .

'Enough!'

The streams of fire died and Suviel felt the Cadence canto simply stop. As Avorst snatched his forelimb away, a man robed in dark blue walked calmly into view, carrying a long, plain staff. Of average height and build, the man had short grey hair, was clean-shaven, and had the milky white eyes of an Acolyte. As he surveyed all before him, Suviel felt a mounting sense of familiarity and dread, and when those eyes gazed straight at her a horrible recognition finally dawned. It was Ikarno's brother, Coireg Mazaret.

The Acolyte Coireg and the nighthunter Avorst looked at each other and Suviel felt some kind of unspoken exchange take place. At one point, Avorst stirred his wings and uttered a deep, angry hiss but when Coireg held up a hand wreathed in green, flashing fire, the nighthunter succumbed, bowing his head and refolding his wings. Coireg then turned his attention to Suviel but before he could speak, Falin dashed over and sank to his knees. Coireg had not come alone and several leather-masked guards leaped forward, swords bared, but he waved them back.

Falin opened his mouth to speak but Coireg quickly took hold of his lower jaw and moved his head from side to side, examining him.

'Half-made thing,' Coireg said, raising a foot to Falin's chest and thrusting him roughly to the floor. A swift, sharp gesture, and three masked guards pounced on him and dragged him bodily away. As his protests and pleadings receded, Coireg turned smiling to Suviel and considered her for a moment.

'A mage,' he said thoughtfully. 'Lesser Power, but skilled.'

'Coireg, what happened to you?' said Suviel.

The Acolyte was momentarily puzzled, then, 'Do you know this outerness? It is now mine, reborn I, living I!' The white eyes shone, boring into her. 'You, too, will give us much, serve as we serve.'

'Never,' Suviel said, suddenly feeling tired and old. 'I will never be one of you.'

Coireg barked his laughter and as the rest of his guards bound her limbs he bent in close and whispered: 'Your flesh, our vessel. Your soul, our clay.'

As they carried her off through darkness in the direction of the High Basilica, Suviel listened in despair as the Acolyte said over and over, 'Reborn I, living I!'

Chapter Twenty-six

Seize the enemy's city and you wrap yourself in risk.
Every wall becomes both front and rear, every gate
holds the key to calamity, and every meal eats at the
future. Yet you are where you want to be, and the
enemy must come to you.

Marshall Gostrian, *The Endless Battle*, ch. 7, xiii

At last, the waiting was over.

'Yarram's men are in position near the Riverside Barracks, Lord
Commander,' said the black-garbed runner as he stood panting
at the doorway. 'His scouts will begin dispatching the sentries in
several minutes.'

The small but crowded room was suddenly alive with a tense
expectancy. In the glow of a hooded lamp on the floor, faces took
on looks of eagerness, or composure, or stored-up hate as officers
quietly sheathed thrice-whetted blades, or pulled on gauntlets, or
tightened armour straps.

'Good,' said Mazaret, turning to a couple of men dressed in
the rough garments of labourers. 'You and your people know
your tasks?'

'Aye, milor', we do,' said one as they stood, their air of readiness
and coiled threat belying their stolid appearance. These were
Kodel's most valuable spies, men who volunteered over a year
ago to live in Besh-Darok, noting the enemy's every strength
and weakness in preparation for just such a day as this.

'Then be swift and merciless,' he said. 'There must be no one to raise the alarm when we follow.'

Each gave a sombre nod then slipped out of the front door and off into the night. When they were gone, Mazaret issued the brief, final orders to his officers, especially Cebroul, a young banner-lieutenant he had put in charge of the attack on the Ironhall Barracks. All left by a passage leading to the rear of the building, a disued tannery, till only Mazaret, his aide, and Medwin remained.

He looked at the mage. 'What is happening at the palace – have you learned anything more?'

Medwin sighed, fingers tugging on his grey beard, now clipped and neat. 'It is . . . difficult to be certain of these things when one is a passive observer, especially when the powers involved are so strong. But the rite is continuing, this I know.'

'I understand,' Mazaret said, nodding. 'Our troops will be here soon. Let us wait outside.' Then to his aid: 'Dim that lantern and bring it.'

Outside, the air was cold and clear without being icy. The front of the tannery faced the rear of a warehouse across a dark, deserted alley. This place had been carefully chosen as a staging post – the warehouse was abandoned and in a state of semi-collapse, there were few dwellings nearby, and the alley was a lightless gulley which ran, with few interruptions, straight towards Mazaret's objective, the Imperial Barracks.

Standing in the darkness, cold and alert, Mazaret thought about the great city of Besh-Darok and its tens of thousands of citizens lying asleep and unsuspecting. Many a time in the last few years he had envisaged his return as a glorious victory, a bright and joyous triumph conducted in the open for all to see. Yet here he was, about to dash through the shadows towards desperate combat in the service of an uncertain purpose. Cloaked figures would be stealing across back courts, or dropping from overhanging eaves to subdue guards with the silent flash of knives or the twist of a knotted cord around the neck. Accuracy and surprise were vital – according to Kodel's spies, the city forces, including the watch, outnumbered Mazaret's by almost two to one. But they were mostly confined to the three main barracks and several guardposts scattered across the districts. If they could be taken quickly and with the minimum loss of life, then the city would awake to freedom.

But if we lose the advantage of surprise, we risk setting some of the people against us, he thought. *And if Bardow and Kodel fail to halt that foul sorcery, our hours are numbered.*

At least Tauric and his companions have the Armourer with them, and if Yarram follows my advice, they will be out of harm's way . . .

Then he laughed a soft, wry laugh, and Medwin gave him a puzzled look.

'It's all right, my friend,' Mazaret said. 'I have just realized that all of us are risking everything just by being here, yet we pretend that somehow there are degrees of danger in this pit of hazards.'

'That is not a comforting observation,' said the mage.

'Alas, neither is our situation.'

Medwin was about to answer when he glanced past Mazaret and said, 'The men are here.'

In shadowy double files they approached along the alley from the south, all buckles, metal armour and weapons muffled by cloth, all footsteps deadened. Mazaret watched them approvingly for a moment then went over to the officer at the front of the leading company.

'Kalno, pick up the pace to double-time and follow me.'

With that, he set off at a steady trot towards the Imperial Barracks, and behind him the rustling sussurus grew, the thud of rag-wrapped feet and the hiss of cloth on cloth merging into a rushing, drumming sound, a river of warriors flowing after him down the alley.

The Imperial Barracks was an austere, three-storey building erected nearly two centuries ago in the reign of Emperor Mavrin. It had no windows below the top floor and a barrier of fenced pillars surrounded the square drill yard laid out before the main entrance, a large pair of doors flanked by burning torches and long banners in dark colours. As it came into view, Mazaret saw three hooded figures straightening from a pair of motionless forms sprawled in front of the entrance. Two of them went to the doors with sets of keys while the third came out to meet Mazaret, who had meantime brought his troops to a halt.

'All is well,' the scout said. 'The sentries on the roof have been disposed of. Only those at the rear postern gate remain, and your men must be there, ready to rush the inner guardroom.'

'They will be,' Mazaret said, turning to nod at one of his officers. A moment later, fifty or so soldiers, mostly knights of the Order, peeled off from the main body and hastened round to the rear of the barracks. The remaining 200 Mazaret led across the flat, empty drill yard and up to the doors as they were pushed open by the scouts.

Within was a square hall where only a pair of nightlamps burned, one either side in cressets on the plain mortared walls. Swords and maces were drawn and bucklers were stripped of their muffling rags, as they advanced into the hall. Prearranged squads were moving towards the doors of the dormitories to the left and right when those same doors burst open and armed soldiers rushed out to the attack. With a dreadful crash of metal and men's voices, battle was joined.

Mazaret cursed inwardly, realizing that they had been expected, and the hollow fear of ambush bloomed in his stomach. Then a moment of swift appraisal with a keen eye allayed much of his fear – the enemy numbered no more than three score with a dozen of them fanned out at the back of the hall. This was no ambush, but a delaying action. He bellowed orders, and with most of a full banner-squad at his back he charged the enemy at the rear.

One soldier came at him with a hooked poleaxe. He ducked the lunge, swung his sword with all his might and sliced the attacker's leg off at the knee. Another shoulder-charged him as he came up out of the crouch, a fist-held dagger driving towards his chest. Mazaret grabbed the soldier's wrist, twisting it as they fell together. The soldier's face went from horror to agony in a second as his own dagger punched into his vitals. As he screamed in pain, Mazaret pushed him away, scrambled to his feet and took up his sword from where it had fallen. Grimly pleased that few of the enemy still stood, he cried 'To me!' and tore open the door at the back of the hall.

A wide corridor led straight to the guardroom at the rear of the barracks. It was deserted, and when they emerged from the postern gate his worst fears rose up in his thoughts once more.

Bodies were strewn around the small courtyard, a few still moving, most deathly still, and all were bloodied. A few knights staggered in from the shadows of the street to tend to the wounded, and some of Mazaret's squad went to help. Mazaret found a sergeant propped against the outside wall, a torn-off surcoat sleeve tied about a deep shoulder wound, and a moment's terse questioning confirmed his suspicions. More than 150 of Yasgur's men had poured out of the postern gate as the Order knights were arriving.

'They were taking no captives,' the sergeant said. 'They just marched right over us and out.'

'Where were they heading?'

'Towards the river, milor'.'

Mazaret nodded. And the old Chapel Fort. *It's just what I'd do*, he thought as he got to his feet and shouted for his officers.

Back inside the barracks, the fighting was over and a handful of prisoners sat on the floor at the centre of the hall, guarded by twice their number. Mazaret eyed them coldly as he gave orders to secure the building and have the wounded brought in. Meanwhile runners arrived with news – Yarram's assault on the Riverside Barracks was a complete success with no casualties and nearly 300 prisoners. But at the Ironhall Barracks, some of Yasgur's men had barricaded themselves inside after a spate of furious skirmishing – Mazaret's men had suffered a score of fatalities, among which was Cebroul.

And when Mazaret asked Medwin about events in the palace, the mage was scarcely less encouraging.

'Bardow and Kodel and their men cannot gain the inner chambers,' he said, wiping his hands on a scrap of cloth torn from the dorm curtains. He had been attending to some of the wounded and his formerly spotless robe was streaked with blood. 'The palace guard is putting up considerable resistance, despite the powers of Bardow and the mages accompanying him. They appear to have some sorcerous protection.'

'What of the ritual? Has it been completed?'

Medwin gave a tired smile. 'Were that so, neither of us would be alive to wonder. No, it continues to grow by the minute. You remember the Hall of Audience?'

'I do.'

'Well, that is the place and it is webbed, entwined with spells, each one of staggering magnitude and a purpose I am still unable to fathom—'

A soldier dashed into the hall from the rear and hurried to salute Mazaret. 'My lord, the bridges are in flames!'

Mazaret stared at him for a frozen instant, then took him by the shoulder and said, 'Show me.'

From the step at the postern gate Mazaret gazed out at the great, night-darkened mass of Besh-Darok. Much of the southern district had been built on hills and other higher ground, and he was able to look across clusters and rows of roofs, towers and cupolas, all sloping down to the river Olodar. Wharfside torches and the big oil-fired dock lamps scribed the river's wide S-curve through the city, and now two burning bridges added their own hot glows. Sparks flew up, floating with the clouds of wind-caught smoke which were spread in a long smear east towards the bay. Even as they watched, fire bloomed in several places all along a third bridge, and Mazaret knew that Yasgur's men were using oil. Then another of Kodel's hooded scouts appeared at the courtyard entrance, breathing heavily.

'Lord Commander Mazaret?' he said, looking from face to face.

'I am he,' Mazaret said.

The scout came over and sketched a bow before speaking in a low voice. 'Milor', I bring grave news.'

Mazaret inhaled deeply, steeling himself. 'Go on.'

'Commander Yarram regrets to inform you that Lord Tauric and his companions are trapped on the north bank. The Bridge of Spears and the Queens' Bridge are impassable, and he cannot spare men to hasten to the bridges in the east of the city . . .'

Mazaret fought down the twin tremors of anger and panic that shook him from within. 'And he wants to know if I will send some of my own troops, am I right?' He leaned closer to the man. 'But I wager that all the river's bridges will be ablaze very shortly. Thus, I want you and your brothers to find another way across the Olodar. The Lord Tauric must be found and brought back safely – any other outcome is unacceptable.'

The scout met his gaze for an unwavering moment, then swallowed, averted his eyes and nodded. 'It will be as you command, milor'. We shall bring the throne's heir back.'

'I know you will,' Mazaret said, putting as much confidence into his voice as he could. 'We are all the Earthmother's sons, and as we fight for her, so she works her will for us.'

There were unbidden cheers from the men in the yard, along with a shouting of Tauric's name, yet Mazaret kept his gaze on the scout. 'Now go.'

The scout whirled and was gone and as Mazaret went back inside, with tiredness tugging at his eyelids, he thought, *In the Mother's name, boy – what hazard are you courting now?*

Tauric hurriedly pressed the moist cloth against his nose as the wind blew another tail of dense smoke across their rooftop refuge. When the scout first brought them up here, after the Queen's Bridge was set afire, it seemed the perfect hiding place, a shelf concealed on three sides by peaked roofs with the fourth facing the river. Now it was starting to feel like a trap. Everyone's eyes were watering from the sting of the smoke and hair and garments were dusted with ash while uncovered skin bore red marks where embers had landed.

'How much longer is he going to be?' he muttered when the smoke cleared.

The Armourer gave him a withering look out of red-rimmed eyes. 'As long as need be, so save your voice.'

Tauric shrugged and stared morosely out at the city south of the river. There were a few street lanterns lit, but they were limited to the more prosperous districts on the hills and upper slopes. After dusk most of the houses and workshops of ordinary people dwelt in a gulf of shadows, broken by the bright little islands of alehouse lamps or the glow of a forge working through the night. By stark contrast, the Imperial palace was a monument to light; torches burned on every one of the four tiered walls and in every window of the High Spire. Once the abode of the Khatrimantine emperors, it was now Yasgur's den and a lair for his creatures, and by night it resembled a vast ship riding over the crest of a dark, dark wave.

'The fire from one of the bridges is spreading,' said Aygil.

The standard-bearer was lying full-length further up one of the sloping roofs, peering north over the peak. Ignoring the Armourer's disapproving frown, Tauric edged over and carefully climbed up to join. Aygil waited till he was settled before wordlessly pointing.

It was the northernmost bridge, the Bridge of Spears. It was a mass of flames spanning the river and buildings on either bank were now ablaze. By the fierce glow Tauric could see crowds of people trying to fight the fires, forming bucket lines that stretched down to the river's edge, and his heart went out to them. *These are the people I'm meant to deliver from injustice and pain. Yet we've brought them only suffering . . .*

Then another great curtain of smoke swept over them, obscuring everything. Beside him, Aygil was seized by a racking spasm of coughing and as Tauric held on to him, someone shouted his name. Glancing over his shoulder he could just see through the haze the Armourer, standing, beckoning.

'The scout has returned . . . we must leave now!'

Relieved, Tauric tried not to be hasty as he helped Aygil down from the roof and over to the open trapdoor. A few of the Companions had already descended and one stepped back to let Aygil go before him. Once all seventeen were down in the loft, coughing and murmuring among the crossbeams and crates, the Armourer turned to the scout, a short, wiry man with a permanent sardonic smile.

'What's this way back to the south – is one of the bridges still passable?'

'Nay . . . be as well to wish for a boat for there's not an unholed one on the north bank.'

'We could swim,' Tauric suggested.

The Armourer shook his head and the scout chuckled. 'Wrong season, laddie. The waters're full of poison worms and ripperfins, and the currents are fast, deep and treacherous. There'll be no way across the river this night.'

Dislike glittered in the Armourer's eyes as he gave the scout a poke in the shoulder with one gauntleted forefinger. 'Stop these games and tell me how we can get back,' he growled, then almost as an afterthought, 'and what is your name?'

The scout stared at him with eyes hard as flint and for a moment Tauric expected some kind of cutting reply, but instead he just smiled. 'I am known as Racho, O nameless one, and the only escape is through the Black Sluice.'

To Tauric's surprise, the Armourer uttered a deep, throaty laugh. 'I must speak to Kodel about you, little man. You have a talent for unpleasantness.'

'What is the Black Sluice?' said Tauric.

'The main sewer for the north of the city,' said Racho, visibly straining to keep from grinning. 'It feeds into the Eshel, an offshoot of the Olodar, and thence into the bay.'

'So we get to leave along with the shit and whatever else people throw out,' added the Armourer.

There were suppressed groans from Tauric's Companions, at which the Armourer gazed about him unsympathetically. 'Don't be complaining – I'm thinking of adding it to your training roster once this local disturbance is over.' Then he turned back to the scout. 'Are you certain about this? I don't want to find out later that there was another, quicker way.'

'On my father's grave, ser, I swear. The sluice is the only sure way outside, and our people control the slurry house. They will provide you all with waxed canvas overclothes.'

'Very well, then we shall go. Ser scout – you may lead the way.'

Racho smiled and bent to haul open a trapdoor in the floor.

The building was a thick-walled townhouse whose doors were locked and the windows bolted and shuttered inside and out. But the diminutive scout had a key for the back door which opened silently on well-oiled hinges to reveal a small, walled courtyard and three hooded figures, bows raised and aimed. Lightning fast, the Armourer snatched a dagger from his waist, then slowed as the archers lowered their weapons.

'Our own,' Racho said levelly, but glanced at Tauric and rolled his eyes upward in mock exasperation. Tauric fought the urge to laugh out loud.

'Good,' the Armourer said, sheathing his knife. 'We will proceed in single file led by myself and this pair.' He indicated two of the newcomers, then jabbed a finger at the third. 'You will bring up the rear with good ser Racho.'

All three scouts looked at Racho who just nodded, once. The Armourer, seeing this, gave a thoughtful grunt and looked at Tauric. 'Where will you walk, my lord?'

'Where . . . ah, at the rear, ser. Aygil still needs help.'

'As you wish.'

Tauric watched him lead the Companions quickly from the yard, privately astounded that the Armourer had actually asked him where he wanted to be. But why? It could not be because he was suddenly displaying the glowing talents of leadership – perhaps Kodel had a hand in this . . .

'An interesting man,' said the scout Racho. 'I never thought to find him here, playing such a part.'

'You know him?' Tauric said as they helped Aygil out of the yard and down a smoke-wreathed back alley after the rest.

The scout was silent for a moment or two, which was filled by the sounds of the city around them, shouts, screams, running feet. Then finally he spoke.

'The last time I saw him was fifteen years ago. Our village

owed fealty to a minor lord whose house was bound by marriage to the great sept of Ironkeel. Our dour comrade was the Ironkeels' forgemaster, and their mage. He was often seen in the hills near our village, prospecting for seams of ore.'

'Where was this?'

'In the Islands of Mist, east of the Drowned Realms of Lelorandelas.' The darkness of his hood could not entirely hide his sad smile. 'Beyond the Wilderan Sea.'

'You're from Keremenchool,' Tauric said, surprised.

'As you call it.'

Tauric let his voice drop to a murmur. 'So . . . what is his name?'

Racho chuckled, shook his head. 'That I would keep to myself. He may not thank me for being loose-tongued with it—' He stopped in his tracks, wide-eyed and staring over Tauric's shoulder. 'Gods, is the whole city going to burn?'

Tauric followed his gaze and almost cried out. A gap between two buildings afforded a view which took in part of the river and the districts leading up to the Imperial palace. Tiny figures were rushing along the palace walls as black, spark-laden smoke roiled from windows at the top of the High Spire itself. As Tauric watched in horror, a sound came to his ears, a harsh inhuman moan carrying across the roofs from the palace. It rose in pitch to an agonized shriek, like a thousand swords given voice, and finally ended in a single, thunderous crack reverberating across the city. At the same time, great gouts of fire erupted from the High Spire's topmost windows. Indistinct fragments arced away in flames and showers of sparks, and a jagged section of wall fell, tumbling slowly to crash on the battlements below.

Tauric stared, aghast. Before leaving with Yarram's men, he had learned from Bardow that Alael was up in that tower, and that Bardow and Kodel would try to bring her out.

'Quick!' Racho said, grabbing his arm. 'We must hurry – now!'

Alael! he thought as he and Aygil stumbled after the scout, *in the Mother's name, live!*

*   *   *

A short time before, while Tauric and his Companions were still
languishing in their smoke-hazed refuge, Alael had been standing
on sore feet near the throne in the Hall of Audience and trying
to shut out the sound of sorcery.

The Hall of Audience was a great oval chamber, its high roseate
walls hung with many exquisite tapestries depicting the cities and
regions of the vanquished Empire. Towering grey granite columns
bore hooks where unknown objects had once been displayed, and
the floor in front of the throne dais was a detailed map of the
entire continent of Toluveraz, executed in a mosaic of gems and
coloured marble.

Once, Alael was sure, it would have been polished and shining
– now it was obscured by a huge pattern scribed upon the floor.
Clusters of shallow grooves spread out from the foot of the throne
dais, some coiling, or forming spikes or repetitive motifs, while
others curved smoothly through the twisted intricacies towards
five end points where the others converged. Pale green light glowed
in every groove and at every intersection sat a small copper bowl.
There were scores of the bowls, each full of the green glow and
emanating a quiet ringing sound.

Alael, ankles aching, stood at the foot of the throne dais
steps, within a small incised circle from which all the grooves
originated. Next to her was a waist-high stand upon which lay
a plain, curved dagger and a strange, vaguely egg-shaped thing
apparently crudely carved out of grey-brown wood. At first it
was the dagger that scared her, but now the wooden egg caused
a deeper, darker dread.

Behind her, holding her neck and wrist ropes, was the man
called Dow Qrren who had kidnapped her north of Oumetra and
taken her to Sejeend. Alael hated him more than the Acolytes or
the Mogaun shamans, for he had carried out his treachery behind
a mask. And it was a base treachery – more than once during
the journey to Besh-Darok he had boasted of the kingdom that
would be his when the Lord of Twilight at last trod the earth.
Alael thought he was a self-deluding fool.

A yellow-shirted servant approached from the other end of

the hall and muttered to Dow Korren for a moment or two. Korren cleared his throat discreetly then spoke: 'Brother Galred, the rebels have taken the Imperial and Riverside barracks, but Ironhall is still holding out. Those attacking the palace have reached the anterooms on the floor below where their advance has been halted. The captain of the guard, however, is begging for reinforcements.'

Two black-robed Acolytes stood at the far side of the glowing floor pattern, shoulders hunched over, studying the lines. The elder of the two, his grey hair tied back in warrior style, glanced up from the bowls being carefully placed by his companion. Alael looked away from the white-eyed gaze.

'I care not,' said Galred in a high, hoarse voice. 'If that Bardow and his hedge wizards were at the doors to this hall, I could keep them out and not even raise a sweat. And I do not care for your presumption in naming me "brother" – you are not a Nightbrother, nor have you any of the five stigmata. In future, you will address me as "your serenity". Is that clear?'

Alael heard Korren swallow before answering but could not tell if it was from fear or anger. 'Indeed, yes, your serenity.'

'Excellent. Of such obedience are empires forged.' The Acolyte Galred turned to his assistant. 'Brother Miras, are we ready for the Vraoleach Dor?'

Miras, a black-haired youth with cadaverous features, bowed to Galred. 'The last of the tethering bowls are in place and the five mouths have been well positioned.'

Galred gave a satisfied nod. 'Our brothers are with the Great Shadowkings, and the Weaving of Souls awaits death, agony and power.' His white eyes regarded Alael and this time she could not look away. 'Once, the Lord of Twilight was the All-Highest until his lesser siblings betrayed him. Soon he will assume his rightful dominion and all who oppose him shall be swept away. Miras, your duty awaits.'

The younger Acolyte, his face expressionless, walked carefully across the pattern, robe lifted slightly to avoid touching any of the bowls. He knelt on the floor a few feet in front of Alael, facing away, robe wrapped tightly about him as he hunched forward over his hands. Alael saw no knife and discerned no movement, but suddenly a dark fluid was rilling along the grooves from in front of Miras, kneeling still and silent.

It was blood. Mouth dry, Alael watched it spread throughout the pattern, including the circle where she stood.

Then Galred, who had meanwhile walked around the pattern, stepped into the circle with her. Involuntarily, she cringed.

'Fear is good, child,' he said. 'But shackles are better.'

She knew what he meant. On her arrival at Besh-Darok, he had placed an invisible guardian over her which weighed down her limbs and mind whenever she tried to evoke the Lesser Power.

'The time is upon us,' Galred said. 'Korren – know that the heat will be so great that you may wish to shelter in one of the side galleries. Or you may stay and observe.'

'I shall stay, your serenity.'

'As you wish.' He stared out at the pattern, raised a spidery hand and began to intone barbaric-sounding words in a strange, deep animal-like voice. Veils of radiance sprang up from the blood-filled grooves, a glittering, shifting maze with brighter spears of light rising from every intersection where a bowl sat.

'Child, give me your hand.'

There was a forceful compulsion in the words that could not be resisted. Galred's fingers were bony, dry and hot around her wrist, pushing the knotted rope up to her elbow. Before she could react, his other hand came up and jabbed something pin-sharp into her arm.

'Worry not,' he said. 'There will no pain.'

An utter numbness was creeping down into her hand till she could no longer feel Galred's grip, not the shape of his fingers nor their squeezing pressure, nothing. Galred then guided her hand over to the wooden egg, saying, 'Grasp the seed. You still have the use of the hand.'

As she did so, he picked up the dagger. The massed ringing sound of the tethering bowls was growing louder, and her terror was a widening shadow, drowning more and more of the world in darkness.

'Mother-spirit!' Galred declaimed. 'Come forth! Surrender yourself to the Spirit of the World, the Lord of Twilight. I so command by the spilt essence of this, your last true host!'

The blade shone as Galred raised it above his head, empty white eyes fixed on his target, her fingers gripping the thing he called the seed.

And on the edge of the glowing maze pattern, a copper bowl flipped over and its bright spear of light died. The veil leaped higher at that point and a sour note crept into the sorcerous ringing. Galred lowered the dagger, angry gaze swinging round to the pattern.

'Korren,' he said in cold fury. 'Go round and return that bowl to its place.'

Alael felt the ropes around her wrists and neck slacken and saw the tall, bald man hurry around to the bowl. He crouched down, pulled on a gauntlet and gingerly reached through the veil for the bowl . . .

There was a burst of red light and Dow Korren flew backwards, his arm ablaze. He struck one of the wall tapestries and it caught fire as he slid to the floor, beating weakly at his burning arm.

Galred cursed him, dived out of the encircling veil and rushed round to the overturned bowl. But before he could even reach for it, others began tipping over. He uttered a wordless bellow as the pattern veils grew taller and brighter.

'Who are you?' he roared, staring wildly about him at the empty doors, and the deserted high galleries. 'Come out, thou craven dog, and face me!'

Fire from the burning tapestry had spread to others nearby and a grey haze of smoke was starting to thicken. Alael could see her surroundings rippling with heat, yet where she stood the air was cool and untainted. An awful metallic shriek filled the hall and Alael could only cover one ear – her deadened hand would not move from the seed.

Galred seemed to have lost his senses and was flinging fiery knots of power up at the galleries. His hair was smouldering and his robes were smoking from standing so close to the veils of the pattern, but he seemed not to notice. Then he was running back round towards Alael, dagger held before him, murder in his face. He shouted something, which was drowned in the shattering din, and lunged at her.

In mid-thrust, something invisible caught him and hurled him, robes flapping, into the centre of the pattern. Alael saw him breathe in to scream, then she cried out as he was torn limb from limb, joint from joint, flames not blood bursting forth as the pieces of mangled flesh were sucked into the veils along which they flew like flotsam swept up by savage currents.

The veils began to quiver and sway, as if caught in strengthening winds. They curved, bending and stretching towards one of the pattern's five convergence points, five blurred black holes on the floor. Long snakes of black smoke were being drawn in, too, and Alael could feel it pulling at her body and mind as the noise, a horrific iron howl, reached a crescendo.

Close your eyes . . .

The voice was in her head, rousing her fear, her panic.

Close your eyes now, my last true one . . .

She did, just as the world broke apart in a blinding, deafening crash that went on and on and on . . .

When the terrible sounds faded, when the stench of burnt things filled her nostrils, and when she realized that she was curled up on the floor, hugging something rough and heavy to her chest, she opened her eyes.

Blackened, charred floor and walls, small fires still burning fitfully here and there, fragments of a shattered column, melted and glassy, and a great jagged hole in the wall through which she saw a sky of broken clouds and stars. And from the gap came a breeze to stir the ash which lay everywhere.

She never knew he was near until a hand reached down and wrenched the seed away from her exhausted grasp.

'This bauble will do . . .' His voice was cracked and full of torment. 'I'll have my kingdom yet . . .'

Ignoring her pleas, he took hold of her arm and began dragging her across the filthy floor, even as thuds and bangs came from the doors to the hall. Halfway to one of the side galleries he fell, gasping in pain, but before he could seize her again there was a smashing, breaking sound and the doors flew open to a triumphant chorus of shouts. With a cry of frustration, he clambered to his feet and lurched off ino the gallery shadows.

Seconds later, friendly hands were helping her to sit, or offering her water. Then Kodel was kneeling next to her, a moistened cloth in hand and gently wiping her face.

'Look for the seed,' someone else was saying. 'It must be here.'

Alael shook her head, assailed by guilt and loss. 'I lost it,' she said brokenly. 'He took it and I couldn't stop him.'

'Who?' Kodel said quietly.

'Dow Korren,' she said, and began to weep.

Chapter Twenty-seven

Hot the blood,
And cold the knife.
Let Death feed upon death,
And Life betray life.

Eshen Karedu, *The Tale of the Revenger*, ch. 9, iv

When the hot, charred wind had cooled and trailed away to nothing, when the ghostly lines of the Hall of Audience, drenched in fire and ash, had finally faded, there were only five figures standing in a forest clearing ringed by torches.

Byrnak inhaled deeply and breathed out, long and shuddering, and strove to keep his surging relief from showing. He was still himself, still whole. As his own power had flowed out to join the others in the abortive Weaving of Souls, he had seen into the depths of the unfolding spectacle – the pure, unwavering devotion of the Acolyte Galred, and the aura of untapped Lesser Power that surrounded and permeated the girl. And the seed of the Mother, not a vessel, rather a channel from the Earthmother's realm into the world.

Byrnak had felt the potential within the seed, the crushing immensity of the power which they had come close to possessing. But the mountain had not fallen, the torrent had not burst through, and his soul remained unwoven. Silently, secretly, he was glad.

Not so secret that I cannot know how weak you are, said the shadow within.

An image of a bloody eye flashed across Byrnak's sight for an instant and he gritted his teeth in anger. His unwelcome companion had taken to sending unsettling visions, gory nightmare fragments which would flit and flicker behind his eyes.

Gnaw on your old bones, he thought. *The day will come when I shall be free of you, I swear.*

On that day, it will be your bones that I gnaw.

In his mind's eye, Byrnak saw grinning, bloody teeth.

'Is this truly the best you could contrive for our purposes?'

The spectral figure of the Hidden One stood before Ystregul, whose broad, bearded face was a picture of simmering rancour.

'You could have done better, no doubt.'

'I rather fancy that I could. For one, I would have had half a dozen Acolytes in that hall, and a dozen—'

'Clearly, brother, you misunderstand our relationship with the Acolytes and their relationship with Yasgur.' With his head lowered slightly, and his glittering eyes hooded, his grin was unpleasant in the torchlight. 'The prince has never allowed more than two of the Nightbrothers within his city.'

'The opportunity was there, brother,' the Hidden One sneered. 'You should have made better preparations—'

'What could have prepared us for an unseen opponent?' Byrnak said smoothly. 'One who could overmaster a senior Acolyte?'

The Hidden One tilted his helmed head to glance in his direction. 'Since we have already encountered unexpected difficulties, such caution should have been part of the plan.'

'You are quick with scathing comment, brother,' said Thraelor. 'Yet we have heard no proposed stratagems from you.'

Like the Hidden One, Thraelor and Grazaan were attending from afar, their forms mistily opaque. Neither wore the concealing helms and their attire was opulent without being gaudy, Grazaan an unsmiling, grey-haired man in white and pale blue, Thraelor a tall, beautiful youth in black and emerald.

'I have my own schemes,' the Hidden One said. 'They are well laid and more certain of useful fruition than this . . . posturing.'

'But we have seen no evidence of these schemes,' Thraelor

pointed out. 'What else can we do but pursue other means of
completing the Weaving?' He smiled as he looked at Byrnak. 'And
you, brother – have you a course of action we might consider?'

'Why, no.'

A frown creased Thraelor's perfect brow and the delicate,
almond eyes narrowed. 'None at all?'

Byrnak laughed. 'Brothers, need I remind you that I was given
command of the Mogaun host? When your plots and intrigues
come to naught, it will fall to me to crush these upstarts and
bring them under our power and our will.'

'That is comforting to know,' Thraelor said blandly. 'But there
are other alternatives yet to be ventured.' He turned to Ystregul.
'As we have already proposed.'

Disdain crossed Ystregul's heavy features. 'Gorla and Keshada?
Too time-consuming. There is no way of telling what our enemies
may achieve during a span of weeks. No, there are other ways of
securing our purpose . . .'

Byrnak and the others listened as he outlined a new plan. The
Hidden One stood with arms crossed through it all, and nodded
firmly when Ystregul finished.

'Yes, this may serve,' he said. 'Provided these servants of yours
will obey us without question, and will not be turned against us
by our unknown adversary.'

'They will be ours,' Ystregul said, clenching a fist before him.

'Then you have my support. Call upon me when it is time.'

As he faded away, Byrnak noticed Thraelor and Grazaan
exchange a look.

'There are risks in this,' Grazaan said. 'The mages will fight,
and such conflict may endanger the end we mean to attain. Then
there is Yasgur – he may baulk at carrying out your orders.'

Ystregul's grin was a study in malice. 'Oh, Yasgur will play his
part. I intend to send one of my servants to help him overcome
any reluctance. As for the mages, their powers will be greatly
subdued.'

'Very well,' Grazaan said, though without apparent enthusiasm.
'You may rely upon my involvement.'

Thraelor nodded. 'Mine also.'

'We see that Yasgur and the vanguard are less than an hour from Besh-Darok,' Grazaan said. 'We shall be ready when he arrives.'

Both he and Thraelor turned to walk away and between one step and the next their forms dissolved, melting from sight. Byrnak smiled at this graceful departure.

'And you, brother Byrnak – what is your decision?'

Still staring at the place where Thraelor and Grazaan had been, Byrnak said, 'As before, I shall aid the common effort.'

'Without any misgivings or exceptions? How trusting of you.'

At this, Byrnak spun to face him. 'Not so! My doubts are many – this plan of yours is wasteful and extravagant, and takes no account of the adversary who, you may recall, throttled your last great strategy. You may have heard that one of my servants foiled an attempt by our enemies to seize the Crystal Eye.'

The sudden change in tack neutered some of Ystregul's anger. 'I heard differently. So?'

'Can we be sure that the Imperial rabble have not unearthed some other god-wrought talisman from a lost age, one strong enough to defeat a senior Acolyte?'

Ystregul shook his head. 'My attack will be so swift that no mage in Besh-Darok will be able to stand against us. After that, there will be little more than a thousand rebels facing Yasgur's army.' He smiled. 'The blood sacrifice of more than a dozen mages coupled with the Vraoleach Dor should be more than enough to fuel the Weaving of Souls.'

'Such certainty.' Byrnak could not keep the contempt out of his voice. 'Your self-confidence will eat you, brother. But until then, I will continue to work with you. After all, there is always a chance that you might succeed.' He tugged on a pair of plain rider's gauntlets. 'Now, you must excuse me – the chiefs of the Host are awaiting my commands. Don't linger too long in the shadows, brother.'

So saying, he clapped his hands once and the circle of torches went out. But he had taken only a few paces towards the edge of the clearing when the torches flared into life again.

'The darkness comes at my behest, brother.'

From the clearing it was a short downhill walk to the valley along which the Host of Clans was encamped. Here, night was banished by the glow of many hundreds of cooking fires, and the air was heavy with smoke and the smell of horses. Few tents had been erected for this brief pause, and looking down the valley Byrnak saw a sea of men clustered about the fires, or gaming for petty gems or tokens, or curled up in blankets, asleep. Standards and banners stood among the crowds – some were crude regalia of bones and rusted armour, or ragged pieces of cloth daubed with an eye or a dagger, while a few others were well made from tapestry fabric, adorned with golden emblems, or hung with knotted cords of silk.

One such stood before his own modest tent, a long banner of blood-red cloth bearing the device of a rayed sun pierced by an upward-pointing black sword. It had been a gift from Welgarak, chief of the Black Moon clan, who had insisted that the general of the Host of Clans must have his own standard. At first he had agreed out of expediency, but then some warriors (most notably from the Bearclaw, Black Moon and Iceskull clans) began adopting the emblem and now Byrnak experienced an obscure pleasure whenever he saw it.

Around a fire near his tent sat his assistants and his personal guards. The former were an assortment of tutored slaves and talented misfits, while the latter number a dozen battle-hardened warriors donated by a few of the clan chiefs. They all rose at his approach and once he had dealt with scout reports, a handful of complaints and petitions, and given the orders to strike camp, he was able to turn towards his tent.

But Obax was there, standing at the entrance, and before he could say anything, the Acolyte was using mindspeech.

Great lord, an exalted visitor awaits you within.

He moved aside as Byrnak stepped up to the tent flap, glanced frowningly at him for a moment then pushed on through. It was warm inside, the air full of the taint of hot tallow from the lantern glowing on the table beyond which stood a translucent figure, his head concealed by an ornate helm.

'Why are you here?' Byrnak said bluntly.

'Out of curiosity,' said the Hidden One. 'And to bring a warning.'

'Were you that offended by my comments earlier?'

The Hidden One made a dismissive gesture. 'You clearly don't trust our brother the Black Priest, yet you are willing to work with him. Also you put forward no plans of your own. Why is this?'

Byrnak smiled. 'You don't understand – I don't trust a single one of you, and I especially don't trust you. As for working with our honoured brother, I am content to let him and the rest of you scheme your schemes and make your mistakes . . . for the time being.' He stroked his chin thoughtfully. 'Is that what you were going to warn me about, the perfidy of the Black Priest? Well, I have him under my regard, as do you, I'm sure.'

'He almost succeeded in the attempt to tap the seed of the Mother,' the Hidden One said. 'If he had, it would have focused all that power in his hands alone, and that would have been the end of us.'

Byrnak wagged a finger at him. 'It was you, wasn't it? You were the one who undid all his spells.'

'I have my agents, and they have theirs. But realize this – he will try again, thus we should be on our guard.'

'I am always on my guard,' said Byrnak.

The Hidden One raised a hand to his helm and it vanished, revealing a strong-featured man, his hair a flaming red, his eyes dark and secretive, and his mouth betraying a hint of cruelty. Byrnak almost laughed out loud.

'I am still less inclined to trust you,' he said.

A shake of the head. 'As you wish. But it is in your interest to watch the Black Priest and tally his work and deeds, for he will move against us all, I am certain of it. The question is how and when.'

Then, in an eyeblink instant, he was gone. Byrnak, thoughts

dark and troubled, stared at the empty air then went back outside, shouting orders for the tent to be broken down.

The night was like a dream of cold wind and darkness through which Gilly rode, just behind Yasgur as he led the vanguard along the country road to Besh-Darok. Next to Gilly, on a spirited black horse, was Ghazrek, Yasgur's second-in-command, and in front of him, riding next to Yasgur was the old man, Atroc, his threadbare cloak flapping, threads streaming and slowly unravelling from its worn edge.

It had been an eventful three days since departing Arengia. Twice they had fought furious skirmishes with bands of brigands, and both times Yasgur had been saved from 'accidental' misfortune, once by Ghazrek whose outswept buckler caught an arrow meant for the prince's throat, and later by one assailant who leaped onto Yasgur's horse to grapple with him, only to be impaled front to back by a flung spear. Those responsible, both Bloodfists, were sent back to rejoin their clan and the Host. Yasgur meanwhile pressed on, with a gulf of mistrust widening between himself, his advisers and their few sworn guards on one side, and the 200 or more Doubleknives and Bloodfists and their shamans on the other.

But a further burden had come to Yasgur earlier that night when a bloodied rider arrived from Besh-Darok with the grim report that the city was in the hands of rebels. Yasgur immediately dispatched riders with orders for the two halves of his great army, then set out for Besh-Darok. Soon after, one of them returned accompanied by the aged adviser, Atroc, who brought the more welcome news that the army which had set out for Sejeend had turned back and was less than two hours from Besh-Darok's walls.

They had left the wide plains of Kalen behind as the road curved through the wooded hills west of the city. There were many small towns and hamlets scattered throughout these hills, some of which Gilly knew from his travels in Mazaret's service. This countryside had been heavily cultivated from the earliest of times, parcelled off into fields, farms, orchards and private estates with their own woods and gardens. Scouts came and went, and a few times they encountered parties of torch-bearing wardens and rangers whose belligerence quickly cooled on recognizing Yasgur's standard.

Besh-Darok was an uneven glow less than an hour away, partly hidden by a wooded ridge. As the city drew ever nearer, Gilly's mind turned to thoughts of escape. It could only be the Knights and the Hunter's Children who were now in command of Besh-Darok and Gilly was determined to join them, even if Yasgur's army would soon assault the walls.

Escape, though, seemed a slim prospect while six Mogaun riders were watching over him with a diligence born of malicious glee, almost as if they were hoping for an excuse to pounce. He had already suspected two of being his keepers, but it was Atroc who pointed out the other four, soon after his arrival.

'The one with the spear is in case you dodge the two nearby riders,' the old Mogaun had said, matter-of-factly. 'The one with the bow is there if the spear misses, and those two, the ones without armour, will chase you down were you charmed enough to evade the rest.' Atroc had grinned, not unkindly, and patted Gilly on the shoulder. 'See how we value your companionship, southman?'

They were deep in the darkest hours of the night by the time the road came to the ridge. The slope before them was steep and overgrown, a thick tangle of trees, thorns and shadows, but the road curved to the right, staying on level ground. Gilly eyed the dark wall of foliage, trying to discern details – weren't there a couple of old smugglers' trails that led over the ridge? If he could spot one amid the shadows, and if he could get to it without taking an arrow or a spear in the back, then he could lose any pursuit in that dense undergrowth. He was already on the ridgeward side of the column, with Ghazrek more than an arm's length away on his right. The trick would be to get Ghazrek between him and those watchful warriors, or perhaps fake a fall, somehow provoke his horse into throwing him . . .

Then there was a shout from up ahead and Yasgur slowed the vanguard with a raised hand as one of the scouts came riding out of the murk. One of Yasgur's retainers fumbled with a hooded lamp as the prince and Atroc conversed with the scout in whispers. By the lamp's tapered yellow glow Gilly saw the scout hand a wadded cloth to Yasgur who partly unfolded it and examined it for a moment before thrusting it into his saddlebag.

The next moment, Yasgur was leading the column in a furious gallop after the scout who was already riding off the way he had come. Gilly had to spur his horse roughly to keep up with Ghazrek, who cast him a frowning glance, and the other Mogaun who pressed closely around him. He cursed inwardly – at this speed, spying out the secret trails would be next to impossible.

After less than a mile the vanguard slowed once more as the scout turned along a narrow track which climbed the steep face of the ridge. In front of Gilly, Yasgur and Atroc were engaged in a quiet yet animated discussion which ended when the slowing horses brought Gilly and the other front riders close. Interesting, he thought.

The undergrowth on the slope was a dense entwining of poisonous dogivy and wallthorn, and the air beneath the trees was chilly and damp. The track, which had clearly once been wider, passed over two brooks and round a time-worn rocky outcrop before the crest of the ridge came into view. There had once been a fort here: the tumbled remains of its walls, rounded by centuries and moss, bore mute testimony to the square lines of its ancient design. Once, too, the ground all about it had been cleared, perhaps even salted, but down the years tenacious grass and bushes had taken hold across the area, right back to the impenetrable wood many yards away.

Torches burned amid the ruins and figures moved there as the vanguard approached. Yasgur and Atroc dismounted, as did everyone else, almost 200 riders gathering in a wide crescent to watch. Six hooded Mogaun warriors – members of Yasgur's special scout band – came forward with three prisoners and forced them to kneel. As Yasgur strode forward to meet them, Gilly examined the captives, all youths not yet in their maturity, and his gaze came to rest on one that he thought familiar, a fair-haired young man whose face was full of dignity and despair.

Recognition came in a sudden leap, bringing in its wake a dismay that he felt in his stomach. The boy was Tauric, the heir to the Imperial throne. But what was he doing outside Bēsh-Darok if Mazaret and the others were in control of it? And why had they been so cruel as to tie his amputated arm behind his back?

Yasgur was clutching the cloth brought by the scout, unfolded and trailing on the ground as he walked straight towards Tauric. The cloth was a white flag bearing the device of the Fathertree, symbol of a dead emperor and a shattered empire. When Yasgur came to halt before Tauric, he gestured with his empty hand for the youth to stand. As he did so, a tense stillness hung over the ruins and a chill went through Gilly at the sight of this meeting.

'I've heard of your arm,' said Yasgur. 'I would see it.'

At his nod, one of the hooded scouts cut Tauric's bonds and held up his right arm. A brown sleeve and gauntlet were stripped away to reveal gleaming metal from elbow to fingertips. Excited murmurs and whispered charms against evil passed among the watching warriors, and Gilly stared in amazement.

'A fine piece,' Yasgur said. 'Is it sorcerous?'

'I . . .' Tauric faltered. 'I do not know.'

Watching Yasgur, Gilly was sure he saw a hint of uncertainty behind the stern, bearded features and wondered if he knew who Tauric was.

'You risk much with that arm,' Yasgur said, and held out the flag. 'And this.'

'Sometimes risk is in the blood,' Tauric said calmly.

'Is that why your troops have seized my city?'

'It is no crime to regain that which was stolen!'

Yasgur smiled slowly, as if satisfied, and to Gilly's eyes a look of mutual acknowledgement seemed to pass between them.

'Now I must decide what to do with you,' Yasgur said. 'I could send you to the Council of Chiefs, who would not treat you kindly. Or I could send you to the Acolytes in their fastness, and they would be harsher still. Or I could just torture you myself.'

From the gathered warriors came laughter and jeers, and faces lit up with glee. Gilly felt a tremor of dread.

'But would that smooth the return of my city?' Yasgur went on. 'Would that safeguard my subjects, who have already suffered much from this insurrection? No – Besh-Darok is mine—' A hand came up clenched in a fist then stretched out to point at Tauric, '—just as you are mine.'

Yasgur gazed fiercely about him, looking many of the Doubleknives and Bloodfists in the eye, an open challenge to his audience.

'I have decided what will be done,' he said. 'These three shall be sent to the city with a simple message for their fellows – leave Besh-Darok within the hour and you shall not be hindered. If that span expires and you yet remain, then my army shall fall upon the city and every one of you will be slain without mercy.'

A shocked silence greeted these words, and Gilly saw many of the assembled warriors glare at their commander with unconcealed hate. Yasgur, however, turned to Tauric.

'My words must reach your captains without alteration – swear that you will repeat them as I have said them.'

But before Tauric could answer there was a commotion among the onlookers and a gaunt figure carrying a plain staff stepped forward. It was one of the two shamans sent with the vanguard by Byrnak, a Bloodfist by the name of Jaroul. His bony form cast a long shadow as he pointed at Yasgur with the forked head of his staff.

'You dishonour the memory of your father,' Jaroul said. 'The mighty Hegroun would not have made such spineless agreements with the enemy—'

'Who are you to say what my father would or would not have done?' Yasgur cried, stung to fury. He moved towards his accuser. 'You forget who is your master here!'

The shaman raised his staff, and scores of warriors rushed forward in groups. Amid the noisy scramble, Gilly was grabbed by a cluster of hands and thrust to the ground while Yasgur, roaring his anger and swinging his fists, was overwhelmed by a mob of Doubleknives. Elsewhere, Yasgur's few personal guards were ruthlessly butchered, and Ghazrek went down beneath a flurry of blows.

Untouched by the tumult, but closely guarded, Tauric and his companions could only stare in helpless amazement.

At last, out of the confusion a kind of order emerged. Gilly found himself kneeling next to a dishevelled but alert Atroc and a bruised and bloody-lipped Ghazrek. Yasgur was also kneeling a few feet away, bound and gagged, while all the warriors gathered closely around in a rough semicircle. Gilly could feel the heat of their bodies and smell the pungent taint of days-old sweat. But most of all, there was the sense of expectation.

Some warriors behind Yasgur stood aside and the shaman Jaroul came forward, smiling. After him, supported by two brawny Mogaun, was the other shaman, a smaller man wearing little more than stained rags held together with animal gut. The man was deranged – his pale eyes wandered and rolled in their sockets, perspiration gleamed on ashen skin and a dry blood trail marked his chin from where he had bitten through his lower lip. His hand twitched at his sides and only his keepers kept him on his feet.

Jaroul watched him with obvious pleasure then reached out to Yasgur and, none too gently, wrenched the gag from his mouth.

'Your fate was in your hands, O prince,' he said mockingly. 'You could have commanded that the enemy be broken and crushed, but you chose otherwise. Thus it is now your fate to be shackled and caged.'

Yasgur tried to spit in his face, but only white droplets came. The shaman uttered a cracked laugh then turned to his mindless companion. With both hands he grasped the man's head, spidery fingers spread across ears and temples, thumbs holding open the upper eyelids as he stared into those restless orbs.

'All is ready, master,' Gilly heard him whisper. 'The furrow awaits its seed.'

He withdrew his hands, stepped back and gestured to the two warriors who tightened their grip. For a moment, nothing. Then a trembling began in the little man's arms, as if he were cold, a quivering which travelled up to the shoulders and the head. The shaking grew till the man's entire body was juddering and his head was nodding and jerking upon his neck. Beneath his rags, his chest was fluttering as his breath wheezed and inarticulate grunts came from his twisted mouth. In the lurid glow of nearby torches held aloft, it was a ghastly sight.

Just when it seemed to Gilly that the man was on the point of death, his convulsions changed to a retching which soon became deeper and drawn out. No one spoke in the fearful stillness, as finally there was one expulsive exhalation which went on and on for long seconds, the widened mouth exposing a pale, dry tongue. Animal terror shone in the eyes and for an instant they glanced over at Gilly.

Someone in the crowd gasped, followed by others, then Gilly saw it, a greenish radiance emerging from the agonized shaman's mouth. Then the bright core of it appeared, a burning emerald mote which slowly slid over the bottom lip and off into the air. It drifted there for a moment, the focus of all attention, then in a blurred streak of motion flew straight at Yasgur.

Instinctively, Yasgur turned his face away and Gilly was not the only onlooker to cry out when the bright green speck struck the prince's cheek and buried into it. With blood pouring from the wound, Yasgur lurched sideways, still bound hand and foot but thrashing and bellowing in pain and fear. Pandemonium erupted. Warriors scrambled back from him while others pushed forward to see, and over the noise came the voice of the shaman Jaroul shouting futile orders.

At length, the crowd went oddly silent and drew back, and Gilly saw Yasgur getting to his feet, his stance poised and relaxed, his hands holding severed pieces of cord. But now a pale green nimbus clung to him, a pearly veil which shifted and glittered faintly, casting a sickly tinge across a face whose eyes were full of evil power and whose lips smiled a smile of hungry anticipation.

'Mighty Hegroun!' cried the shaman, throwing himself at the prince's feet. 'We are your servants – command us!'

Hegroun? Gilly thought in stunned dread. *What foul sorcery is this?*

The man named Hegroun ignored the outburst, instead side-stepping the prostrate shaman and with a predatory litheness moved towards where Tauric still stood, hands bound again behind his back. The young heir scarcely flinched when the possessed chief leaned in close to study him, letting the green aura brush against hair and face.

'I can smell him in you,' Hegroun said. 'You share his blood, and his fate.' He turned to survey the crowd, his piercing gaze coming to rest upon Atroc. 'Well, old man, still alive, eh? Still meddling?'

Atroc inclined his head. 'Each to his own nature, lord.'

Hegroun snorted. 'You have changed not at all. Even when you say little, it is still too much.' He looked at the shaman. 'Tie the boy to a tree and have the men gather kindling, then get me a spear. Let us see if he burns as well as his father.'

There were whoops of delight and eager hate at this, and the clustered crowd of Mogaun riders dispersed in groups to gather foliage. As Tauric was dragged struggling over to a slender tree, Gilly cursed aloud and received a casual cuff from his guard. Beside him, Atroc just watched with a kind of cold intensity.

Then Gilly saw one of Tauric's captors topple to the ground, a feathered shaft through his neck. There was the whirr of more arrows and several agonized cries as some torchbearers fell, dousing or dimming their flames. Hegroun and the shaman were shouting orders amid the gloom, then behind him Gilly heard the thud of arrows into flesh and turned to see his guards lying in their death throes. Instantly he leaped up and was about to dash across to Tauric when dozens of flaming missiles began falling out of the night sky. Panicking warriors ran from the ruins, only to encounter their own horses, released and driven to stampede. Many were trampled before the horses swerved towards the ridge's nothern slope.

As he ran and dodged the burning missiles – clods of grassy earth soaked in oil – Gilly spotted the Hegroun creature carrying a spear and loping towards Tauric. A couple of men bearing swords stood near the boy, working on his bonds. Then he was free, and to Gilly's utter astonishment he leaped from the tree and charged straight at the possessed chieftain. Skilfully, he beat aside a spearthrust and with his clenched metal hand struck Hegroun in the face, casting him to the ground.

Hegroun lost his spear but was still agile enough to use his legs to knock Tauric's feet from under him. As the boy sprawled in the dust, Hegroun rose to stand over him, laughing.

Gilly was racing full-tilt towards the chieftain. *I'll have you*, he thought grimly. *Just a few more paces* . . .

Two things happened almost at once. A great dark shape rushed in from the side, a rider on a horse Gilly realized. He saw it slam into the Hegroun creature in the instant before a heavy weight landed on Gilly's back and bore him to the ground.

'I told you we value your companionship,' a familiar voice gasped in his ear while he struggled with his face in the dirt. Out of the corner of his eye he thought he saw the rider haul Tauric up behind him. But then a blow came down on his head and he knew no more.

On boggy ground by a river, Byrnak stood next to an empty, smoking pit while Ystregul stared out at the night. They had all watched the drama unfold atop the ridge near Besh-Darok and now that the other three Shadowkings were no longer ethereally present, Byrnak wondered at Ystregul's composure in the face of what had transpired.

'The boy is lucky in his allies,' he said. 'To escape from such a trap . . .'

'You would know about that,' Ystregul said cuttingly.

Byrnak ground his teeth at the remark and held in his anger, channelled it, made it work for him. 'Such a shame that your servant was foolish enough to let him slip away. Hopefully the rest of them will not be as . . . lacking.'

The Black Priest turned with a gaze full of enmity. 'In life Hegroun was an ordinary man – the others were anything but. Besides, where else can the boy go but back to the city, which will be in our hands anyway before the night is done.'

'So your Acolytes promise you,' Byrnak said. 'But can you be sure?'

'I am certain of every detail, every link in the chain. It will not fail.' He raised a bare hand to point at Byrnak. 'Be wary of testing my patience in this way. I will not be mocked.'

Ystregul turned and stalked back to his horse, accompanied by his small coterie of Acolytes and Initiates, two of whom half-carried a weak, delirious shaman. Byrnak enjoyed a contemptuous smile. He had watched them all work with Ystregul, digging the conical hole, tracing patterns all around it, then standing there, drenched in the harsh emerald glow shining up from the pit, wreathed in vapours expelled by the heat of sorcery. Then with metal rods they had coaxed forth the revenant spirits, rising like a tiny flock of burning viridian pearls which they guided over to the open mouth of the drugged shaman and smoothly down his gullet.

All this Byrnak had observed, with some unknown instinct, some hidden aptitude noting every step and method and fitting them all together in his mind, making him understand. This shaman was linked to one of the two accompanying Yasgur, one the entrance, the other the exit. He recalled a comment Obax had once made, that the Acolytes were artisans of the soul, able to treat a man's spirit like a gemstone, cutting, reshaping, polishing it, even gathering it back together from the grinding scatter of the grave.

Now as he walked carefully across muddy ground back to his own horse, the Hidden One's insistence that Ystregul needed watching over took on a certain urgency. Byrnak already knew which clan chiefs belonged to the Black Priest and which ones might sway to his cause, but of his dealings with the Acolytes he knew next to nothing. Was he in alliance with the entire order, or with just a few of them?

Now remounted on his horse, winding the reins about his hand, he sat listening to the riders' song coming from some way back along the column. The words were simple and moved to the rhythm of a gallop, punctuated by drawn-out syllables. He smiled and looked over his shoulder at one of his personal guards.

'Pass the word – we ride to the attack. That should give them something to sing about!'

Chapter Twenty-eight

Pain, madness and bones –
The harvest of his dungeons.

Jurad's *History of Ordeals*, book vi, 8

Cold, blind and caged, Suviel despaired. The cold was the heavy, seeping cold of a stone-walled chamber utterly devoid of light, and her cage was an upright, lidless coffin of iron into which she was strapped. She wanted to weep but her eyes felt empty and dry. She wanted to cry out but some enchantment had been laid upon her and her voice was a barred gate. The only thing between her and the crushing weight of despair was the cracked shield of her mind.

Against the deliberate blackness of the chamber her awareness instinctively strove to perceive her surroundings, despite her attempts to rein it in. Earlier, when several Acolytes returned not long after her incarceration, her nether-senses had revealed them to her. Faint lines glimmered in the darkness, the curve of a jaw or the glint of an eye, forming the likeness of cruel faces.

'How strong,' one had murmured.

'How fertile,' said another, laughing.

Then a veil of nothingness fell . . . and rose like a slow eyeblink. It seemed to last only moments, but when it lifted she saw that her visitors were gathered about a pale, hooded figure, guiding him from the chamber.

All that had happened but a short time ago, she was almost sure.

Had the pale figure been a fellow prisoner? There were another ten or so silent captives somewhere else in this black stone crypt – she had felt their presences. She recalled old Babrel relating the escaped children's tales of iron caskets adorned with symbols and the terrible rites conducted upon them . . . She shivered as much from the iciness of her flesh as from the coldness of her spirit. She tried to imagine that Ikarno Mazaret was with her, and took refuge in memories of the warm circle of his arms, of the gentle passion of his kisses . . .

After an interval, perhaps an hour, perhaps longer, there were more visitors. This time it was Coireg Mazaret and three Acolytes. She could make out more details this time and could see the hot satisfaction in Coireg's face when he came and stood close by. She felt his breath on her cheek, and it smelled bitter.

'You will give,' he said. 'You will serve.'

Never, she wanted to say but could only mouth the word.

Coireg laughed, a high unpleasant sound. 'My master's fate is hungry – it crushes all others. At this moment, his plan holds the city of emperors in an iron grasp. Soon the nighthunters will fly. Forests will burn, fortresses will fall, and a great empire of shadow will be born. You will see it, you will praise it, you will serve it!'

Voiceless, she could only shake her head and hold on to the memory of Ikarno as nothingness rushed in . . . and rushed out. As before, she looked up and saw her tormentors leading a pale, almost misty form towards the chamber entrance. At the doors, though, the white figure turned and Suviel saw her own face, milky eyes in translucent flesh, gaze back at her.

Then they were gone and the blackness deepened and pressed in on her. All her feelings and her thoughts spun around and around in circles of horror. She struggled for glimmers of hope, strove to remember what had been in her mind before this latest violation. It had been something precious, something beautiful beyond compare.

But nothing came. It was past all recollection, and utterly gone.

* * *

Bardow could hear the sounds of the siege as he and his six-guard escort climbed a long, gloomy stairway which led to the palace battelements. Normally, these stairs would have been well lit, but most of the servants were either in hiding or had left the palace altogether. By his guards' torches, and the occasional wall-shrine votive lamp, Bardow could see that most of the tapestries he had known from years ago were gone. *Trophies*, he speculated. *Or kindling*.

It was tempting to reminisce on happier times, but he had just left Tauric in the sickroom down on the Spire's fifth floor, near Alael's chamber, and his thoughts were grim. It was over an hour since the Armourer and his raiding party had returned with the heir, shortly after which Yasgur and his army had arrived and commenced their assault on the west wall. But according to Tauric's account, Yasgur's body had been seized by the spirit of his father, Hegroun, and it was he who ordered the investment of Besh-Darok. Before the possession had occurred, it seemed that Yasgur was willing to allow the Imperial forces to withdraw from the city unhampered.

The implications of Yasgur's spiritual subjugation filled Bardow with a sense of dark foreboding. The Acolytes were known to be adept in the rending and binding of minds, but wresting the spirits of the dead from the grasp of the earth demanded a far greater magnitude of power. Such as that reputedly employed by the sorcerous Shadowkings Grazaan, Thraelor and Byrnak. If any of them were in the vicinity, the chances of holding out were slim indeed.

At last Bardow and his guards reached the top of the stairs where tall wooden doors, their intricate carvings of the Fathertree scarred by axe and sword, stood wide open. Bardow paused under the arch and leaned against one of the doors to catch his breath.

This entrance gave onto a small balconied landing part-way along the Silver Aggor, the inner wall which surrounded the palace and the High Spire. From it several walkways and drawbridges sloped down to the ramparts of the Golden Aggor, whose walls formed a long diamond enclosing the Silver Aggor, the Courts of the Morning and the Square of Swords. Three narrow gantries crossed, via a couple of column supports, from the Golden Aggor to a nearby section of the city battlements. Torches lit the long ramparts of the city walls, from the south-west corner all the way to the north wall near the weir where the river Olodar entered the city. Beyond the wall, the campfires of the enemy were islands of flame in the night, from which torch-bearing companies marched to assail the walls.

To Bardow the calamity of the situation was immediately apparent. The defenders were thinly stretched, strung out along the walls with some clustered at the gates, while others dashed back and forth to counter enemy attacks. As he watched, Yasgur's troops stormed over the walls at three separate points and it was only after a savage, desperate fight that they were repelled.

We cannot hold, he thought sombrely. *Ikarno must begin the evacuation soon*. Then with a determined stride he set off towards a nearby walkway leading down to the Golden Aggor, closely followed by his escort.

At either end of the long diamond of the Golden Aggor were heavily constructed towers, each durable enough to be reckoned strongholds in their own right. To the south was the Keep of Night, which overlooked a swathe of residential districts and college and artisan wards, while to the north the Keep of Day afforded a sweeping panorama of most of the city. Bardow found the Lord Commander there at the top of the tower, brooding over a map of Besh-Darok while a handful of officers looked on uncertainly.

Girdled by a waist-high wall, the towertop was roughly twenty paces across and partially covered by a semicircular wooden canopy. Torches burned on wrought-iron stands, flames rippling in the night's breeze, and a brazier of embers glowed a dirty orange near the trestle table where Mazaret stood. He turned as Bardow approached and the Archmage could see weariness etched deep in the man's face.

Ah, my friend, we are too old to wage such a war, Bardow thought. *But who else is there?*

'How is the boy?' Mazaret asked.

'Quite well,' Bardow said. 'Robustly healthy, in truth. Although by the time I arrived at the infirmary there was little for me to do – Kodel and his Armourer had tended to Tauric's few wounds, and some chafing caused by the metal arm.'

'He thinks highly of them,' Mazaret said, frowning, and Bardow was surprised at the tone of resentment in the words. Before he could respond, the Lord Commander went on: 'So how did he come to be captured? I must have heard a dozen rumours and a valleyfull of ragtalk about the boy. Give me some facts.'

Bardow related what Tauric had told him, from being trapped on the other side of the Olodar river to their escape via the Black Sluice and the long hike round the city walls. Then the chaotic ambush by Yasgur's scouts, the capture of Tauric and two others which led to the encounter with Yasgur amid the ruined ridge fort and the fateful events which then ensued. As Bardow spoke of Yasgur's possession by his father's spirit, Mazaret's expression grew sceptical.

'Can we be certain of this?'

Bardow nodded. 'The Armourer saw most of it from concealment, admittedly at a distance, but he corroborates all the main details.'

Mazaret uttered a hollow laugh. 'So now we count the spirits of the dead among our enemies.' Shaking his head, he leaned on the table, fingers crumpling the edge of the city map.

The man's despair was starkly apparent, but Bardow knew he had to say what had to be said. 'Ikarno, we cannot hold the city. We must evacuate – now.'

Head bowed, the Lord Commander was silent a moment. 'I know. I have already made . . . preparations.' He sighed and straightened to regard Bardow. 'When the current wave of attacks eases off, I shall signal the men on the walls to begin moving back – Kodel is on his way to the west wall to direct the withdrawal. Yarram and Medwin are heading for the harbour to ready the boats and commandeer others if necessary. When the signal is given, Alael and Tauric will be escorted quickly to the harbour by the Armourer and two-score Hunter's Children. By the time our enemy realizes the truth, we shall already be putting to sea.'

He gave a bleak smile which Bardow matched, inwardly relieved. *How could I have imagined that you would break?*

'I don't want to leave, Bardow,' he went on. 'Sixteen years I've waited to walk these streets again and see the places I knew so well. But the people don't want us here, and we can't fight them as well as the Mogaun.' He paused. 'How bad have the riots been?'

'So far – noisy and disorganized,' Bardow said. 'Some of it has been in support of our cause but violent opposition is growing. Hard as it is to bear, many citizens hold Yasgur in high regard because he has worked with them and brought about much peace and reconciliation. They see us as a return to the chaotic days following the death of the Emperor.'

Mazaret snorted. 'If they think this is chaotic, wait till Hegroun gets his hands on them.' A trace of hesitation came into his demeanour. 'What of Suviel? Have you spoken to her?'

'Not since the night at Adranoth,' Bardow said. 'But I have had word of Gilly. Tauric saw him being held prisoner after Yasgur and his guards were overwhelmed on the ridge.'

Mazaret's sombreness was cracked by a small smile. 'Gilly alive . . . I had feared him dead—'

He paused, suddenly tense, hand raised for silence. Then Bardow heard it, the faint roar of a far-off crowd. Mazaret dashed over to the tower's edge and Bardow followed him, hands gripping the stonework as he stared out. He saw nothing of note till Mazaret pointed suddenly at the far end of the Shaska Road.

'The Gallaro Gate!' he cried. 'They've broken through . . .'

From the Imperial palace below a broad avenue called the Shaska Road ran straight through the city to the north-west wall and the massive Gallaro Gate. Bardow focused his awareness, made his vision deeper and clearer, and saw mobs waving torches as armed men streamed in through the open gates.

'There's no resistance,' he said. 'The mobs must have ambushed the defenders and opened the gates.'

Mazaret spun and gestured at the waiting officers. 'Go about your tasks, gentlemen. May the Earthmother be with you.'

But even as they began to depart, Bardow caught sight of something in the sky, approaching quickly from the west. It was like a fallen star, a bright shimmering core surrounded by a misty, faintly green nimbus, and as Bardow watched it fly over the city walls, dread unfurled in his chest.

'Move your men downstairs, Ikarno,' he said.

'In the name of the Mother,' Mazaret said, 'What is it?'

Before Bardow could repeat his appeal, the bright intruder soundlessly burst apart and dozens of glowing motes rained down on the city. Yet their flights were not simple falling arcs but paths which twisted and turned as if at the behest of some conscious purpose. One such was following a long sinuous curve towards the palace when it swerved sharply and dived towards the towertop of the Keep of Day.

'Leave, my lord – now!' Bardow shouted at Mazaret, then dashed past him towards the wooden canopy. But when he turned, Mazaret was by his side. He was about to warn him when the glowing jewel struck. There was a brief flash and the tower shook under their feet. Chips and slivers of stone flew out from the point of impact. Ripples of tenuous vapour radiated across the flagstones, shot through with glittering webs of viridian power, Wellsource power. Bardow could taste the heavy, sickening strength of it in his mouth.

Then the vapour began to swirl inward, as if seized by an invisible force. Erratic gusts of wind came and went, and some of the torches were snuffed out. The flickering traceries grew brighter as they gathered in towards the focus. Beneath, a flagstone suddenly cracked. The foggy knot of power sank into the towertop, and other nearby slabs cracked. The pieces shifted and slid aside as a tall grey figure rose from the jagged hole in the stonework, as if unbending from a crouched position. It was a bearded, elderly man attired in what might have been an ostentatious, high-collared robe of archaic style, were it not the ashen hue of stone. Everything about the man was a deathly grey, apart from the unblinking eyes which burned with emerald fire.

Dust and grit trickled from the old man as he turned to gaze dolefully at Bardow for a long, desolate moment.

Then he was gliding swiftly across the towertop, clawfingered hands outstretched. Mazaret drew his sword, shrugged off Bardow's restraining hand, and charged at the onrushing apparition. But a single, back-handed blow sent him flying to sprawl semi-conscious by the keep battlement. Bardow backed away, readying the thought-canto of Cadence, but it died in his throat and an instant later hard, pitiless hands took hold of his arms. The grey, eroded face, lit by those terrible green eyes, came in close and Bardow's senses were assailed by a cold mingling of rotten flesh and rusting iron.

'Everything must come to its end,' the terrible spectre said in a voice like dust. 'The Void wills it.'

Bardow gaped in fear and confusion, and a nagging familiarity with those doom-laden words. Then his feet were hanging free as his captor, still holding him, rose into the air and smashed through the wooden canopy. Shattered pieces of timber flew and the tower fell away beneath him, and to either side Bardow spotted other struggling figures being carried aloft, towards the top of the High Spire. As he strove to master his helpless terror he suddenly remembered the origin of those words and stared at the old man with horror-filled recognition. For it was Tokrin, Orosiada's companion and the first Archmage, dead long, long centuries ago.

Grief and despair tore at him as he hung limp in that unbreakable grasp. Yet even as the dark, broken gap in the side of the High Spire swallowed him, he refused to concede the territory of his embattled hope, or to surrender his courage.

Not while I live, he thought. *Not while I live*.

Together in the darkness of a gallery alcove, Tauric and Alael rested in hiding. Their long, panic-stricken run had finally come to a halt here and all Tauric could be sure of was that they were at least four floors above the infirmary.

In his mind, he saw again the chaos that had erupted there. After the departure of Kodel and Bardow, he had been sharing food and water with Alael in a small chamber off the hall where the sick and wounded had been quartered. He had been talking of growing up in the greathold of the dukes of Patrein when he was interrupted by a massive crash from out in the hall. Screams and shouts cut the air and when he and Alael emerged from the chamber they were confronted by a terrible sight.

Hanging in mid-air was the slate-grey figure of an old, gnarled woman in tattered garments, dust and flecks spilling from her detritus-encrusted limbs as she tried to advance upon the Armourer and half a dozen Hunter's Children.

Suddenly aware of the two youngsters, the Armourer bellowed: 'Run – now! Save her . . . hide!'

At that moment, the ragged crone had swooped down at the Armourer with arms held wide. One of his men moved to shield him while lunging at her with a spear, which snapped against her midriff. Mouth gaping in a black-toothed grin, she grabbed the soldier by his arm, swung him off his feet and dashed his brains out against a nearby stone column.

Aghast, Tauric and Alael turned and fled through an open archway to a corridor beyond and up the first set of stairs they found. Now, as Tauric felt his pounding hearbeat slow, he and Alael huddled in the dim alcove and listened. All they could hear were far-off, muffled cries and what could have been the hammering sound of doors being broken down.

'We can't stay here,' murmured Alael. 'We have to go and help, somehow.'

'We should,' Tauric agreed, feeling ashamed at the way he had panicked so blindly. 'But you're the one with the power . . .'

She met his troubled gaze, and laid her hand on his metal arm. 'I'm sorry about what happened in Oumetra . . . I was not fully in control of it. Sometimes . . .' She averted her gaze and sighed. 'Sometimes it seems to direct me and I've little choice.'

'Where does it come from?'

She shrugged. 'I don't think it's the Lesser Power – I've never had to use thought-cantos. It's certainly not from the Wellsource, and it can't be the Rootpower although Uncle Volyn used to say that there were similarities.' She bit her lip. 'I could probably focus it through your arm again, though.'

'Perhaps we should practise a little beforehand,' Tauric said.

'Perhaps,' Alael said, straightening to peer outside the alcove, glancing either way. 'First, let's find a window or a balcony so we can see what's happening.'

They left the alcove and moved stealthily along a high corridor decorated with carvings of dances, processions and hunts. Golden lamplight came from a couple of wall-niches and the carven figures seemed to shift and writhe. Soon the corridor ended at an archway leading into a large hall. Once through they paused to look about them.

The hall was about thirty paces across at its widest and had once been a ballroom. The marble floortiles were in the shape of masks, a wide interlocking black and white pattern over which strangely curved balconies hung, their balustrades formed from intricate flower-and-leaf railings. Beneath them were a series of screened booths, where dalliances and assignations of one type or another would have taken place. A few lamps burned up on the balconies, casting enough light to reveal the leavings and pieces of broken furniture which had been swept into the corners.

Alael glanced at Tauric and silently pointed at a high gallery on the far wall. Looking up, he was able to make out, through a doorway at the rear of the balcony, a patch of cloudy night sky. When he looked down Alael was already on her way across the floor to an iron staircase which spiralled up to her goal. Irritated, he hurried after and only saw the grey revenant glide from a shadowy side passage at the last moment.

In front Alael gasped in terror, and froze. It was in the form of a knight encased in full armour of an ancient, barbaric design. Heavy overlapping plates covered the torso, a kirtle of scale mail hung down to the knees and a helm enclosed the head. There were narrow grilles for the eyes and mouth, from which a green radiance shone. Like the crone down in the infirmary, the knight was a death-like grey from top to toe and coated in dust and grit.

Tauric leaped past Alael and swung his blade at the knight's neck, aiming between helm and gorget. There was a tremendous, reverberating clang and Tauric felt fierce vibrations down to the hilt. It was like striking a boulder. The grey knight reeled back, seemed to notice Tauric for the first time and fumbled for the scabbard at his waist. There was a grating sound, and trickles of powdery rust as he drew forth a corroded broadsword. Then, uttering strange whispers, he attacked.

'Tauric, be careful!' Alael cried out from behind.

Parrying a succession of slow but powerful blows, Tauric could make no answer. He began to retreat back the way they had come, meaning to lead the revenant away from Alael. But a scream rang out and to his horror he saw a second ashen apparition, cowled and robed, rising into the air with Alael held kicking and struggling in an iron grip. The grey knight seemed to lose interest in Tauric and floated up to join its fellow, who was carrying Alael towards the open door she had spotted earlier.

Drenched in panic, Tauric dashed to the spiral iron stairs and climbed them three at a time to the top. Sword at the ready, he threw himself after Alael's abductors, who were gliding through a short passageway to an outside balcony. He had taken just a few paces when something in the darkness caught his foot and he sprawled forward, hands out-thrust to break his fall. He felt a sharp pain in one hand, but ignored it as he scrambled to his feet, snatched up his sword and darted out onto the balcony.

Far above, two forms, ash grey against the clouded night, drifted up to the top of the High Spire and slipped out of sight. In frustration Tauric hammered his sword hilt on the stonework, then winced at the pain. The fall had rasped layers of skin from the heel of his hand and the blood had made his grip slippery. He was breathing hard but his mind was strangely clear and calm. *I have to get to the top*, he thought, resheathing his sword. *Somehow I've got to get up there*.

He turned to hasten back inside, but his foot encountered in the darkness the thing that had tripped him. A moan came from the shadows and, startled, he realized that it was someone's leg.

'Who's there?' he said, stepping back. 'Who are you?'

After a moment, a man's wheezing voice answered: 'Not mine . . . says it's not mine . . .'

The leg was drawn back and with grunts of effort the man crawled out of the inky shadows on his knees and one hand. The other clasped something round against his chest. Then he paused, sat back slightly, and raised his face. Tauric caught his breath and stared. Despite seared and blistered skin, and the poor light, Dow Korren's features were still recognizable.

'Not . . . mine . . .' he gasped then toppled forward onto his face and lay still as his final breath rattled from his throat. The object he had been holding rolled to one side, a dark egg shape which Tauric regarded for a long moment before reaching down with his sword hand to take it. And the moment he touched it, the moment the blood on his fingertips met its surface –

In his head, the sun.

In his body, a voice like the roar of a thousand rivers saying: **This is not for you!**

It was dark within the swaying, shuddering wagon, and it stank of badly cured animal furs. Gilly was lying face down amid a jumble of them, wishing he could tell the waggoner exactly what he thought of him. But his hands and feet were bound and his mouth was gagged with a filthy rag which muffled all his grunts and curses.

It could have been worse, he thought. *If they hadn't gagged me, I would be tasting it as well as smelling it. Or I could be up on the city walls with a sword in my hand, waiting for hordes of screaming Mogaun to come after me.*

He had no way of knowing what was going on outside. After Yasgur's ghastly possession and Tauric's escape, he had been put on a horse, tied to its saddle, then led at a gallop with the rest down to meet Yasgur's army. Once there, he was bound hand and foot and slung into the back of a malodorous, barrel-roofed wagon which for the next hour or so moved from place to place. He could not see the siege but he could hear it, the clash of weapons, cries and shouts, the shrieks of the dying, cheers at success, collective moans at setbacks.

Then there was a tumultuous mass roar of triumph and the wagon had suddenly jerked into motion again. Now, as a rumbling vibration came up from the wheels, indicating a cobbled road, he knew that they were entering Besh-Darok.

One of the gates is open, he realized, and for a moment wondered if Mazaret and Kodel had surrendered. But outside the cheering had subsided to the sound of many marching feet, not the sound of a victorious army.

Then the wagon lurched to a halt and a moment later he heard the canvas flaps at the rear part as someone bearing a lantern climbed in.

'You do not look comfortable, southman,' said a familiar voice. 'But you got something soft to lie on, heh?'

Bony hands seized his shoulder, rolled him over and helped him sit up. Then the gag was pulled down.

'At first I thought these skins smelled worse than you did, old man,' Gilly said. 'Now I'm not so sure.'

Atroc chortled and shook his head. 'You make a good insult, ser Gilly. One of your ancestors must have been Mogaun. Now listen.' He moved the lantern closer along with a small sack and sat down on a bundle of furs. 'My master is as much a prisoner as you, enslaved in his head by his father, that vicious old bandit. I want to bring back my prince but I need your help, southman. So?'

Gilly gazed open-mouthed at him for a moment. 'I could have escaped to be with my friends, but you stopped me – and I don't know how because you're as scrawny as a mountain goat – and now you want *me* to help *you*!' He put venom into his sneer. 'You can help me by untying my hands and putting your throat between them . . .'

Atroc snorted. 'I was wrong about your ancestors – with all that noise, one of them must have been a marsh-hog. Look, drink some of this, maybe sweeten your mood.'

From his sack he took a small wineskin and filled a clay beaker which he offered. Gilly eyed it suspiciously and shook his head. 'You first.'

Looking mildly offended, Atroc put the beaker to his lips and downed a generous mouthful. Then he held and tipped it so Gilly could drink. The wine's heavy richness surprised him.

'You are quick to distrust,' Atroc said.

'And with good reason.'

'It is a great sorrow to me that you have not the eyes to see and the ears to hear what is before you.' He leaned in close. 'Learn to trust, southman. There is an honourable purpose in what I do, so you must trust me—'

Someone outside shouted Atroc's name and the rear flaps rustled.

'Especially now!' With that, Atroc firmly pushed the gag back into Gilly's mouth, stifling an angry outburst, then turned to greet the newcomer.

Even clothed in his son's body, Hegroun's presence seemed to fill the wagon. The glittering green nimbus had faded to a faint aura which served to emphasize his physical appearance by giving every detail a certain lustre. Buckles, straps, the scored iron surface of his breastplate, the dense wiry blackness of his hair, the red smear of blood on the blade of the handaxe thrust into his waistbelt – Hegroun was the personification of gory war. He glanced at Gilly with casual malice, then turned to Atroc.

'Well, old man – is my sacrifice ready?'

Gilly blinked. *Sacrifice?*

'In a moment, mighty one. First, I must get . . .' Atroc went to the rear, leaned out of the flaps to converse with someone who helped lift a cannister of some sort into the wagon. Then Gilly saw the thick iron grills and the orange glow of embers and realized that it was a brazier. With padded cloth protecting his hands, Atroc puffed and strained as he brought the brazier over. Gilly watched in frozen dread as the old man then took a variety of implements from his sack, tongs, pincers and hooks which he placed head first in the embers.

'How long?' Hegroun said. 'I feel the presence of the Lord of Twilight – he is hungry for this one's pain and blood.'

'The irons will be ready in a few moments, my lord. How fares the battle?'

'The craven dogs flee to their kennel of a palace. But the Shadowkings have sent their servants after their seers and shamans – there is nowhere they can hide.'

Gilly could only grit his teeth while enduring the baking heat of the brazier and the trickle of sweat on face, neck and chest. *He said to trust him*, he thought as the torture tools began to glow. *But to do what?*

Then Atroc picked up his wineskin and sloshed the contents noisily. 'Would my lord care for some wine while he waits?'

Hegroun, eyes fixed on the brazier, grunted his assent and held out a hand. Gilly watched the old man fill the beaker again, take a drink from it then place it in Hegroun's hand. The warlord drained the beaker in a single gulp and, without looking up, held it out for more.

For a still moment, no one moved. Then the beaker slipped from Hegroun's fingers. The warlord looked round, astonishment turning to fury, his face lit sharply by the lantern on the floor as his hate-filled eyes looked at Atroc.

'You . . .'

His voice was a creaking whisper. He tried to lunge at Atroc but his legs gave and he fell to his knees. His outstretched, grasping hand flopped nervelessly by his side.

'I have unchained your mind, O mighty lord,' Atroc said. 'Your moorings are slipped, and my friend here will bring the tide that will sweep you away.'

'I will . . . eat your heart,' Hegroun gasped. 'The Acolytes will hang your soul on a hook . . .'

Ignoring the threats, Atroc bent to loosen Gilly's gag.

'In the Mother's name, what have you done to me?' Gilly said.

'What was necessary.' Atroc's manner was suddenly stern and compelling. 'Hegroun I have subdued with two potions in combination – you have had only the second, in the wine of course. It relaxes the bonds of the mind and will allow me to send your spirit into Yasgur's head and bring him back to himself.'

A chill went through Gilly and he glanced at Hegroun, now slumped back onto a heap of furs.

'I must do this, southman. You will be a beacon, a stormlight for my prince to follow. Help if you wish. You will be unable to hinder me.'

Before Gilly could reply, Atroc uttered a few syllables and sketched a swift gesture. A thin, glittering line sprang into being, joining Gilly's forehead to Hegroun's. A formless roaring erupted in his ears as Atroc, the brazier, the wagon and everything shrank and dwindled away to nothing.

A long, high corridor in shades of blue, walls, floor and ceiling covered in elaborate carvings. Filmy banners hung low, rippling slowly as he walked by. He passed ornately dressed courtiers who bowed and curtseyed all the way. A broad stairwell led down into gloomy halls, from which other stairs descended further. Down into the bowels of the palace he went till he came to a door of pale green marble. A ruby key on a chain about his neck unlocked it and he stepped through.

He was on a sandy beach, nostrils full of the smell of brine and seaweed. Mist blurred whatever lay out to sea but could not conceal the immense form lying stretched out upon the waters, rocking gently with the waves. It was Hegroun as he had been in life, a tall, hawk-featured man with a black mane and moustache. His huge murderous eyes watched Gilly come down the beach to splash through the shallows and wade further out. With a last glance at the prone, floating giant, he dived beneath the waters.

Into the dark and glimmering depths he swam. Before

long, a great dark building emerged from the murk and as he drew near, its outer walls brightened, illuminated by himself. The walls were thick and rough, with many small windows placed without order or purpose across them. Looking through them he saw other walls within, also with a variety of openings, and realized that the building was a cruelly designed maze. As he searched for a way in, he noticed faint glows and movement inside. By the time he found an entrance, a gleaming black door, the glows were brighter, the movements nearer and more frantic.

Waiting and watching, he caught sight of Yasgur struggling towards the door while fighting off a host of shadowy, snake-like creatures. Eager to help, Gilly raised his ruby key to the black door and it swung open. He then darted in, grasped the weakening Yasgur by the arm and dragged him out of the maze. The ashen, translucent snake things tried to ensnare him but shrieked and dissolved at his touch.

Once free of the maze, they floated swiftly to the surface, breaking through to fresh, clean air and the thundercrash of a storm overhead. The tide was going out, carrying the gigantic, weakly struggling Hegroun with it. As they waded to the beach, Gilly heard a splash behind him and turned to see one of the opaque snake creatures rear up out of the waters. It had Hegroun's face.

'You have made a blood-enemy this day, son of the fox!' it said, and lunged at him . . .

With a rush of sensations, he found himself back in the wagon with a haggard-looking Yasgur crouched nearby, shaking his shoulder.

'Thank the spirit of the Void, he is back with us!' Yasgur stared into Gilly's eyes. 'Atroc told me of your offer to help me. I will never forget what you have done today – never!'

Gilly glanced up at Atroc, whose expression was one of thoughtful amusement. His bonds had been cut and he rubbed his face, trying to think of something to say.

'Duty and . . . and honour demanded no less of me, lord,' he said.

'As it does of me,' Yasgur said grimly. 'I know those who called up my father from his grave and sent him against me. I know their names, and I will pursue them, whatever their powers. Foul sorcery will not stay my revenge.' He regarded Gilly. 'I must agree a truce with the rebels in the palace, and soon. Will you be my messenger?'

'Gladly,' Gilly said. 'Once this clever old man gives me something for the hammering in my head.'

Atroc shook his head while fumbling through the pouches on his belt. 'Can't take his wine. Definitely no Mogaun ancestors.'

Chapter Twenty-nine

Under Night's shadow,
Let the dead hoist their ancient banners and
Let the living fall and bleed and die.
I care not, for I am the earth
And I drink deep.

Calabos, *The Black Shrine*, ch. 11, vi

The air in the tunnel was chill and dead from centuries of slow circulation through the stone maze of the Ordeal, but to Keren it was like wine. She relished the way it flowed icily down her mouth and throat and left an ache in her chest, especially after she had passed through one of the Wards. She had lost count of how many she and Orgraaleshenoth had traversed in their slow ascent, instead concentrating on the weaving of each one, the tone of its intent, the fabric of its punishment.

She vented a black laugh. Not that the final few Wards had presented any kind of genuine difficulty, for she had grown in strength as they progressed while the barriers had become steadily weaker. Oh, the voices of power that were in her now!

Keren went to the nearby wall, pressed her hands against the rough surface and let her iron senses sink into the stone. Before long she could hear the taut nets of ancient energies which permeated the towering mass of the Oshang Dakhal, and hear the rock itself singing, reverberating; hear the winds of the night gusting and wearing away at the crags and pinnacles; hear the click of talons and the beat of wings as the Acolytes' creatures stirred from their caverns and took flight; hear the pain of prisoners in their pens. And then hear footsteps approaching . . .

She opened her eyes and saw the Daemonkind Orgraaleshenoth stride into view. He had once again adopted the tall, haughty form of Raal Haidar and like Keren he possessed an aura which brightened the surroundings.

'I was listening to the song in the stone.'

'There are songs in everything,' the Daemonkind said.

'Yet, hard as I listened, I could not hear the Crystal Eye or anything that it might be.'

Orgraaleshenoth nodded. 'It was cunningly wrought to conceal itself from sorcerous perception by masking its powers and attributes. It is also able to protect itself by negating any kind of sorcery directed against it within a certain area.' He smiled thinly. 'A quality I have just verified. But Trevada is a place brim full of the Acolytes' dark workings, and by seeking out certain subtle absences of power I have deduced that it resides in a tower above the High Basilica.'

'How shall we get there?'

He indicated the way up ahead. 'The tunnel passes through an empty cave, then under the floor of the Basilica Hall and emerges in a chamber behind the altar. Nearby is a set of steps going up to the tower.'

Keren waited for him to turn and lead the way, but he made no move.

'Do you want us to rest?'

The Daemonkind gazed at her with unfathomable azure eyes. 'No. Before we continue I must fulfil my promise and return your flesh and bone to what they were.'

She drew back in alarm. 'But you know that I want to become one of you and return with you!'

'Only because I have made you my servant for a time.' A wintry smile came to his lips as he raised a hand. 'We are the ones who serve – we do not create servants.'

'But wait—'

Change swept through her, a tidal wave of brute sensation rushing up from her extremities. She cried out, reeled against the stone wall, felt sharp points, felt her skin catch on the rasping surface. Trembling, she made herself stand as the wave crashed on through her, flooding every corner of her being. Awareness of herself as a collaboration of elements brought unwelcome news in its wake – she had a nagging headache, her stomach felt unsettled, and she had pulled a muscle in her shoulder.

'The power I gave you is still there,' Orgraaleshenoth said. 'Can you feel it?'

She could. It was like a low, single note thrumming in her, becoming clearer as the wild edge of physical sensation began to subside. Keren tried to recall how she had been before, remembered a sense of invulnerability, an outer numbness, a cluster of iron voices within. Great power and great solitude.

'Your body is as it was, but your spiritual essence is changed forever,' the Daemonkind said. 'Even if you decide to remain here, you will always have an affinity for the Realm of Ruin.'

'I still wish to return there with you.'

'Then come.'

He turned and walked on, and Keren followed.

The Mogaun host swept through the night towards Besh-Darok, leaving a wide swathe of smoking ruin in its wake. Fences and huts were destroyed, fields and gardens churned into mud, dwellings put to the torch, stores ransacked and any resistance savagely put down.

Byrnak looked over his shoulder at the great dark mass of riders, their banners streaming, their standards swaying as they rode. Several bore his own sun-and-black-sword sigil, and he smiled. The Host had grown since departing Arengia and now numbered a little over 14,000 mounted warriors. The sheer brute force of it stirred a feral delight in him, but that was tempered by his awareness of Ystregul.

Thoughts of the other Shadowking made his delight fade into a smouldering hate. For all that Byrnak had been named the

Host's general, in reality the army was divided. Byrnak led the right wing, and Ystregul led the left, each made up of their own followers, while a few maverick tribes kept to the centre and rear. With large clans like the Redclaws and Blackmoons, Byrnak had the numerical advantage but Ystregul had the support of many shamans who were being hurriedly schooled in the secrets of the Wellsource by his coterie of Acolytes.

He glanced at Obax, who rode next to him, and saw those pale ivory eyes staring back.

Your consternation is clear, my lord. Is it the Black Priest's stratagems which trouble you? The Acolyte's mindspeech was a quiet whisper in his thoughts, yet seemed louder than the galloping thunder of the Host.

This is so, he replied. *But my thoughts keep returning to those of your brothers who are aiding him so eagerly.*

Obax looked uncomfortable. *Great lord, each of the Shadowkings possesses a fragment of our god, and we have faith in the strength of the Lord of Twilight's will, that through mysterious paths and workings shall all of his divine facets be united. It is our task, and our burden, to serve to the full.*

And have you served me by talking to the other Acolytes and discovering Ystregul's plans?

I did speak with them, my lord, but I learned nothing conclusive.

Nothing conclusive . . . Byrnak let his contempt show. *Is it not possible that Ystregul has swayed your brothers to his cause, and that their faith is now in him?*

Obax was about to reply when shouts caught Byrnak's attention. He reined in his horse and looked northward to where many warriors were pointing.

The entire left wing of the Host was veering away towards a high ridge nearly a mile from Besh-Darok, the same ridge where Yasgur was seized by his father's spirit. There had been no previous agreement on this, no messages given, no signals, no signs. Rage filled Byrnak and his hands longed to grasp Ystregul's throat. But he kept his fury in check and beckoned one of his officers.

'We are to follow,' he said, as if it was already determined.

'Pass the order to the other chieftains.' Then he turned to Obax. 'Come with me!'

Without pause, he spurred his horse into a gallop, riding past the clusters of tribes and bands. Spears and flags were brandished and hoots and cries went up when he passed by. As he and Obax drew near the head of the great column, a group of riders broke away from it and rode back to meet them. Both parties slowed to face one another a short distance from the constant din of thousands of horsemen.

There were five of them, four Acolytes and one Flegros, chieftain of the Rockwolf clan. Flegros had long, unbraided hair, tallow-blackened eyes, and wore a long red coat over leather and mail. He made an obeisance from his saddle, but the black-robed Acolytes just sat and stared at Byrnak, a couple of them smiling openly.

'On behalf of our master, I present profound apologies to the great lord Byrnak,' Flegros said, insincerity in every word. 'But it was judged imperative that we pause by yonder ridge so that all the Shadowkings may gather in preparation for the coming battle.'

'No mention of this was made previously,' Byrnak said, his temper rising.

Flegros shrugged. 'It was thought that you would immediately understand the situation and give appropriate orders, great lord. As is the case, I see.'

Yes, he thought. *Understand who considers himself the master.* In his mind's eye he pictured Flegros reduced to a pile of charred, smoking bones and had to fight the urge to strike the man down on the spot.

'Remind the Black Priest that the attack on the city must start soon,' Byrnak said through gritted teeth. 'Before Hegroun kills everyone in it.'

'That now appears unlikely,' Flegros said. 'Yasgur's seer managed to cast out the shade of Hegroun and free the prince.'

Byrnak smiled unpleasantly. 'Another triumph for your lord and master.'

'A minor setback. We shall—'

Just then, one of the Acolytes raised a hand and Flegros fell silent as the man addressed Obax.

'My master wished to know your reponse to his offer. Will you accept?'

Strike down this disrespectful vermin!

Half-agreeing with the outraged godhead, Byrnak gritted his teeth and decided to watch and listen.

'My reply remains as it was when the offer was made,' Obax said levelly. 'And will remain so in the future. I cannot accept.'

'So you say. The offer, however, remains open.'

With that, the four Acolytes wheeled their horses and rode back towards the head of the Host, closely tailed by Flegros. Byrnak watched them go then gave Obax a dark, penetrating look.

'I take it that they asked you to join them,' he said. 'You should have told me about that.'

'I did not think it of importance,' Obax said. 'But I will accept whatever punishment you decide upon.'

Ah, punishment. You will all taste it to the dregs.

'I shall forgo punishment, this once,' Byrnak said with iron resolution. 'Just remember that where Ystregul is concerned, everything is important. Now, let us return to our warriors and persuade them that this is all part of the great plan!'

The meeting took place in a furniture warehouse by the river, in a long, low-ceilinged storeroom lit by glass-sided lanterns and smelling of sawdust. When Mazaret arrived, Yasgur was already there, accompanied by two bare-armed guards and the elderly seer Atroc whom Gilly had mentioned. Mazaret had Gilly with him, and a couple of staff officers, and a head full of frayed nerves. When Gilly had appeared with an amazing story and Yasgur's offer of a truce, Kodel was nowhere to be found so Mazaret had no choice but to carry out the task himself.

Now he was sitting at a scored, notched carpenter's trestle across from Yasgur, who was giving a brief account of his possession by the spirit of Hegroun and how Gilly and Atroc had brought him back. Despite its lurid, macabre nature, it tallied with what Gilly had said earlier and had several details in common with what had happened atop the Keep of Day.

'It was always my intention to send the boy Tauric back to you, not torture and kill him,' Yasgur said. 'Is he well?'

'He was in the High Spire when the stone monsters fell upon the city,' Mazaret said, feeling weary. 'The inner palace is cut off – the doors barred, the stairs wrecked, corridors collapsed, so we do not know what is happening.'

Atroc nodded. 'They want our deaths, even for us to be their slaves in death.'

Yasgur shuddered visibly, fingering his oiled black beard, eyes full of a simmering anger. 'I will tell you this – when the Host of Clans arrives, I will not submit to their commands, or surrender my walls.'

'You mean to fight your own people?' Mazaret said.

'I must, for they are in thrall to evil creatures claiming to be messengers from our god.' Yasgur leaned forward, face full of intensity. 'It is they who have blackened the honour of my family and my clan by tearing my father's spirit from his grave, making him their servant and sending him against me. When they come to Besh-Darok I shall hurl defiance in their faces and resist them with all my strength.' He narrowed his eyes. 'I still have another army coming from the north. It should be here by dawn.'

'With respect, that may be too late,' Mazaret said. 'The last scout reports I received suggest that the Host will be here in less than an hour. Those stone monsters may have completed their vile purpose well before your army arrives.'

'Yes,' Yasgur said sombrely. 'Which is why I shall attack the false messengers as soon as they draw near to the walls, ride out and catch them unawares. If we can kill one or both of them, we may halt whatever is happening in the High Spire and prevent a catastrophe.' He gave Mazaret a pensive look. 'Will you join me? Will you bring your men to this fight? I will not hinder you if you wish to withdraw – these sorcerers have powers beyond reckoning.'

Mazaret scarcely needed to consider the proposal. 'While I have friends and allies held in fear of their lives in the palace, I cannot leave. We will stay, and we will fight.'

Yasgur smiled and held out his hand, which Mazaret grasped. At that moment, there was a commotion at one end of the storeroom and one of Yasgur's men entered at a rush, breathing heavily.

'My lord, news . . . from outwith the city. The Host has turned aside . . .'

'What?' cried Yasgur, leaping to his feet.

'One of the mounted scouts reports that the clans are taking up positions on this side of the old fort ridge, yet they are not setting up camp.'

'Why do such a thing?'

'Because of their servants up in the palace,' Atroc said, his voice heavy with dread. 'Something terrible is going to hatch out . . .'

There was an awful, still moment, and Yasgur looked straight at Mazaret. 'Then we cannot – we dare not – wait for the enemy to come to us.'

Standing up, ignoring the aches in his limbs and back, Mazaret met the chieftain's dark gaze, understanding fully the enormity of what he was saying. 'An attack by night?'

'Half my men are still outside the city,' Yasgur said, grinning a fierce grin. 'We would have some advantage of surprise.'

Mazaret felt that teetering, hollow feeling of fateful risk, of stepping out over the great unknown, then nodded. 'I agree,' he said, and the two men shook hands once more, settling the matter.

'This is madness,' Gilly said to Atroc, who was pouring pale liquor into four thimble-sized cups. 'Insanity.'

'In such a situation,' the old Mogaun said, handing him one of the tiny cups, 'what other choices are there?'

It was in a long gallery lined with mirrors and bronze statues that the third revenant found him. The gloomy light of failing lamps sent jagged shadows across the walls as it glided soundlessly towards him, arms spread wide, each hand grasping a slender-bladed dagger.

As before, Tauric obeyed the vast inner voice and faced the oncoming apparition with the cold weight of the Motherseed held to his chest. Odours of bark, leaves and moist earth began to percolate through his senses and he could feel a strange heat building in his head, moving down his arms and hands, into the seed, while on came the revenant, its grey-as-granite countenance frozen in a grimace of pain, its cankerous green eyes seeking him out.

The heat filled his head, made it feel like a furnace. Sweat dripped from his chin, trickled down his arms. Then, when the revenant was mere yards away, the seed cracked open and spewed forth a cloudy mass of white fibres finer than hair. The pale cloud flew at Tauric's attacker, engulfed it in mid-air, long strands winding, spiralling about legs and arms.

The revenant slewed to a halt, tearing at the fibrous skeins which were spreading across its skin, burrowing into cracks and cavities. In its struggles, the creature drifted towards Tauric, who stepped back, forced to watch the awful sight. The white fibres thickened, became tendril rootlets digging into the unnatural flesh. Stony fragments clicked on the polished marble floor, falling through trickles of powdery grit.

The revenant uttered a harsh, hoarse sound full of despair and swung into the wall, shattering a tall mirror. The left side of its body, from shoulder to groin, suddenly sheared away and crashed to the floor. It drifted back along the corridor, scraping against the wall as it went, smashing more mirrors, toppling statuettes from their niches, creating a cacophony of destruction.

The end came when the crippled monster collided with a protruding ledge and broke apart. Smothered in a net of white tendrils, the pieces struck the floor one after another. Tauric felt the dammed-up tensions within him relax and pour away, leaving him light-headed. On the floor near his feet, white rootlets writhed slowly about the statue of a young boy falconer, and as he watched they began to melt, dissolving into vapour . . .

Enough, my supplicant. Leave this place. Resume our upward progress.

The voice seemed to make his skull vibrate and he raised a hand to his head. He could not be sure whether or not the voice was the same one he heard amid the skirmish at the keep in Sejeend, but it wanted to steer him like a boat or a lamb. He had to strive against the weight of its compulsion, and concentrate on keeping control of himself.

He heard footsteps from up ahead in the corridor, and turning he saw a brown-robed, hooded figure step through a door which swung shut behind him. Clutching the Motherseed to his side, he ran along to the door, found it unlocked and entered into a dark, narrow passage. Small rooms containing dusty tables led off to either side, but Tauric kept on to the end where a door opened on a long, high room. Books and parchment rolls filled an entire wall along the room's full length, except for where several shelves and their contents lay in a heap near where Tauric stood. The library had three windows, each inset with darkly patterned stained glass, but the only light came from a candle burning on a large iron stand encrusted with drippings of wax. A hooded figure sat at a cluttered desk nearby and only turned when Tauric approached. A trembling, rag-wrapped hand came up, palm outwards.

'No please . . . come no closer . . .'

He stopped and stared, alarm fluttering in his stomach. Windings of cloth covered the man's hooded head and neck.

'For your own well-being,' the man continued in a well-bred but hoarse voice. 'I suffer from yellowblight, you see . . .'

Revulsion and pity warred in Tauric, but curiosity kept him from fleeing.

'Why are you here?' he said. 'Are you one of Yasgur's people?'

'Not I, young ser. The Acolytes keep me here to watch over the library for them, thus keeping anyone else away. I was once a scholar in this city, but my studies led me into folly.' The voice rang with bitterness. 'But you are a stranger to these lands – your accent is of southern Khatris, perhaps even Patrein . . .'

This one is dangerous – I will destroy it.

'No!' he cried, forcing himself to keep the Motherseed tucked under his arm. He stepped away from the diseased scholar. With his free hand he wiped sweat from his face and tried to ignore the heat that was flooding through his limbs. 'Forgive me,' he said shakily. 'This thing which I carry has a will and a purpose I cannot fathom, but I need its protection and it needs me . . .' He gave a despairing laugh. 'Or so it seems. I only know that friends of mine are being held prisoner on the topmost floor – I must find a way there and help them.'

The hooded scholar nodded. '"Unseen, the Unknown is in the saddle and rides us all",' he said, as if quoting lines, then pointed at the far end of the library. 'Beyond that door, choose the first archway on the left and take the spiral steps in the corner – that's one of the servant stairways. They sometimes join rooms that are several floors apart.'

'My thanks,' Tauric said, inclining his head in respect.

Fool.

Making no response, he shifted the Motherseed to a more comfortable position and hurried from the library.

The scholar watched the youth leave and sat unmoving for a few moments, then stood and calmly began removing his outer garments. The hooded robes were tossed aside, revealing a long coat over an embroidered tunic and kilted trews. The rags were stripped from his hands and the windings from his head. The face was old and bearded, with hollow cheeks, webs of wrinkles and a furrowed brow. And everything about him, from finger-rings to tongue and teeth, was the grey of old, cold stone, except for the eyes which shone a feverish emerald and betrayed a weary sadness.

The revenant stepped away from its cast-off disguise and approached the nearest stained-glass window, carefully unfastened the latch and swung it open. He rose off the floor and a moment later was ascending the outside of the High Spire. At the jagged hole left by the Acolytes' abortive spell-making, he slowed and glided into the gloomy, pillared Throne Room. Light came from a few torches in wall-brackets, and from the nets of Wellsource power holding the mage prisoners in small groups. By such poor illumination he could see what a charred, cinder-strewn ruin the hall had become. Yet court was being held, after a fashion. Almost a score of revenants were arrayed on the steps to either side of the throne, whose occupant watched the newcomer with undisguised contempt.

'Well?'

The revenant stopped at the foot of the dais and bowed his head. 'Majesty, another of us has returned to the dust.'

A clenched fist slammed down on the arm of the throne.

'Who is this man? The girl says that he's just some merchant prince from Yularia—'

'By your pardon, majesty, but it is not a man but a boy who has the seed.'

'You saw him?'

'I spoke with him, majesty.'

'And here you are. Yet it appears that the seed is not in your possession, Argatil. How can this be?'

Argatil, once Archmage and Imperial adviser, straightened and stared at his accuser. 'Sire, the boy is your son. Your child by the Duchess of Patrein.'

Korregan, twenty-seventh monarch of the Khatrimantine Empire, regarded the former Archmage with a green gaze. 'Are you certain? Yes, I expect you are. So Illian's offspring survived all these years ... Still, we must have the seed ready and waiting for our master, and soon.' He pointed at the pair of revenants who had captured the girl. 'You two, take this sentimental fool and go after my esteemed son. Use him as a decoy, or even kill the boy if you have to, just bring me the—'

Then a thin smile crept over his leaden countenance. 'On the other hand, perhaps I should attend to this myself. After all, there are some things that only a father can do.'

The crest of the ridge was busy with horses and their riders looking for any kind of shelter from the fine, steady rain. With dawn still an hour or more away, torches hissed in the damp air and hastily made fires crackled as the Mogaun boiled up crocks of beverage from an assortment of tubers and seeds. At the centre of the activity were the ruins of the old fort. One massively built corner was still standing, its stones gleaming in the rain, its accumulated burden of small bushes and saplings sending strings of drips to the ground below.

As Byrnak climbed over the eroded remains of the outer wall, he saw that Grazaan and Thraelor were already present, as were a group of Acolytes. They were gathered by the fort's overgrown corner wall, marking lines on ground and stonework, and did not look up at his arrival.

'Greetings, O general,' said Thraelor.

'Brothers,' Byrnak murmured in reply as he crossed to the pair of opaque figures. Grazaan was still a dour-faced, grey-haired man while Thraelor remained a tall, handsome youth. Both were attired for battle, Grazaan in the heavy, battered trappings of a mercenary while Thraelor wore a suit of armour seemingly modelled upon the shells of sea creatures. But in colour it was a glassy red, gleaming like translucent blood. Thraelor smiled, regarding Byrnak with cat-like eyes.

'It appears that the Black Priest's timing does not sit well with you, brother.'

'Nor does it with us,' Grazaan said bluntly. 'But that is trivial next to his carelessness and his negligence.'

Byrnak nodded slowly. 'Yasgur.'

'Exactly. He habitually overstretches himself and exposes us all to potential disaster.'

'His arrogance is undermining all we have gained,' said Thraelor. 'For all we know, the Motherseed may no longer be in Besh-Darok. If this new strategy of his fails, we must pursue other alternatives.'

'Such as Gorla and Keshada?' Byrnak said. 'A long, slow task—'

'But certain,' said Grazaan. 'Our domination of this land would be complete and irreversible.'

Uncertain, Byrnak shrugged. 'Our nameless hidden brother might be swayed,' he said. 'But what of Ystregul?'

'Let us see if he survives his latest endeavour, first,' Thaelor said, glancing past Byrnak. 'Enough – he approaches.'

The rain was growing heavier and gusts of winds tugged at the robes of Ystregul and his servants as they trooped into the ruined fort, each bearing a wooden staff. The Black Priest inspected the markings made by the Acolytes then turned to face the other Shadowkings and gave a stiff bow. At that moment, the spectral, helmed form of the Hidden One stepped out of nowhere and sauntered over to join the others. The look of poisonous anger that trembled in the Black Priest's features just then gave Byrnak an immense inner pleasure.

Ystregul mastered his fury and lifted his gaze to stare at the sky. Fine droplets of rain swirled about and over him, yet Byrnak saw none touch his face nor mar his full, perfectly black beard and hair.

He will betray you, said that familiar darkening voice within his mind. **Strike him down while you can.**

Be silent, was his only reply.

'The time is upon us,' Ystregul began.

'Again . . .' muttered the Hidden One.

'The past awaits, the future awaits, the very heavens await the return of the Lord of Twilight. Mountains will be hewn into temples, the seas will open and the sun will give forth wine when the Prince of Dusk walks upon the earth . . .'

Byrnak felt a chill at the words, and sensed a thread of dark anger winding its way through his thoughts.

'The moon will be our banner, the shadows shall breed with shadows, and all the realms will become as one.' Eyes glittering with an unfettered voracity, he raised his staff and turned to his dozen or more servants, saying, 'Begin!'

Gathered in a rough semicircle, the Acolytes pressed the tips of their staves to points in the designs they had scribed on ground and wall. As each began to murmur a harsh incantation, a vivid green radiance spread quickly through the patterns. The rain hazed the hot, bright symbols and tenuous vapours began to rise.

'Brothers,' said Ystregul. 'Lend me your strength.'

It was no effort to reach for power. The Wellsource was always there and for Byrnak, drawing upon it had become as easy as breathing in. Channelling it to Ystregul demanded a conscious shaping of the flow, giving it direction. And all the time part of his awareness was observing the Black Priest, watching for any hint of treachery.

At the focus, Ystregul seemed taller, his presence dominating the gathering. Enclosed by a restless aura, he stood facing the patterns, one hand grasping his staff and guiding its burning tip across the intricate weave. Raising his free hand, he uttered a deep-throated cluster of syllables – brutish, primal sounds – and swept his hand down. The air twisted like a membrane bitten by invisible jaws, and the mossy wall behind rippled and faded into a view of the throne room in the palace at Besh-Darok. The grassy ground with its symbols blurred into a fire-blackened marble floor upon which more symbols glowed, sustained by grey forms wielding rods of brightness. Across the gloomy hall, a slight female form sat huddled at the foot of the throne steps, watched over by a green-eyed guardian.

Byrnak was concentrating on Ystregul's actions, as were the other Shadowkings. Their mistrust was almost tangible, yet Ystregul himself seemed innocent of any dubious machination and fully intent on preparing for the ritual, concealing nothing. Then he noticed that the man's head was slowly turning, not far, just enough to give Byrnak a piercing sidelong glance and a wide malicious grin.

'The Acolytes!' said the Hidden One suddenly. 'They are—'

Before Byrnak could react, the Black Priest, the Acolytes and everything vanished in a dazzling, blinding burst of light. A monstrous thunderclap shook the ground and a rushing force picked Byrnak up and threw him backwards. Instinct and anger seized the Wellsource for him, and he slowed his flight and set himself back on his feet. A thick cloud of fumes and steam was already dissipating, revealing nothing but a charred wall and scorched ground with a few clumps of burning grass. Ystregul and his Acolytes were gone.

'That traitorous filth!' said Grazaan. 'Where did he go?'

'To the palace, of course,' the Hidden One said. 'Where the Motherseed is, where the power will be.'

There was a sudden cry from Thraelor, whose beautiful features were contorted with alarm and fury. 'He attacks my city! . . . with nighthunters!' Then he disappeared. In the next instant Grazaan, without any explanation, did the same.

An eery silence fell, then Byrnak became aware of sounds of fighting from the darkened terrain around the ridge, sounds that were coming closer. He felt torn between a kind of shocked lack of purpose and a hatred of the Black Priest so extreme it seemed to exist apart from himself.

'His followers are attacking yours,' the Hidden One said, then gave a dry laugh. 'There was not much he wanted left whole behind him.'

'How sure of himself he is,' Byrnak said. 'I envy such certainty.'

'Certainty! A mask for stupidity, a flaw which will break him.' The other's voice was full of contempt. 'I am not done with him yet.'

'You mean to go to the palace?' said Byrnak. 'I will accompany you—'

'I am already there, but you should stay here and salvage something from this wreckage,' the Hidden One said. 'Be patient – I will send him to you.'

Then he too was gone.

Byrnak stared out at the concealing night, focusing his awareness, searching.

Obax . . . Obax . . . bring the clans to the ridge . . .

Lord, we are fighting our way towards you, but the Black Priest's vassals are ferocious and their shamans wreak much havoc.

How soon?

Minutes, great lord, but there is other news from our scouts . . . they say that Yasgur is riding forth from Besh-Darok with the Imperial rebels at his side. Should I order a portion of your men to attack them?

A third will be sufficient, then bring the rest here.

There was a wordless assent and as Obax's presence, the taste of his personality, faded from Byrnak's thoughts, something else emerged from the veils in his mind and rang through all his inner halls and chambers.

A dark and baleful laughter.

One moment Alael was staring at a misty door in the wall of the Throne Room, and the tall, robed man who stood beyond it with several others. Then there was a flash of light and the door was gone, and the tall man was leading his followers across the great hall.

He stopped before her, gazing down. She felt dwarfed by his height and broad-shouldered physique, almost smothered by his presence. But she would not be cowed and made herself look up at the dark hunger of his eyes.

'What a countenance of innocence this is,' said the man, whom she knew to be Ystregul, the Black Priest. 'Yet even if her spirit were blackened and base, it would matter nothing – her blood is the key which will open the way to the domains of the eternal. All I require now is the lock—'

'I know you!'

A grey stooped figure came forward, the one who had returned without the Motherseed. Alael felt a stab of pity at the despair that was writ openly on his aged stone features.

'Who might you be?' said the Black Priest.

'One who knows you well.'

'Ah, yes – you are Argatil.' Ystregul stared in contempt. 'Do you know where my seed is?'

'I know you – I have seen your face reflected in a thousand swords, in the patterns of blood spilt upon the ground, in the smoke rising from razed towns and villages, in the stones of dried-up riverbeds, in the carrion of battlefields—'

'You do not know me, old man,' Ystregul said in a low voice heavy with menace.

But Argatil went on. 'I have heard you weeping with joy

at the altars of pain. I have seen your hand in the ruins of
the ages—'

'You have never seen me!' Ystregul said tightly, angered.

'I can see you now, even behind that mask you are wearing . . .'

Uttering an inarticulate cry, Ystregul hurled a burning knot
of green fire at the revenant Archmage. For a second Alael saw a
smile of weary peace on Argatil's face . . . then it struck, and with
a terrible cracking sound he shattered. She gasped in fright and,
in reflex, covered her head with her hands as the pieces rattled
and clattered all about.

The Black Priest stood staring at the destroyed revenant with
something akin to fear in his eyes. His lips moved as if in some
inner dialogue, but he made no sound. Knowing she was in the
presence of madness, Alael glanced away as tears came.

'So you disposed of the old dotard, my lord. Good.'

She looked up and the sight made her catch her breath in
dismay. The revenant emperor Korregan had returned, bearing
a shocked, unresisting Tauric, who was clasping to his chest the
Motherseed. The Emperor floated over to Alael, deposited Tauric
next to her then alighted at the edge of the floor pattern and
bowed very slightly to the Black Priest. Ystregul had regained his
composure and smiled at the forced show of obeisance.

'Your loyalty will be rewarded,' he said. 'In the domains of the
eternal I shall need many lieutenants, many governors—'

'Give me a body,' Korregan said. 'Give us real flesh, skin and
bone as was promised. Then we will do whatever you ask.'

Alael glanced at Tauric who sat, dazed, beside her.

'What happened?' she said. 'How are you feeling?'

'She wouldn't stop him,' he mumbled. 'He came for me and
the seed . . . did nothing . . . I . . .' He clutched her arm, his eyes
wild. 'That . . . thing is not my father! It can't be . . .'

'The promise will be honoured,' Ystregul was saying. 'First,
blood must flow upon the seed, opening the way. Then—'

'Then there will be nothing,' said a voice. 'Because you will
be nothing and he will be everything.'

Visibly startled, the Black Priest whirled to stare, along with everyone else, at the armoured figure sitting on the throne. The armour was golden, almost amber, and all its parts were ornately worked with images of lizards and snakes and adorned with spines. A grotesque full mask-helm was likewise decorated.

'Ah, my faceless brother,' said the Black Priest, relaxing slightly. 'Faceless, nameless and spineless . . .'

'You are his puppet, Ystregul. You think that you are pursuing your own purpose, but he has laid out the path for you, all the steps, all the tasks that will give him the power you dream of.'

'Such ravings are proof of an addled mind, brother,' Ystregul said. 'Leave this place while you may.'

The figure on the throne, whom Alael guessed to be one of the other Shadowkings, laughed softly.

'You hear him, do you not? Whispering black thoughts to you, all the day and all of the night, sometimes begging, sometimes demanding, but always there, waiting.' A gauntleted hand pointed. 'I know you hear him because I do too, and like me you will not give it all up for him.'

'Leave now. I shall not make this offer again.'

'Yes, life is not so bad that you would voluntarily end it – for him. Is that not so?'

'Your armour is tarnished, brother,' Ystregul said. 'Let me polish it for you.'

He swept his staff before him in a swift arc and a bright bolt of power sprang forth. Simultaneously, all his servants unleashed sorcerous attacks, a howling barrage of spikes, nets and spears that lit up the great hall. A storm of fire and radiance raged around the throne but its occupant, seemingly unaffected, stood and spread his arms in a dramatic gesture. Bright spines burst from his armoured form, all speeding unerringly towards each and every one of his assailants. Some were thrust backwards, while others lost fragments or limbs. One of them, a gaunt bowman who was launching fiery arrows from several feet up froze in mid-motion and fell to the floor with a mighty crash.

Crouching on the floor while the waves of deadly force flew to and fro above her head, Alael almost jumped when Tauric seized her hand.

'Look – they're getting away . . .'

Across the hall, the mages who had been under guard were sidling along the wall and moving towards the main doors now that all the revenants were otherwise occupied. Tauric pointed at an archway to the right of the throne dais. Alael nodded and together they began crawling towards the arch. They were almost two-thirds of the way there when Tauric suddenly gasped and slumped onto his side.

'Tauric, what's wrong?' Alael said, panicking.

'. . . Won't let me . . .' he said. 'She wants . . .' The words dissolved in choking sobs and moans of pain as he lay there with the Motherseed held in the crook of his arm.

'No, you won't be leaving just yet!' said a harsh voice.

Glancing over her shoulder she saw against the flaring battle of sorceries the ashen form of the revenant Emperor Korregan gliding towards them. Her gaze immediately went back to Tauric's metal arm, remembering how she had used it to tap into her own wild power. Then she saw the seed, grabbed it in desperation and swung round to face the oncoming danger.

At once it began rising from within, like a stormfront. She could taste it in her mouth, a pungent heat and a pure whiteness she could sense but not see. The pursuing revenant was now only yards away and Alael was trying to will the burgeoning power into breaking free when a bright spear flashed down from near the throne and struck the revenant in the side.

With a sound like a hundred hammers smiting a hundred anvils, the grey Emperor burst apart. Fragments large and small flew in all directions and Alael, eyes tight shut while turning away, felt the stings of shards and splinters on her face and neck, bare arms and hands.

Then it was over and she looked down at her hands cradling the heavy Motherseed to her chest, saw the chips and slivers embedded in the skin, and saw the blood that was trickling down to where her palms were pressed against the seed's cool, grained surface . . .

Now my revenge shall begin.

It took her a moment to realize that the vast, resounding voice had come from her own throat, had been shaped by her lips.

From the other side of the high chamber came a roar of fury. 'No! – that power is mine!'

As Ystregul lunged across the chamber, Alael felt herself being lifted up amid a coruscating silvery aura which was thickening in opacity by the second. Tingling waves of hot and cold raced all over her body and the veins and arteries on her arms and hands pulsed with vivid rainbow hues. It was terrifying, but it was beautiful.

Fear not, child. You will come to no harm . . .

She felt herself rising into the air, yet cushioned on all sides. Looking down she saw that the glittering aura had coalesced into a semblance of prodigious legs and to either side were the blurred shapes of huge arms. *Am I within the body of a god?*

Ystregul came running, hurling bolt after bolt of havoc. The great form which had engulfed Alael stretched out an arm and swept him up. At once green and black flames wreathed the massive silvery hand.

I could destroy this part of you, betrayer, but it would do nothing to ease my grief. No, I will send it back to its brothers and when you regain your unity in flesh I shall come for you.

'Never!' Ystregul howled. 'I will never be extinguished!'

BE SILENT!

The great arm, limb of silver and mist, was flung out swiftly and the hand released the Black Priest, who streaked across the hall and out through the hole in the wall. Then the godlike being turned its attention to the other Shadowking near the throne and in two strides was standing over him. Revenants swooped out of reach, their battle forgotten, and to one side Alael noticed Tauric crouched by the throne steps, gazing up at her in stark amazement.

The Shadowking in his golden armour began to rise into the air.

Let me see what you're made of.

The armour and the helm melted away to reveal a muscular man in a white tunic and leggings, his features taut with fury. As Alael stared in disbelief she clearly heard Tauric utter an anguished cry of denial.

For it was Kodel, Sentinel and leader of the Hunter's Children.

Chapter Thirty

From the soil of Black Loss,
Watered by Hate's bitter rain,
The strangling vine of Revenge sprouts.

Gundal, *The Doom of Gleoras*, ch. 4, xii

Mazaret led his 500 riders at a steady gallop across a wide, muddy field towards a long stretch of woods. There was some kind of minor affray taking place at the far end of the field but there was no time to investigate. Mazaret caught the taint of smoke on the air and by the time they reached the edge of the wood he could see the fractured glow of trees burning on the other side. And hear the sounds of battle.

The night-shrouded farms and estates all around the old fort ridge were full of the chaotic shambles of planless war conducted after dark – deadly pursuits, individual duels, the dazzling flare of sorcerous powers, skirmishes and ambushes. But at that moment there was only one conflict that Mazaret wanted to take a hand in.

Riding north they came to an old cart track and followed it west through the wood. A few birds burst from cover at their passing and a dog tied up outside a ramshackle cabin barked furiously. Then Mazaret ordered the column to slow as the leading ranks emerged from the tree line and beheld a dire scene.

Perhaps 400 yards away, Yasgur and his men were drawn up on a low hogsback bare of bushes or any substantial cover. The blazing trees burned like gigantic torches and cast a lurid ochre glow upon the sight of massed Mogaun raging around the trapped soldiers, driving in with spear and blade while others launched stones and arrows.

The battle had not gone all the Mogauns' way. Much of the intervening distance was littered with trampled bloody debris, bodies of men and horses, smashed carts and broken weapons. The heaps of slain, of both sides, grew larger towards the hill.

For desperate moments Mazaret sat and eyed the savage spectacle. It was hard to be certain of numbers in such poor light, but he reckoned there to be at least 2,000 Mogaun warriors grouped in bands and attacking with no apparent co-ordination. Yasgur had only a few hundred, formed in steady ranks with shields locked, and they were being gradually whittled away by the enemy's sporadic assault.

The choice before him was stark. He could retreat, returning to a city in the grip of vile sorcery. Or he could lead his men in a headlong charge and break through the encirclement in the hope that he and Yasgur would have the strength to fight their way to the ridge.

He smiled grimly – in the end the choice was no choice at all.

Mazaret snatched his sword from its scabbard, whirled it over his head and uttered the battle-cry of a lost empire: 'The Tree and the Crown!'

His men took up the cry as they rode at his back from the wood and spurred their mounts into a thundering gallop across the ruined field. The ground was cluttered with the wrack of battle, and sodden with mud and blood. Near the hill, hundreds of Mogaun riders milled around, unprepared for such an attack, and by the time the tribal horns began blaring a warning the rebels were more than halfway to their goal. Fifty yards on, a jostling band of Mogaun warriors turned to face the oncoming charge, but Mazaret's captains had already chivvied and prodded his men into a broad wedge with himself at the apex.

Some of the Mogaun had second thoughts about meeting such

a furious onslaught head-on and were frantically reining their mounts aside. Others were bolder or more foolhardy and Mazaret suddenly found himself hurtling towards a bushy-bearded warrior wielding a long woodcutter's axe. Mazaret threw himself sideways in the saddle, dodging a wicked slicing blow, then slashed out with his own blade, and hand and axe fell to the ground in a shower of blood.

Then he was ascending the hillside towards a double rank of shields which were parting to admit the reinforcements. Some Mogaun bands tried to take advantage of this but swift action by Mazaret's captains on both flanks kept them at bay. As he steered his horse into the relative safety of the shield wall, Yasgur cantered over to meet him.

'Your valour knows no bound, Lord Commander,' he said. 'As too, my gratitude. Now, what news of the rest of the army?'

Mazaret was too tired to keep his dismay from showing, and shook his head. The army had been more than halfway from the city to the ridge when they had encountered a pitched battle between rival parties of Mogaun. Both sides, thinking the rebels to be enemy reinforcements, turned and attacked them. Moments later, another force of Mogaun rode out of the darkness and straight into the army's right flank, and the disciplined column dissolved into a chaos of furious, blind fighting.

Mazaret had been in command of the right flank and the rearguard, and when he had realized the gravity of the situation he had gathered what men he could and sought to circle north around the confusion. Later he learned that Yasgur had taken similar measures, except that he had headed onwards, driving for the ridge, only to be halted by greater forces. Of the core of the army, comprising the bulk of the heavy cavalry, there was no word or sign.

'But we still number nearly a thousand, my lord,' said Mazaret. 'And we have discipline and a purpose.'

'Yes,' Yasgur said. 'Against our combined forces, they cannot stand.' He stared across at the dark mass of the ridge and the flashes of green fire that lanced down at indistinct groups trying to ascend the western slope. 'We could feint towards the south, drawing those attackers, then charge up the—'

'By the Tree!' Mazaret said. 'What is that?'

A glowing object, its shape vaguely manlike, soared over their heads towards the ridge and arced straight down into the ruined fort. There was a burst of light, then an odd, shifting glow began among the ruins.

'It seemed to come from the direction of the city,' Mazaret said.

'Whatever it may be, my friend, we cannot stay here.' Yasgur clapped a hand on Mazaret's shoulder. 'Ready your men while I give orders to my captains. At my signal we shall break this shackle of horsemen and carry the fight to our enemies. And may the gods smile upon us!'

The almost-deserted Throne Room seemed to overflow with the night's cold air. Torchlight shone from an upper gallery and a glass oil lantern glowed on the floor near the centre of the great chamber, amazingly untouched by all that had happened only a short time before. But nothing could compare with the soft pearly radiance emanating from the massive figure which stood before the throne.

From where he stood, Bardow watched the manifestation of the Earthmother as she drew the remaining revenants to her and, one by one, took back their spirits into her keeping. Periodically another stone form, empty of its animating shade, crashed to the floor, joining the other heaps of rubble scattered around the dais. But it was the real, living Alael about whom he was concerned, his worry prompted by memories of old fables of gods visiting mortals. Such tales told of a body of light which drew upon the strength of a worshipper, and the fatal consequences of too long a visit.

He glanced over at Medwin. When all the other mages had slipped away during the battle between the two Shadowkings, Medwin had decided to stay, despite a twisted ankle and a wound in his shoulder. Now, on an overturned stone trough by the main door, he sat next to Tauric who was a picture of misery, hunched over with his head in his hands, both flesh and metal. Bardow regarded that remarkable limb for a moment, and wondered how deep Kodel's plans and purpose went.

He smiled wryly to himself. *To think that all along one of the Shadowkings have been among us. We need more than eyes to see this struggle through. Pity we don't have Kodel himself to question.*

After unmasking the Shadowking, the Earthmother had treated him with a contempt similar to that meted out to Ystregul, and had hurled him through the hole in the tower wall and out into the night.

As he reached a decision in his thoughts, Bardow nodded to himself. Then he made a slight hiss to catch Medwin's attention, and with mindspeech said: *Wait here.*

The elderly mage gave a weary nod and Bardow, gathering all his courage, came out from behind a wide pillar and strode down the central aisle. At the foot of the throne dais he stopped and bowed.

'Greetings, O Queen of Life and Death,' he said. 'Accept our praises, we beg of you, and be welcome.'

I need no invitation from such as you. The mages were among the least devout of our followers, yet they drank deep from the rivers of our beneficence, our richness. Save your empty praises, thou empty vessel. Your fear would be better received.

'All gods are feared,' Bardow said before he could stop himself.

The radiant head, a misty semblance of womanhood, turned to regard him. Bardow felt a part of himself quail beneath that terrible, implacable gaze and he had to avert his eyes, concentrating instead on the hazy figure of Alael, hanging with eyes closed inside the shimmering torso.

I have no time to debate meaning with you, mage. Say what you wish to say, then depart.

He breathed in deep. 'Great Earthmother, the girl on whom your presence rests grows weaker by the moment. Now that you have vanquished your foes, will you not have mercy and relinquish Alael to us before her life is spent?'

Mercy? The air cracked with the word. **No mercy was shown to my beloved by the betrayer! No hesitation, no regret, not a hint of remorse have I sensed from that foul murderer, or from the band of paltry spirits he has become. But I will have my revenge upon him when he becomes whole again, by whatever means.**

As for this girl, the bearer of the blood – she is strong and has much yet to give, and I will not do her harm. But I am not done here yet – see, they are coming!

Thoughts whirling with the implications of all this, Bardow turned, following the Earthmother's outstretched hand. A new breeze was stirring the ash on the floor as the air near the hole in the wall began twisting and tearing, and a cold foreboding seized his thoughts.

For long, long moments Suviel struggled to remember the name of the woman who had freed her from the chamber of caskets and was helping her up these steep, stone stairs. The trembling weakness in her limbs was secondary to the strangeness now occluding her mind, making it seem like a house full of locked rooms once open to her. She knew she was in Trevada and that Bardow had sent her here to take back the Crystal Eye. But how she had got here, and who this woman was . . .

Name and past refused to come to mind, a stubborn gap that made her curse under her breath. Whoever she was, Suviel owed her freedom to her, freedom from the sense-draining blackness, the cold iron casket, and the visits from the Acolytes and . . .

Coireg. The name resounded in her, unlocking a stream of images and feelings. The Acolytes gathering around her, the period of insensibility, the half-seen pale figures that were led away. She blinked away tears and breathed in shakily. Would she ever regain what Coireg and his foul coterie had stolen?

A little strength was coming back into her legs and she was able to stumble up the spiral steps with a touch more ease. She tried to shrug off the helping hand but the woman just frowned and maintained a firm grip on her upper arm. It seemed to emphasize her weakness, yet she felt oddly glad of it.

Further up the cold, gloomy stairwell thoughts of Coireg still swirled in her mind, along with the image of another man, tall and grey-haired, strong blue eyes and a kind mouth . . . A confused welter of emotion sprang up in her mind's eye view of this man, yet he was a mystery to her. She steered her thoughts in the direction of her master, Bardow, but the tall man was there, too, talking with the Archmage, laughing, looking at her, and smiling.

Who are you? she thought. *Why are you important?* And she sobbed quietly, wishing at that moment that Coireg was here so that she could throttle the life from him with her bare hands.

'Please,' the woman said. 'You must be silent.'

'I'm sorry, I . . .' Suviel shook her head, dabbed her eyes with a torn fold of her robe. 'I should be stronger than this.'

'I know what they did to you,' said the woman. 'You must have been strong to survive it this well.'

'Thank you, Nerek, but I . . .'

Nerek. The name came unbidden to her lips and took her unawares with an upsurge of feeling and a scattering of images. Nerek – the arrival in Trevada, the encounter with the spirit-shackled children, the shifting personas within Nerek, and the subsequent stumbling through darkness which led to their capture, and long before that – Keren . . . and the evil sorcery of one named Byrnak.

For a moment she was sure she was about to tug an entire net of memories out of the darkness, but it slipped away.

'We have to keep moving,' Nerek said. 'If we are to reach the Crystal Eye before . . . before her . . .'

Suviel stared, confused. 'Before who?'

The eyes were like stone in the weak light. 'The other one, the sell-sword, the one I was made to be like. She was brought here by the Daemonkind creature – it used her to gain entry to the maze below, and has lent her powers.' Nerek frowned. 'There is a bond between us which grows stronger as we draw nearer. I see what she sees, glimpses and glances, and I hear the thoughts that flutter at the edge of her words. She thinks she wants to become one of the Daemonkind, but fear and doubt eat at her certainty.'

Suviel could scarcely grasp what Nerek said – a Daemonkind? But there was something else more pressing. 'What is that you want?' she said, almost fearing an answer. 'Why are you helping me?'

'I know what I was and I know what was done to me,' Nerek said, then looked at her. 'I spoke to him ... the other part of me, for the first time a few hours ago while locked in that cell. I felt his agony and his betrayal, and now we both want revenge. Helping you take the Crystal Eye from this place will be—'

She was interrupted by a low rumble and Suviel felt the stonework at her back quiver.

'The Daemonkind and Keren,' Nerek said. 'They are battling the Acolytes and their nighthunters in a courtyard outside the Basilica. We must be on our way.'

Together they hurried up the stairs with Suviel still leaning on Nerek's arm. As they climbed she tried to picture where they might be in the great complex of the High Basilica. She remembered the series of courtyards that encircled the Basilica, the official chambers within, and the level of vestibules that lay below the Congruence, the imposing hall of ceremonies. But all else eluded her.

As they passed a wood-framed archway there was a shout, and glancing through it Suviel gaped to behold a group of Acolytes, with Coireg in the lead, racing up a long sloping corridor. Before she could react, Nerek pushed her away with one hand while a vivid green nimbus flickered into being around the other. Suviel stared as she raised the glowing hand under the arch and, with a gasp that was half triumph, half punishing effort, made a tugging motion.

There was a creaking, snapping sound and the corridor beyond fell in with a deafening crash. Grit and dust billowed out as the two women stumbled coughing up the steps.

At the top was a locked door whose mechanism Nerek destroyed with a touch. Stealthily they emerged in a square, lamplit room which bore signs of recent abandonment – a skillet of water boiling over a lit fire, half-eaten meals on the table, and a beaker lying on the floor, its contents darkening the unvarnished wood. Through an open door was a smaller room with a table and chairs, a rack of spears and a battered leather trunk, and a second door which led outside.

It was still night and Suviel caught an acrid trace of smoke on the cold, dead air. The black mass of the Basilica loomed over the courtyard and she could hear a muffled din of battle coming from the other side, a nightmarish medley of shouts, roars and other less definable sounds. Quickly they darted across a blighted circular lawn to a portico, then pushed through heavy wooden doors which swung ponderously shut behind them, cutting off all noise. Inside, a pair of ceiling-suspended lanterns revealed a wood-panelled corridor, its walls dotted with pale areas where portraits and other artefacts had once hung. Open doors to either side exposed deserted rooms whose dust and debris suggested many years of disuse.

'Where are we going?' Suviel said. 'Where is the Eye being kept?'

'In some kind of tower above the Basilica,' Nerek said. 'I have listened carefully to her thoughts, and she seems to think that behind the altar in the main temple there are stairs leading up to it.'

'But . . . the Congruence has no altar,' Suviel said, following her through another pair of doors at the end of the corridor.

Within they paused. The immense Congruence was full of a smothering darkness punctured by a scattering of lamps whose jewelled glows seemed to float amid the blackness rather than illuminating it. And there was an altar, a slope-sided monstrosity with carving-cluttered surfaces that glinted like bronze in the light of a nearby lamp. It should not be this dark, Suviel thought. Even at night. Then she looked up.

Long swathes of ash-grey cloth were just visible, hanging all along the inward-curving ceiling, masking the Congruence's huge stained-glass windows which, she recalled, depicted scenes from the history of the Fathertree. No vestige of light, from sun or stars, could ever find its way in here.

Stealing through the funereal gloom towards the altar, Suviel's sense of revulsion deepened as she detected a sickly sweet perfume and under it the taint of rotting flesh. As they drew level with the altar she saw objects upon it, a long knife, several charred bowls, a small pile of shrivelled roots, and a wide, dark stain across the surface. Nerek urged her on as she slowed to look closer.

'We cannot linger. They are very near this place—'

A deep, insistent hammering began at the other end of the Congruence, shattering the silence, echoing back and forth. Then a jagged section of the far wall burst inward and a tall hulking form stepped through, wreathed in dust and a shimmering aura. Blazing golden eyes surveyed the murky interior, settling on Suviel.

I will have the Eye, little mage. Do not stand in my way.

A smaller figure appeared by the Daemonkind's side, a woman dressed only in a long, pale shift but veiled in a similar nimbus of power. It was Keren. She stared over at the two by the altar, at Nerek, and Suviel sensed something unfathomable pass between them.

Then there was a mass roar of voices, and scores of Acolytes with green fire in their hands rushed in by the doors to either side. At the same time, there were tearing sounds from above and pieces of masonry and glass fell crashing among the the benches as winged shapes swooped down. Suviel staggered towards the doorway behind the altar, kept from falling by a watchful Nerek. With a last backward glance she saw the Daemonkind and Keren hemmed in by flaring webs of Wellsource power and fending off the flame-breathing nighthunters. She also caught a glimpse of a murderous Coireg moving in her direction before Nerek hauled her though the door and up the steps.

In a daze of desperation and fatigue, she stumbled up the steep stairs, one hand gripped by Nerek, the other leaning on the stairwell's stone hub for support. Utter exhaustion dragged at her mind and body. It seemed that every force of evil was harrying them, and she wondered if she would have the strength to make use of the Crystal Eye even if they found it.

When they reached the top, she knew she had nothing left. The tower room was square, with pillars on three sides which were otherwise open to the elements. A vigorous breeze made it bitterly cold, and Suviel seemed to recall that before the invasion this place used to be a private meditation platform for the chancellors of the academies. From here one could see across the peaks of Prekine to the lands of southern Anghatan and the great plains of eastern Khatris. And below the narrow surrounding ledge was a perilous drop onto the roof of the Basilica which sloped down to meet the crags and the sheer face of the Oshang Dakhal.

Head swimming, Suviel sat down heavily on a weathered wooden bench while Nerek crouched beside what looked like a stone casket set into the flagstone floor. She closed her eyes, weariness almost singing in her nerves, and could feel vibrations coming up through the bench. She whispered a prayer to the Earthmother that Keren would somehow survive.

A moment later, a cracking sound made her open her eyes to see the stone casket gaping wide and Nerek turning with both hands holding a pale blue sphere swaddled in white cloth.

'Take it,' she said. 'It would be my death to try and use it. This is meant for you.'

Suviel sighed. 'I am empty,' she said, regarding the orb, its opaque radiance, the unmarred perfection of its glassy surface which caught few reflections in the dimness. She had only ever seen it twice before, both times at public ceremonies and from a considerable distance. Then it had been the focus of many minds and much veneration, but now it seemed to have no presence, no aura that she could discern.

'I am empty,' she whispered, but still reached out and took the Crystal Eye.

At once from below came a shrieking roar of rage, but for the moment Suviel was oblivious. It was as if every locked room in her mind sprang open, releasing a myriad memories. The faces and names of family and friends were hers again, as were the recollections of her days as a scholar here in Trevada, her time in Besh-Darok, the war, the long years of secret resistance. And Ikarno Mazaret.

That you were taken from me, she thought. *May that never happen again.*

There was a thunderous, reverberating crash from below and the tower shook. Nerek rushed to stand at the head of the steps and Suviel, her weariness washed away, rose from the bench.

'I may be able to use the Eye to take us somewhere safe,' she said.

There was a rumble of falling stonework and Nerek turned to nod, green radiance limning her features. 'That would be a good thing,' she said. 'Before they dig away the rubble.'

Before Suviel could reply something struck the tower with violent force, knocking them both off their feet. A few pillars cracked and pieces of masonry fell over the ledge. Suviel felt a hand around her ankle, looked and saw that it was Keren, creeping towards her with an inhuman glow in her eyes.

I know the odour of your spirit, mageling, came the Daemonkind's voice from nearby. **No matter where you fly to, I can hunt you down.**

Then Nerek was there, leaping across from where she had fallen, reaching down to wrench Keren's grip away from Suviel's leg. Tightly clutching the Eye to her chest, Suviel retreated to stand with her back to one of the pillars. The two women were locked in a deadly embrace, hands about each other's necks, auras contending. Suviel turned and saw the Daemonkind standing on the ledge outside the pillars, calmly watching her.

I must have the Eye, mage-woman. Freely given, it would bring great aid to my people.

'And thus betray *my* people?' Suviel said with scorn. 'I think not.'

Your companion will soon be defeated. Give me the Eye and I will carry you both to safety.

Suviel laughed aloud and stepped between the nearest pillars, out onto the ledge. It was still colder out here, and the gulf of black emptiness yawned dangerously below her, yet her mind was clear and prepared. As the Daemonkind had talked, the Crystal Eye had shown her many things about him and his race, most importantly things she needed to know now.

'Just as you did in the Realm of the Fathertree?' she said. 'Again, no.'

The Daemonkind turned to face her along the line of columns. His form was dark and hulking, and he had crooked one huge arm round a pillar to keep his balance. Eyes hot as forge gold regarded her.

Hear me, mage-woman, and understand this well – when the Lord of Twilight unites his warring selves, the Crystal Eye will be naught but a bauble set against the powers of his realm. In my realm, however, it would be of great use . . .

'Yet it remains our sole weapon,' she said, watching him, noticing the shift of muscles and stance. 'And I shall not give it up. No, *you* hear *me*, Orgraaleshenoth, prince and deceiver – you have trespassed upon the Realm Between for far too long and it groans with the pain of your presence!'

Your insect whine irritates me, and my patience is at an end.

But before the Daemonkind could leap at her, she clenched her fist as Enfold, the first thought-canto made for her by the Eye, spun into being. A blurring haze appeared around him and for a moment he was unable to move. She knew it would not last long, but it would be long enough.

'Your time here is at an end!' she cried, flinging out an arm to point at the night. 'In the name of the Void – begone!'

From her trembling hand a dazzling mote of light flew forth to scribe a burning line in the air, a line which then tore open. At once a gusting wind sprang up to moan through the pillars. A rippling river of grey radiance poured out of the gap and straight towards the Daemonkind, enveloping him, trying to draw him back. But the creature had wrapped his arms about one of the undamaged pillars, and as he glared at Suviel he raised one leg and stamped down on the ledge.

The tower shook, and a crack appeared across the floor.

But Suviel felt as she had been squeezed out and wrung dry, and was unaware. As the spell had unfolded, the very force of her life and being had streamed out to fuel it, unstoppable as blood gouting from a severed neck. She sank to her knees on the ledge, one hand holding onto the Eye, the other grasping the nearest pillar. Insensibility threatened to overwhelm her but by force of will she stayed conscious, head bowed but determined to finish the task. Then fear surged when she looked up to see the Daemonkind almost within arm's reach. The grey radiance was pulling at him with a fearsome strength, such that his massive legs were hanging straight out. But he had kept his grip and was grappling his way from pillar to pillar towards her.

Then a loud crack came from the column to which he clung and fracture lines began racing across it. He howled in fury and with a mighty effort, hauled himself forward and clawed at the floor, chipping handholds in the flagstones.

But the dragging force of the grey radiance was increasing to the point where something had to give.

Still waveringly conscious, Suviel watched the Daemonkind's exertions with a mixture of awe and dismay. Then she saw the widening black crack inside, on the tower floor. There was a grinding sound, the ledge lurched beneath her, and she knew that there was only one thing left for her to do. As her corner of the tower slowly broke away she summoned up the last shreds of her strength and tossed the Crystal Eye towards the two figures staring from the back of the tower.

Then she was falling amid a shower of disintegrating masonry. Above her, the tear between the realms swallowed the Daemonkind Orgraaleshenoth, cutting off his bellows of rage, and began to close.

She closed her eyes, picturing Ikarno Mazaret with his arms wide and his long face smiling and joyful. She smiled too . . .

A sharp and terrible instant of pain struck, then the door of life closed.

*   *   *

Keren cried out in horror and anguish as the corner of the tower cleaved away. She and the mirrorchild Nerek were on their knees and still holding on to each other, but all the formless hate and wordless hunger had gone. Seeking the death of the other, they had stared into each other's eyes for long, twisted moments and found themselves wanting life. Instants which transformed fear into understanding and cold desire into revelation. Her longings for the power and form of the Daemonkind dissolved like a half-made dream.

Suddenly truly awake, and watching Suviel fall to certain death, a terrible guilt seized her. Keren could only close her eyes and with a choking sob cling to her twin. Something thudded on the floor nearby and as the roar of collapsing stonework receded she was vaguely aware of Nerek making a slight movement.

'Open your eyes.'

She couldn't, not now . . .

'Open your eyes . . .' Hands shook her by the shoulders. 'Open them and look at me!'

Startled, she did so and stared into her own features, only harder, leaner and more cruel.

'She has passed the Crystal Eye into our keeping,' Nerek said, taking Keren's hand in an iron grip. 'And we must use it before the Acolytes dig their way up here.' And she dragged Keren's hand relentlessly down and pressed it against the cold, curved surface of what had to be the Crystal Eye.

All sight blurred in a ghostly blue haze though which strange faces and portents fell. *This way*, a voice said softly through the rain of images, and she caught glimpses of a smiling Suviel beckoning and pointing. *This way*. Fear forgotten, she leaned in that direction and heard an intake of breath from Nerek. The blueness deepened and enfolded her in layer after layer of paradox and meanings insoluble to her.

Then the blueness unwrapped her and the world, and Keren found herself kneeling, shivering, staring down at a fire-blackened, ash-strewn floor next to a yawning gap in a high wall. She was holding the Eye in both hands now, and beside her Nerek was getting to her feet. She looked up and gasped in terror at the great golden figure which loomed over them both.

Where is the mage Suviel?

The towering being seemed composed of a fine, swirling dust of amber and copper motes and in shape resembled the female form. But it was the girl hanging eyes shut and motionless within the giant torso which caught her attention. Then someone else came into sight, a middle-aged man in grubby travelling clothes. It was the Archmage Bardow.

Well, where is she? Is she dead?

'Yes,' Keren whispered. 'Yes, she is.'

The implacable golden eyes regarded her for a moment.

Good. Then all is as it should be.

Keren saw Bardow's face sag with shock and grief. The tall being turned away as if to walk back into the hall, but then melted amid the shadows. As the glowing mist of its form thinned to a fading vapour, the girl sank to the floor and Bardow rushed to her side.

Keren could only sit there, with Nerek's steadying hand on her shoulder. When she glanced outside she saw a city, hills and distant fields, and felt a tearless, numb relief. At last, the dawn had come.

EPILOGUE

Upon an ocean of death,
Cities of pain draw near.

The Black Saga of Culri Moal, xvi, 10

One

After a difficult ride through fields cluttered with the bloody
debris of battle, Gilly found the Lord Commander upon the
old fort ridge, seated at a smouldering fire with a beaker of
mulled wine in his left hand while a physician bandaged his
right shoulder. Mazaret greeted him warmly, sat him down
with some wine of his own, then gave an account of the
night's events. He told of how he and Yasgur had become
separated, then later joined forces and driven their attack towards
the ridge. At that point, it appeared that a battle of sorcery
had broken out amid the ruins of the fort, while from the
sky had come scores of nightmarish creatures, attacking indis-
criminately.

As the Mogaun broke and scattered in panic, Mazaret and
Yasgur had kept enough of their men together to make a
determined push for the ridge. But they had got there too
late. From its foot, where bands of Mogaun fought a desperate
last stand, Mazaret had looked up to see a glowing man throw
the limp form of another onto the back of a nighthunter before

climbing up himself. Then with a few massive wingbeats it had launched itself into the greying sky . . .

Mazaret paused in his tale and dismissed the physician. Then he leaned forward with elbows on knees, his gaze level, iron straight.

'I know why you're here, Gilly. You've hardly said a word, and have just let me talk on and on.' He took a deep, careful breath. 'She is dead . . . isn't she?'

Gilly felt his inner misery slide into a kind of helpless anger, and he cursed Bardow for having forced this black burden upon him.

'Yes,' he said simply. 'But she did not fail—'

'How?'

'There was a struggle in a tower above the High Basilica. She banished one of the Daemonkind and sent the Crystal Eye back with Keren and then—'

Mazaret silenced him with a raised hand. 'It's too much to hear . . . and too little.'

He drained off the last of the wine and without another word rose and walked away from the fire. Gilly watched him go over to where a dozen horses were hitched around a young tree, and untie one. Moments later he was riding from the ruins, down the long slope of the ridge towards Besh-Darok. At the foot, he turned and headed south-west, riding hard as if fleeing the dawn.

Gilly heard footsteps behind him and looked to see Yasgur approach.

'Will his grief break him, ser Gilly?' asked the prince.

'Yes,' Gilly answered in an unsteady voice. 'I believe it will. But what matters is that he heals afterwards.'

And maybe then I can tell him about his brother.

Out across the fields and broken meadows, the first pyres of the battle's dead were being lit, but the rider never looked back.

Two

From a balcony halfway up the Keep of Night, Alael looked down at the gardens of the Courts of the Morning. Birds flitted to and fro in the early afternoon sun, a couple of sheep wandered around grazing, and a solitary gardener tended a large, sprawling heskel bush adorned with violet litrilu blooms. But she took no joy in the sight. A sense of desolate futility gripped her and nothing, not even the flowers and bowls of fruit decorating her bedchamber, could dispel it or the foreboding of her dreams.

She had not wanted to be an instrument of destiny, and had told Uncle Volyn as much during their ill-contrived attempt to flee Oumetra. Thereafter, events had conspired to coerce her into that very role, and now the Lord Commander and Prince Yasgur had offered her the crown.

I have been the Earthmother's thrall, Alael had wanted to scream at them. *How can you offer the throne to the puppet of a god who hungers only for revenge?*

There were footsteps in the chamber behind her. It was Tauric. He still wore the battered leather jerkin, but now a dark blue cloak hung from his shoulders. There was no need to ask how he was – he had the hollow look which came from anguish and lack of sleep. With his metal hand he took a gezel fruit from a bowl at the foot of the bed and came out to join her on the balcony. For a moment he stood still and silent, weary eyes taking in the view of the palace and High Spire with its smoke-blackened upper windows. Then he spoke in a rush: 'I wish I had your power!'

Tears welled in his eyes. Head bowed he covered his face with his ordinary hand while leaning on the stone balustrade with the other. The gezel fell half-crushed on the tiled floor.

'Enemies . . . become friends . . .' he said, voice shaking. 'Then friends turn out . . . to be enemies . . . and m-my real father is a . . . monster . . . !'

Alael's heart ached with pity for him, this boy forced to endure a man's fate. She reached out to draw him to her, to rest his head on her shoulder, and to do the only thing that could be done.

Listen.

Three

'We could break him in body and mind,' said Thraelor with speculative malice. 'I would find that most amusing, in the light of what his creatures did to my city.'

'The consequences would be uncertain,' pointed out Kodel. 'Could it be possible that the fragment of the Lord of Twilight he carries would find another host? What disaster might come of that?'

'Yes,' said Grazaan. 'Better to keep him shackled here for now, and decide his fate later.'

All three Shadowkings then glanced at Byrnak, awaiting his response. He smiled.

In a darkened chamber deep below the Basilica, Ystregul the Black Priest hung before them in a specially remade iron casket. Suspended on heavy chains linked to the corners of the ceiling, the casket covered every part of him except his face. The eyes glared and rolled and the lips mouthed curses and imprecations, but such grimacing happened very slowly and the voice was a low, buzzing sound without sense or meaning. Within the spell cast upon him, time crawled.

'I agree,' Byrnak said. 'But what is to be our purpose now? Are we still intent on relinquishing all that we are in order that the Lord of Twilight may become whole?' He surveyed the reluctant faces, and nodded. 'I thought not. Yet we must deal with him in the end.'

'Could there be some way to employ the Weaving of Souls that does not result in our personal obliteration?' Kodel asked. 'Perhaps we should put the Acolytes to work on the problem.'

Heads nodded.

'In the meantime,' Byrnak said. 'We need to plan the reconquest of our domain. Our hasty brother has all but wrecked the regard and loyalty we had from the clans, and left us with few available stratagems. There is one, however, which offers a much-needed certainty.'

Grazaan gave a wintry smile. 'Gorla and Keshada.'

'Gorla and Keshada,' Byrnak repeated. 'Yasgur and those rebels are too weak to challenge the northern warlords, with or without our help. By the time they feel able to, Gorla and Keshada will be ready, along with our new armies. Which the Acolytes assure me will have many willing spirits.'

Grazaan and Thraelor exchanged a look. 'We shall begin at once,' Thraelor said and the two of them faded from the chamber.

Kodel gave Byrnak a thoughtful look.

'Do you trust them?' he said.

'To carry out the seedings? Yes. I also expect them to seek advantages that suit them.'

'Of course,' Kodel murmured. 'I shall gather together our remaining Acolyte masters and exhort them to explore our problem with the Weaving of Souls.'

Departing, he left Byrnak alone with the imprisoned Ystregul and the compass of his own inner perceptions.

That will have to suffice for you, he thought inwardly. *We will not pay the price of oblivion.*

But the only answer was silence, a deep, secretive silence.

The End
(To be continued in *Shadowgod*)

Acknowledgements

To my agent, the indefatigable John Parker, and my editor the inestimable John Jarrold, and to Steve Stone, artist nonpareil! And to Rob Holdstock and Chris Evans for taking *Waltz in Flexitime* all them years ago.

To my brave readers of the first draft – Dave W, Dave McG, Eric, Ian, Fiona, Alison, Stewart, Derek H, Neil, Phil, Al, Craig, Barry and Niall.

To Stewart Robinson, long-time buddy, soulbrother, musician and guru manqué – without whom I might have ended up an MP or an engineer – and Alison, Bobby, Alan, Dave R and Ann, Colin and Adrienne (and the six-legged beastie known as Tranceport). And to Sue Stuart – great to know we're still friends.

To David Wingrove, writer among scribblers, prince among men, whose unfailing friendship and sharp-eyed criticism has helped me reach higher.

To Bill King, Eric Brown, Keith Brooke and Ian McDonald, the four musketeers of British SF. Salute, mes braves! And to Bill Hicks, who rocked!

To Dave McGillivray, staunch friend and fellow C&C Red Alert addict, and Derek Cameron who knows a good game when he sees one. To Melanie, prog queen of Bexley; and to Antje – Tuus! And to Gary Gibson, publishing magnate and king of the layouts!

To the Glasgow SF Writers Circle, past and present, including Veronica, Duncan, Neil, Gary G, Gerry, Phil, Paul, Al, Irene, Elsie, Graham, Jims Whyte and Steel, Roddy, Barry (the Ferg), Richard, Craig, John, Andrew J, Mike M. Also,

Cuddles, Vince, Brian Waugh, Jim Campbell, Russell, Neil at Fshock.

To Peter and Sarah, and the Cobleys of Leicester, and to the Bradys and the Mackenzies, wherever they may be.

To my English teacher, Ada Lister (nee Matheson) – well, you did tell me not to stop writing . . .

To Iain Banks, Elizabeth K Ewing, Bill Grant, Noel Hannan, Bruce Sterling, Norman Spinrad, Simon Ings, Ken McLeod, Jack Deighton, Charles Stross, and Steve Brown – bestowers of advice, encouragement, inspiration and Tao!

To Nick Mahoney and Ian Sales, for the immortal Lyre and Turkey Shoot. And to JFM for squeegeeing my third eye before I even knew I had one.

To the old Strathents Crew, 1979–83 – they knew no fear! Likewise, the GCCS crowd at Strathclyde Students Union, circa 1983–8.

To the writers who have inspired me by their example, among whom I include (as well as those already mentioned), Harlan Ellison, John Buchan, J.R.R. Tolkien, David Gemmell, Robert Silverberg, George R.R. Martin, Tim Powers, David Brin, J.V. Jones, Roger Zelazny, Vernor Vinge, Jack Vance, Walter J. Williams, Robert E. Howard, and many more.

And for the music that has provided the score for the writing process – Porcupine Tree, Tranceport, Peri Urban, Black Sabbath, BOC, Berlioz, Shostakovich (specifically the 1905 Symphony), Carl Orff (*Carmina Burana*), Vaughan Williams (*Tallis Fantasia* etc), Van Der Graaf Generator, IQ, Yes, Monster Magnet, Paradise Lost, NIN, Sisters of Mercy, The Tea Party, Ozric Tentacles . . .and the rest.

And in no particular order, I would like to offer thanks to Gigantor, Noggin the Nog, Marine Boy, Ben Okri, the Prisoner, King Tut's WahWah Hut, Airfix model kits, the Koei Corporation, and the Café India buffet. Oh yeah!

For more information go to:
www.shadowkings.co.uk and www.deepphase.co.uk

EARTHLIGHT

A SELECTED LIST OF FANTASY TITLES AVAILABLE FROM EARTHLIGHT

THE PRICES SHOWN BELOW WERE CORRECT AT THE TIME OF GOING TO PRESS. HOWEVER EARTHLIGHT RESERVE THE RIGHT TO SHOW NEW RETAIL PRICES ON COVERS WHICH MAY DIFFER FROM THOSE PREVIOUSLY ADVERTISED IN THE TEXT OR ELSEWHERE.

☐	0 7434 0893 4	Talisker	*Miller Lau*	£6.99
☐	0 6848 6036 8	Celtika	*Robert Holdstock*	£16.99
☐	0 6710 2261 X	The Sum Of All Men	*David Farland*	£6.99
☐	0 7434 0827 6	Brotherhood of the Wolf	*David Farland*	£6.99
☐	0 6848 6061 9	Wizardborn	*David Farland*	£10.00
☐	0 6710 3302 6	Downs-Lord Doomsday	*John Whitbourn*	£6.99
☐	0 6710 3300 X	Downs-Lord Dawn	*John Whitbourn*	£5.99
☐	0 6710 2193 1	Sailing to Sarantium	*Guy Gavriel Kay*	£6.99
☐	0 7434 0825 X	Lord of Emperors	*Guy Gavriel Kay*	£6.99
☐	0 6710 3725 0	The Dreamthief's Daughter	*Michael Moorcock*	£6.99
☐	0 6848 6670 7	Silverheart	*Michael Moorcock & Storm Constantine*	£16.99
☐	0 7434 1607 4	The Obsidian Tower	*Freda Warrington*	£6.99
☐	0 7484 0826 8	The Sapphire Throne	*Harry Turtledove*	£5.99
☐	0 6710 2282 2	Into The Darkness	*Harry Turtledove*	£5.99
☐	0 6710 3305 0	Darkness Descending	*Harry Turtledove*	£6.99
☐	0 6710 3398 0	Through the Darkness	*Harry Turtledove*	£6.99
☐	0 7434 1513 2	The Treason of Dortrean	*Marcus Herniman*	£5.99

All Earthlight titles are available by post from:

Book Service By Post, P.O. Box 29, Douglas, Isle of Man IM99 1BQ

Credit cards accepted. Please telephone 01624 675137,
fax 01624 670923, Internet http://www.bookpost.co.uk or
e-mail: bookshop@enterprise.net for details.

Free postage and packaging in the UK. Overseas customers allow
£1 per book (paperbacks) and £3 per book (hardbacks).